About the Authors

Kelly Hunter has always had a weakness for fairytales, fantasy worlds, and losing herself in a good book. She is married with two children, avoids cooking and cleaning, and despite the best efforts of her family, is no sports fan! Kelly is however a keen gardener and has a fondness for roses. Kelly was born in Australia and has travelled extensively. Although she enjoys living and working in different parts of the world, she still calls Australia home.

USA Today bestselling author **Jules Bennett** has penned more than fifty novels during her short career. She's married to her high school sweetheart, has two active girls, and is a former salon owner. Jules can be found on X and Facebook (Fan Page). She holds competitions via these outlets with each release and loves to hear from readers!

USA Today bestselling, *RITA*-nominated, and critically acclaimed author **Caitlin Crews** has written more than 150 books and counting. She has a master's and a PhD in English Literature, thinks everyone should read more category romance, and is always available to discuss her beloved alpha heroes. Just ask. She lives in the Pacific Northwest with her comic book artist husband, is always planning her next trip, and will never, ever, read all the books in her to-be-read pile. Thank goodness.

Second Chance

June 2025
His Unexpected Heir

September 2025
The Prince's Desire

July 2025
Their Renewed Vows

December 2025
A Love Rekindled

August 2025
A Cowboy's Return

January 2025
Their Enemy Sparks

Second Chance:
The Prince's Desire

KELLY HUNTER

JULES BENNETT

CAITLIN CREWS

MILLS & BOON

All rights reserved including the right of reproduction in whole or in part in any form. This edition is published by arrangement with Harlequin Enterprises ULC.

This is a work of fiction. Names, characters, places, locations and incidents are purely fictional and bear no relationship to any real life individuals, living or dead, or to any actual places, business establishments, locations, events or incidents. Any resemblance is entirely coincidental.

Without limiting the author's and publisher's exclusive rights, any unauthorised use of this publication to train generative artificial intelligence (AI) technologies is expressly prohibited. HarperCollins also exercise their rights under Article 4(3) of the Digital Single Market Directive 2019/790 and expressly reserve this publication from the text and data mining exception.

® and ™ are trademarks owned and used by the trademark owner and/or its licensee. Trademarks marked with ® are registered with the United Kingdom Patent Office and/or the Office for Harmonisation in the Internal Market and in other countries.

First Published in Great Britain 2025
by Mills & Boon, an imprint of HarperCollins*Publishers* Ltd
1 London Bridge Street, London, SE1 9GF

www.harpercollins.co.uk

HarperCollins*Publishers*
Macken House, 39/40 Mayor Street Upper,
Dublin 1, D01 C9W8, Ireland

Second Chance: The Prince's Desire © 2025 Harlequin Enterprises ULC.

Shock Heir for the Crown Prince © 2018 Kelly Hunter
Maid for a Magnate © 2015 Harlequin Books S.A.
The Scandal That Made Her His Queen © 2022 Caitlin Crews

Special thanks and acknowledgement are given to Jules Bennett for her contribution to the *Dynasties: The Montoros* series.

ISBN: 978-0-263-41862-0

This book contains FSC™ certified paper and other controlled sources to ensure responsible forest management.

For more information visit: www.harpercollins.co.uk/green

Printed and Bound in the UK using 100% Renewable Electricity
at CPI Group (UK) Ltd, Croydon, CR0 4YY

SHOCK HEIR FOR THE CROWN PRINCE

KELLY HUNTER

PROLOGUE

Casimir, Crown Prince of Byzenmaach, woke with a woman on his mind and an ache in his loins. He rolled onto his back, and let out a groan when the heavy cotton sheet rubbed against him in just the right way to make his hips move again, and then again. Not this again. Not her again—it was the third time this week.

He wasn't impressed.

It took longer than usual to shove those wayward memories of lovemaking aside and roll out of bed. Naked, he padded across age-old silk carpets towards the door that led to the parapet that led to the bathhouse—a domed white marble indulgence that would have found favour with the gladiators of Rome.

Cool air hit his skin the minute he opened the huge double doors, and if he hadn't been fully awake before, he was now. Summer was in full swing in Byzenmaach but here in the snow-capped northern mountains the mornings still held the edge of winter on them and always would. He suffered it because he liked the cool lick of ice on his skin and because it made that moment when he entered the hot pool that much sweeter.

Nothing could ease the tension in his body and clear his mind faster than spending five minutes beneath the pounding man-made waterfall at the far edge of the hot pool and then another five immersed in the still and silent water at the other end of it. Access to the bathhouse was one of the main reasons he'd made Byzenmaach's remote winter fortress his permanent home.

Hedonist. He'd never deny the label. Pleasure-seeking was an integral part of his nature.

It wasn't all he was.

The woman on his mind—Ana—had been a mistake, a youthful indiscretion, a hedonistic folly, and every so often she haunted him. She'd been a student of languages, living in Geneva. He'd been on his way home from delegate talks and bored. The bar where they'd first met had been called the Barrel and Fawn.

Who remembered details like that seven years after the encounter?

The walkway to the bathhouse was open to the air on one side, courtesy of a waist-high stone wall and colonnade arches. The view that greeted him stretched out over the valley below and still managed to impress, no matter how many times he saw it. Once winter hit he'd take the long way round through the palace, but until then he'd enjoy the caress of cool mountain air on his skin. Perhaps it would cool his morning ardour.

It didn't.

Why was it that seven years after the affair, Anastasia Douglas was still his go-to memory when his body sought release?

Why did he remember the way she took her morning coffee when he had hundreds, if not thousands, of more important memories to recall?

Double shot, black, with one sugar, and hot enough to burn.

Her hair, a tousled black cloud that framed exquisite bone structure as she purred her contentment and blew on the steaming black liquid to cool it before setting it to her lips.

He hadn't been the only hedonist in their short-lived relationship. The things she could do with her mouth…

He shivered and it wasn't just because of the cool dawn air.

There'd been something in the air, in the water, on the night he'd met her. Something that had him acting with greater than usual abandon. He'd made the first move, used every bit of charm in his arsenal, and before the night was through they'd ended up naked in her tiny student apartment on the outskirts of the city. He'd stayed the night and instead of leaving the next morning he'd stayed four more nights, turning his back on everything but her. Learning her. Loving her. Ramming into her life and meeting no resistance.

He'd monopolised her nights and infiltrated her days.

They'd lain on the grass in a tiny gated park with his face to the sun and Ana's head on his hip as she read Russian poetry to him in flawless Russian and then again in English. She'd been equally fluent in both languages, or so she'd said—courtesy of her Russian mother and English father—but the results of her translations had been confusing.

Russian poetry was never meant to be read in English, she'd said, which had begged the question as to why she was attempting the impossible in the first place.

She wanted to be an interpreter, she'd said. Maybe for the European Parliament, maybe for the United Nations Secretariat, and to do that she had to be the best of the best. She was practising.

She'd shared her goals and ambitions, her body and her home.

He'd shared next to nothing.

She hadn't known she was talking to the Crown Prince of Byzenmaach, with his impeccable lineage, private planes and castles carved into the side of mountains.

He hadn't told her he was Casimir, dutiful son and heir to the throne, student of politics since he was old enough to stand at his father's knee and listen.

For four days and five nights he hadn't been Casimir, with his dead mother and sister, an ailing father and responsibilities he hadn't been ready for. She'd called him Cas, just Cas, and the freedom to *be* Just Cas had been liberating.

Maybe *that* was why he kept remembering Anastasia Douglas every so often. Her breathy cries and the softness of her skin, the way she'd wrapped around him… maybe he equated her with freedom, or the illusion of freedom. Maybe his longing to choose his own path sat in his subconscious like a burr, never mind that he'd come to terms with his royal responsibilities long ago.

The waters of the bath glinted deep blue and silver in the weak light of morning. Steam spiralled towards the high domed ceiling, and the caress of water on his feet as he took that first step down into the pool made him groan his pleasure.

He liked that the water temperature was almost too hot to bear.

Same way Ana had liked her coffee.

He took another step into the pool and then another, the water now lapping at his thighs, his erection in no way deflated by the sensory experience of cold air followed by the lick of hot water.

Soon he would propose to Princess Moriana from the neighbouring monarchy of Arun. Moriana was smart, educated, well versed in affairs of state and extremely well connected. It wasn't a love match but he wouldn't regret the union. Moriana would be good for him and for Byzenmaach. He *knew* this.

Moriana, not Anastasia.

He tried to turn his thoughts towards his intended, but it was no use. Ana won.

Ana always won.

Turning on his heel, he stepped back out of the pool and headed for the shower, half hidden in the marble recesses beside the far door. He turned the taps, adjusted the heat and let fat water droplets fall to the floor before stepping beneath them. He reached for the body oil rather than the soap and took himself in hand.

Maybe he should find out what Anastasia Douglas was doing these days as a way of getting her out of his head. Maybe she'd be married now and wildly content with her husband and two point three children. Unavailable, unobtainable. No longer the woman who'd loved Cas, just Cas, and wished him happiness.

New memories, lesser ones, to replace the memories that haunted him still. Ana, sated and smiling, all long limbs, alabaster skin and silky black hair that a man could lose his fist in. Ana on her knees for him while he muttered words like *please* and *more* on more than one occasion. Ana, with her open sensuality that had ignited his.

No pressure, no reputation to uphold, no expectations and no demands. Pleasure for pleasure's sake. Quick, clever hands and lips that dragged in all the right places. Tumbling words of fire and passion that his soul understood, even if the actual words had been a mystery to him.

Surely, in his mind, if nowhere else, he could have this.

Closing his eyes and turning his face upwards into the water, he let the memories come.

CHAPTER ONE

'Your Highness, a moment of your time.'

Casimir looked up from the papers on his desk and nodded for Rudolpho to enter. The king's chief advisor looked more careworn than usual but that was only to be expected given that his king, Casimir's father, was dying. Loyal to a fault, Rudolpho had found the transfer of power from Leonidas to Casimir an unpalatable process. Crown Prince or not, Rudolpho was first and foremost the king's man.

And he didn't always like the changes Casimir was insisting on.

Soon Casimir would have to leave his winter fortress and take up permanent residence in the palace in the capital. Soon he would no longer have to bear witness to his father's relentless march towards death. He and his father weren't close. A big part of him loathed the man, and always would. Another part pitied him. And then there was a tiny sliver of Casimir's soul that craved the man's approval.

It wasn't like Rudolpho to hang back in doorways, but the older man still hadn't entered the room and his stance was stiffer than usual. Something was amiss. 'What news of my father?' he asked.

'Your father had a comfortable evening. Morphine

helps. He's sleeping now.' Rudolpho approached the desk, his gaze roving over the neat stacks of paperwork to either side of Casimir's laptop. 'You need to delegate some of this workload.'

'I intend to. Just as soon as I understand exactly what it is I'm delegating.' Some of these duties were new to him. Not many, but some, and Casimir was nothing if not thorough. 'I thought you left the palace hours ago.' Casimir let his raised eyebrow ask the obvious question.

If the king was resting comfortably and Rudolpho had a rare evening off, what was he doing here?

Rudolpho set a yellow courier's envelope on the desk as if he couldn't wait for it to leave his hand. 'The report you ordered on Anastasia Douglas came in. I took the liberty of opening it.'

'You open everything.' Nothing unusual about that.

'Not every report I glance through threatens my ability to breathe. Did you know?'

The older man's voice had taken on a hard, precise edge, with an undertone of something Casimir couldn't quite place. Fear? Despair? Maybe it was disappointment. 'Know what?'

'I'll be in my office,' Rudolpho said, and stalked away, his spine one ramrod line of displeasure.

Disappointment it was. Casimir eyed the offending envelope with deep suspicion before reaching for it.

New memories to replace the old, he reminded himself grimly. Closure, rather than curiosity. Nothing to worry about. He'd asked for this.

So why did his hand tremble ever so slightly as he reached in and withdrew the contents of the envelope?

There were photos, lots of photos, and the topmost image was a close-up of Ana's face. A heart-shaped face, wide of brow and pointy of chin, with eyes to drown in and lips that promised heaven. Strong, shapely eyebrows and lashes, thick and black, made the cerulean blue of her eyes all the more arresting. In this picture her hair had been scraped back into a careless ponytail. In the next photo it framed her face in sultry waves that curled around her neck and shoulders. It was a face to stop a man's breath. Casimir put a hand to *his* face and rubbed hard before turning to the next photograph.

So she'd grown into her beauty. No surprises there.

The next shot was a full-body take of Ana walking up a set of wide outdoor steps—rushing up them most likely, because her body was a study in motion. Slender legs and rounded curves and, again, that loose mane of ebony hair. She wore a dark grey corporate skirt and jacket and had a black satchel slung over her left shoulder. Two more photos showed similar variations on a corporate theme.

The next photo showed her in jeans and a pink short-sleeved T-shirt, standing outside school gates with a young schoolgirl by her side. The photographer had caught them from the rear, as Ana adjusted the shoulder strap of the girl's backpack. So she was a mother now—good for her. Hopefully she had a husband to love and a solid family life. Casimir looked to her hand to see if she wore a wedding ring but the photo didn't allow for that level of detail.

The next shot was a formal school photo of the child.

At which point the world as Casimir knew it simply stopped.

There was no sound. No air.

Grey threatened the edges of his sight.

No.

Yes.

Casimir had had a sister once. For seven years he'd

had a sister three years younger than he was. And then the rebels to the north had taken her and when his father hadn't agreed to their demands they'd killed her and sent back pieces to prove it.

His mother had never recovered. She'd taken her own life a year later to the day, leaving her husband and her son to carry on alone.

They didn't talk about it, Cas and his father. They never had and probably never would. Therapists had been out of the question—too much potential for exploitation to ever let someone inside the young Prince of Byzenmaach's head, so Cas had survived as best he could.

The pictures of his mother and sister remained prominent in the palace—a permanent reminder of failure, loss and grief. One of the first things he'd do as king would be to remove them to a rarely used dining room and shut the door on them.

Such a small and petty command for a new monarch to give.

He couldn't look away from the picture of the girl. The cloud of unruly black hair, the cowlick at the child's temple, the aristocratic blade of her nose.

Those eyes.

He put his hands to his own eyes and rubbed, but the picture was still there.

There would be no getting rid of this.

More pictures followed and each one brought with it a barrage of conflicting emotions because from a distance the kid could be any young girl, but up close…up close, and especially around the eyes—the hawkish, tawny-gold colour of her eyes…

The photo of her twirling in the garden, arms outstretched as if to catch the dust motes in the air…

Heaven help him, he was ten years old again, only

this time he hadn't left his sister alone in the garden to go and get a jar to catch the praying mantis in, and when he came back she hadn't been gone.

Taken.

Kidnapped.

And never coming back.

Weakness didn't sit well on him but he'd rather cut his own eyes out than look at another photo of Anastasia Douglas's daughter. Cas closed his eyes and concentrated on the formerly simple act of breathing.

The clink of glasses and a bottle thudding down on the table prevented him from doing either. Rudolpho was back, and with him a glass and a bottle of Royal Vault brandy. Age spots and veins stood out on the older man's hands as he poured generously and pushed the glass into Casimir's hand.

'I don't know the royal protocol for this,' Rudolpho said gruffly. 'But drink. You're white.'

'She's… It's…' Cas took a steadying breath. 'It's not her.'

'No. It's not her,' Rudolpho said evenly. 'But the likeness is uncanny. How far did you get?'

Wordlessly, Casimir picked up the photo of the child in the garden. Rudolpho winced.

'Summarise,' Casimir said.

Rudolpho sighed and stared momentarily at the brandy. Casimir gestured for him to have one and succeeded only in offending the man. Rudolpho was a product of an earlier era and would no more sit and drink with Casimir, Crown Prince, than fly. It wasn't done. It breached a thousand protocols. 'The child is six years old and has a British birth certificate, courtesy of her being born at the Portland Hospital in London and her mother's chosen nationality.'

Now it was Casimir's turn to wince at the thought of a child of Byzenmaach claiming a foreign nationality.

'The mother is Anastasia Victoria Douglas,' Rudolpho continued. 'Twenty-six years of age. Marital status: single. Occupation: interpreter for the European Parliament and the United Nations Secretariat. Currently residing in Geneva, where most of her work is.'

'And the father?' He had to ask. He already knew.

'Father unknown.'

So.

Casimir, future king of Byzenmaach, had an illegitimate six-year-old daughter. A daughter who was the spitting image of his long-dead sister.

'Your name isn't on the birth certificate,' Rudolpho pointed out quietly. 'Maybe the child's *not* yours. Maybe Anastasia Douglas doesn't *know* who the father is.'

Cas silently rifled through the photos for the headshot of the girl in school uniform and held it up.

Rudolpho could barely bring himself to glance at it. 'Maybe the mother has a weakness for amber-eyed men. My point being that the girl's mother hasn't contacted you in seven years. She hasn't asked you for anything, least of all acknowledgement. She provides amply for the child. The girl has a roof over her head, good schooling, loving grandparents. The child is intelligent. She won't lack for life choices.'

'Are you suggesting I don't acknowledge her?'

Rudolpho stayed silent.

'That's your counsel?'

'Or you could bring her here,' Rudolpho said finally. 'And do your best to protect her.'

Temper soared. 'You think I can't?' Never mind that Casimir had been the one to leave his sister unprotected in the first place. 'You think I'm like *him*?'

'I think…' Rudolpho paused, as if choosing his words carefully. 'I think this innocent bastard child looks like your sister reincarnated. She'd be a target for your enemies from the outset. Front page fodder for the press.'

Silence fell again, the deeply unsettling kind.

'This stays between us for now,' Casimir said finally.

Rudolpho met his gaze. 'It can stay between us for ever, if that is your wish.'

Could he do it? Casimir glanced at the pictures strewn across his desk. Could he really shut her out the way he'd shut out all memory of his seven-year-old sister and too-weak-for-this-world mother? Pack all the pictures away and never look back?

Could he really continue on as if the girl simply didn't exist?

The child was his blood. *His* responsibility. His to protect. 'What's her name?' he asked gruffly.

'Your Highness, the less you know the easier it'll be to—

'What's her name?'

'Sophia.' Rudolpho sounded defeated. 'Sophia Alexandra Douglas.'

A fitting name for the daughter of a king.

Had she known? Had Anastasia Douglas known who she was getting in bed with?

'Your Highness—'

'Enough!' Whatever it was, he didn't want to hear it.

'Your Highness, *please*. Sleep on this. Think carefully before you expose the child to Byzenmaach, because there's no coming back from that. They'll take her and shape her into whatever they most desire, and you'll have to protect her from that too.'

'The way my father never did for me?' Casimir asked, silky-soft and deadly.

Rudolpho remained silent. Never would he speak ill of the king he'd served for over forty years.

'Are you asking if I can accept this child as a person in her own right—with strengths and flaws of her own making? Can I protect her from the expectations of others? Do I know how to be a father to a child who carries the expectations of a nation on her shoulders? Is that your *concern*?'

Rudolpho said nothing.

'I *was* that child,' he grated. 'Who better to defend her exploitation than me?'

Casimir scowled and reached for his drink again. He knew exactly what his father would do with this information, and it would be as Rudolpho said. Use the girl to shore up a nation's hope until legitimate heirs were produced, then cast her aside because she no longer fitted in the Byzenmaach monarch's perfect world. She wouldn't have it easy here. No child of Byzenmaach ever did.

The desk, this room and everything in it stank of duty and the weight that came with it. 'You really think a part of me doesn't realise that the kindest thing I can do for both of them is to leave them alone?'

All that, and still…

'She's mine,' he said. '*My* child. *My* blood. My responsibility.'

The bottom line in all of this.

And yet.

And yet…

Could he really expose the child to the dangers that awaited her here in Byzenmaach?

'There's one more thing.' Rudolpho eyed him warily. 'We weren't the only ones watching them. Anastasia Douglas and her daughter were already under surveillance. There was a team on the house, and another in place at the girl's school. As far as we could ascertain, their focus was the girl rather than the mother.'

Dread turned his skin cold and clammy. 'Who were they?'

'We don't know. They disappeared before we could deal with them. They're good.'

Not good.

'I've ordered a covert security team to watch and wait for additional orders,' said Rudolpho. 'I don't think it wise to involve your father in any decision-making at this point.'

His father only had days to live. That was what Rudolpho meant. 'I'll handle it.'

'If you need additional counsel—'

Casimir smiled bleakly. 'I don't.'

CHAPTER TWO

ANASTASIA DOUGLAS DIDN'T usually attend black-tie fundraising events at the director of the United Nations Secretariat's request. She was a lowly interpreter, one of many, even if she did have a reputation for being extremely good at what she did. She commanded five languages instead of the average three and was conversationally fluent in half a dozen more. She could navigate diplomatic circles with ease, courtesy of the training she'd received at her Russian diplomat mother's knee. She had an intimate understanding of world politics, and enough corporate mediation experience to be of use when conversation got heated. All good things for a career interpreter's toolkit.

It still didn't explain why she was here in Geneva's fading Museum of Art and History, talking black tulips with the Minister for Transport's wife. The ticket would be held for her at the door, the director had said. It was important for her to be there, he'd said. Someone wanted to meet her in person, in advance of securing her services.

It would help mightily, Ana thought grimly, if she knew who that person was.

Twenty more minutes and Ana would cut her losses and make her exit. She was drawing enough unwanted attention as it was—possibly because she'd put her hair up and was wearing the simple black gown her mother had bought her for Christmas. It had a discreet boat neckline, no sleeves, and clung to her curves like a lover's hand. Very little skin was showing. The dress was more than appropriate for such an event, and yet…

It didn't matter that she never particularly wanted to draw the male gaze, she drew it regardless. And the female gaze and the gaze of the security guard stationed at the door. Sex appeal, mystery, an air of worldliness—whatever it was, people always stared. Some envious, some dazzled, others covetous. No one was ever neutral around her.

When Ana had fallen pregnant at nineteen, with barely any knowledge of the father and no way to contact him again, her mother had been horrified. All those plans for Ana to make a powerfully advantageous marriage, gone. All Ana's formidable allure spent on a man who didn't want her.

Only he had wanted her.

For one glorious week Ana had been the centre of a laughing, passionate, attentive man's world and she'd gloried in it. He'd smiled at her in a bar and she'd felt the warmth of it all the way to her toes. He'd put a hand to the small of her back and held the door open for her on their way out and she'd stumbled beneath the heat of it all.

Clumsy Ana, when she'd never been clumsy before. All lit up at the touch of his hand.

So young. So utterly confident that the pulsing connection between them would last for ever. For one unforgettable week she'd found heaven here on earth. And then he'd left without a word, no farewell and no forwarding address.

He's married, nothing surer, her mother had said.

You don't have to have this baby, she'd said months

later. *You could move on with your life. Continue with your study plans.*

Wise words from a woman Ana had always respected, only Ana had never quite been able to turn that stolen week into nothing. Never quite been able to wipe it from her consciousness.

She'd been nine months pregnant before she'd even figured out who Cas, *her* Cas, was. Not married. Not some feckless con man who'd needed a place to stay for a week.

He'd been the Crown Prince of Byzenmaach.

She'd woven that information into something she could live with; of course she had.

He hadn't left her because he wanted to; he'd left her because duty to his crown demanded it. His father had forbidden it, and he'd fought for her, hard, but been overruled. He'd spent weeks in a dungeon, clamouring to get out and return to her. *Yeah.* Ana smiled ruefully. That last fantasy had always been a favourite.

Far better than the bitter knowledge that she simply hadn't been a suitable choice for him and that he'd known it from the start and chosen to love her and leave her regardless.

She hadn't got in touch.

The Transport Minister's wife had exhausted the topic of tulips. By mutual consent they headed towards a larger circle of people, allowing Ana to drift away, towards a Grecian bust, champagne glass in hand. She rarely drank, although at an event such as this she would often take a glass of whatever they were offering. She liked to think it made her fit in.

The sculpture wasn't the most impressive one in the room but studying it served the purpose of separating her from the crowd. She stood alone. Approachable. Any potential employer could introduce themselves now, in private, assuming they wanted to. If they didn't, not a problem. She *had* enough work lined up to keep her and Sophia living comfortably for quite some time.

No one could accuse her of not giving her daughter a good start in life.

She felt the presence of someone at her side before she saw them. The movement of air, a dark shape in her peripheral vision. She turned to look at him, and felt the bottom drop out of her world.

She'd have known him anywhere, never mind that it had been years since she'd seen him last. She'd mapped that face with her lips and fingertips, and left not one inch of his body unexplored. Broad of shoulder and long of leg, his shoes were black and shiny and his shirt was snowy white beneath his black suit. His hands were in the pockets of his trousers, stretching the fabric taut across his abdomen and the top of his thighs.

Hurriedly, she turned her attention back to the Grecian bust, giving it far more attention than it deserved. Her palms felt suddenly slick and she longed to wipe them down the sides of her gown. Instead she wrapped both hands around her glass and tried to ignore the thunderous beating of her heart.

She hadn't forgotten him, no, she could never do that. She woke to a living, breathing reminder of him every morning and fed her cheese on toast.

'Hello, Ana,' he said quietly.

'Cas.'

'Been a while,' he said.

'Yes.'

'You're looking well. A little pale. Must be all that working indoors.'

'You know where I work?'

'I had you investigated.'

'Oh.' *Stay cool, Ana.* There was still a chance he didn't know about Sophia. 'Why?'

He smiled grimly and shook his head. Shrugging those powerful shoulders as if to say he didn't understand it either. 'In truth—which is more than you deserve—my father is dying and I need to marry soon. The woman my country has in mind for me is a princess from a neighbouring principality. We've been informally promised to each other since we were nine years old and I wanted to do right by her before making it official. I wanted to put you—and the week we once shared—out of my mind for good.'

'That's right. You're the Crown Prince of Byzenmaach.' She smiled, because she knew the power in her smile. '*In truth*, that was something I deserved to know all those years ago, when you graced my bed. Don't you think?'

Now it was Casimir's turn to study the Grecian bust. 'I don't disagree,' he offered finally.

She looked at his proud profile and wondered for the umpteenth time why he'd done it. Spent the week with her, pretending to be someone he was not. Was his life really that bad that he'd needed to escape it? Or had he too been blindsided by attraction?

'A lot of my choices would have been different had I known who you really were,' she said.

'They always are,' he replied somewhat grimly.

'So you had me investigated.' Carefully, she picked up the earlier thread of their conversation. 'How is that supposed to help put me out of your mind for good?'

'You were supposed to have developed flaws.'

'What kind of flaws?'

'Any kind at all.'

'Should I have lost teeth and grown warts?'

'Yes.' The glimmer of a smile chased the shadows from his eyes, but only for a moment. 'You were supposed to have moved on.'

'I *have* moved on. We had a good time. It's done.'

'You're the mother of my child,' he countered flatly.

Right. That.

As for Ana's response, she'd prepared for this day. She had words in place in at least five languages.

'You're wrong.' Those were the first words in her arsenal. She glanced up to see how he'd taken them. Not well, if his fierce and unforgiving glare was anything to go by.

'Do I need to order a DNA test for the child?' he enquired silkily. 'Because I will if I have to. I will regardless, so let's move past denial. We both know she's mine.'

If denial wasn't working, try reason. 'Walk away, Your Highness. You don't have to be here.'

'You say that as if it's an option.' He kept his voice low but anger ran like a river beneath his words. 'It's not.'

'Marry your princess, produce an heir to your throne and forget about me and mine. It *is* an option.' She turned imploring eyes on him. 'I'm well set up. I can provide for my daughter. You *don't* have to be here.'

'Does she ask about her father?'

Ana squared her shoulders and told it like it was. She'd tackled that question back when Sophia had been four years old. Not Ana's finest moment. But the lie had fallen from her lips and there was no taking it back. 'I told her you were dead. No one knows who Sophia's father is. *No one*. Not even my parents.'

'You say that as if it's something to be proud of.'

'Isn't it?' she said haughtily. 'Think of it as protection rather than oversight, and maybe you'll see where I'm coming from.'

His lips tightened.

'I found out who you were purely by chance.' Ana had the advantage so she pressed it. 'I was nine months pregnant at the time, you were long gone and I'd already made the decision to raise my baby alone. I saw your picture in a Middle Eastern newspaper one of my mother's guests had left behind. Suddenly your joy in the little everyday things we did made so much more sense. As did your disappearing act at the end.'

Needing distance, she walked around the statue, putting it between them even as their gazes stayed locked. 'I researched you; how could I not? I read about your sister's death and your mother's suicide. Your father stood tall throughout.' Ana badly wanted to reach out and run her fingers over the cold, smooth marble, but it wasn't allowed. 'I remember looking at the pictures of him and thinking how stalwart he was. The widower king who held it together, with you at his side…ten years old and so determined not to disappoint. You were your country's last hope. You still are.'

She'd watched him walk away once before; she could do it again. 'I'll never know why you took up with me in the first place, but you left me behind for a reason, maybe for a whole lot of reasons. So I left your name off my daughter's birth certificate for a reason too.' She stared at him, willing him to understand. 'Go home, Your Highness. I've got this.'

'Come with me,' he offered gruffly, his gaze never leaving hers. 'Bring her.'

This wasn't how the conversation ever went in her imagination. In her imagination he walked away, relieved by her silence. 'You haven't heard a word I said.'

'On the contrary, I'm listening very carefully. You seem to know broadly what's at stake, which makes this meeting easier than expected. I discovered my daughter's existence three days ago. I want to meet her.'

'No.' She took a careful step left, partially obscuring him from her line of sight. 'That's not advisable.'

He tilted his head, the better to keep her in view. 'It wasn't a request. I have a jet waiting and a security team in place outside your house, awaiting orders.' The smile he sent her was a worn and bitter thing. 'I'm sorry, Ana. I had hoped for a more leisurely approach but circumstances beyond my control are against it. I need you and Sophia in Byzenmaach.'

'No.'

'For your own protection, as well as mine,' he said. 'Perhaps it's you who needs to listen a little more carefully. Because it's not a request.'

There were other ways he could have gone about getting access to the child. Official, less invasive ways but all of them took time and time was something Casimir didn't have. He'd carved out the hours and minutes it took to come here to collect them, and even gaining that amount of freedom had been harder than carving granite with bare hands. He didn't have time to ease himself slowly into Ana and his daughter's life.

They had to come to him.

'My car is out front,' he said.

'Mine is in the car park.'

And if she thought he would allow her to drive it back to her house, she was mistaken. 'Someone will make sure your vehicle is returned to your apartment.'

'I need to go to the ladies' room,' she said next, glancing around as if weighing her options.

'By all means.' He nodded towards the severely

dressed woman who stood by the stairway, her eyes sharply trained on them. 'Katya will escort you.'

Ana swayed suddenly and he stepped closer and put his hand to the small of her back to steady her. Her skin was warm beneath the thin fabric of her dress and her breath hitched. It was all he could do to stop from lowering his head to the curve of her neck and breathing her in. Desire hit him, stronger than the desire he'd felt for her all those years ago. A staggering certainty that this woman would always be the woman he measured all others against. 'Are you afraid of me?'

She glanced at him and their gazes caught and held. She feared him now, this woman who'd once offered him all that she had to give. He could feel it in the slight trembling beneath his hand.

'I'm afraid of what you might take from me, yes.' Her quietly contained reply made honesty seem like strength.

'Perhaps I'll share,' he muttered as he took her drink and gave it to a passing waiter. 'Right now my father is ill, I need to return to Byzenmaach and I don't have time to waste. I could have sent strangers to collect you, but I thought you might prefer a familiar face.'

He hadn't wanted her or their daughter to feel the terror of abduction.

He steered her towards the exit and Katya fell silently into step beside them. Another security type stood waiting by the door to the museum, holding Ana's coat over one arm. Ana faltered when she saw him and Casimir slowed his steps to match.

'Cas, please. I don't want this.' She looked at him imploringly and put her hand on his sleeve to hold him back. 'I know what will happen once you claim her. She'll be in the spotlight. A target for those who oppose you. I don't want her to be a target. I want to keep my daughter safe.'

It had been seven years since they'd breathed the same air, but her effect on him was as potent as he remembered. He wanted to touch and he wanted to take. Sip at her lips and drive them both mad, until memories became their reality.

'That's what I'm trying to do. On my grave, Anastasia. I will keep you and your daughter safe.'

She let him escort her out of the museum and towards the waiting car, and Casimir was grateful for her acquiescence. Approaching Anastasia in public had been a calculated risk that his security team had advised against. They'd wanted to approach her at her home. He'd wanted to make his approach while the child wasn't with her and he'd only had an evening to do it in. Easy enough for him to pull strings and arrange for her to be here this evening.

She got into the car without comment and he followed, as his bodyguards peeled away, one towards another vehicle, the other sliding into the front seat beside the driver. He had a team of eight in place for the pickup. Four here and four more at Ana's house. Overkill, but he was taking no chances. He could see the trembling of Ana's hands as she clenched them together in her lap. The trembling didn't stop, so with a shaky huff of breath she shoved her tell-tale hands beneath her thighs and sat on them.

'Better?' he said.

'Interpreter training didn't encompass fearlessness in the face of abduction.'

'You're doing very well.'

Ana cut short what might have been a bitter laugh and looked out of the window as the museum swept from view. He let her be, more content with the darkness of the car and the silence, and her presence, than he had any right to be.

'What's wrong with your father?' she asked finally.

'Cancer.'

'How long does he have left?'

'Days.'

She nodded, and he appreciated her lack of false platitudes for a man she'd never met.

'Do you want Sophia to meet him?' she asked next, and it was a fair question. One he had yet to answer for himself.

'I haven't arranged it.'

'Because your father will be disappointed that you spawned a bastard child?'

'Because Sophia is the image of my sister at that age and my father is not always lucid,' he countered. 'He'll see what he wants to see rather than reality, and I would protect her from that kind of confusion.'

'And what will you see when you look at Sophia?' she asked.

'I don't know.' Truth again, and it sat uneasily on him after a lifetime of concealing his innermost thoughts and feelings. 'Ask me again in fifteen minutes.'

'Casimir, Your Highness, I'm not ready for this.'

Neither was he, but he was doing it. 'My father resides in the royal palace in Byzenmaach's capital but that's not where we're going. We're going to my private residence instead. It's a fortress under lockdown. There will be no press. No courtiers. You'll be safe there.'

'I was safe here,' she said.

'No, Anastasia. You weren't. You and Sophia were already under surveillance when we came looking for you.'

'I don't believe you.' She looked mutinous. 'We *are* safe here. Safer than we'd be with you.'

He reached into the pocket of the seat in front of him and drew out an envelope and handed it to her. 'This is all we've been able to come up with on those who have you under surveillance.' She opened the envelope and photos spilled out. 'That's the school's new contract gardener. He's a Byzenmaach national with ties to those who took my sister.'

Ana said nothing as she flipped to the next photo, but her lips tightened.

'Your new neighbours of three months. They live across the road from you. The woman is a Byzenmaach national. She's the granddaughter of the speaker for the Northern mountain tribes of Byzenmaach. He unifies them. He's also the one who ordered my sister's abduction. That or allowed it to happen. That's her real husband, by the way. He's Swiss. We don't know whether he's part of your surveillance team or not.'

Ana's hands trembled but she firmed them up fast and flicked over to the next photo. This one was of her sitting at a café with a co-worker. Her neighbour sat two tables away, reading the paper. 'So they watch. So what? They haven't done anything.'

'Yet.' He laid it out for her as plainly as he could. 'The Northern rebels are ruthless. Sophia is of royal blood and may be used against me. I'd rather have her at my side than see her in their clutches. I've already seen one show of theirs and I don't need a repeat performance.'

'Cas.' She shook her head, clearly not wanting to believe any of it. 'I can't— This isn't my life.'

But it was. 'I'm sorry, Anastasia. Had there been no other eyes on you I might have been able to leave you alone. Not saying I would have, but it was an option. That option ceased to exist the moment we identified who else we were dealing with. At that point I *had* to step in. Now that I have there's no coming back from that. Not for any of us. The world you woke up to this morning is gone.'

She said nothing.

'If it's any consolation this is an equal opportunity disaster. The world as I know it shattered too, the moment I discovered I had a daughter.'

'How very even-handed,' she said faintly.

'Isn't it. You always were fluent in understatement.' He'd always found it vaguely entertaining. 'How many languages are you fluent in now?'

'Six.'

'Your UN résumé says five.'

'They missed one.'

Not exactly reticent when it came to her skill set. Maybe that was a good thing, given the political world he was thrusting her into. 'Which one did they miss?'

'Yours.'

He blinked. Calculated the benefits of her being fluent in his native tongue and there were plenty. 'Thank God for that.'

'God has nothing to do with it. I learn fast. I was bored one day and picked up a dictionary.'

'You'll assimilate faster if you can speak the language. You may even be able to work as an interpreter for the palace.'

'Why would I want to do that? I've already achieved my workplace goals,' she snapped.

So she had. 'Will the UN allow you to work remotely?' They might. He'd not object.

'Casimir, I don't know exactly what you're thinking, but my career is here. I've worked hard to build it and I have no intention of throwing it away because you think Sophia and I would be safer in Byzenmaach. You have a problem on your Northern borders? Fix it. And then we can all get on with our lives.'

'It's really not that simple.' He'd expected resistance. Possibly not quite this much resistance, but still... He'd come prepared to bargain. To say whatever he had to say in order to get her on that plane. 'Anastasia, please. Take some leave from your work, come with me to Byzenmaach—where I need to be and where I can protect you—and let us work through this. You're right. These people may not be a threat to you or Sophia. Maybe they want to welcome you into their community with open arms and treasure you both for reasons unknown. It's possible. But right now we don't know what they want from you. What if I ask for a mere two weeks of your time? Enough time to build a case either for or against you and Sophia returning to Geneva. Right now I don't consider that an option but perhaps you can convince me otherwise. I'm not an unreasonable man. We can negotiate.'

She handed the photos and the envelope back to him and stared out of the car window by way of reply.

'The palace will provide amply for both you and Sophia. Money won't be an issue.' Possibly not the point but still worth mentioning.

'Thank you,' she grated, still not looking at him. 'Being dependent on someone else for the roof over my head, the clothes that I wear and the food in my mouth has always been one of my primary goals.'

'Irony, right?'

She cut him a look that could have shredded steel.

'Just checking. Some people wouldn't have a problem with being kept, given the circumstances.'

Although it seemed unlikely that she would be one of them and make life easier for everyone.

'Independence is hardly a character flaw,' she said. 'Try thinking of it as a strength.'

'I'd like to.' He really would. He just didn't know how much of an asset it would be when navigating the demands of royal existence.

Ana lived in an apartment just outside Geneva's UN precinct. By the time they reached it, a cold, illogical fear had begun to assail him. His daughter was in there. A daughter he'd never met, who was the image of his sister. A daughter who thought him dead.

'Ten minutes,' he said as he exited the car and leaned against the bonnet. 'Clothes, passports, belongings you can't live without. Whatever you're likely to need for your stay, bring it.'

'You're not coming in?'

'Am I invited?'

'You hijack my life and yet you stand here and ask for an invitation inside? What are you, a vampire?'

'I'm courteous.'

She laughed as if she couldn't help it, a sudden brightness in a night full of shadows and wrongdoing. 'You're everything I never wanted and can't forget,' she said. 'Presumably you've prepared for meeting your daughter as ruthlessly as you prepared for everything else.'

'Yes.'

She paused, both hands to the little blue door of her house. 'If you remember nothing else, remember this. If you hurt my daughter…if you ever make her feel less than the beautiful, innocent child she is… I will make you regret it.' Her voice was shaking and so were her hands but she turned to spear him with eyes fiercer than any eagle in his aviary. 'I will protect my child with my last breath. It's what mothers do.'

'Not in my experience.'

'Maybe you need more experience.' She turned away from him, put the key in the lock and pushed it open. 'My warning stands.'

He watched her enter, squared his shoulders and followed. He knew nothing of parenting, or of six-year-old girls, except that maybe, just maybe, they liked playing in royal gardens and catching dragonflies. That and they were expendable political pawns.

God help them all.

A cluttered hallway. A teenage babysitter who stood nervously when they entered the living room, a blue bedroom door—not quite closed. A sleeping child, half buried in bedclothes. These were the images that stayed with him, even as he boarded the plane forty minutes later with both Anastasia and their daughter in tow.

He hadn't been able to stand in that doorway as his daughter awoke, he'd returned to the living room—now minus the babysitter, who had been dismissed. He needed to put some physical distance between them so he could prepare himself for the moment. How to introduce himself to a six-year-old girl who thought her father dead? A child whose life would never be the same now that he'd claimed her as his?

Ana watching him from the doorway to the living room, a child's backpack in hand. He remembered that part.

'There's still time to change your mind,' she'd said. 'You could walk out that door and never look back. You'd never hear from me again. Whatever we had, whatever we once did…it never happened. I will take it to the grave.'

'She's mine.' He'd spread his hands wide. 'She's in

danger because of me. What kind of man would I be—what kind of father would I be—if I simply stepped back and let it happen?'

I am not my father.

Therein lay the crux of it.

And here they were on the plane. Ana getting the little one buckled into a seat for take-off. The child sleepy and wary of everything and everyone, the mother equally wary, her attention divided wholly between her daughter and him. There was a bedroom on the jet. A supper room if anyone was hungry. There was comfort here, and luxury. He didn't know whether to be relieved or concerned that Ana seemed to have no care whatsoever for the trappings of royalty or the security team that now surrounded them.

She'd brought the child to him in the living room of her house, both her and the girl hastily dressed in clothes for travelling. Jeans and a soft green pullover for Ana. Jeans, a teal T-shirt and a soft pink jacket cinched at the waist for his daughter. Sophia's ponytail had been slightly lopsided, her amber eyes still bleary with sleep and she hadn't reminded him of his sister at all in that moment. She hadn't reminded him of anyone he'd ever met and that was as it should be.

It had allowed him to breathe.

She was a skinny little thing, this child of his, but she'd met his gaze fearlessly.

He'd crouched down, one knee to the ground, and held out his hand for her to shake it. 'Hello.' No way he'd been able to get his voice to come out smooth so he'd settled for gruff in the hope that it would hide some of the emotion welling in his chest at the touch of his daughter's hand.

'Sophia, this is His Royal Highness, Prince Casimir of

Byzenmaach. He's an old acquaintance,' Ana had said. 'And a prince.'

'And your father,' he'd said. Like ripping off a Band-Aid. *Get it done, get it over with.*

The girl had flinched and looked to her mother for confirmation.

'Not dead,' Ana had said somewhat helplessly, and left it at that, and his daughter's wary gaze had returned to his face.

'Your eyes are like mine,' she'd said.

'Yes.'

'Maman says you have a castle,' the girl had said next.

'Yes.' Yes, he did, and he wasn't above using it to impress. 'Would you like to see it?'

'No,' she said.

'And we have puppies,' he'd said.

'What kind of puppies?' She was hard to impress, this daughter of his.

'Wolfhounds.' He'd wondered if a six-year-old would know what that meant. 'They're big and shaggy and built to protect the animals in their care. Wolfhounds are almost as big as ponies, which we also have.'

'Nice try,' Ana had murmured, but, hey. Whatever worked. He wanted his daughter to arrive in Byzenmaach with castles, ponies and puppies on her mind rather than fear in her heart for the unknown.

Ten minutes into the flight he turned on his phone to find three urgent messages waiting, all of them from Rudolpho. 'Flight time is five hours,' he said to Ana as foreboding washed over him. 'There's food, a bed through there with a television screen on the wall. Children's movies.' He'd even stocked up on those. 'Make yourselves comfortable.' He stood and nodded towards the sole woman on his security team. 'Katya will see to your needs.'

Ana eyed Katya with the deep distrust one might afford a rabid dog. 'And what will *you* be doing while we make ourselves at home?' she asked finally.

Casimir wasn't used to having his movements questioned, but for her he made an exception. 'I have some calls I must attend to. There's an office area at the rear of the aircraft.'

'I still have questions,' she said.

'Rest now.' He wished he had that luxury. 'There are some books on Byzenmaach in the bedroom if resting or television doesn't appeal. English editions. Arabic editions.' He'd offer books in his native language now that he knew she could read them. 'You're the mother of a royal bastard and you're about to gain unparalleled access to me and Byzenmaach's most trusted advisors. I want you knowledgeable when it comes to our history, our customs and our politics. I need you to be aware of the political battles in play around you and because of you.'

Not for Anastasia the kind of life his mother had led. Sidelined. Stripped of her voice and unable to influence even the most basic household decisions. Not for Casimir the choices his father had made.

'You expect me to inhale all this knowledge in five hours? From a pile of books?' she said.

'Well, I hear you're very smart and I did choose the books rather carefully,' he offered, deadpan. 'It's a start. I'm arming you with the tools you'll need to navigate my world. Knowledge that will prevent you from becoming a pawn for the ruthless. I *want* you to think for yourself. I *need* you to be able to protect yourself and our daughter. I will never deny you knowledge or a voice.'

She looked at him, and there was something wholly vulnerable in her gaze. A tiny break in her defences against him. 'Is this who you really are? No pretence?'

'This is me.' His world and his choices exposed. Sometimes self-serving, sometimes in service to the crown, sometimes in need of an anchor he didn't have but, heaven help him, he tried to be a fair and just man. And if he could be that for strangers he could sure as hell try to be that for her.

'Okay,' she said quietly.

'Okay,' he echoed, and fled before the sudden sizzling tension in the air between them got too much for him.

CHAPTER THREE

FIVE HOURS AND fifty-eight minutes later, after the flight in the royal jet followed by a helicopter ride, Ana stepped into another world.

Casimir had brought them to a pale stone fortress that shimmered in the moonlight. Floodlights lit the cobblestone courtyard that doubled as the landing pad. The walls of the fortress stretched towards the sky and dark mountains loomed menacingly to either side of it.

Ana couldn't imagine a more remote place.

'They're expecting you,' he said, as a security guard lifted his sleepy daughter from the helicopter and placed her in Ana's arms. 'The south wing is yours for the duration of your stay; they were my mother's rooms and the rooms I used throughout my childhood.' He gestured for a tall, bearded man waiting at the edge of the cobblestones to come forward. 'This is Silas. He'll see to your needs. I'm afraid I have to return to the capital this evening.'

'You're leaving?' If she sounded panicked it was only because she was. He'd stayed in his office for the entire plane flight and had said less than two words to them in the helicopter. Granted, the helicopter was a noisy beast, not conducive to conversation, but still...

'It can't be helped.'

'Why are you leaving? Where are you going?' Ana

clutched Sophia closer. 'Why go to all this trouble to bring us here if you're not even going to *be here*?'

'I'm sorry,' he offered. 'I'll return as soon as I can.'

'You can't just leave us here! I don't even know where here is!'

That'd teach her to take the word of a prince as something worth having.

'You're at the winter fortress in the Belarine Mountains of Byzenmaach. This is my home and the people here are loyal to me. You can trust them.'

'Why on earth would I trust them when I can't even trust *you*?'

He looked torn in that moment. Not to mention utterly weary.

He took her aside, his hand at the small of her back guiding her way, and it was a gesture she'd never forgotten, not to mention a response she'd never experienced with any other man. Desire washed over her, pure and fierce and more potent than ever. Desire laced with fear.

She closed her eyes and drew in a shaky breath. 'I want to trust you to do right by us. I want to believe I've done the right thing by coming here. But I don't know you. I never did. All I know is that you come into my world and turn it upside down and I lose.'

He pressed his lips to her temple and then hesitated before lifting her chin and pressing a kiss to the edge of her lips. His lips were soft and warm and so gentle, and if Ana's eyes fluttered closed and she suddenly wanted this moment to last for ever it was only because all else seemed so harsh.

'I don't want to lose any more,' she whispered, and he pulled away and drew a breath more ragged than hers.

'Neither do I. Believe me, neither do I.' Slowly, almost reluctantly, he tucked a stray strand of hair behind her ear. She leaned into his touch, and maybe it was because he was the one familiar thing in a world that was cold and dark, and maybe her soul would always cry out for his touch no matter what.

'I wanted to help you get settled. I wanted to show you my home, and I will but not tonight. My father is on his deathbed and I've been called to his side. That's what all the phone calls were about—that's where I'm going. And that is no place for a child.' He put his fingers to her chin and tilted her head until she met his gaze. 'We do take care of our young around here, no matter what you might think. Get Silas to show you the puppies. They're real. It's all real.'

'For you,' she said, and he smiled wryly.

'For all of us.'

Ana watched him leave in the helicopter, a fading red light in the bleak night sky, and only once the tail light had disappeared did she realise how cold it was and how heavy six-year-old girls could be. She took a deep breath and felt Sophia's arms tighten around her neck.

'Maman?'

'Hush, baby. Everything's okay. We'll find ourselves another bed soon.'

'Indeed you will,' said the bearded man, bowing slightly. 'Ms Douglas, would you like me to carry the child?'

'No.'

He bowed again. 'Then please let me lead the way to your rooms.'

'Thank you.' She too could be courteous. And it had been one hell of a long evening.

The bedroom suite he took them to was truly fit for a queen. Silk wallpaper adorned the walls. Heavy brocade gold covers graced the bed and Ana wondered whether a body would suffocate beneath the weight of them.

His mother's rooms, he'd said.

The one who'd lost her daughter and committed suicide.

She put Sophia down and fingered the heavy coverlet while the bearded man, Silas, looked on in silence. The floor was a pale grey stone and the ceiling soared high above them. An open fire crackled in the hearth and uniformly shaped logs had been stacked beside it.

There was a breakfast room, a dressing room, a bathroom suite and a nursery, all of it too vast and imposing to contemplate. Tears pricked at her eyes as she stood there, barely holding it together. She closed her eyes, wrapped her arms around her waist and tried to imagine the comfort and familiarity of her snug apartment, but it was no use. She was thousands of miles away and drowning in uncertainty.

Casimir had come for them with conviction in his eyes and promises to protect her on his lips and she'd trusted him to do right by her.

When had he ever done that?

Opening her eyes, she faced her fear as two other people she didn't know brought her and Sophia's luggage into the room and began to open it.

'Leave it,' she snapped.

Her five-minute packing effort; her mess to sort. Their bad luck to be waiting on a woman who didn't want any of this.

The fortress staff withdrew without a word, all except for Silas, who seemed as immovable as the stone beneath her feet. 'We've been warming the suite for two days,' he said. 'I regret that we're not quite ready for visitors but you came as quite a surprise. The chill should be off these rooms by tomorrow and then we can make lighter bedcovers available.'

Castle-warming. Attempting a smile at this point would only bring tears. 'Thank you.'

'What time would you like breakfast?'

'What time is it?' She'd lost track of time, not to mention time zones.

'A little after two a.m., Ms Douglas.'

Right.

'Or you can pick up the phone when you wake, dial one, and let us know when you would like to breakfast.'

She nodded. 'I'd like to ring my parents and let them know where we are. Can I do that from this phone?'

'Of course,' he said. 'Dial zero, then the country code, then the number. It will dial straight out.'

'Thanks.' Not a prisoner then. Not quite. 'I'll do that tonight.' Wake them up. Have a conversation with her parents that she'd been avoiding for almost seven years.

'Of course,' he said again. He turned to Sophia, bowed slightly and left.

Ana waited until the door had closed and they were alone before looking to Sophia. Her daughter's gaze slid towards the nursery room door, her face a study in uncertainty.

'So this is Casimir's castle,' Ana began.

Sophia nodded.

'Big, isn't it?'

Sophia nodded again.

'It'll be better in the morning when we can see it properly. You want to sleep with me tonight?'

A more vigorous nod.

'I can tell you a story before we go to sleep.'

'A story about a princess trapped in a castle and a dragon who comes to save her?' Sophia asked.

'Sure.' They both knew that particular story well. Where were their pyjamas? She hadn't packed winter ones. Why hadn't she packed winter clothes for them?

'Can there be a donkey and a dying king?'

'Yes,' Ana said, still rifling through their suitcases. She knew that story too.

'That man—Cas—he said his father was dying.'

'Yes.'

'And then he *kissed* you.'

Yes. That. Her daughter wasn't used to sharing and Ana had no explanation whatsoever for the kiss. 'Okay, we'll add a dying king and a prince—who is a donkey—to the story.'

'Is he really my father?' Sophia asked abruptly, and there was a world of hurt in her voice and no little accusation.

'Yes.'

'You said he was dead.'

'I know. I thought—' *I thought it better to tell you that than the truth.* 'I thought wrong.'

'What does he want?' Sophia asked next.

'Right now he wants to protect us.' Give the devil his due. 'And then I think he wants to get to know you.'

'You're not leaving me here and going home, are you?' Fierce golden eyes were even more breathtaking when they were vulnerable.

'No. I will never do that.'

'Promise?'

'I promise. What else do you want in this story?'

'No frogs.'

'Got it. No frogs.'

'And no kisses,' Sophia said fiercely.

'Not even a mother's goodnight kiss for the princess?'

Sophia hesitated. 'Am I a princess?'

Pyjamas! Finally. 'Here. Get changed and jump into bed and then there will be storytelling. As for whether you're a princess or not… I don't know. Your father's a prince. He's about to become a king. But he and I aren't married, and that complicates things. It's something else to ask when we see him next.'

Mothers were wise, and it was their duty to make chewable that which was complex. Or, in this case, to avoid talking about Casimir altogether.

'So. Let me tell you a story about a castle and a dragon and a princess. You want to hear it in Russian or in French?'

An hour later, Sophia was asleep and Ana was in the other room, castle phone in hand and too afraid to use it. She needed advice and with that came confession. For seven years she'd shut her parents out as far as the identity of Sophia's father was concerned. They'd helped her get back on her feet after Sophia had been born. With their financial help she'd been able to continue her studies and find childcare for her baby. They hadn't let her fall. They'd supported her.

But they'd never, ever understood her choices.

She barely understood them herself.

She made the call and started pacing the moment she heard her mother's voice.

'I don't want you to worry,' she said to begin with, and knew it for an opening that would guarantee exactly the opposite result.

'I'm in Byzenmaach with Sophia…and Sophia's father,' she said next, and, yeah, she truly failed at giving reassurances. 'Let me start again.'

'Anastasia, breathe,' her mother said, so she did.

'Now, start from the beginning.'

'Oh, you really don't want me to do that.'

'I really do,' her mother said gently. 'If this is about Sophia's father, I really do want you to start from the beginning.'

She couldn't do it.

'Let me start for you,' her mother said next. Still calm. No judgement. 'You were nineteen and I'd just sent you away from me for the very first time. A new country for you. A bright future. I knew you were precocious, passionate, full of life and I wanted new experiences for you. New people to meet and worlds to explore. I thought I'd prepared you.'

'You did. Mama, you did. None of this was your fault.'

'And then you met a man.'

'He was twenty-three, and he was everything.' Ana gave her that in the hope that her next words would come more easily. 'He said his name was Cas and that he'd been attending a political summit in Geneva. He stayed with me for a week. It was a good week. A week out of time and place—I was so captivated by him. And then he left. You know he left.' She closed her eyes. 'I found out who he was just before Sophia was born, and then it made sense. What he'd done. Why he went away and never looked back. He's the Crown Prince of Byzenmaach. Sole heir to the throne and he's promised elsewhere. His father is dying and he'll be king within days. I didn't know that to start with, but I've known for a while.'

Silence held sway while her mother digested her words. Her mother was a political animal, first and foremost. Ana didn't need to say any more.

'And now he wants Sophia,' her mother offered at last.

'Yes.'

'Oh, baby,' her mother said, and there was no solution in those words, just a deep well of compassion and unshed tears.

'So I'm here, in Byzenmaach, trying to find a way forward that doesn't involve giving her up or me turning into some kind of royal wallpaper without any agency or life of my own.' That was the sum of it. The end result of all those decisions made long ago. 'I'm sorry I never told you who he was. I never thought he'd return. I thought it better that no one knew. Safer for everyone.'

'Oh, Ana.'

'Don't make me cry,' Ana said fiercely. 'I can't cry here. I can't show weakness. They'll know I'm not enough. That I've never been enough.'

'You have *always* been enough.' Her mother had slipped into Russian, a sure sign of emotions fully engaged. 'I am so proud of you. I have always been proud of you. And if he left you because he couldn't see your value, that's *his* loss. And your advantage.'

'Mama, what do I do? Can I fight a royal family for Sophia and win?'

Her mother's silence echoed what she already knew.

'What do I do?'

Her mother drew a deep breath. 'So he's about to marry?'

'I don't know. I think so.'

'What are your feelings for him?'

'I don't know.'

'Oh,' her mother said.

'What do you mean, "*Oh*"?'

'I mean he's it for you, and always has been.'

'No!'

Maybe.

'Okay, maybe feelings are involved and I'm not as immune to him as I'd like to be. He's...more than he used to be. More of everything.'

'This is bad,' her mother said. 'Anastasia, listen to me. You keep your feelings for him to yourself for now. It's to his advantage that you still care for him, not yours. Negotiate first. Confess your attraction later. Or never. Never would work.'

'Got it.' Ana stifled a snort.

'Anastasia, your experience with men is—'

'Limited. I know. But when you've had the best why settle for less?'

'He wasn't the best. He left you. Remember that? Because I do.'

'I remember.'

'You never gave anyone else even half a chance. You threw yourself into your work, and that worked for you and continues to do so. But don't try and tell me you live for your career. Because I live for mine, and God bless your father for putting up with me in that regard, but you're not like me. You don't have that compulsion. You work because that was the plan before he came into your life and you were determined to stick to the plan afterwards. And you have. And I'm proud of all that you've achieved. But your work is not your life's ambition. It's just ambition.'

'Mama, I don't—'

'You want the fairy tale, Anastasia. An identity of your own, the man you love at your side and children in your life and in your heart. Sophia and more. That's your life's ambition. Correct me if I'm wrong.'

Ana nudged her forehead gently against the wall, phone at her ear and bare feet on cold stone. 'You're not wrong.'

'It's not too much to ask for. This I believe. Will he give that to you?'

'No.'

'Negotiate,' said her mother, and this time Ana laughed helplessly.

'With what?'

'Yourself.'

'You mean the one he left all those years ago? Couldn't hold his attention for more than a week?'

'His mistake. He didn't realise what he held.'

'Maybe he did.'

'*Or* you can take a good look at him without the rose-coloured glasses of youth and this time you look for the flaws in him.' Her mother's voice had firmed. 'Embrace him or not, but see him for who he is and bargain hard for your future and Sophia's. I raised a daughter with brains as well as heart. Don't prove me wrong.'

'So find his weakness and exploit it?'

'Well, that's another way of putting it,' her mother said drily. 'That or make him see you and want you and love you the way you should be loved.'

'How is that easy to do?'

'It can be.' Her mother sighed. 'If he's the right one for you, it's as easy as breathing.'

'I'm not breathing, Mama. I'm holding my breath.' She looked around the room, at the ceilings high above her with their intricate plasterwork, at the silk wallpaper and the paintings on the walls. 'I don't know how to do this.'

'You're not alone. Remember that. There's strength in that. You have us, and Sophia. You *know* love and that is the strongest force in the world. Does he know love?'

Ana thought of the man and his history. His duty and his resolve. 'I don't know.'

'Step one,' said her mother. 'Find out.'

CHAPTER FOUR

CASIMIR'S FATHER DIED sixteen hours after Casimir reached the royal palace. Casimir had sat at his father's bedside and occasionally held the older man's hand and tried to feel something other than bone-deep weariness. His father had rallied at one point, enough to realise that Cas was there, but beyond that there had been no real communication.

Cas would never know what words his father spoke at the very end; they'd been unintelligible. He didn't need to know. His father had never spoken any words of love in Casimir's presence and Casimir would have been astonished to hear any, even here at the end of things.

When his father took his last breath, Cas felt nothing. No sorrow. No grief. He knew grief and this wasn't it. He just felt blank.

He waited five minutes before calling the physicians in. Five minutes that he spent with his head bowed and his hand still clasped in his father's until finally he felt a small stirring of some kind of feeling, even if it was only relief for the end of his father's suffering.

His father was at rest now. No more brutal physical pain for the man who'd once been king. This was a good thing.

When he opened the huge double doors of his father's

bedchamber and stepped out into the anteroom, every man and woman waiting stood and snapped to attention.

'It's finished,' he told them. 'The king is dead.'

Rudolpho was the first to respond. 'Long live the king.'

And there it was. Another king for the Byzenmaach throne.

His father's endgame finally realised.

Casimir rubbed at his face, beyond tired and way beyond lucid. Sixteen hours at his father's bedside. Twelve hours of travel before that, with collecting Ana and Sophia somewhere in the middle of it. A full day's work before he'd even left to go and get them. Thirty-six hours since he'd last slept and still more to do before he could rest. 'I'm going home,' he said.

'Your Majesty.' Rudolpho again, eyeing him as cautiously as one might survey a ticking time bomb. 'There are rooms here. Surely—'

'I'm going home,' he said again. He'd stood vigil to the bitter end and no one could fault him. Duty had been served and all he wanted was to get out of this place and breathe for a while before he had to return.

Ana was waiting for him. That, more than anything, drew him like a lodestone. 'Make it happen.'

'Yes, Your Majesty.' Rudolpho bowed and Casimir almost groaned. He'd spent a lifetime preparing for this moment, and here he was acting like a petty two-year-old. 'I also want every portrait and photo of my sister and mother gone from these palace walls by the time I return. All bar the two in the portrait gallery. They can stay.'

Someone gasped. This wasn't going well. That second command could have waited a decade or so before being made. Casimir had waited all of seven minutes. He smiled grimly and tried to explain himself—another first in a day of firsts. 'Put them in a room somewhere and shut the door on them. My family will never be forgotten—not by me, not by any of you. This I know. But this palace has served as a shrine to the dead long enough. No more. Not one minute more.'

People bowed their heads. His father's people, not wanting to make eye contact.

His people now.

He'd carried the hope of a nation on his shoulders for years and it was finally time to deliver.

'I will serve,' he rasped. 'To the best of my ability I will serve you all. When have I not? But I am *not* my father, and things *will* change around here. Not in five years' time, not in ten. Change starts now.'

It wasn't until he and Rudolpho were approaching the helicopter ten minutes later that the old advisor deigned to talk about Casimir's first words in his new role.

'Good pep talk,' Rudolpho offered drily. 'You could have warned me about wanting to take the portraits down.'

Could've. Didn't. 'I wanted to see their reactions for myself.'

'And what did their reactions tell you?'

'That some will always resist change and others will embrace it.'

'You didn't need to issue a royal command to know that.'

Casimir smiled mirthlessly. 'I also learned that the people of Byzenmaach are willing to give me more leeway than I expected, going forward. And I'm going to take it.'

'You'll be needing a new chief advisor, I presume,' Rudolpho offered tightly.

'No. I want you to stay on in the role, but there's a

catch. I don't want the kind of silent subservience you gave my father. I know how you work. You sidle in sideways, using your considerable diplomacy skills to smooth over problems that you knew my father would never outright address. That stops. For forty years you've had the pulse of a nation at your fingertips. Now you have a voice to go with it and I expect you to use it, because I'm listening. I'd like to see if together we *can* fix what my father would not. Are you up for it?'

'Your Majesty, I am most definitely *up for it*, as it were. Although not entirely fluent in your vernacular.'

'That's all right.' Casimir allowed himself a smile. 'You'll learn.'

The first thing Casimir saw as he approached the winter fortress by air were the flags flying at half-mast. So they knew and there would be no need to say it again. The king was dead. Byzenmaach was his now, not that it mattered here in the cradle of these mountains.

The people here had always been his.

By the time they'd landed and he'd reached the entrance hall, it seemed as if the entire castle staff had either seen or heard the helicopter land and dropped whatever they were doing.

People lined up to one side of the door. People who'd cared for him since he was a child. People he cared for, like Silas and his wife, Lor. People like Tomas the falconer and Saul the stable master.

God help him, he was tired.

But he did what he had to do. He started at the top of the line and took an old groundsman's hand in his and let the man offer his condolences. He would speak to his people until there was no one left in line that he hadn't touched and listened to. He would do this because, unlike his father's courtiers, he owed them.

He looked away from the person in front of him just once—looked up to see how far the line stretched—and there stood Ana at the foot of the stairs, with Sophia beside her. He smiled, and maybe it was a mere echo of the smiles they'd shared all those years ago, but it was real.

She looked well rested and coolly composed. Guarded, which wasn't surprising. He'd all but abandoned her here. She lifted her chin and stared him down as if she belonged here and he had some explaining to do, dead father or not.

Ten more minutes and he'd be at the end of the line and facing her and the daughter he'd barely come to terms with.

If this was protocol, Ana didn't know her part in it, other than to hover by the foot of the stairs with Sophia at her side and wait for Casimir to approach them.

Casimir's father was dead. Byzenmaach had a new king and he was it, as evidenced by the security staff who accompanied him. Hard-eyed men and women in dark suits, they took up positions in corridors, by doorways and on the stairs.

Not alarming at all.

Cas made a point of greeting every person waiting to speak with him. He shook every hand and accepted a lone poppy from a wizened woman who couldn't possibly still work for him. He patted the woman's hand and whispered something that made her smile, and then he reached Silas and his wife, Lor, and Ana was surprised at the strength of the embrace they shared. Words passed in that embrace, none of them spoken. Whispers of the boy he'd once been and exactly where such a boy might have found a comforting hand.

And then he turned his gaze on her and Sophia and the conflict in his eyes rendered her silent.

She was here at his request, sure enough, but she had no idea if he wanted her and Sophia where he could see them.

He smiled at her then, a touch of wry amusement in the curve of it, and in that instant became the man she'd once known.

'My condolences,' she said, so stilted and formal, but she didn't know what else to say.

'Thank you,' he said quietly. 'Ana. Sophia. Once again I must apologise for leaving you to your own devices. It appears my skills as a host are gravely overrated.'

'We have puppies,' Sophia said by way of reply, and it was the right thing to say. Or perhaps it simply wasn't the wrong thing to say.

'*Do* we?' he said.

'Do you want to see them?' her daughter asked.

'Yes.'

'They're Jelly's,' Sophia added. 'They're very special. Lor says you named Jelly the First when you were a kid.'

'I did,' he said.

'This mother dog is Jelly the Eighth. Which means one of the puppies has to be called Jelly the Ninth.'

'Have you chosen which one yet?' he asked.

'Yes.' Sophia rushed ahead and then stopped abruptly at the first security guard, glancing back at Cas to see if he was following and then at Ana. Or perhaps she was simply looking for permission to proceed.

Ana stood frozen, not knowing her role in any of this. And then Casimir turned to her and pinned her with a questioning gaze as well. 'Coming?' he asked.

Yes. Even with the way she usually drew public gaze, she was hard pressed not to flinch beneath the weight of *this* crowd's gaze. Wariness. Suspicion. Not from Silas or Lor, who she'd spent most of the day with, but from others, yes. She could feel the crawl of judgement on her skin.

It made her straighten her shoulders and lift her chin as she walked towards him. 'Thank you for coming back here this evening,' she said when she reached him.

'Did you think I wouldn't?'

'I didn't know. I know nothing of the duties of a king.'

They reached the kitchen, not that it was like any other kitchen Ana had ever been in. This kitchen had storerooms of its own and a long central bench. Three hearths, only one of which was functional. One of the other fireplaces held Jelly the wolfhound and her puppies. Sophia approached them with a confidence borne of innocence, dropping first to her knees and then to her belly, her ponytail off-centre again and her too-short jeans hiking halfway up her calves. She wasn't wearing shoes. Who wore shoes inside a house?

Unless, of course, the house was a royal fortress.

'This one's Little Jelly,' Sophia said, gently stroking one of the puppies while Mama Jelly looked on indulgently.

Wolfhounds were placid and tolerant, Ana had decided. This one was, at any rate.

'How can you tell?' Casimir asked.

'She has a white tip on her tail, just like Big Jelly.'

'I think Sophia's going to be a geneticist,' Ana murmured, given all the questions she'd asked about eye colours today. 'Have you eaten?' Not that it was her place to ask, but it was as good a question as any. A regular question without any ulterior weight to it. 'Lor's been baking all day.'

'I'm not hungry,' he said, but he went into a side chamber and returned shortly after with a bottle of whisky. He knew where the tumblers were and enquired, with the tilt of the bottle, whether he should fill a glass for her.

'No,' she said.

'Something else?' he asked as he poured himself one.

'I'm fine.'

'What have you been doing today?' he asked next.

'That's really what you want to talk about?'

'Yes.' A weary smile crossed his lips and softened her heart. He looked to their daughter, the wolfhound and the puppies. 'Talk to me of carefree things.'

'We baked with Lor and made Turkish delight.'

'My favourite,' he said.

'So Lor said.' Ana knew a lot of things about him that she hadn't known before this morning, including the fact that dead King Leonidas had been a good king, a merciless opponent, an indifferent husband and a hard father to please. 'Then we saw falcons and horses and hand fed them both. Then there's the bathhouse,' she added, and was rewarded with the glimmer of a smile.

'You found it?'

'Oh, I did,' she said reverently.

'You liked it?'

It was a Roman gladiator's bathhouse built of marble, with steaming hot pools of varying temperature and a waterfall. A soaring domed roof added majesty. 'I want to take it with me when I leave.'

'You're not the first to want that.' His gaze drifted to Sophia again. 'I know we need to talk about what I have in mind for you both. I should be free of my most pressing commitments by Wednesday at the latest.'

It was Saturday night.

'Cas.' As beautiful as this place was, she couldn't just abandon the life she'd built on the off-chance that the new king of Byzenmaach could schedule her in. 'I need to understand what you want from us now, not next week. I need you to prioritise our custody talks. Can you do that for me? Because I guarantee that if you can't do that I'm going to assume that you will *never* put your daughter's needs first.'

He met her gaze squarely. 'Tell me what you want going forward.'

'Ideally? The security threat you spoke of gone, full custody of my daughter, and my life in Geneva to resume.'

He nodded. 'I'm working on the first, no to the second, no idea about the third. Like it or not, your daughter is a part of the royal family of Byzenmaach now and, by extension, so are you. Complications will ensue.'

'I want to meet with you tomorrow to talk about a way forward for us all,' she continued doggedly, keeping her mother's words of negotiation firmly in mind. 'I want to talk about the kind of compromises we may *both* need to make. No lawyers. Not yet. Just you, me, a problem to solve and our goodwill.'

'I have meetings all morning.'

'Or…you can toss my current goodwill back in my face and we can embark on a very public, very bitter custody battle. Then we can get *all* the lawyers involved,' she murmured. 'UK lawyers. Human rights lawyers. *Your* lawyers. Keep in mind that when it comes to eviscerating reputations I have a great deal less to lose than you.'

Those fierce tawny eyes of his narrowed. 'Where'd you learn to negotiate?'

'The UN.'

He smiled mirthlessly and lifted the glass to his lips for another hit. 'Right.'

'I'm not nineteen and naïve any more, Casimir. I can't

afford to be. And you're not twenty-three and running from your responsibilities. Or are you still doing that?'

'Ana, leave off. You've got your meeting tomorrow. I'll make time.'

'Thank you.' It didn't feel like victory. Instead, it felt a whole lot like kicking a man when he was down. She sipped at her drink as he studied his daughter and the puppies as if they were puzzle pieces he couldn't quite place. And this time when he spoke he didn't look at her.

'My father used to say to me, "You need to marry and produce an heir, Casimir, for the sake of the throne". I used to tell him there was plenty of time for that, and when I turned thirty I would do my duty by him and by Byzenmaach. Until then, I didn't *want* to be bound within marriage. I didn't want to bring children into my world. Because I knew I'd fear for their safety in a way that I've never feared for my own.' He ducked his head and ran a hand through his hair before turning his gaze on them again. 'For what it's worth, I was right. Some of my fears for your safety and for hers aren't even based in reality. They're just shadows. Intangible. Present only in my head, and I don't know how to get rid of them.'

'Maybe I can help,' she offered quietly.

The look he gave her in return was a shadowy, twisted thing.

'Even if it's simply to cut you some slack when it comes to intangible fears based on some of your more formative experiences,' she said. 'In return, you might cut me some slack when it comes to my fear of losing Sophia to a glittering, privileged world I cannot access.'

'Done,' he muttered. 'I am no monster to deny a mother access to her child. We'll work something out.'

'What are you going to do about a legitimate heir?' It

wasn't an idle question. Clearly, he needed an heir. That was his reality. 'I'm assuming Sophia will never inherit?'

'Correct. Sophia will never rule Byzenmaach. It doesn't make her any less valuable in my eyes. She's my daughter and I am more than glad she exists, and I am…grateful…' he chose the word as if trying it on for size '… I am grateful you are here with me today. Both of you. Like this.'

'You have no other family left.' She tried to imagine herself all alone in the world, and couldn't. She too would cling to whatever slim thread presented itself. 'Better this than nothing.'

'That's not it.' Her gaze met his and held and he was the first to look away. 'Hell, maybe it is.' He took a drink. 'Do you ever think about back then? About what we had?'

'Yes.' Pointless denying it.

'Good thoughts?'

'Sometimes,' she offered. 'We were very good at some things. Sleep wasn't one of them.' She watched his lips tilt slightly and knew she wanted more of that and less of the duty-bound monarch who'd entered his fortress and set to making sure his people were comforted.

'There wasn't much cooking happening either,' he rasped.

'You couldn't cook. That was blindingly obvious.' She looked around the huge catering kitchen that was Lor's domain, for all that the older woman was staying out of it at present. 'And now I know why.'

'Never saw the need to learn,' he admitted. 'Do you still live on apple Danishes and sunshine?'

'Sometimes I try.' Not often. Too many sweets and her curves tended to get out of control. She wondered if he'd clocked the changes in her figure in the same way she'd noticed the increased breadth of his shoulders and the muscles in his thighs. She wondered if he was looking for traces of the laughing girl she'd once been in the same way she was waiting for him to be the person she remembered. The one with the smile she'd never had to work for. The one whose body had been hers for the taking.

He'd had her every which way and then some.

She hadn't forgotten.

'Yeah. It's not hard to look back on that week with a certain amount of fondness.' Even his wrists, currently half covered by the snowy white cuffs of his shirt, conjured memories of their lovemaking. Of her pinning his arms above his head the better to get at him, and of him letting her. 'And then you left.'

He said nothing.

Nothing to explain.

'So. Do you have any other illegitimate offspring I should know about?' she asked.

'No.'

'Are you sure? I mean, you didn't know about Sophia until now. Maybe there's more.'

'There's not.'

'How do you know?' She was goading him now, for no real purpose other than she wanted to hurt him the way he was hurting her.

'Because I've never been as careless as I was with you, neither before nor since. Nor have I ever deceived another the way I did you.'

And wasn't that adding fuel to an already lit flame. 'Then why did you do it? *To me!* What did I ever do to you to deserve that kind of treatment except love you? *I don't understand.*' She'd never understood.

'I saw something I wanted and took it. I never thought beyond the moment as to whether I could keep it. Never a good idea.' He stood abruptly and drained his glass.

'But it's done now, and it's time to move forward. Perhaps after you put Sophia to bed you can come and find me. We can try more negotiation, maybe even work our way up to argument.'

'Will you even be awake? When did you last sleep?' And why did she care?

'Centuries ago,' he offered. 'You have the advantage. Take it or leave it.'

'I'll take it,' she said.

Casimir knew he was making a mess of things when it came to his dealings with Ana. Incorporating her and Sophia into his life was never going to be easy—and this was only the beginning. They'd had only the tiniest taste of the security needed to keep them safe, and no encounters whatsoever with the press. Even if he had been willing to let his daughter live in Geneva some of the time—and he wasn't—fundamental changes would have to be made to the way they lived.

Casimir's bedroom provided the solitude he so badly needed. Cold meats, cheeses and breads had been laid out on the sideboard. Lor's doing, most likely, for she well knew his tendency to skip meals when at the palace.

Shower first, eat later. He needed the smell of death gone, never mind that all he had to do was close his eyes in order to conjure a vision of it.

He stripped as he walked towards the bathroom. Stood naked under the stinging spray and finally let the significance of this day enter the guarded chambers of his heart. His father was dead and he still couldn't summon true grief for him. He tried to think back, and further back again, but couldn't call up a memory of his father ever letting his royal façade fall. It wasn't done. Duty to the throne had been everything.

Casimir *knew* what his father would do with Sophia in this situation. Use her as a panacea for the nation and milk her resemblance to Claudia for all it was worth until a *real* heir could be produced. What would his father have done with her after that? Shipped her back into obscurity? Married her off in service to Byzenmaach alliances? Either way, his father would never have allowed a daughter close enough to be missed.

His father would certainly never have allowed any wife or mother of that child—or even the child herself—any say in those decisions.

I am not him.

That sentiment right there was his weakness when it came to dealing with Ana and Sophia. Was he to be so bound up in proving himself a more reasonable man than his father that he forgot to voice what *he* wanted out of this? To raise a daughter who had no doubt whatsoever as to her father's love for her. That was a primary goal of his.

And there it was again, that insidious comparison to his upbringing. His father's influence worming its way into every breath.

His father was dead.

And if Casimir felt only a bone-deep relief, so be it.

It wasn't the hard-hearted indifference his father had tried to instil in him and for that he would be grateful. His father was dead and he had a daughter who lived and breathed and he wanted nothing more than to have her within reach so he could get to know her. He didn't want to parent her alone. He didn't want to cut Ana out of her life.

He wanted them both within reach, and when it came to Ana…

When it came to her he'd always wanted more than he could afford.

Why was it that the mere thought of Anastasia Douglas could make even the most exhausted version of himself rise to the occasion?

New memories to replace the old, and now he had one of her waiting for him on the stairs to his fortress and smiling when he looked her way. He had one of her pouring him a drink, all understated care and compassion. Her smile when she'd told him she'd already discovered the sensory pleasures of the bathhouse. He'd not forget that any time soon.

Still too open and honest for her own good, this new Ana.

Still way too inclined to look at him and let her gaze linger on his fingers and his mouth, his body and the rise and fall of his chest. It was still there, that overwhelming awareness of each other. He still wanted her with every breath he took.

And she wasn't indifferent to him.

It was going to make negotiating a pathway forward more difficult for all of them.

What else did he want from her? That was the question. Forget the demands of the monarchy for once. Forget his father's example when it came to dealing with women.

What *else* did he want from her if he could have it?

Apart from her—wholly naked and pleading—beneath him.

Five minutes later he emerged from the shower, his skin still dripping and his towel slung low around his hips. He felt a little more human, a little more alert, and no more the wiser.

Ana stood waiting for him.

'Silas told me where to find you,' she said.

'Did he tell you to walk right on into my private quarters?'

'You invited me.'

So he had. The why of it still escaped him. He was too tired for negotiation and at a disadvantage. If she pressed him for concessions he was likely to give them. Was it loneliness that had made him extend the invitation? Did he have any idea why he was doing this?

All food for thought.

'This room is the mirror of the one I'm in. Only warmer.' Her gaze never left his skin. 'I was looking at it before you came in. Shouldn't you be putting some clothes on?'

'Perhaps if I'd known you were here...' Although, given the hot colour stealing through her cheeks, he might have left them off just for her. 'Nothing you haven't seen before.'

'You look like an Egyptian king.'

'Well, you know. Romans, Egyptians. Relatives. All of them.' She couldn't seem to drag her gaze away from him and he knew that if she kept it up he'd be reaching for her within minutes. 'Do you feel like swimming? I feel like swimming.' He walked towards the door that led to the walkway that led to the bathhouse. She'd know where he was heading soon enough given that her rooms had the mirror image layout and bathhouse access. 'You don't look as angry with me as you did in the kitchen.'

'I'm trying to be a grown-up. Also, you've had a hard few days. I'll give you that.'

'Always with the compliments,' he said. Broken moonlight banded the stone floor and faintly lit the way. 'Coming?'

'You say that a lot.'

'King,' he said. 'People wait on my command.'

'Even your lovers? Even your friends? When does equal exchange happen?'

Rarely, and maybe that was part of his problem. 'Perhaps you can show me how it's done.'

She fell into step beside him, their shoulders brushing every so often, never mind that the walkway was comfortably wide enough for two.

'How's this going to work?' she murmured. 'You swim, I talk and if you don't like what I have to say you disappear underwater?'

'Well, it *could* work that way,' he murmured agreeably. 'Or you could swim too.'

'No costume.'

'Are you expecting me to wear one?' Now there was a thought he hadn't entertained.

'Sophia wants to know if she's a princess,' Ana said next. 'My mother also wants to know about Sophia's princess status. I don't know what to tell them.'

'Officially, no. Unofficially, yes.'

'Good luck explaining that to a six-year-old.'

'My sister's duchy lies vacant. I find it fitting that it goes to Sophia, in which case she'll hold the title of duchess. There is a castle to go with it. A very pretty one. Will that suffice?'

The walkway chilled his skin. Talk of tiny princesses did likewise. Ana's presence heated it. All in all, there was balance.

'Are you really serious about making Sophia a part of the royal family?' she asked.

'Did you think I wouldn't be?'

'I thought you were offering us protection on an as-needed basis. Not…incorporation.'

'I'm offering both. She's my daughter too, Anastasia. My blood. I have a duty of care. Had I known of her existence—'

But he hadn't known. He'd never, ever thought there'd

be those kind of consequences. Ana had been so determined to have a career.

'I should have known about her. Followed up with you. I should have made it my business to know.' He was not flawless. He could admit that. 'Now that I do know I will not do wrong by you. Sophia will need a nanny while she's here. Tutors,' he continued, and his daughter wasn't the only one who'd need tutoring. 'Would you object to me providing a tutor for you? I would have you educated in royal protocol and diplomacy so that you in turn can guide our daughter. I meant what I said about not cutting you out of Sophia's life. That's not what I want.'

She was silent a long time after that, and he wondered if he'd offended her. He hadn't, had he? He'd offered a service. Politely.

They reached the bathing room and stepped inside, and he'd switched on the underwater lights before she finally answered.

'I don't object to being tutored,' she murmured. 'I would like to be involved in helping Sophia make the transition from ordinary girl to... Duchess.'

'I'll make it happen,' he said. He padded towards his favourite pool. It was smaller than the others, hotter, and set back into the shadows. No underwater lights for this pool. It was all dark, lapping water and unspoken promise.

'Have you made any progress when it comes to knowing why we were under surveillance in Geneva?' she asked.

'Not yet.'

'What happens when the two weeks is up and your people still don't know what they want?'

'You stay here.' Where he wanted her.

'If safety is to be an ongoing issue for Sophia, why

not simply put protection measures in place for us in Geneva?'

Because they wouldn't be enough for his peace of mind. 'I want to make you an offer,' he told her instead. 'I want you and Sophia to live in Byzenmaach on a permanent basis. In return I will do everything in my power to ensure your career as an interpreter continues.'

'In Byzenmaach,' she said flatly, her eyes shadowed.

'That's right. I can offer you ongoing comfort and security in any number of living situations. Not necessarily here. You could have more independence than this. You could create new career opportunities and the palace would help with that. I truly don't regard the offer as a bad one.'

'*This* is your idea of negotiating a way forward for us all?'

Yes. 'And now you speak and tell me what you do and don't like about the offer. And I listen and take it into account.' He dropped his towel and walked to the side of the pool.

'Are you deliberately trying to distract me with your naked self?' There was frustration in her voice, liberally mixed with something that sounded like want.

'All's fair in love and negotiation. Is it working?'

'Well, you're even more spectacular naked than I remembered, so I'm going to have to go with yes.'

'Are you coming in? It's very pleasant.'

'I know it's very pleasant,' she muttered grudgingly, but she made no move to undress. 'I want Sophia to live with me in Geneva. She can visit you at weekends.'

'No.'

'I want to keep working for the UN.'

'A travel account will be set up so you can move freely between countries and residences. You'll have more freedom to pick and choose the work you undertake than you ever had before as a single mother. You're good at what you do, Anastasia. I have every confidence you can turn my offer into a career-enhancing move, assuming career progress is truly what you're interested in.'

She scowled at him and said nothing.

'It will, of course, be necessary to inform the palace of your plans from now on, whether you're in possession of Sophia or not. You'll have access to my secretary.'

'And do I get to know *your* every move from now on?' she enquired a little too dulcetly for comfort.

'You will know where Sophia is at all times.' His daughter was going to need a secretary of her own at this rate. 'She will, of course, have a security detail on her, no matter where she is. She's a target now.'

'And you'd like me to thank you for making her one?'

It didn't seem likely that she was going to thank him for any of it. Casimir let the hot spring water soothe his body and quiet his mind. 'I'm currently undecided as to the type of security you will require on an ongoing basis,' he told her.

Ana had stopped to toe off her shoes. The noise the zip of her skirt made carried across the water with a sibilant hiss and gave him a moment's warning before the dark material pooled at her feet. Her legs glowed porcelain pale and her underwear was tiny and white. Casimir swallowed hard.

Whose idea had it been to get naked and swim? Because the stirring in his body declared it a bad one.

He cleared his throat. 'Are we still negotiating?'

'Is that what you call this?'

Her top had joined her skirt on the floor. Her bra was nothing but lace and shoestrings but at least she kept it on as she knelt at the side of the pool and trailed her fingers in the water. 'I am not a puppet to be made to dance on your strings. I have opinions. A life to lead.'

'I'm listening.'

'Casimir, whatever it is you think you're doing…listening's not it.'

She had more curves than she'd had at nineteen. His body thought it'd be a fine idea to reacquaint himself with them, map them with hands and lips, see how they fitted.

'Hell with it,' he murmured. 'The press will never leave you alone once they get a good look at you. You're getting a full security detail as well. And a press liaison. They're going to eat you alive.'

'There you go again. Telling me what's going to happen.'

'Or you could go without the press liaison and beg me for one later, once the damage has been done. Trust me; if you want to have control over any of this, you need to control your own spin. I'm giving you the means to do that.'

'Uh huh.' She slipped into the pool with barely a splash, the water licking at her skin and raising goosebumps, never mind its warmth. Her eyes were dark and troubled when they landed on him.

'If—once you've become more accustomed to your role within the royal scheme of things—you find this to be overkill, let me know and I'll back it off a little,' he offered.

'You really do think you're negotiating.' She sounded more amazed than grateful. 'What if I don't *want* to live in Byzenmaach and be connected to the throne?'

'It's not all bad, Ana. Money and comfort will never be a concern for you again.'

'They never *have* been a concern of mine. I live comfortably enough already.'

'You will have influence.'

'Over who? Over you?'

'When it comes to our daughter you will always have my ear,' he told her.

'What good is that? Your ears don't work. All you do is talk.' Her eyes skittered to his lips. When she raised her gaze to him again, those all-seeing eyes were knowing and somewhat resigned.

'You bore a royal child, Anastasia. Surely you knew that some day it would come to this.'

'No, Cas. I bore *your* child. The child of the man I met seven years ago. The one who made me feel loved and cherished and brought me hot croissants from the bakery every morning. The one with the sweet tooth and the wicked tongue. We were careful—you were there. Pregnancy wasn't part of your plan or mine. And still it happened and you were already long gone. I bore a love child, not a royal one.'

He'd lied to her. There was no getting past that. He had no excuse for his deceit other than he'd met her and fallen utterly in thrall. One week, just one, in which royal duty hadn't ruled him.

'I'm resentful.' She drew closer. 'Damn right I am. Last time you came into my life you changed the shape of it completely. You're doing it again.'

Tension. So much tension between them and only part of it due to argument. Still so strong this invisible thing between them. 'Maybe I want to leave your life in better shape than I left it in last time,' he said.

'Maybe you just want what you can't have.'

Maybe he did. She didn't back away when he bent his lips to hers. He kissed her gently, at first. A hello that devolved into piercing heat within moments. She tasted of sweetness and surrender, succour and temptation, and the need in him was so big. Seven years since he'd lost himself to this and he needed it again with a ferocity he couldn't quite handle.

This night, with his father dead and not yet buried and the weight of the crown heavy on his head. This place that had always been a haven to him. This woman, whose passionate surrender had never failed to rouse him. Peel away the layers until she breathed only for him, Casimir the man and not Casimir the king.

The kiss deepened as he splayed his hands around her waist and drew her in. One hand to the small of her back now, as his erection met supple skin.

'You still want me,' she murmured.

'And you want me.' He dipped his head to her neck, to the swell of her breast and then to its peak and proved his point.

She proved it again when she scored her nails across his neck and kept him there.

'Just so you know,' she murmured raggedly. 'If you take me now and marry another, I will make your life a living hell.'

'I'm used to it,' he muttered, and claimed her mouth again.

She didn't fight him. Not when he took her to the steps leading down into the pool and laid her out on them before they both drowned. Not when he worshipped her with kisses and covetous hands. His hand to her ankle as he raised her knee to her breast. A kiss for the hollow behind the knee. The roughness of his cheek and chin against the flawless skin of her inner thigh. Delicacy after that, as he set his mouth to her. No need for a map; he already knew how to read every twitch she made and memory did not fail him.

She came on his tongue with a cry and a shudder that

started deep within and rippled out, and nothing else mattered but conquering her all over again, with him inside her this time. He'd never been bare inside her before and he wanted to feel it.

It would be madness to risk it.

'Whose idea was it to trade my bed for marble?' he muttered as he eased her away and helped her to her feet.

'Yours.'

'Bathing *after* sex. Remind me next time.' And then he was dragging her through the door and out onto the walkway. He'd taken all of two strides before another fantasy took hold. Him. Her. Stone walls and a valley far below them as he slaked his need for her beneath the moonlight.

He didn't think they were going to make it to the bed.

He pushed her up against a stone column, his fingers laced in hers and hers above her head. She uttered a broken curse and sank into his kiss as if born for it.

'I never forgot,' he whispered, knowing it for confession. A power exchange he could never deny, no matter what happened going forward.

'I wept when you left,' she said between kisses.

One hand was to her wrists now, his other around the curve of her buttock to urge her closer, her leg outside his—he'd dreamed of this, here in the moonlight. 'I dreamed of you.'

'And I of you.' Her admission came with razor edges. 'Be careful, Casimir. People break.'

More curses, all his as he buried his head in the curve of her neck and held still. Trembling as she trembled beneath him. It had been like this their first time too. All heat and need, no thought in any of it. She'd borne his child, all alone, and stayed alone afterwards if reports could be believed.

He believed.

'Forgive me.' As he claimed her mouth again and trailed his hand from her wrist down her arm and the hollow of her underarm, around the back of her waist. He lifted her to meet him, centre to centre as she wrapped her legs around him and her arms around his neck. 'Tell me you want this.'

'I want you.'

He pushed in on a groan and smothered her keening wail with his mouth. All the way in until he was buried as deep as he could go, no barrier between them. This wasn't just sex, up here at the top of the world with ancient stone on one side, the valley below and stars looking over them. It never had been just sex between them.

This was devotion.

He began to move, breath harsh and flesh willing, and Ana flowed with him, supple and pliant. They fitted, their bodies completely and effortlessly attuned to each other, and pleasure soared. He'd missed this.

Needed it.

'Please,' he begged, and she kissed him again, giving him everything, convulsing around him and he in turn held nothing back. Not the yearning, the regret or the cruel whip of hunger still riding him.

New plan. We're getting married, he thought.

Gathering her close, and knowing full well that she was still too far gone for speech, he carried her to his bed.

Ana woke with the dawn, aching and pliant. The bed beneath her was unfamiliar but the man beside her wasn't. She knew his touch and the scent of him. The warmth of his skin beneath her cheek and the hills and valleys of his chest. He had a broad chest narrowing to a trim waist and a perfectly curved bottom. He was plentifully endowed, long and thick, and knew exactly how to use that which he'd been given. Last night he'd revealed exactly how well he remembered her lovemaking preferences.

Only man who'd ever been able to make her scream. She'd been so lost in him.

Forget all her scruples and the complications arising. She'd only seen him.

They'd exhausted what their bodies were capable of last night, not surrendering to sleep until the early hours of the morning. Still naked, both. Still craving the connection of skin on skin, as if determined to let nothing come between them.

In the darkness of the night, here in this secluded fortress, it had worked for them.

And now morning was stealing in.

Ana closed her eyes, the better to shut it out, her lips to his chest and her tongue slipping past her lips to taste him. The salt on his skin, the hardening nub of his nipple, oh, she liked that. Enough to fit her lips to the circle of dusky flesh and suck gently.

He woke with a shuddering breath and wound his fingers in her hair. 'More,' he said in a voice still thick with sleep, so she dragged her lips across to his other nipple.

The man had a monarchy to serve and a father to bury. Once dawn broke he would belong to them and not to her and maybe he'd break her heart all over again.

But it wasn't dawn yet.

CHAPTER FIVE

CASIMIR WOKE IN a bed that had seen enough hard use that the bottom sheet had come free of its corners. The top sheet rode low on his back; any other coverings had long since left the vicinity. The bed was a wreck and Casimir was draped across the middle of it, on his stomach.

With Rudolpho and a loaded breakfast tray staring impassively at him.

'What time is it?' he muttered.

'Eleven.'

Eleven? He'd had a meeting with Augustus—*King* Augustus of Arun—and his sister, Moriana at ten in the city. And last night he'd forgotten to tell Rudolpho he wanted to cancel it. 'My meeting—'

'Rescheduled.'

'To when?'

'Two p.m. I took the liberty of deciding you needed to sleep. I am not without eyes or ears, Your Majesty. Or experience when it comes to what people need but won't ask for.'

'You presume a lot, old man.' Even if he was right. Cursing, Casimir rolled out of bed and strode towards the bathroom as Rudolpho set the tray down on the table by the window and opened the curtains to let daylight in. 'Does the press have my tribute to my father?'

'It's been playing all morning. They want more.'

They always did. 'Set up a press conference for Monday at noon. I'll give them everything they never wanted and more. I'm giving Claudia's duchy to Sophia.'

He'd reached the bathroom and the older man had not followed him. The silence was not encouraging. Grabbing a towel, he slung it around his hips and turned back, eyebrow raised as he sought Rudolpho's opinion.

'That's...one way of incorporating her,' Rudolpho said finally, still fiddling with the curtains.

'And I'm marrying Anastasia Douglas.'

Rudolpho stopped dead.

'If you have something to say, say it,' Casimir said.

The older man cleared his throat. 'When?'

'When do I want you to say something?'

'When do you intend to marry this woman no one knows?'

'After the burial. After the coronation. After I claim Sophia as mine. It's the next logical step.'

'Logic,' Rudolpho echoed, and side-eyed the bed. 'Does logic have *anything* to do with this?'

Probably not. But after last night with Ana he felt more at home in his skin than he'd ever felt before, and he wasn't giving up on that without a fight. He could see the future now, in all its splendour. And Ana was an integral part of it. 'You sound sceptical.'

Rudolpho smiled tightly. 'That's what chief advisors are for. What of your relationship with Moriana of Arun? There is an understanding there.'

'Moriana's been in no more of a hurry to marry than me.'

'But she does want to marry eventually. And she's been promised a king.'

He knew it. And he was that king. 'I'll get her another king. Theodosius of Liesendaach.'

He didn't think it possible for Rudolpho's eyebrows to rise any more but they did. 'The wastrel?'

'He's surprisingly reliable. The wastrel image is carefully cultivated.'

Rudolpho wasn't buying it.

Never mind. He didn't have to convince Rudolpho. He had only to convince Moriana. 'Onto more immediate concerns,' he prompted. 'I want Sophia's image in the press restricted as much as possible. She's the innocent in all of this, just as Claudia was innocent of the crimes committed against her. The daughters of Byzenmaach must be protected.'

'That's the message?'

'Yes. Comparisons with my sister will be inevitable. Use them.'

'And the mistress who kept your child from you all these years? The one you now intend to marry? How would you like us to spin *that*?'

Be careful, Casimir. People break.

'We tell the truth. She didn't know who I was because I never told her. We had one week together. I left her to return to Byzenmaach and my duties here. I looked her up recently on an ill-advised whim. Romance ensued. We're madly in love and looking forward to our wedding.'

'*That's* the line you want to spin?'

Casimir studied the older man. 'You don't like it?'

'Not at all,' the other man said. 'It's—'

'Idiotic is the word you're looking for.'

The words had not come from Rudolpho. They'd come from the doorway, and the voice was decidedly feminine. Ana stood there, fully dressed in grey trousers and a scoop-necked black T-shirt that emphasised all her curves. Her make-up was perfect and she'd pulled her hair back into a sleek chignon. The warm and willing woman who'd given herself over to him so completely last night was nowhere in evidence and in its place a mask of cool and steely composure graced her features. He knew such masks well. He used them regularly.

'Marrying you will protect you from the worst of the slander,' he offered.

'What's a little slander to a king's gold-digging mistress? I'll get used to it. Who knows? I might even cultivate it to my benefit. I'm not marrying you.' She sounded quite adamant.

'Why not?'

'Because you didn't ask!' The tirade that followed was rich in a language he didn't know; nonetheless he got the gist of it. 'I will marry for love, Casimir, or not at all,' she said at last, in English. 'And you don't love me.'

'But the sex is good.'

She smiled, fast and reckless. 'I can get good sex anywhere. I don't need your assistance.'

Oh, it was *on*. If she wanted an argument she'd get one. 'Is that so?'

'Count on it. And will you at some point in existence put some clothes on?'

He smirked; he couldn't help it. 'Still distracting, right? Rudolpho, that will be all for now.'

It was a battle for who wanted to get gone faster, Ana or Rudolpho.

'I'm not marrying you,' she yelled from somewhere outside his room, her composure a thing of the past. 'You're a self-obsessed, insufferable lunatic.'

'No, I'm making the best of a bad situation. Lunch at twelve on the terrace,' he yelled back. 'You and me.'

Nothing by way of reply.

'I'll wear clothes,' he offered, and wondered afresh at her capacity to bring out his playfulness.

Still nothing. He stalked to the door and watched her retreat. The rigid shoulders were at odds with the delectable curves of her buttocks. Her sleekly tamed hair a stark contrast to her passionate soul. 'Last night you said that if we made love and I then married another, you would make my life a living hell,' he said to her retreating form. 'I believed you.'

And then the devil rose up and he baited her some more. 'I took it as a wedding proposal in and of itself. Your proposal to me.'

She still didn't look back.

'I said yes,' he added helpfully, and at this Anastasia turned.

'I want a DNA test for my daughter,' she grated. 'She can't be yours. She's too bright!'

'You're right. We *are* going to need a DNA test for Sophia in order to satisfy Byzenmaach. But I'm convinced.'

Her eyes narrowed with deadly intent, a subtle reminder never to put her in charge of a pitchfork.

'Can't talk now,' he said. 'I need to shower. I smell like…' he sniffed at his shoulder '…you.'

'I'm leaving. I'm going to bribe your helicopter pilot with good sex and get him to take us somewhere *you can't go.*'

He sent her an angel's smile. 'Good luck with that. See you at noon.'

The garden terrace, Ana discovered, overlooked a walled garden full of espaliered fruit trees and whimsical flower beds. Surrounded by twelve-foot stone walls and divided by low internal walls that acted as heat banks, it overlooked the stables, and beyond that a narrow mountain pass. Apart from a few scattered outbuildings for animals there were no other dwellings here. Isolation ruled this fortress, no matter how many luxuries they tried to soften it with.

Sophia walked the garden with Lor, collecting hardy herbs and vegetables that grew at this altitude and the wolfhound, Jelly, walked with them, never venturing far. It was the dog's first foray away from her puppies, and Ana had no idea how they'd coaxed her there or whether she walked with them willingly, trusting the safety of her offspring back in the kitchen. It was almost noon, and she'd been waiting for Casimir to arrive for the past ten minutes.

First he demanded she be somewhere and then he didn't show. It was a sign, she decided grimly. How many more signs did she need before she got the message that on a list of his priorities she rated very low?

Marry him and have him run roughshod over her life for evermore? No, no and no.

He came up beside her, his footfall on bleak grey tiles unencumbered by greenery. It was two minutes to twelve and she couldn't even fault him for being late.

'I don't know how you stand it here,' she said by way of greeting.

'What don't you like about it?'

'Apart from the isolation? My inability to leave at any time.'

'It takes all day by horse to get over the mountain pass but it can be done,' he said. 'There's a village on the other side. Or it's half an hour by helicopter to the capital. No time at all, really.'

'*If* you command the helicopter. Or the horse.'

'Fair point.'

He scrubbed up well in dark trousers and a white collared shirt, open at the neck, and dark sunglasses. His version of informal wear, perhaps. And he smelled better than he looked.

'Are you sniffing me?' he asked with a tilt to his lips that said he didn't mind at all.

'No. It's just…the soap here is good.'

'I hadn't noticed.'

'All citrus and woodsy. You're probably too used to it.'

'You weren't in my bed this morning when I woke.'

'Well, I was in it when Lor requested my presence because my daughter was awake and wondering where I was,' she said drily. Lor had been uncharacteristically subdued. Ana had been mortified.

'Were you embarrassed?'

'Yes. It wasn't my finest moment. You bring out the worst in me.'

'And the best,' he said. 'I don't know what you bring out in me. The desire to live a more carefree life, perhaps. Rudolpho thinks I've gone mad. He's never seen this side of me before.'

'You should probably take that as a warning. I'm a bad influence.'

'You might be right. I've scandalised Rudolpho. He's reminding me I have a funeral and a coronation to attend before I can even start thinking about a royal wedding.'

'He seems a sensible man. You should listen to him.'

'He's served my family for forty years.'

'You should definitely listen to him. Before you make a very large mistake.'

'My offer is genuine, Anastasia, no matter what you think. I want to marry you.'

'For convenience.'

'It would be convenient, yes. Byzenmaach has been

without a female role model for a very long time. I dare say they'd welcome one.'

'Yes, and they've been promised one—a proper one. Moriana, isn't it?'

He ignored her question completely. 'You could become that role model if you put your mind to it. Think of it as a new career.'

'No, thank you. I already have a career.' Was he trying to sell her on the role? Because she wasn't buying. 'I don't envy you your status. You can keep your royal trappings.'

'And that's why you'd make a good queen. It's not all bad, Anastasia. Being able to wield influence on a grand scale can be rewarding. You can showcase the causes you're passionate about. Shine a light on situations that need improving. There can be downtime too. Like this morning, for example. Nothing to do. Are you hungry? I'm hungry.'

And lunch was being served. The table had been set when she wasn't looking. The platter of breads, meats, cheeses, pastries and fruit would mean no one left the table hungry. The linen napkins were green with white daisies on them and the flower arrangement was informally whimsical. Her mother would have set a similar table for a casual Sunday get-together, although there'd probably be more salad involved.

He looked towards the table and somehow read her thoughts.

'It's not all formality and perfect table manners,' he offered.

'Who's joining us?' The table was set for three.

'Our daughter, is she not? Don't you usually dine with her?'

Her fault entirely that she'd interpreted his invitation

to mean her alone and not Sophia as well. Sophia was the only reason Ana was here in his presence at all.

There was wariness in Sophia's eyes as Ana approached. So far this morning, she had been having a wonderful time what with no schoolwork to do, animals to tend and Lor dancing attendance on her.

'Lunchtime,' Ana said when she reached them, and Lor looked up and nodded and Sophia looked towards the balcony and frowned.

'With him?'

'Yes. With him.' Was Cas still a prince until his coronation? When did he take the title of king? There was so much about his world that she didn't know.

Sophia took her outstretched hand. 'I don't think he likes me.'

'Why wouldn't he?'

Sophia's hand tightened in hers. 'What if I don't like him?'

'That would be a problem.'

'You don't like him.'

'Not true. I like him well enough at times. Shall we wash our hands at the tap?'

They washed, and then Lor was there with a tea towel in hand so that they didn't wipe their hands on their clothes. They reached Cas eventually and he saw them seated and took the chair opposite both of them. Sophia studied him solemnly. 'Maman says your father is dead.'

Casimir nodded. 'He is.'

'*Dead*, dead or dead like you?'

'*Dead*, dead.'

'Maman says I look like your sister,' Sophia said next.

'You do.'

'Where is she?'

'Dead.'

'*Dead*, dead or dead like you?'

'*Dead*, dead.' He turned towards Ana, a little wild-eyed around the edges. Conversations with morbid six-year-olds could do that to a man. 'And how are your parents?'

'They're very well. We spoke to them yesterday.' He probably didn't want a rundown on the sense of betrayal her parents had felt at not being trusted with her secret for the past seven years. For all their support, they'd never seen her silence as anything but her lack of trust in them.

'Am I going to be a princess?' Sophia said.

'Do you want to be a princess?' Cas glanced up from the act of filling his plate.

'Would I have to stay locked in the tallest tower of the castle and be guarded by a fire-breathing dragon?'

The plate-filling stopped abruptly. 'No. You wouldn't have to do that.'

'Fairy tales,' Ana murmured. 'Always a nightmare.'

'Would I have to stay here?' Sophia regarded him anxiously.

'Sometimes,' he said.

'Maman doesn't want to stay here.'

'I know.' The glance he slid Ana was enigmatic. 'So, for now, perhaps we will have to find somewhere else for you and your *mère* to live, and you can visit me here when you would like to practice being a princess. And when you want to see Jelly the Ninth and Alberto the eagle owl.'

'Alberto the eagle owl?' Sophia regarded her father with owl eyes of her own.

'You haven't seen Alberto the eagle owl yet? He came here when he was very young and sick and didn't know to be afraid of people handling him. Tomas the falconer hand raised him and uses him today to help settle other injured birds that arrive here scared and afraid. He's big, very big, with orange eyes and ears that stick out and can go up and down and sideways and he can hear very well.'

'Does he come when you call?'

'He does. I like that in a bird. But he's asleep now, and I would not abuse my power by rousing him for no good reason. Perhaps later this evening when he is awake we can call him and feed him.'

'Will Tomas be there?' asked Sophia.

'He usually is when it comes to feeding the birds.'

'Tomas doesn't like me,' Sophia announced.

'Oh?' Casimir studied his daughter coolly. 'How do you know?'

'Lor took me to see the hawks in the big cage while Tomas was there and when he saw me he looked like he wanted to cry. And then he didn't look at me again the whole time and then he left and he didn't even say goodbye. Everyone else here says hello *and* goodbye.'

'I see,' said Casimir.

'So he doesn't like me.'

'I really don't think that's the problem.'

Sophia waited for more but Cas had clearly said all he was going to say on the subject of Tomas and his lack of goodbyes. 'Eat,' he said instead, pointing to Sophia's plate, at which point she dutifully pushed a tiny tomato around her plate with a fork.

'What does Alberto the eagle owl eat?' she asked.

'Dead things,' said Cas. 'Preferably still warm.'

'Boy, do you have a lot to learn about father-daughter conversations,' Ana murmured and he smiled, brief but sure.

'I thought I was doing rather well. Staying on topic.'

'Are you sure you don't have a dragon?' asked Sophia. 'Because this would be a good place for a dragon to live.'

'No dragons,' he said firmly.

'Because it could come when you called. Down from the mountains to guard the princess from the evil frogs.'

'Do we have evil frogs?' he asked with considerable calm.

'Yes,' said Sophia. 'They're very big. But they don't have ears.'

Cas silently offered to fill their glasses with juice. 'You can add to this conversation any time you like,' he told Ana.

'Wouldn't dream of interrupting.' It wasn't a regular family conversation, by any means. Ana had no experience when it came to sharing her daughter, and Casimir had no experience with daughters at all, but somehow she was enjoying herself.

They ate. Cas and her daughter talked about all manner of things. From places they'd been to favourite foods to good names for puppies. Only when a butterfly landed on a cake and Sophia held out her hand to attract it did he falter, standing up with an abruptness that made them stare, and sent the butterfly flying off into the garden.

Sophia followed its progress before turning reproachful eyes on Cas.

'Sorry to startle you,' he muttered. 'I need to be…not here. Excuse me.'

'Yes, of course.' Not that he needed anyone's permission to leave, but the man seemed downright rattled. 'Everything okay?'

'Saw a ghost,' he muttered, and Sophia's eyes widened. He looked at his daughter and winced. 'Not a *ghost*, ghost,' he corrected rapidly. 'We don't have ghosts here. At all. Ever. Or dragons. No dragons here.'

'Cas?' Ana murmured.

'What?' He sounded entirely too grateful for the interruption. Lost, for once, as opposed to entirely too much in charge of his world.

'You're making it worse.'

'I know,' he said, a proud man, utterly undone by a small girl.

Ana smiled.

'Not funny,' he muttered.

'Oh, come on.' It was a little bit funny. All that towering helplessness in the face of butterflies and evil frogs. 'Thank you for inviting us to lunch. Great idea. We could do this again tomorrow.'

His eyes widened in dismay. 'I, ah, may have other stuff on.'

'What kind of stuff?' asked Sophia.

'Kingly stuff,' he offered.

Ana grinned. Oh, this was good. 'Do tell us more. Are there donkeys involved?'

She knew with absolute clarity the moment when he fell. When he stopped being a man of duty and surrendered utterly to absurdity. 'No donkeys,' he said. 'Unless you'd like one?'

'I'd like one,' Sophia said, and Ana smiled beatifically. This was too easy. The man needed more practice if he intended to take on her and Sophia both.

'Right,' he said. 'Right. A live donkey?'

Both Ana and Sophia nodded.

'Just checking,' he said. 'I really do need to go and rule...something.'

'Enjoy,' she said. 'And thank you once again for our lunch invitation. Did you have fun? Even with clothes on, I had fun.'

CHAPTER SIX

Ana found him in the library later that afternoon. The large walnut table that ran the length of the room like a spine had been covered in newspaper clippings and photographs, some of them yellowed with age. He smiled when she came in and once more she sensed a deep weariness in him that he kept carefully hidden.

'Am I interrupting?' she asked.

'I don't mind. It's time for a break anyway.'

'That's what Lor said. She said you were back from your meeting and sent me to woo you with talk of coffee and something called Borek, which apparently you like.'

'Pastry,' he murmured. 'Predominantly with a meat filling, although you can use anything. Meat pie.'

'Simple tastes.'

'Borek is *never* simple.' Given enough prompting, this man would play. She kept catching glimpses of the man she'd once known, and that man had been irresistible, never mind his secrets.

'Lor says they'll be hot from the wood-fired brick oven in ten minutes.' Lor liked to do things the traditional way here. 'What are you doing?'

'Choosing a photo of my sister to release to the press tomorrow, and seeing what they've already got so that I can better predict what will be regurgitated once they get wind of Sophia. Are there any photographs of Sophia online?'

'No.'

'Good. That's good.'

Ana stepped forward to take a better look at the photographs spread out on the table. She'd read the newspaper articles about his sister's death when she'd first researched him but she hadn't revisited them in years. She picked up an informal photo of his sister in what looked like this very library. The resemblance to Sophia was uncanny.

'The press release I read said your father refused to negotiate with the kidnappers.'

'Correct.'

'What did they want?'

'Water.' Casimir hesitated, as if warring over what to say next. 'There were plans afoot to build a dam in the mountains. It was a good plan for its time but, as always, there was opposition. Villages to be relocated, environmental studies to be done, water distribution rights to be negotiated with the mountain tribes to the north—a proud, fierce people who didn't always suffer my father's rule in silence. My father had been meeting with them. Trying to appease them.' Casimir's lips twisted in mockery. 'That was his interpretation, anyway. He invited their leader to the palace to continue discussions. I remember meeting the man.'

'What was he like?' she asked softly.

'Kind.' The word seemed wrenched from Cas's mouth. 'Kind to a small boy who had forgotten his place and barged into his father's library unannounced. In my defence, I did not know they were there. All I wanted was a book on birds for Tomas. Anyway—' Cas shook himself as if trying to remove the memory from his soul '—

my father and this man fell out and my father refused all water rights for the mountain tribes. Negotiations ceased. Petitions from the north went unread. My father's advisors tried to soften his stance, to no avail. My father was a proud and unyielding man. No one could sway him. People say he brought what happened next upon himself.'

Ana's gaze flicked to the pictures on the table. 'What did happen next?'

'How does one force a man to realise that he's taking away the future of a people?' Casimir said bleakly. 'It's very simple, really. You take away *his* future and you try to make him compromise. But they made a mistake, the people who came for Claudia and for me. They only took one of us.'

'Why?'

'Because they couldn't find me. Such a stupid thing, really. They had someone on the inside, a palace guard, and had chosen their time carefully. It was dusk. We were always allowed to play in the maze garden in the hour before dinner, and dinner was always served at dusk. The kidnappers expected to find me and my sister both. Unfortunately for them, I'd gone to the kitchen to get a jar to put a dragonfly in. Claudia had caught one and wanted to show Tomas before releasing it again. She was a gentle soul, my sister. She was seven years old, I was ten and I should never have left her alone in that garden.'

'Surely no one blamed you?' Ana couldn't comprehend anyone blaming Claudia's abduction on him. 'Where were all the *other* palace guards?'

'Absent. In on it. Diverted from the scene. Take your pick.'

Oh.

'The first ransom demand came within hours. Generous water rights for the mountain tribes in return for my sister's release. My father refused to negotiate. The next demand was accompanied by Claudia's hair. They offered to return Claudia in return for him. He refused. The demand after that was accompanied by Claudia's dress. Me for my sister. My father laughed at that one, and refused them yet again. And then they got creative.' His voice held an echo of old despair. 'That's not common knowledge.'

'Those choices weren't choices,' she said bluntly.

'The first one was. He wouldn't even negotiate. All the recommended procedures. He didn't follow any of them.'

'How do you know that?'

'I was there.'

'You were *ten*. I can't imagine you were included in every briefing.'

Casimir smiled bitterly. You'd be surprised. My father was big on having me learn by example.'

'And what did you learn?'

'That I will never be like him. No matter how hard he tried to mould me in his image, I am my own man. I would have traded water rights for Claudia and to hell with my pride and my fury. I'd have negotiated.'

He stood, head bent, as if staring at the photos and newspaper clippings on the desk, but she didn't think he was seeing any of it. 'What did your mother think?'

'I'll never know. She took to her rooms the day Claudia's dress arrived and reappeared six months later, brain addled and addicted to sedatives. Didn't even manage to get out of bed the day of my sister's memorial service.'

Ana tried to imagine sending Sophia out to face a day like that while Ana stayed in bed and pulled the covers over her head. One child was gone, sure enough, but the other one had been right there and hurting, and very much at the mercy of a ruthless king.

'She wasn't a strong woman,' Casimir offered quietly. 'But I loved her very much.'

God. She didn't know how to comfort this man, didn't think he'd accept it if it wasn't cloaked in sex. But she wanted to help him, truly she did. And she wanted, more than anything, to spirit him away from all of the grief spread out in front of him.

'I've waited a long time for the crown, Anastasia. I aim to create a bright and prosperous future for all of Byzenmaach's children, and if that means dealing once again with my sister's kidnappers I'll do it. If it means admitting how I wronged you all those years ago and offering to do what I can to fix that now, I'll do it. It's not wrong to want to fix what is broken.'

So fierce, this new king for a new age.

So very, very alone.

'I think you should release these three pictures to the press.' She pointed towards three photos that had already been set to one side. 'And then I think you should get someone, or several someones, to put this stuff away. Then I think you should help me wrap Lor's pastries in a picnic basket and take me halfway up the mountain to where the watch fire used to burn. I want to sit on a rock in this Godforsaken place and look around me and see everything there is to see. I want you to show me the beauty in it.'

He looked at her appraisingly, but he didn't say he couldn't do it. 'You'll need hiking gear.'

'I have sandals and jeans. And I'm prepared to make do.'

Two hours and one breathtakingly steep hike later, Ana sat at the edge of the world and watched falcons soar. She was huffing and red-cheeked on account of the thin mountain air, half her hair had slipped its ponytail and was wrapped around her face and her calf muscles would never be the same again, but it was worth it.

Because Casimir was smiling.

She flopped back against one of the huge torch fire supports, closed her eyes and let her breathing return to regular. A royal helicopter sat on a cleared patch of even ground almost a hundred metres below them, and they'd scrambled the last hundred metres to the watch tower. Well, to be fair, Cas had traversed it with the agility of a mountain goat and Ana had scrambled alongside him until at last he'd held out his hand to her. The last part of the climb had been the steepest bit and also the easiest because of that strong, steadying hand with the blunt nails and the coiled strength behind it.

When they'd reached the top and he'd let her go, she'd felt the loss of his touch more than she cared to admit.

Eyes still closed, she scraped her hair back with her fingers and redid her ponytail. When she opened her eyes again she caught Casimir's gaze.

'Okay,' she said. 'Maybe that might have gone a little better with hiking gear.' But they were alone; Casimir's security team had already been up here and pronounced the area clear and then disappeared into the ether. Cas had then flown her up here, just the two of them, because of course he could fly a helicopter just as well as any pilot could—all-weather jacket, aviator glasses, khaki trousers and hiking boots included. 'So where are we?'

'Falconer's Pass,' he said. 'Named for obvious reasons. It's a World Heritage area. Plenty of endangered bird species here. And the watch towers.' He pointed behind her, towards the other end of the pass. 'There's one over there. And there's one up there, on the ridge of that mountain. See it?'

She followed his gaze, shaded her eyes from the sun and nodded, before moving forward and choosing a big broad rock to sit on, close to the edge of the cliff. She wasn't living dangerously on the edge, even if it felt like it, as she sat and drank in the view. 'Do you need pie? I need pie. I *deserve* pie.'

So he slid the pack from his back and sat beside her and spread Lor's picnic offerings on the rock. He withdrew a slim leather-bound book from the backpack as well and set it to one side of the food.

'You brought a book?' Ana paused in the act of stuffing her mouth full of meat-filled pastry, not the slightest bit less tasty for not being warm.

'It's about a hero called Pechorin,' he said and handed it to her. 'I want to hear it in Russian.'

'But the book is in English.' She checked a page of it with the flick of her fingers. 'And you don't speak Russian.'

'Never stopped you before,' he murmured. 'Listening to you translate is very peaceful, for some reason. Except when you get bored and start inserting random commentary in Lithuanian. Which I understand.'

'Hnh.' No point speaking with her mouth full so she waited until it wasn't. 'So what's so good about this story?'

'I don't know. I've never read it.' He picked up a pie and ate it with far more appetite than she'd seen him display at the lunch table.

'Lunch wasn't so long ago,' she said with the lift of a teasing brow.

'Lunch was extremely stressful,' he countered. 'It's entirely possible I ate less than our daughter did. And she ate one tomato.'

'And a green bean,' Ana informed him. 'Sophia snacks in Lor's kitchen—possibly in much the same fashion you do.'

'Oh,' he said.

'Thank you for spending time with her today,' Ana said next. 'She's very curious about you. You're a remote and romantic figure for her at the moment.'

He looked out over the valley below them and frowned. 'That's not...right. That's not who I want to be in her eyes.'

'What *do* you want her to see when she looks at you?'

'I would have her see someone who cares for her welfare and tries to do right by her.'

'What about love? Would you have her see your love for her?'

He cleared his throat. 'You're assuming I know how to show such a thing.'

Maybe she was. 'Give it time,' she offered lightly. 'Maybe it'll sneak up on you.'

'Did you love her from the start?' he asked, and there was a question with no easy answer. She nodded and blinked sudden moisture from her eyes.

'Did you ever not want her?' His eyes were sharp and saw too much.

'You have a lot of questions.' Ragged words to cover a ragged start when it came to Anastasia's feelings for her daughter.

He nodded, but instead of pursuing it he cleared the food away and picked up the book. 'Will you read to me in Russian? For old times' sake?' he asked, and she took the book and he settled back on the rock with his head resting against the backpack and, after a moment, Ana settled down next to him with her head resting against his chest. It was firm and warm and his hand came up to smooth the hair at her temple and the delicacy of his touch made her close her eyes and long for yesteryear.

She opened the book and her eyes and began to read

about a man embarking on a journey. Four pages in, she started summarising in Lithuanian and wore Casimir's sun-spelled objections with a grin.

Ten pages in she started another story altogether. A story only she knew. An answer to his questions. She told it in Russian because it was better that way and because she'd have never been able to tell it in English.

'I discovered I was pregnant six weeks after you left,' she began. 'Nineteen years old with my lover gone, a baby in my belly and all my study plans shot to hell. I couldn't stop crying for what I'd lost and I couldn't stop remembering what we'd found. I was so in love with you. I'd never felt that way before. I was blind with it.'

She turned a page and read the first couple of lines before continuing her own story. 'I tried denial when it came to the baby growing inside me. Maybe it'd go away the same way you went away and I'd smile and be relieved and pretend to have no regrets. It didn't work. My pregnancy continued. At four months I went to the doctor to start proper antenatal care. At five months I told my parents. Your name never came up. Lonely times for me, my friend. Very lonely, with no one to confide in. I think you know that feeling well. Even better than I do.'

She took a breath and turned a page. 'You knew where I lived even if I had no idea how to contact you. You'd made me feel so loved. There was a part of me that still hoped you'd be back. How could you not be back?'

Cas shifted beneath her and Ana paused. But then he settled, his fingertips at her temple again. 'Keep reading,' he muttered.

'I was nine months pregnant when I saw your picture in a newspaper and realised who you were. *What* you were. I was at my parents' house for the weekend and braving their constant well-meaning interrogation. A baby due almost any day and me still refusing to name the father. I sat in the bath with my belly and my memories and cried myself a river because I knew then that you were never coming back.'

She stopped speaking then. The words on the page were too blurry to read.

'Go on.' His voice was rough and drowsy. Or maybe it was just rough.

'I'm looking for the words,' she said in English. 'They're hard to find.'

She turned another page and closed her eyes. 'Hardest thing I've ever had to do, letting you go. Letting the *thought* of you go. The happy family fantasy. Some days I didn't want to get up in the morning. Life would continue on regardless, and I didn't want to be there. Maybe I do know how your mother felt.'

She could feel the rise and fall of his chest, the gentle press of his fingertips against her hair, although the stroking had stopped. Maybe he'd fallen asleep. She switched back to English. 'Are you still listening?'

'I'm listening.'

More English. 'There's not a lot happening in this story. It's very boring.'

'No, it's not.'

She turned a page. 'It's just a description of place. Mountains and a cottage built against a cliff. Bleating sheep and growling dogs, a crackling fire and some smoke-blackened posts. Sounds ominous.'

'In Russian, Anastasia.'

'You are so right. Why is it that things always sound better in Russian?'

'It's your mother tongue; it's comforting. You've heard it since the womb.'

'My mother has a beautiful speaking voice,' she said,

by way of a distraction. 'You'll fall in love with it. People do.'

'You didn't fall far from that tree, did you?'

'I am taking that compliment and basking in it.'

'Good,' he murmured. 'Read.'

She closed her eyes and began to speak.

'You missed the birth. Not that I blame you. I'd have missed it too if I could because it was brutal. And then my baby was born and she was so beautiful and I fell in love all over again in a different way. And I thanked God for her and for bringing you into my life.'

She felt Cas stroking her hair and it soothed her and helped her speak again. 'I got up. Every morning I got up and I studied and took every bit of help my parents offered and I built us a life and I vowed to never regret what happened between us. I *want* to love like that again. I know I can. But it's never quite right with anyone else. And then you come back, offering everything and nothing. A fairy tale life when all I've ever wanted was your love. And for all your fine lovemaking, you've never offered that.'

She stopped speaking and turned the page, tried to read what was written there, and then Casimir's hand curled around the book and closed it as he dropped it on the ground beside her.

'Marrying you makes a lot of sense, I know that. I just don't know if I can do it and not get lost in you again,' she whispered, and then he was kissing her, slotting his mouth against hers and blotting out the sky. He gave as much as he took and he took everything she had and she thought she tasted tears and maybe they were hers.

It was minutes, maybe years, before he released her and lay back down again with his eyes closed.

'We need to leave soon.' His fingers traced the back

of her hand before entwining with hers. His eyes were still closed and his voice was still rough. 'Best we return before dark.'

'Well, we wouldn't want Tomas the falconer to have to send out the owls.' Ana tried for humour and managed stupidity instead.

'You're right,' he said as he got to his feet and held out his hand to haul her up. 'I'd never hear the end of it.'

Casimir excused himself when they got back to the fortress. He made calls he'd been putting off all day and then sat down to work on his speech for tomorrow. He called Rudolpho in to help and if the older man knew Casimir's request as nothing more than a futile need to control events he couldn't control he made no mention of it. He simply loaded Casimir up with work and sat alongside him and worked his own way through a share of it.

Six pm came and went. Lor delivered their dinner on trays.

'You're different around Anastasia Douglas,' Rudolpho said as they ate. 'Less rigid. More relaxed.'

'Sometimes,' Casimir said. More often than not he was a mess.

'Why?'

Good question. Somehow she made him feel lighter. As if the responsibilities he shouldered could potentially be shared. 'I don't know why. She's always had that effect.' He studied the older man's expression but could read nothing from it. 'Ana brings humour and strength to adversity. And brutal honesty, she brings that too. I like being around her. I can loosen my own reins, and know that she can more than hold her own. What do you even call that?'

'A gift,' said Rudolpho.

'I haven't treated her well in the past.' Understatement.

'Then I trust you'll treat her with more care this time.'

'That's it? That's all the advice you have for me on the matter?'

'I'm not a dating advice column.'

Good to see Rudolpho taking Cas's command to speak up so much to heart.

Eight p.m. came and Rudolpho left. When the clock struck eleven, Casimir knew himself for whipped. Pushing too hard. Trying to cover every angle of his upcoming speech to the nation when all he had to do was say what he had to say and follow through on it.

Easy.

He made his way to his bedroom, stripped down to skin and headed for the pool. Ritual or hedonism, he didn't care. He needed this.

He sank into the water of the main pool tonight and made his way to the far end, where the waterfall flowed when the pump was on. When the pump wasn't on and the sheet of water not falling, the area boasted a wide lip, just beneath water level, where a person might rest their arms while pillowing their head on the edge of the pool. He leaned back, stretched out, closed his eyes and tried to will the tension from his body.

He hadn't really expected Ana to be waiting for him. She'd shared his bed last night, refused his marriage proposal this morning, and made him splinter into a thousand pieces up on the mountain, with her telling a story she'd never told before.

Because Casimir spoke Russian now. Not fluently, not without an accent, but he'd understood every word she'd uttered in the language, and he knew now what she wanted from life. What she was really holding out for.

Love.

Above all, she wanted someone to love her and cherish her as she should be cherished.

The main problem, as he saw it, being that he didn't know how to love anyone. He who'd spent so long keeping people out of his heart and his head that he no longer knew how to let anyone in. A man apart. A man alone. A man who ruled.

The boy who was born to be king.

CHAPTER SEVEN

ANA COULDN'T SLEEP. She'd risen from her bed, slipped the wrap someone had left in the bathroom around her nakedness and stargazed from the darkness of her balcony until her memories of hot flesh and ravenous lovemaking had dimmed. She stayed out there, drawing patterns between the stars, until her flesh grew cold and clammy but still her mind was full of Casimir.

Casimir the man, not Casimir the king.

She couldn't get the butterfly from lunchtime and Cas's reaction to it and his conversations with Sophia out of her head. It was as if he'd wanted to connect with her but didn't quite know how. Given his upbringing, he probably *didn't* know how to be part of a family unit, but she couldn't fault the man for trying.

He'd made more of an impact on his daughter than he knew. He was no longer 'that man' or 'the prince' or 'the king' as far as Sophia was concerned. He was Cas who liked owls but didn't like butterflies. At some point he would stop being Cas and become Papa and then it would be *My father said...* and *My father gave me...* A puppy, a pony, a castle.

Tutors, for mother and daughter both. *Heaven help her.*

She couldn't get his stupid marriage proposal out of her head. There was a time when she would have joyfully said yes. She could still say yes. Bury all her doubt and uncertainty and craving for love beneath an avalanche of practicality. Embrace life as a royal consort. Remain wholly in her daughter's life. *Trust* the man to know what he was doing when he'd made his offer of marriage in the first place.

Two weeks, he'd said when he came for them. *A mere two weeks of your time. We can negotiate...* Now he was offering her a place at his side and a marriage that would decidedly *not* be in name only. Forget about her old life. Learn how to be what he needed her to be—mother to a duchess and consort to a king—and maybe one day she'd feel more at home and less utterly out of her depth. Forget those wild dreams of Casimir loving her with all his heart. Instead be content with what he was offering.

Compromise.

The air on the walkway was too crisp. The view was too superb. This walkway was the jewel in the fortress crown, loading her senses until they were raw. The shy moon and the shadows, the lick of air on already cold skin. She thought of Casimir, the man who'd haunted her dreams for years and who'd taken her again last night with a hunger she'd been powerless to resist. When it came to pure passion he would always win.

Whether he offered love or not, she wanted him.

When darkness fell and the world disappeared, she always wanted him.

He was in the pool when she pushed the door to the bathhouse open, his head tipped back, his arms spread wide and his legs stretched out before him. Hedonism or crucifixion, she didn't know. All she did know was that she felt his presence like a blow to her already overloaded senses.

He lifted his head to look at her, his eyes dark with

secrets, and he watched in silence as she sat at the edge of the pool and delicately dipped first one foot in the water and then the other. Her robe stayed on, firmly tied at the waist.

For now.

Hot water caressed her feet and ankles and lapped at her calves, but it was Casimir's gaze that burned. She felt it on her skin, on her breasts until they peaked for him, high on her arms, the curve of her shoulders.

She lifted her arms to her hair and bundled it in a loose knot high on her head. It might stay up, it might not; that wasn't the point.

The ravenous heat in Casimir's eyes was the entire point of the exercise.

He tilted his head back to rest against the lip of the pool again and watched her with hooded eyes.

'How are you?' she murmured.

'Today, after lunch with a daughter I don't understand, I angered a princess I was supposed to marry, disappointed her brother who happens to be a neighbouring monarch, and broke a promise I made to my father.' He closed his eyes. He didn't move. 'And then there's you.'

She studied his face in the half light. The arch of his brows, the cut of his cheekbones and the hollows beneath, the sensual generosity of his lips. 'You told Moriana you weren't willing to marry her?'

'Yes.'

'Because of me?'

'Yes.' He opened his eyes and levelled her with his gaze. 'Last night—right here in this room—I chose you. You asked me to.'

She held his gaze, wholly troubled now. 'Words spoken in the heat of passion are often unreliable. Last night I spoke without thinking things through.'

He smiled mirthlessly. 'I spoke true. I would marry you. I want to marry you.'

'Because it's convenient,' she muttered.

'Because it's *more* convenient than any other union I might make, that's true. It rights a wrong. It keeps you wholly in Sophia's life. Isn't that enough?'

'It's kind of only half the fairy tale.'

'Fairy tales aren't real,' he murmured.

But love was. 'What—' she took a deep breath '—what would I have to do if I married you?' She couldn't believe she was even considering it.

'I'm sure someone will have a list.' He smiled again but there were shadows.

'Would there be more children involved?'

'Yes. I need heirs. Legitimate ones. Is that a problem for you?'

'No.' She'd always wanted more children. Likewise, Sophia had always wanted a brother or sister. Or both.

'Would I still be able to work? Outside of official palace duties?'

'Why would you want to?' She had his attention and it burned.

'I've worked hard for my career. I'm proud of it. It helps define who I am. Who I think I am. Without that identity I become…less.'

'Or you could bring those career skills to your new position and become…more.'

'And maybe, just maybe, I'd like to be able to get out of the palace bell jar every now and then. Be me again rather than a creature bound to royal duty.'

'Now there's an argument I can understand,' he murmured. 'It'd be nice to be able to move between worlds and maintain balance in both. I'll not stop you from trying.'

'You don't think it can be done?'

He shrugged. 'I've managed to escape this life and the duties involved exactly once in thirty years. That was when I met you. And I didn't exactly maintain my balance.'

Oh.

'If there's a way to be both king and my own man, I haven't yet found it. Maybe with certain people I can be the man and not the figurehead. Maybe finding balance in a life such as this isn't about the work you do but about the people you allow through. And maybe for you, as royal consort and not born to this life, your experience will be different to mine. You already have another life you can access and I have no objection to you trying to merge the two. Parents, friends, work colleagues— bring them through. *Make* this world work for you. You're strong enough.'

Flattery would get him everywhere.

'Your language skills would be of value to me,' he added wryly. 'Your listening skills would be an asset. You would not lack for political intrigue.'

She looked down past her knees to the water. The picture he'd painted was not an unpleasant one. There were worse lives to be had.

'Would Sophia object to us marrying?' he asked next. 'Is that what's stopping you?'

'No. I don't think she'd object.'

'Then what's stopping you? Because I know you're attracted to me.'

'What gave it away? My unfailing ability to fall into bed with you at a moment's notice or my reduced brain capacity whenever I see you naked?'

'I'm naked now,' he pointed out. 'And you're still thinking.'

'Yes, but not particularly well.'

'I agree. Because you're still saying no to my proposal.' He came to her then, sleek shoulders and silky skin, the water running off him like raindrops down a window pane. Hot hands on her waist, plucking at the tie of her robe before sliding beneath and finding skin. 'Marry me.'

It was hard to stay focused, with his fingers dipping lower and his lips nibbling their way up and over her ribs. 'No.'

'Why not?'

'Because you don't love me.' It was the same answer she'd already given him, only this time it was harder to give. Possibly because his lips had just closed over her left nipple and, oh, he was good at that, sending streaky, jagged slivers of lust through her body. She could feel herself moistening, her legs widening in invitation.

'Do you remember the night we met?' he said as his fingertips drew lazy circles on her skin.

She hadn't forgotten. A shadowy bar and a glance that led to another glance. A smile, the offer of a drink, and then the slow roll of the pad of his thumb across her inner wrist as he'd introduced himself. His fingers had been hard and calloused and he'd been Casimir, just Casimir, and she'd thought him a man who worked with his hands.

He still had them, the calluses.

'I'd never had anyone look at me the way you did,' he murmured. 'No titles. No expectations. Real life didn't come into it.'

'Mine did. I showed you everything.' He'd had a good look around, poked through her hopes, her dreams and then left. 'You lied to me.'

He reached out and caught the fist she'd made of her hand. He stroked her knuckles with the pad of his thumb, stroking her fingers open one by one and then he put her palm to his cheek. His stubble rasped over her skin as he leaned into her touch.

'You rip my heart out every single time,' she whispered.

'Not this time. There are no lies left.' He pressed his lips to her palm and she closed her eyes then and tried not to picture him. All that did was enhance her other senses. The puff of breath against her skin, the touch of his other hand, wet and warm against the back of her neck as he drew her effortlessly closer and transferred his lips to the blade of her cheek, the curve of her jaw and finally, finally to her lips.

He sank into the kiss as if it was the next breath he needed to take.

No words of love from Casimir, King of Byzenmaach, but his body was wide open to her and always had been.

Take it, every line of his beautiful body screamed it, even if he would never say the words. Take *me*.

She led him from the pool and stood him beneath a steaming shower. She towelled him dry, starting at his feet and working her way upwards, peppering his body with kisses while he shuddered and wound gentle hands in her hair and begged for more.

She took him to his bed and made him beg some more until he turned her on her back and entered her, smooth and slow.

'Mine,' he whispered, which wasn't the same as *I love you* and never would be.

'Not yours.' Not even if her body and half her brain said otherwise. 'You can't own people any more. Didn't you learn that at school?'

His grin flashed white in the darkness of the room. 'I didn't go to school. I had tutors.'

'That explains...' She sucked in a breath as his lips grazed her nipple. Whoever had taught him how to worship a woman's body had taught him to excel. 'Your arrogance.'

He withdrew to the point where she feared complete loss, then put his thumb to her centre and slid back in, hard and slow, and made her moan.

'I do allow some people a hearing,' he murmured. 'For example, you could tell me what you wanted me to do to you next and I'd do it.'

The notion that he was hers to command in the bedroom hit hard and made her eyes close. 'I want you to kiss me and keep moving.'

He obliged with a smile, so she buried her hands in his hair and held fast while her body clung and trembled on the precipice of fulfilment.

'See how reasonable I can be?' he whispered against her lips, before stealing her breath.

She broke the kiss and gasped for breath. 'Less talk, more—' She was losing the fight for coherence. 'More.' More of everything.

'Mine.' There was that word again, and there was an implacability about it this time that burrowed beneath her skin like a brand. 'No one else gets to see you like this.'

'Possessive.' She could be possessive too. 'That works both ways.'

'You have me,' he said. 'No marriage to someone else, no heir from anyone but you. That's what you asked for. That's what I've agreed to.'

'I didn't—oh.' A scrape of his fingers across her too-sensitive nipple and the pleasure-pain soared. Maybe she had suggested...something...of the sort. He was kissing her again, the snap of his hips driving her relentlessly towards completion. 'It's not that simple.'

'It really is that simple. I've been thinking about it a lot.'

'Argumentative.' His parents really should have socialised him more.

'Enlightened,' he argued. 'Do you trust me?'

'No.' As he set his teeth to the curve of her neck and bit down hard. 'I'm so close to coming.'

'Do it,' he whispered. 'I want to watch.'

And then she was soaring, clenching, clamping down hard as he surged into her with a muttered curse and began to fill her up.

This was what she remembered most about their time together. The way their bodies talked, no words required. The way he opened up and gave until there was nothing left to give, and nothing more important in this world than being with him.

The morning after began with Ana's groan as Casimir put a hand to her shoulder and tried to nudge her awake. She'd returned to her room in the early hours of the morning rather than share his bed. He'd resented it then. He resented it still, but there'd been no convincing her otherwise. She'd wanted to be closer to Sophia, his daughter, who'd woken with the dawn and was presently keeping Lor and the wolfhound puppies company in the kitchen. Ana had asked to be woken before he left so here he was, keeping his side of the agreement.

An agreement made before he'd realised she'd be returning to her own bed.

How did one wake a woman who didn't want to be woken? Cold water? Brass band? Surely four hours sleep was enough for anyone?

'Press conference,' he murmured as she burrowed into

the bedclothes and tried to make a cave out of them. 'Wake up.'

'More sleep,' she muttered, and then the impact of his words hit home and she sat bolt upright. 'Oh, hell. Press conference.'

'There we go, consciousness. Knew you could do it.'

She spared him a glare from her collection but it was counterbalanced somewhat by the wild tumble of her hair and lips still swollen from greedy kisses throughout the night.

'How is it you look so fresh and rested this morning?' she grumbled. 'You're an incubus, right? You feed off my sexual energy and it gives you enough power to rule the universe.'

'I've had four hours sleep,' he countered, which was more than he'd had in a while. 'And a shower.'

'You do seem rather attached to the whole getting wet thing.' Her gaze started somewhere in the vicinity of his suit trousers and finished somewhere around the shirt collar he had yet to button properly.

'Checking me for marks?' he asked and she shook her head.

'I don't leave marks.'

'Not where people can see them, at any rate,' he murmured, and she smiled a little helplessly. 'I leave for the capital in half an hour, assuming you want to come with me.'

'I do.' She tried scrambling off the bed with a sheet still modestly attached to her person, but gave that up for a bad idea around three seconds later, and headed for the bathroom fully naked.

'Nothing you haven't seen before, right?' she asked over her shoulder as if she knew full well where he was looking.

'Right.' Which didn't stop him from appreciating her nakedness.

'So do I get to be in the audience for this press conference?' she asked next.

'Absolutely not,' he told her. 'It's a circus.'

'I follow politics,' she said. 'I translate for the UN and the floor of the European Parliament. Circuses are my business.'

'But this circus is about you.'

'Exactly why I should be there,' she said. 'And if I am going to be there, where better than in the thick of things? No one knows who I am yet. I can be anonymous.'

She'd reached the bathroom and the last of her words came out muffled. He followed, the better to hear her, or see her, or maybe he wasn't quite ready to put distance between them yet. 'It will be televised. Watch it then.'

'It's not the same. Television coverage will only focus on you. I don't only want to focus on you. I want to focus on the journalists too. The mutterings, the sideways glances. Put me in the room as an interpreter attached to some fictitious international newspaper.' Her hand-waving became more enthusiastic. 'I'll take notes.'

He glanced at her, darkly amused. 'I assume you're expecting Sophia to stay here.'

'Wait—what?'

'Where else would you put her?' he enquired dulcetly. 'In the press gallery too?'

'How about in a nearby room?' she asked.

'No. You're welcome to come with me to the capital, Anastasia, but Sophia stays here.'

'In whose care?'

'Lor's care. Which is where she is now.'

'Why can't Sophia come with us and stay in a nearby

room packed full of security guards while you give your speech and I watch from the crowd?'

'Because she'd be noticed getting off the helicopter and she'd sure as hell be photographed getting back on it.'

'So?'

Ana had so much to learn about image cultivation. He barely knew where to start. 'I don't want to introduce Sophia in person yet. The images we want on the front pages tomorrow have already been chosen by me and vetted by press aides. I know what I want to see and I know how to make it happen. Sophia stays here.'

Ana narrowed her gaze. 'I'm trying to pinpoint exactly which breath it was when you stopped being a... lover and started being an autocratic ass again.'

'King,' he said.

'Mother,' she countered tranquilly. 'You don't *get* to be king when it's just you and me and we're talking about Sophia's movements. We get to be *parents* and make joint decisions.'

'Then, as one parent to another, I'm asking you to consider my words. Your presence at the palace today can be explained away to some extent. You can be part of my advisory team. Sophia can't. She'll be noticed. She's better off waiting here.'

He thought there might more argument to be had but after a moment Ana nodded curtly. 'How long will we be gone?'

'I can have you returned directly after the conference, if that's your preference.'

She nodded again.

'Stop rubbing yourself red,' he snapped. 'What are you trying to do? Wash me away?'

'I'm trying to get clean.' But the ferocious scrubbing stopped and softer soaping resumed. 'I'm just...nervous.'

That made two of them. Not that he could let anyone see his nervousness. Not today and especially not during his inaugural speech.

'Wear your dark trousers and the white shirt you wore the other day and you'll fit into the press gallery easily enough. But you'll stand at the back alongside two of my security people and when they say it's time to go you'll leave without protest. Are we agreed?'

'Do I have a choice?'

'In this, no.' Not when her protection was concerned. 'I need your word that you'll co-operate or I'll leave you behind.'

She'd started scrubbing hard again and this time his hand shot out to stop the abuse of skin. His hands were gentle as he showed her how to wash without scouring but his voice was hard when he spoke again.

'I can't be giving my speech and worrying about your safety at the same time. Give me your word that you'll do what my security team tells you to do.'

'Are you always this paranoid?'

'Always. And not without good reason.'

She couldn't hold his gaze. 'You have my word.'

'We leave in twenty minutes,' he offered.

And left her to it.

CHAPTER EIGHT

ANXIETY RODE ANA hard as the helicopter drew away from the winter fortress. She didn't like leaving Sophia behind, even if she could understand Casimir's reasons for not taking her with them today. Sophia would be cared for here, of that she had no doubt. Her daughter was resilient and seeing Ana leave for work was nothing new.

And still, Ana had never felt such anxiety at the sight of her daughter becoming a speck in the distance.

'She'll be fine,' Casimir said from his seat beside her. He wasn't flying the helicopter today; he'd taken a back seat, alongside her. Behind them sat four security guards. His favourites, Ana thought. His most trusted. The ones who'd been with him before when he came to Geneva, the watchful Katya amongst them.

That had been what…four days ago?

It felt like longer.

Casimir was already dressed for his press conference, or so Ana assumed. Black suit, black tie, white shirt. She was wearing what he'd suggested. Dark trousers, white shirt, a short-cut jacket and low heels. Clothes from a suitcase packed in a hurry, back when they'd agreed she'd only be here for two weeks. She'd kept her make-up to a minimum and scraped her hair into a bun. She'd had twenty minutes to shower and dress. If he wanted her more presentable, he had to give her more time. 'How do I look?' she asked anxiously. 'I didn't bring many clothes.' And she certainly hadn't brought her best clothes. The kind he wore on a daily basis.

'You're beautiful,' he said. 'You always are.'

'I know how to make the most of what I have,' she continued doggedly. 'And I know this outfit is okay for today. That isn't to say that I wouldn't take advice from your people about what to wear, and what Sophia should wear, once you've acknowledged her. Do you have those types of advisors available?'

'Fashion advisors for women? No. It's been a long time since the monarch has needed to dress either a princess or a king's consort.'

'I mean, we have more clothes at home. They're just not *here*. We're only going to be here two weeks, and apart from that I didn't know what we'd need and I still don't know. I know what kind of clothes are acceptable in Geneva—no problem there. I'm just not sure what's acceptable here.' New country, unknown expectations and a public more than willing to crucify her. 'Never mind. I'll figure it out. It'll be fun. Lots and lots of fun.'

'You're nervous,' he said.

'Very.' She clasped her hands together and tucked them between her knees. And not just about clothes. He was about to lay claim to their daughter. There would be no turning back from that.

'I'll ask Moriana to take you shopping. She'll know what's appropriate.'

He sounded serious. He looked serious.

'This would be the Moriana you were supposed to marry, yes?'

'Yes.'

'Yeah, let's not do that.'

'Why not? Do you expect her to hold a grudge?'

'She might.' The woman was losing not just a kingdom but him too. 'How long has she waited for you?'

He had the grace to look slightly discomfited. 'I wouldn't call it waiting on me, as such. Moriana had things to do too. She has a degree in politics and fine arts. Charities to oversee. Her brother's coffers to empty when it comes to the royal family's art collection. She's been busy.'

'Uh huh.' Busy *not* pursuing anyone else, by the sound of things. 'Do you *know* that Moriana's heart isn't involved?'

'I'm sure.'

She wanted to believe him.

'You don't believe me,' he murmured with a half-smile. 'I am very charming, it's true.'

He could be. That was the problem.

Charming. Forceful when he wanted to be. Not to mention confident and assured. 'Are you nervous about the press conference?' she asked.

'I'm not concerned about giving the speech. I'm well prepared. The aftermath could get interesting.'

'Will there be question time?'

'Yes.'

She could only imagine the kind of questions he'd be fielding. 'Good luck with that.'

'Like I said, I'm well prepared.'

Clearly, arrogance could be an asset at times. She looked out of the window at the grey and rocky plains beyond the valley. It was desolate country. Water, or the lack of it, was an issue here. 'If you need a scapegoat today, it's okay to use me. My reputation's disposable.

Blame me for not telling you that you had a daughter if you need to. It's the truth.'

He looked strangely offended by her offer. 'You don't think any of the blame here is mine?'

'That's not what I said.' She looked down and laced her fingers together. 'You have a crown to claim, a monarchy to protect and a daughter to present in the best possible light. They're all important things.'

'And you think *your* reputation's not important?'

'I already have a reputation as a young single mother. People often assume certain things about me because of that. All I'm saying is I don't have a monarchy to lose. You do.' He'd started working on it at his father's side when he was eight years old. 'So be ruthless if you have to. I won't hold it against you.'

He looked down at his own hands then and the rest of the trip passed in silence until a city came into view at the far end of that barren tableland. It was a walled city, medieval in approach. Red roofs and grey stone walls dominated the cityscape and a palace sat clear in the middle of it like the pupil of an eye. There were no skyscrapers—it wasn't that kind of place. There were no big bodies of water. Instead, a series of circular canals ribboned outwards from the palace. What greenery there was looked carefully tended. 'Where does the city's water come from?' she asked.

'A river to the north,' he said. 'Water's precious here. We need more of it.'

'Did you ever build that dam in the mountains?'

'No.' His beautiful lips thinned. 'That project never went ahead. We've a project afoot between Byzenmaach and three neighbouring principalities to jointly address our water shortfall using new technologies and old. I'll be speaking about it today. Selling it.'

'Will it be hard to sell? If it's needed?'

'Ask me tomorrow,' he said with a smile that bordered on mocking.

The royal palace was grander and more ornate than the winter fortress. Soaring spires and covered walkways surrounded a central courtyard big enough to host several football games at once. Ana walked with Casimir and, beyond a curious glance or two from some of the palace staff, no one paid any attention to her at all. They entered an office and the bodyguards stayed outside. Rudolpho waited for them inside the room with a slender file in hand.

'The list of journalists and cameramen attending the press conference,' he said and handed the file to Casimir, who opened the file and began reading.

It was barely nine a.m. and the speech wasn't until twelve. Ana was used to being discreetly present in a room, but never before had she had absolutely no role to play at all.

They *knew* she was there. Rudolpho's narrowed gaze practically eviscerated her. 'I can arrange a private tour of the palace for you this morning, should you be interested.' Polite words to mask her removal.

'Perhaps later,' she murmured. 'Don't mind me. I'm fine where I am for now.' Doing nothing. Feeling wholly out of place and of no use whatsoever. She headed for the bookcase behind the desk. 'I'll read a book on…' she looked closer '…international monetary policy.'

'*I'll* give her the tour.' At last Cas spoke, his attention still on the file. 'Rudolpho, do we have anyone on staff who can function as a wardrobe mistress and fashion advisor to Ana and Sophia?'

'No.' It was an unequivocal reply. Enough to make Cas glance up with a frown for the older man.

'What about the Lady Serah?'

'I can arrange to have the Lady Serah meet with Ms Douglas and Sophia, yes,' said Rudolpho and turned towards Ana. 'His New Majesty may not beg you to leave the lady in question in her current role, but I will. She's my best function planner, has twenty-two years' experience in the role, and her social acumen and statesmanship is unsurpassed.'

Casimir's gaze clashed with Rudolpho's. 'Then I suspect she'll know fashion. Will she not?'

The older man nodded curtly, his gaze dropping to the floor.

'Perhaps she'll be able to recommend someone more suited to a wardrobe consultancy role,' Casimir continued. 'Set up a meeting between her and Ana for today at eleven o clock.'

Rudolpho nodded and left without speaking. Ana watched the advisor leave and shut the door behind him before turning to Casimir. 'What was that?'

'A difference of opinion that has nothing to do with the Lady Serah. When it comes to Rudolpho, I'm all for encouraging outspokenness. It's a slow process but we're getting there.' Casimir seemed unconcerned. 'He's worried about the press conference.'

'You don't have to babysit me if you'd rather concentrate on preparing for that. Like I said, I can read.' She glanced around the room, which looked as if it belonged in the mid-seventeenth century, never mind the computer on the desk. 'Or practice my needlework. Correspond with my parents with the aid of a fountain pen… Plenty to do.'

'Come. We can start with the armoury. It's full of seventeenth and eighteenth-century pieces.'

Of course it was. 'I always wanted to be a knight,' she said.

Ten minutes later she had her head in a helmet and her hand in a gauntlet, trying them on for size. 'They're a little heavy,' she said. 'But otherwise the perfect camouflage and protection required for a spot of shopping in the city, followed by coffee. Then music and dancing, a quick swordfight and then some rutting.'

'Rutting?' he said.

'I'm very earthy. You are too when you're naked. Where's my sword? And yours. You can be my man at arms.'

'Why would I want to be your man at arms when I can be a king?' he countered, but he was pulling a sword from the rack as he said it and holding it out in front of him.

'You'd do it for the freedom,' she said. 'Freedom from service.'

'I'd be serving you instead.' He was surprisingly good with that sword. 'And there would be drudgery.'

'Or you can be a bard. No drudgery, just music. Do you play an instrument?'

'I'd make a terrible bard and I'd starve.' He picked up another sword, swung it and then presented it to her. 'I'm sticking with the king business. It's what I know. All I need is the right queen and I'm set.'

'The poor woman.'

'She won't be poor.'

'She won't be free.'

He frowned. 'That again. What would convince her to give up her freedom for a king?'

'Love.' She kept telling him what she wanted. Over and over, spelling it out for him. 'She might do it if she loved her king enough. And if he loved her back.'

'Kings can't afford love.'

'I don't believe that.' Ana lowered the sword but kept the helmet in place. She needed the protection of him not being able to see her face. 'Love is free. What you can't afford is any more loss.'

He didn't answer. Instead he put his sword back and helped her remove her armour too. 'There are two more places I want to show you,' he said, picking up a jewelled dagger, crossing the room and pushing it into a slot in the wall.

An entire section of stone wall slid aside to reveal a vault with a huge steel door. He stepped up to a control panel, let it scan his right eye and the door clicked open with a hollow whoosh and a light inside came on.

'What is this?'

'This is where we keep Byzenmaach's crown jewels.' Cas opened the door wider and gestured for her to lead the way.

Trepidation at entering a vault warred with deep curiosity as to what she might find on the other side of that door. Curiosity won.

'So how does it work? The acquisition and use of crown jewels?'

'First of all, they don't belong to me; they belong to the monarchy. This, for example, is the crown.' He stopped in front of a crown behind a glass case. 'I'll wear it at my coronation. It's a ceremonial piece and likely won't be seen again until my successor is crowned. We have sceptres, orbs, daggers and rings—each of them a cultural icon with a specific purpose.' He steered her towards another glass case, this one filled with daggers. 'And then there's the jewellery worn by the women of the royal family. Want to see it?'

'Oh, come on, stop torturing me. My appreciation for fine jewellery is alive and well. Of course I want to see it.'

The women's jewellery was kept in steel trays that

slid out at the touch of Casimir's thumbprint on a wall pad. There were trays of rings, trays of necklaces. Tiaras.

'Normally, the royal consort would also have a personal collection held elsewhere but after my mother died, all her jewellery was rolled into the royal collection. Brooches, earrings.' He pressed his thumb to another wall pad and four more trays slid out. 'Bracelets, pendants.'

'Do these have to be worn at specific times?'

'Some do. And of course the more formal pieces are more suited to more formal functions. All have a history that the wearer needs to acknowledge.' He picked up a diamond ring and held it up to the light until it flared a brilliant white. 'This was my mother's engagement ring. Given the state of her marriage and her subsequent suicide, I doubt any monarch will choose to offer it to their future bride.'

'You're superstitious?'

'Maybe a little.' He held it out towards her. 'Would you wear it? Assuming you had agreed to marry me, of course.'

'Which I haven't,' she said. 'But no. I wouldn't wear it.'

He returned it to its velvet-lined spot and picked up another ring. 'What about this one?'

It was an old-fashioned emerald-cut diamond, with a baguette either side. 'It's lovely.'

He picked up her hand and slid it onto her engagement finger. 'It was my great-grandmother's. Sixteen carats and flawless.'

'Uh huh.' She couldn't help but admire it. 'Pretty.' She took it off and gave it back to him.

He put it back, only to put yet another ring on her finger. This one was a brilliant cut stone that flashed intensely pink in the light. 'My grandmother's pink diamond. A gift from her husband on their fiftieth wedding anniversary.'

This one was beyond beautiful. The pink colour giving it a warmth that the others, for all their brilliance, simply didn't have.

'Which do you prefer? This or the one before it?'

She looked at him sharply. 'Are we shopping for an engagement ring?'

'Of course not. Apparently I'm not getting engaged.' His wry smile could have cut these diamonds. 'I'm showing you the royal collection.'

She studied the ring again and couldn't help but admire the way it flashed and the elegant simplicity of the design. 'It's very beautiful,' she said and then took it off and handed it back to him. 'Thank you for the tour.'

He moved to another tray and picked up a necklace set with diamonds and large sapphires, with the biggest sapphire of them all hanging pendant style, as the centrepiece. 'Try this.'

'What? No!'

'C'mon. I'm offering. Your appreciation for fine jewellery is alive and well, remember?'

He took her hand and led her to the end of the row and turned her around so that she stood directly in front of a full-length mirror. He stood behind her while he fastened the necklace around her neck, and the stones were cold but his fingers burned.

'Oh, wow.'

He dealt deftly with the first button of her shirt and then the next, before pushing the collar aside with his fingertips. By the time he was done and her shirt was half hanging from her shoulders, her nipples were erect and his heated gaze was not on the sapphires.

'Stunning,' he murmured. 'The Connaach sapphires have never seen such a setting.'

'They have a name?'

'They do. There are earrings, a pendant and a tiara to match. They date back to the time, and the Court, of Marie Antoinette.'

'That's...very impressive. Take it off.' His gaze met hers in the mirror.

'They're not the first thing I see when I look at you,' he said.

'What *do* you see?'

'Strength.' He slid the necklace from her neck, dragging it low across the swell of her breast first. 'Passion.' He settled her shirt back into its proper position. 'Loyalty.'

She rebuttoned her shirt while he put the necklace away and made the trays of jewellery slide back where they came from.

'You never took a husband,' he said. 'You've had no long-term lovers these past seven years. Why not?'

'You think I stayed alone out of loyalty to you?'

He turned and warily watched her approach. 'I don't know.'

'Have you had lovers these past seven years?' she asked.

'Yes.'

'So have I.' His expression darkened and Ana shrugged. 'Nothing serious, it's true. But I'm open to the idea of walking through life with the right person at my side. I never shunned that thought.'

'But you shun me.'

'You don't love me.'

'But I care about your wellbeing. And there's passion between us. Respect for each other's needs. I've promised you my loyalty. What kind of love do you *want*? Explain it to me.'

He was opening up another sliding tray and picking out a pair of black cufflinks.

'I want the kind where two people stand at each other's side in the middle of this huge and crazy world, with every option known to man open to them, and they know, without a shadow of a doubt, that there is no other place they'd rather be. Love is not an intellectual puzzle. It's a feeling.'

He pocketed the cufflinks. 'Thank you for explaining.'

'You don't understand, do you?'

'I do understand. I've just never felt that way.'

'I know. Why do you think I keep refusing you?'

His smile didn't reach his eyes. 'Could have been any number of reasons. Or a combination of reasons. I like to think that by talking about it with you I'm narrowing it down. Come. I want to show you something else.'

'*More* treasure?'

'Of a sort. This one's practical.'

It took them five minutes to get out of the palace building and another ten to walk through the garden and down the vast expanse of lawn to the southern end of the palace grounds where a two-storey stone building stood. It wasn't small. A dozen huge windows ran the length of both floors, and the lower floor also displayed climbing roses of deepest apricot on its walls. Lavender lined the pathway that ran the length of the building and the garden beds here were the most impressive yet—stuffed full to overflowing with shrubbery, more roses, rosemary, thyme and other more tender herbs.

'This is a cook's garden,' she said, breaking off a tip of lavender and putting it to her nose.

'Yes. It serves the palace kitchen. My grandmother

used to live here, the one whose ring you preferred. She was very fond of her garden. The dower house also has the advantage of being situated within the palace grounds but fully separate from the palace itself.' They reached the corner of the house and turned into the shade of the building. 'I'd like you and Sophia to consider living here on a permanent basis.'

'Excuse me?'

'They duchy I plan to give Sophia is some distance from the capital. This is a better living option for you both, although you will, of course, be free to visit the duchy from time to time.'

'It's too big.'

'I will, of course, pick up the running costs and ensure you have all the staff you need. Some of the rooms are small, if I remember correctly. I don't remember my grandmother's house being austere.'

He took her through an iron gate and into a walled vegetable garden full of fruit trees and nursery plants. Definitely not austere, this part of it. It was kind of frenzied and haphazardly organised. A mixture of old and new and everything in between. But thriving. And there were bees. Probably royal bees.

'The gardeners use this as a plant nursery. It seeds the palace gardens. All this would move somewhere else, of course, were you to accept the offer. And there's the conservatory. Also used by the ground staff and gardeners.'

The conservatory was a huge glass semicircle extending from the house and bursting with greenery. 'The house was mothballed when my grandmother died.' He pulled out a brick that formed part of the wall beside the doorstep, stuck his hand in the hole and pulled out an old-fashioned key.

'Seriously?' she said. '*That's* your security?'

'Needs updating.'

It was clean inside the house, dark but not damp, and as Cas started opening curtains and taking covers off the furniture Ana began to see the appeal. The house was far too big for two people but the common rooms were lovely and the bedrooms were of a size that people wouldn't get lost in.

She opened the door to an ancient bathroom, beautifully tiled in saffron and gold, with a circular bathtub big enough for two. A skylight hovered over it, the same size and shape as the bath. 'This world of yours…it's a little opulent.'

He stood in the doorway, arms folded across his chest, watching her as she took it all in. 'You like it. It reminds you of the bathhouse.'

It did remind her of the bathhouse. 'I could fill it with exotic dancers. You could have a harem.'

'You're tempted.'

'Don't be smug.' But he was correct. If he really was looking to incorporate Sophia into the royal family, this would be one way to do it. A way that allowed Ana some autonomy. From him.

'You could turn some rooms into a business centre. Build a business from here. The house already lies within the palace's security parameters, which makes me very happy,' he offered quietly. 'It would make my security team happy. It would save money.'

'What about my life in Geneva?'

'Anastasia.' He looked torn. 'That life is gone. I'm trying to give you choices. That's not one of them.'

Up until now she'd resisted truly digesting that notion. This house, this fresh new *option*, was forcing her to.

'I'm sorry,' he said.

'No, you're not.' Anger had to be directed somewhere.

'Believe me, I am. I know the value of freedom, even if I've never had it. I can hear in your words and your voice the value *you* put on it. I'm trying to make it up to you.'

'With things.'

'Yes. With things. Useful things. Pretty things. Things that may be of value to you, going forward. Opportunities.'

He turned away to stare towards the bathroom door. 'I'll be moving into my father's old quarters in the summer palace soon. The Byzenmaach monarch resides at the summer palace. Tradition demands it.'

'Even though you prefer your winter fortress?'

'Even then. And even though I would live nearby, you would have complete privacy. This would be your home. I would not venture here uninvited.'

He wanted her to say yes to this. He couldn't hide it. Not with his words and not with his eyes.

'Show me the second floor,' she said.

The second floor was even more inviting than the first, full of sunshine and windows and intimate corners. He took the covers off the sofas and the sideboards in the living room and unrolled the floor rugs and a little more grandeur crept into the space. She could make it less daunting, more lived in. It was indeed an option she could work with. A place from which to learn how best to navigate his world.

Ana looked through a couple more rooms, and Casimir said nothing. A muscle flickered in his jaw. 'We're going to need a couple of wolfhounds,' she said.

'Done.'

'And the gardeners can stay, provided we have full garden access and get to sample the spoils on a random basis.'

He smiled, just a little. 'You will never be without flowers or fresh produce again.'

CHAPTER NINE

THE ROOM THE press conference was to be held in had a podium, several centuries' worth of royal portraiture, and standing room for around one hundred people and their equipment.

Ana stood at the back of the room, not quite a part of things, not quite an outsider. A palace pass graced her neck, two security guards hovered within reach and exit strategies had been discussed. When told to leave by Security, she would leave. She'd given her word.

So far, the press people in the room had barely spared a glance for her. One or two had glanced her way a second time and their gaze had slid to her press tag. Today, she was an employee of Associated Press TPR. Whoever they were.

And then Casimir entered and strode to the podium and silence fell. He looked out over the room and paid her no more attention than anyone else, even though he saw her. He wore a stern and solemn expression and she wondered if he knew he looked older than his years.

He probably did.

If she'd learned anything in the previous half-hour in Casimir's office, with Casimir running through lines of his speech and Rudolpho peppering him with insulting questions, while yet another aide brushed his suit and fastened the cufflinks Casimir pulled from his pocket and handed to him, it was that Casimir and his entourage were consummate professionals.

Only when Rudolpho had presented Casimir with a ring to wear had Casimir faltered.

'It's been resized,' said the older man and Casimir nodded and slid it on his finger without another word and went back to running lines. But he fisted his hand and rubbed the thumb of his other hand over the ring until Rudolpho stopped with the questioning in order to stare pointedly at the offending behaviour.

Casimir scowled, but the ring-rubbing stopped. 'I'm ready,' he said.

Casimir started his speech with a tribute to his father. He talked political achievements and ongoing projects. Ana had heard variations on this speech a thousand times in her capacity as a translator, but it was nicely done and spoke of stability and the alignment of vision.

'I want to talk about water next,' he said and the reporters collectively moved forward. 'For a number of years now, I've been in talks with our neighbouring monarchs—Augustus of Arun, Theodosius of Liesendaach and Valentine of Thallasia. We propose the construction of a water supply system that weaves its way across many borders and regions. It is intended to supply all those in need and the water-harvesting techniques and recycling plants will be at the forefront of technology. As an individual nation we could not afford it, but together with Arun, Thallasia and Liesendaach we can make it work and reap the benefits. Detailed plans are in the press kits available to you as you leave here today and there's one part of the plan that I want to emphasise, beyond all measure.' He took a breath and his jaw seemed to harden. 'No matter who you are, no matter where on our borders you live, no matter what you've done in the past, I invite you to the negotiation table. Your presence is welcome, your opinions are welcome, and your water needs will be considered.'

He paused and looked out over the gathering, as if to let his words sink in. 'I do not dwell on the past. I will not sit back and let fear and hatred rule this monarchy. For the sake of your children and mine, it's time to move forward.'

'Did he just invite the northern mountain tribes back to the negotiation table?' Ana heard one reporter mutter to his cameraman.

'Yep.' The two men exchanged a glance that spoke of deep concern.

'Leonidas will be turning in his grave,' the first one said.

Personally, Ana would rather see Leonidas of Byzenmaach burning in hell for his sins, but maybe that was just her. She shifted from one foot to the other and kept her mouth shut as Cas began to talk of family next.

He talked of his sister and dark days indeed and he spoke of his mother. As pictures of them came up on the viewing screen behind him, he spoke to them. Sometimes with joy, sometimes in sorrow. Always with utter sincerity.

He was good at this.

And then a picture of Sophia appeared. 'I mentioned earlier that I would see old animosities die for the sake of Byzenmaach's children,' he began. 'This is my daughter.'

Ana recognised the park in the background and the clothes Sophia was wearing. The photo couldn't have been more than a week or so old. But Ana hadn't taken it. She crossed her arms over her chest defensively, set her mouth in a firm line and wondered what other surprises this speech of his would bring.

Cameras clicked like crickets at dusk as Casimir continued. 'Her name is Sophia Alexandra, she was conceived seven years ago and I am very, very protective of her.'

Another photo went up—another picture of Sophia. 'As you can see, she bears a strong resemblance to my sister. Sometimes...' he cleared his throat and his gaze sought Ana's '...sometimes she takes my breath away with a gesture or a look that I remember from another time. It hurts my heart and I have to remind myself to look forward, not back. At the same time I can tell you that there is no better motivation for wanting peace and understanding between neighbours than having this child in my life.'

Another picture, this one showing Ana from behind and Sophia at the school gate. Where had he got these pictures? Why hadn't she realised someone had been taking them? Ana felt a twitch between her shoulder blades, as if someone had painted a bullseye on her back.

'My daughter has lived a sheltered life away from the press. Her childhood has been a happy one, and I would see it continue. Any attempt at invasion of her privacy will be met with a security force some may consider excessive. My reply to this is simple. Consider what Byzenmaach—what I—have lost.'

There was one more picture of Sophia, spreadeagled on the floor with Jelly the wolfhound and the little black puppies, her ponytail sloppy and tilted to one side as she oversaw the feeding. Jeans, no shoes, a faded blue Tee—a little girl in all her innocence. The setting showed a stone floor and walls that gave nothing of the location away but hinted at age and grandeur. Protection of the young. The picture was perfect.

He glanced down at the podium and smiled wryly. 'I know you'll have questions and have anticipated some of them. Ladies and gentlemen of the press, the mother of my child is fluent in six languages—including ours—and is an interpreter for the European Parliament and the United Nations.' He touched the ring on his hand briefly, and Ana wondered whether he did so for luck or for courage, or whether the gesture was a totally unconscious one.

'Until now, my daughter and her mother have lived independently of the Byzenmaach monarchy. That is about to change. My daughter will soon begin to take on the roles assigned to her as a valued member of this royal family. She will occupy the duchy formerly held by my sister and will henceforth be known as the Duchess of Sanesch. I thought it fitting. Any questions?'

Oh, dear Lord, were there questions.

Was he married?

Had his father known of the girl?

What of his relationship with Moriana of Arun?

Casimir, King of Byzenmaach, smiled grimly and began answering the questions that suited him.

No, he was not yet married.

Relations with Moriana of Arun were amicable. He had enormous respect and admiration for the princess but marriage was unlikely.

Ana saw sideways glances and raised eyebrows at that one.

The questions continued, a mad jumble of sound with the occasional moment of breathless silence while everyone waited for his answer.

'Are you serious about resuming water negotiations with the very same people who murdered your sister?'

'Yes.'

'When can we see the child in person?'

'When I see fit.'

'What is your relationship with the mother? Do you ever plan to marry and have legitimate heirs? What good is a bastard daughter?'

That last one caused consternation, both within the press and the royal aides assembled. A line had been crossed, a challenge issued. Casimir's fierce hawk eyes turned predatory.

He stared at the reporter who'd dared ask the question. He let the silence build and the reporter squirm for a very long time.

And then he let his displeasure fill the silence just that little bit more.

'This *illegitimate daughter* you shun so quickly is a gift,' he offered finally in a voice that dissuaded argument. 'She has many names in my household—Sophia, Little One, Beloved. *Bastard* is not one of them.'

More buzz from the press at that.

'If history teaches us anything, it is this,' Cas continued. 'It is no easy task to stand beside a king and risk public crucifixion on a daily basis. It is no easy task to live with the constant threat of violence against your own self or your loved ones. The strength required to do so is enormous. Yet here I stand, your king, asking a child in all her innocence to do exactly that. To stand at my side and believe that I can keep her safe. To make her world a better place. Make no mistake, I will see it done.'

Ana's bodyguard touched her arm, albeit briefly, and glanced towards the rear door of the room, before heading towards it. Ana followed reluctantly. She'd given her word. Another security person, this one a man, fell into step behind her. They stopped at the door itself.

Half in, half out, allowing her a view of Casimir still. Casimir caught her gaze and held it for a heartbeat. And then he turned back towards the screen.

A new photo came up, a shot of Ana. Make-up-free and with her hair piled high atop her head in a messy ponytail reminiscent of Sophia's, she wasn't looking straight at the photographer, but rather appeared to be staring intently at something in the distance. Ana tilted her head and tried to place the background. The park in Geneva, near where she lived? No. The walled garden at the winter palace? Ana frowned. The cloistered walkway? Yes.

'There's one more person I'd like you to meet. Not in person today, but soon. Her name is Anastasia Victoria Douglas. She's twenty-six, of English and Russian descent, the mother of my child, and one of the strongest women I know. Which is good news for me and for Byzenmaach. A strong royal consort is a blessing for all.'

Cas looked her way again and a flicker of some undefined expression crossed his face. Sorrow? Apology? *Royal consort? What was he doing?*

'We will be married within the year.'

A picture of two children racing through a garden came up on the screen, a huge wolfhound loping alongside them, and for a moment Ana would have sworn the girl in the picture was Sophia. But it wasn't Sophia. It was Casimir and his sister.

'He's finished,' murmured the bodyguard. 'Go.'

The door closed behind them and minutes later Ana was back in Casimir's office, with the bodyguards stationed just outside. Casimir joined her not thirty seconds later and shut the door behind him.

Ana took one look at him and felt her self-control shatter. 'What was that? What the *hell* was that?'

'Necessary.' Casimir wasn't in the mood for criticism. He'd done what he had to do. He'd gambled it all.

For a woman who looked alarmingly pale, her voice certainly seemed to radiate a lot of heat. 'I *refused* you. In what world does *no* translate into *I'm marrying you within a year*?'

'You're not indifferent to me, Ana.' Surely she could do him the courtesy of admitting it. 'You could come to love me. You're already halfway there.'

'I know that. You know that. *Every man and his falcon at the winter fortress knows that.* Doesn't mean I said yes.' She started pacing and he leaned back against the edge of his desk and watched her work off some of her temper.

'You gave me permission to destroy your reputation in order to preserve mine.'

'Still not a yes!'

'It was a foolish offer and I refuse to do it.' He crossed his arms, trying to get a read on the extent of her distress but she wouldn't stand still long enough for him to properly see her face. 'I want my people to value and protect you, Anastasia. I want stability for Sophia. This is the way to do it.' He drew the ring she'd admired from his pocket and held it out to her.

'No,' she snapped. '*Hell*, no.'

'You liked my mother's ring more?'

'Casimir, I'm not doing this.'

'You want love as well,' he said. 'I'm getting there. I'm willing to work towards it.'

'It's not *work*,' she grated, and then his office door opened and Rudolpho stormed in.

'What the *hell* was that?' the older man said, and then his gaze took in Ana and the ring and he paled. 'God have mercy. You haven't asked her yet?'

'I'm doing it now.' Obviously. 'So if you'll excuse me, I'll get on with it.'

Rudolpho closed his eyes and put both palms to his face. He let out a laugh that sounded ever so slightly hysterical and then wiped his face. 'Your Majesty, I've known you since you were a baby. I've bounced you on my knee. I taught you everything I know about statecraft. And less than a week into your reign you invite the northerners back to our table and announce a wedding when you haven't secured the bride yet? Are you deliberately trying to end your reign? Because I *know* I taught you better than this.'

But Casimir was done with statecraft. 'For thirty years I've been a perfect puppet for this country. No more. I know what I stand for and I know how I want to proceed. I've made my choices very clear. Now all I have to do is get everyone else on board with the plan.'

Rudolpho shook his head. 'You do realise you risk being exiled?'

'We'll see.'

'You could have at least told me what you planned to do today. I thought you were dropping one bombshell. The existence of your daughter. You dropped *three*.'

'I concede that announcing my wedding may have been a mistake.'

'And your plans for the dam?'

'Not a mistake.'

Rudolpho's bleak black gaze encompassed them both. And then he turned on his heel and left.

Casimir sighed heavily.

'Casimir, what are you doing?' Ana asked almost helplessly. 'You're running roughshod over people! Including me! You can't *force* people to do what you want them to do.' She put her hands to her cheeks. Then she crossed her arms in front of her defensively and tucked her hands beneath her armpits. 'I'm not marrying you within a year.'

This really wasn't going according to plan. 'But you will if I fall in love with you. I'm already halfway there.'

'You are nowhere near there!'

He ventured closer, stopping only when he stood in front of her. Close enough to see the sweep of individual eyelashes and the panic in her eyes. 'Hand,' he said and took her fingers in his and raised her knuckles to his lips. She stared daggers at him but she let him do it.

He turned her hand over and placed his lips to her palm before placing his grandmother's ring in it and closing her fingers over it. 'Keep it,' he said. 'It's yours now. Whether you wear it or not.'

'I'm not wearing it.'

'Have a little faith in me,' he said. 'You were right when you said I can't afford any more loss. I'm not losing you again. Therefore I'm going to love you the way you want to be loved.'

'I admire your resolve, Casimir. It's outstanding. But let me repeat something I said to you before. *Love is not an intellectual puzzle!*'

A brief knock on the door announced the arrival of Rudolpho, phone in hand. The chief advisor's gaze swept over them, sharp eyes missing nothing. 'You're not engaged yet,' he said flatly.

'Not yet,' Casimir said blandly. 'But I did give her the ring, should she ever wish to wear it.'

'Excellent, Your Majesty. No engagement and a royal heirloom worth millions lost to a foreigner.'

'Who's on the phone?'

'His Majesty Theodosius of Liesendaach requests that you take his call,' Rudolpho said, heavy on the pomp and ceremony. 'His Majesty Theodosius said, and I quote,

"Put that moron who just screwed Moriana over and stole my bad-boy crown on the phone."' Rudolpho relayed the message with unadulterated pleasure. 'I gather he watched the live broadcast.'

Cas smiled fierce and free. 'Excellent.' It wasn't the response either Rudolpho or Ana had been expecting if the worried glance they shared with each other was any indication. 'Rudolpho, see to it that Anastasia gets back to the winter fortress this afternoon. She's had enough.' Cas turned to Ana next. 'Unless, of course, you need more time for wardrobe meetings. How did that go?'

'Badly,' she said. 'Thank you for asking.'

'I've arranged a secretary for her,' Rudolpho said. 'One of my best.' *You owe me*, the older man's tone suggested.

'I also gave her the dower house,' Cas said. 'It'll need to be staffed and made habitable.'

'Of course, Your Majesty.' A muscle in Rudolpho's jaw twitched. 'Anything else you'd like to give her? Your kingdom? Saturn? Or may I get back to putting out all the *other* fires you've lit?'

'By all means, put them out. I'll even help.' He turned to Ana. 'I'll find you later.'

She glared at him. 'And Rudolpho and I will find you a therapist.'

She swept from the room, with Rudolpho right behind her, but she kept the ring. It was right there in her tightly clenched fist.

Casimir ran a hand across the back of his neck, his body thrumming with the aftermath of freefall. He'd planned for this. Maybe not all of it but most of it. Squaring his shoulders, he lifted the phone to his ear.

'Theo, my old friend. You saw the show?'

'I did indeed. A six-year-old daughter born out of wedlock and a future Queen Consort no one's ever met? I can't top that. It's going to take years.'

'Don't forget the water management plan.'

'Yes, let's not forget the only thing I did know about beforehand. Talk about burying the lead. I'll be on camera within the hour, endorsing the bold new regional plan and congratulating you on your upcoming nuptials. Which... I have no words other than: I hope the hell you know what you're doing. And how's Moriana? Is she even speaking to you right now?'

'About that. I was thinking you could ask her to Liesendaach to—'

'No.'

'—value the royal art collection.'

'I know exactly what my collection is worth. Why do I need the harridan's opinion?'

'You don't. But she needs a face-saver, and you're—'

'Egregiously reckless, feckless and immature. Her words, not mine.'

'I was going to say available,' muttered Casimir. 'And kind-hearted.'

'Debatable,' his childhood friend said drily.

'So what if you and Moriana fight a little?' They never stopped. 'You like it. It keeps you battle-honed.'

'And perpetually wounded.'

'One photo of you looking smitten with her. That's all she needs.'

'That is not what I need.'

'I don't want to see her take a public press battering over this.'

'Well, I'm sure that could have been avoided had you not to all intents and purposes been practically engaged to her *for the past twenty years*. Damn you to hell and back, Casimir, what were you thinking? Do you think it's been pleasant, her having to wait on your whim? She was relying on you to come through for her.'

Cas looked at the phone. He'd heard similar from Augustus, but Augustus was Moriana's brother and naturally protective. Theo, on the other hand, was traditionally not in Moriana's corner. Not ever. 'Hello? Is this Theodosius, despoiler of women? Because for a moment there I thought I was talking to someone who cared about a woman's feelings. Someone deeply invested in the fact that their only female friend of over twenty years might be hurting.'

Silence, then, 'Screw you. You were perfect for her. The golden couple. You never put a foot wrong and now this.'

'She's not broken-hearted.' Casimir tried again. 'I've spoken to her and she's angry, yes. Resentful, yes. Not shy about voicing her displeasure at being made to feel like a fool. But we've never been intimate, not once in all these years.' And that was more than Theo ever needed to know about Casimir's relationship with Moriana.

The silence on the other end of the phone was deep enough to drown in.

'Seriously?' Theo said finally. 'What are you, a monk?'

'Compared to who? You? Yes.'

More silence, and then, 'I'll ask her out. She will refuse and then I'll be done with it.'

'Thank you.'

'You're welcome. Hey, Cas—' Theo's voice had softened '—we're finally doing it. All those years. All our plans.'

'I know.'

'Asking you to offer the northerners a seat at the negotiating table was a big ask, but you did it. I've never been more proud of you. I've never been more proud of anyone.'

Casimir rubbed at his chest to ease the sudden tightness there. 'Thanks.'

Theo cleared his throat. 'Anyway. I'm hanging up now, you ungrateful cur. Some of us have work to do.'

'Call Moriana.'

But he was talking to a dialling tone.

Forty minutes later, Casimir put the phone down and headed for the outer offices where Rudolpho and various other royal aides held court. 'You all saw Theodosius's press conference?'

Everyone nodded.

'Augustus of Arun will follow within the hour, as will Valentine of Thallasia,' he told them. 'It's all been scheduled.'

'What of the north?' asked Rudolpho, his eyes sharply assessing.

'I've had no communication with the mountain tribes to the north,' he said. 'They heard of the new water plans when you did.' He glanced at the clock. 'I don't know if or when we *will* hear from them. Tomorrow I'll send them a formal invitation to negotiation talks here at the palace and ask them to nominate a representative. See if that encourages a reply.'

Rudolpho sighed heavily.

'You disagree with my strategy?' Casimir asked coolly.

'I know who we're likely to get by way of an envoy.'

'You liked him well enough once.'

'That was before I knew what he was truly capable of. You'll barely be able to guarantee him safe passage.'

Rudolpho was right. 'Then he can come to the winter fortress, where I *can* guarantee safe passage.'

'You would put him within a mountain range of your daughter? Of your future wife?'

'I'll send them elsewhere.'

The older man sighed again. 'There's no dissuading you from this course of action, is there?'

'I'm fully committed. I have been for years.'

'You planned this. You and Liesendaach, Arun and Thallasia. When?'

'Years ago. Back when we were young men dreaming big.'

Rudolpho stiffened. 'Why didn't you *tell* me?'

'You would have been duty-bound to tell my father and he would have destroyed any fair hope of these plans ever gaining traction.'

'Your father's been dead for four days. You could have told me what you planned to do during the hours and hours we spent working on your speech last night. A speech you *did not give*.'

'I gave parts of it.' But his chief advisor was right. 'I could have told you my plans. I chose not to.' Casimir looked around the room at the other aides, some of them pretending to work, others not bothering to hide their avid interest in the conversation. 'I've been waiting years to right old wrongs and if you think I haven't planned these next few days and what needs to happen in order to gain the confidence of my people down to the second, you're wrong. Theo, Augustus and Valentine will stand with me because it benefits us all. Formal letters of invitation to peace talks will be sent north.'

He stood tall and squared his shoulders. 'You know me. For thirty years I have stood at my father's side and been what he wanted me to be. What Byzenmaach needed me to be. I have served. I have learned from my father's mistakes. And I will not let my country stagnate and fail any longer. If you don't like my vision for the future, if you are not capable of dealing fairly with those I bring to the table, there's the door.'

No one moved.

'Right,' said Rudolpho. 'Let's get to work.'

Ana returned to the winter fortress just in time to catch the afternoon news and a replay of Casimir's speech. She watched it with Lor, who had a faintly proud smile on her face and nodded when it was done.

'Congratulations on your engagement,' Lor said, but Ana was already shaking her head.

'I'm not… We're not…engaged. I didn't agree to that. Casimir made a mistake.'

Lor said nothing.

'But the rest of it was good,' Ana said in a small voice. 'Excellent. He's an accomplished statesman.'

'Your mother phoned while you were at the palace,' Lor said. 'She too offered her congratulations.'

Ana winced. 'I should probably call her back.' She sent Lor a wan smile and figured she should probably call from the privacy of her room.

'Ana.' Lor stopped her at the door. 'Ms Douglas.'

'I thought we'd moved past Ms Douglas,' Ana said.

'He's a good man.' Lor twisted her hands in her apron. 'He was a good boy. Loyal to a fault, even when his emotional needs were not being met. And they were very rarely met. He might not show it, or say it, but he cares for you and the little one. I can see the change in him.'

'He doesn't know love,' Ana said. 'He doesn't know how to let anyone in.'

Lor lifted her chin. 'Then teach him.'

Love wasn't something that could be taught, decided Ana as she walked into her room and picked up the phone.

Manners could be taught. Languages could be taught. But love was different.

Her mother answered on the fifth ring and Ana wasted no time in getting to the point. 'We're not engaged,' she said. 'No matter what you heard during the press conference. Casimir was mistaken.'

'He tried to force your hand?' her mother asked sharply.

'No.' *Yes.* 'I gave him mixed messages and maybe slept with him again. Marriage came up as an option, a possibility, nothing more. He needs a wife and an heir. I'm a convenient option.' She tried to keep her voice steady as she spoke. 'I said no.'

Her mother said nothing.

'He wants us to remain in Byzenmaach,' Ana said next. 'He's very security-conscious.'

'And I know why,' her mother said. 'I made it my business to find out.'

'What else did you find out?' Never underestimate her mother's talent for gathering information.

'That he has his work cut out for him. His father divided a nation.'

'He knows that,' Ana said. 'You saw the press conference? What did you think of it?'

'I thought the water plans for the region were visionary, his olive branch to the rebels on his northern borders was reckless, and his family history tragic. His protectiveness when it came to you and Sophia made me weep with both joy and fear, for he has shown his weakness.'

'He doesn't want me to go back to Geneva,' said Ana.

'Neither do I. The damage is done. Stay where he can protect you.'

'He's offered me the dower house on the palace grounds.'

'Good. I hope there's room for visitors,' her mother said.

'There's room for a football team.' Ana stopped pacing and leaned back against the wall instead, and to hell with the gilded wallpaper. If it rubbed off, it rubbed off. Walls were meant for leaning on. 'Mama, he's a good man. He's trying with me and Sophia. He wants us around. I have a ring in my pocket that he wants me to put on my finger and it'd be easy, so easy, just to do it and become part of the royal machinery that surrounds him, with all the protection it affords. I said no.' She closed her eyes and thumped her head gently against the wall.

'What's stopping you?' Her mother's voice soothed, even as it demanded answers.

'He doesn't love me. I'm just convenient. A righting of wrongs and a means to an end.'

'And you've slept with him,' her mother said.

Ana sighed. 'Resistance is non-existent. He wants, I oblige, and we both win.'

'But you still said no to his proposal.'

Ana thumped her head against the wall again. Gently, but still... 'I could love him. Easily.' In a heartbeat, assuming she didn't already. 'I could be happy here. Sophia would have a father. There would be more children. I could keep working as a translator and keep that side of me functioning. I'm interested in Casimir's plans for Byzenmaach and I'm not politically naïve. I could be of use here.'

'I'm listening,' said her mother, and that was another thing she did very, very well.

'But he doesn't love me, Mama, and I don't know if he ever will. And I think if I married him and he never grew to love me, I would break. I don't want to break.'

Not again.

'I'm going to conquer this world,' she continued. 'I'm going to carve out a place in it and maybe one day...'

She took a deep breath and exposed her deepest desire. 'Maybe one day I'll stand at Casimir's side, secure in the knowledge that he loves me as dearly as I love him. But not today.'

'That's my girl,' her mother said.

Six hours later, Casimir walked into his bedchamber at the winter fortress and caught his breath at the sight before him. Soft lamps lit the drinks on the sideboard. Beside them sat a plate of misshapen chocolate chip cookies and a haphazard posy of flowers. The posy was an odd mixture of clover leaves, violets, crooked twigs and pretty leaves that a small girl might collect in her hand. A note sat next to the posy, with an arrow pointing towards the cookies. *For my king*, it said. *Love from Sophia*, and he felt a tiny hand reach for his heart and take hold.

An envelope sat beside it, not quite flat, and he knew what it was before he reached for it. His grandmother's ring fell out into his hand, but it wasn't the ring he was interested in. She'd left him a note, and his hands shook as he opened the folded paper.

Not yet. I don't want either of us to make a mistake. As for your unification speech for Byzenmaach, it took my breath away with its vision and generosity towards old foes.

For your protective introduction of Sophia and of me, I can only say thank you.

Sleep well, Casimir. I'll see you in the morning.

She wouldn't wear his ring, but nor had she left him. That was something.

CHAPTER TEN

THREE DAYS LATER Ana was quietly going round the twist. She had plenty to do; that wasn't the problem. Arrange for her and Sophia's belongings to be sent from Geneva to the dower house. Acquire clothes for them both that they could wear on their first official outing with Casimir. Try and arrange schooling for Sophia, and wasn't that an endeavour of gigantic proportions. Most of all she got to watch an increasingly stern Casimir as he left every morning for the capital and returned every evening with a bleak gaze and a weary smile.

The factions to the north hadn't responded to his invitations yet.

Rudolpho counselled patience but Casimir didn't want to hear it.

Lor simply shook her head and refused to talk about it.

When it came to the matter of schooling for Sophia, Ana sought Lor's counsel above all others. The older woman knew things and had endless patience for Ana's questions.

'Am I really asking the impossible by wanting Sophia to go to school?' Ana asked as they sat at the computer and studied the list of schools Ana's new secretary had sent through. 'What do royal children normally do?'

'There's no hard and fast rule.'

'Casimir said he had tutors.'

Lor nodded. 'Even before the tragedies he rarely mixed with other children. Only other royal children who came visiting. Augustus and Moriana. Theo of Liesendaach—and what a tearaway that one was. Valentine of Thallasia and his sister—those two were designed to break hearts, I've never seen more beautiful children. They were Casimir's friends. He keeps them close.'

'I'm getting that.' Three of them were kings in their own right and fighting just as hard for regional reform as Casimir. 'Did they go to school or did they have tutors too?'

'Augustus and Moriana went to school. Theo too.' Lor frowned. 'Valentine and Amira, no. They had tutors.'

'What do you think I should do when it comes to schooling Sophia?'

'I think she's a gregarious girl who needs to go to school, make friends and have as normal an upbringing as possible, under the circumstances.'

That was what Ana's mother had said too. 'My daughter is down in the aviary with Tomas, learning what to feed orphaned baby birds. I have no doubt that half a wolfhound pack is sitting at her feet and when she's finished with the birds I guarantee she'll con someone to take her to visit the little pink saddle and the little Arabian mare that have miraculously appeared in the stables. I think the normal upbringing ship has sailed.'

Lor snorted. 'You could always ask Casimir about the saddle. And the pony.'

'I would if I ever saw him before bedtime.' And there was the crux of the problem. 'Does he always work this hard? Because, honestly, Lor, there should be two of him.'

'It's a difficult time.' Lor shrugged and pulled away from the computer, standing and reaching for the shawl she'd slung over the back of her chair upon entering Ana's office—a word that didn't quite fit the airy parlour with the view of the walled gardens and beyond that the grassy plains and then the mountains. 'Casimir feels he has something to prove. Something to fix. You're welcome to try telling him he doesn't.'

'Yeah, thanks. Trouble is, I like what he's trying to do. I think it shows courage, vision and strength. I want him to succeed.' Every day when she saw what he was aiming to do and the challenges he faced she wanted that for him. She stood abruptly. 'I'm going for a walk to try and clear my head. I might even make school decisions while I'm at it.'

'Take your coat and don't wander far,' warned Lor. 'There's a front coming in from the west. The weather will turn.'

'I'll take Sophia too. We may not make it past the stables,' Ana replied, although maybe she'd get punchy and venture beyond the castle walls.

She found Sophia at the falconry with Tomas and watched for a while as they finished tending the baby birds. Tomas had infinite patience, with both the birds and her daughter, and if every now and then his smile hinted at painful memories he couldn't quite hide, no one spoke of it.

Tomas told her about the selection of weatherproof coats at the stables, behind the tack-room door, and frowned down at Sophia before finally deciding that her little pink parka and ankle boots were okay.

Sophia needed new clothes more suited to her new life; Ana had already received that memo. They were on their way.

The new pony's name was Duchess, Sophia informed her. Duchess liked carrots, apples, a heated stall and little girls. Sophia knew all the horses in the stalls—of course she did. Names *and* temperaments. Which horses would hang their heads over the doors to be petted and which bad-tempered beasts to stay away from.

They'd make a stateswoman out of her daughter yet.

Sophia was happy here. With Lor and Silas at her beck and call, and all the animals. Sophia didn't care about her current lack of schooling at all. She was learning more than she ever had. Some things *were* working out just fine.

They slipped outside the stable doors and beyond the fortress walls in search of wildflowers, and started along the bridle path towards the mountains. They'd done it before. Just them, the ground underfoot and the sky. The security guards could see them from the fortress walls and were content to give them the illusion of freedom. She and Sophia would walk the fields for a while and then return. No harm done.

A carefree hour later, somewhere on a bridle path, the weather closed in around them. One minute the sun was shining and the next minute clouds were rolling in and bringing a heavy mist with them.

Ana turned back immediately, Sophia's hand in hers and Lor's warning in mind, but it was too late. The air was turning to soup and Ana could no longer see six feet in front of her. They'd been able to see the fortress a minute ago and they were still on the track. Nothing to worry about. They couldn't be more than a kilometre or two away.

'What is this?' asked Sophia, waving her hand through the mist.

'It's a cloud, and we're in it. I think it came over the mountain and fell on us.'

'Will it float away again?'

'Yes.' *When?* being the pertinent question. 'Meanwhile—' she looked at the track, only to find it disappearing as she spoke '—we sit.'

'And then what?' asked Sophia dubiously.

'We sing.' And hope someone came for them or the enveloping fog moved on so that they could see their way home again. Ana wasn't picky. Either one would do.

Casimir had got into the habit of finding Ana and Sophia whenever he returned to the fortress. The mere sight of them was usually enough to quiet the demon inside him that wanted to lock them away and keep them safe.

He still hadn't heard from the tribespeople to the north. Four days since his speech; Rudolpho counselled patience and said they'd have to speak amongst themselves before replying, and Theo had counselled similarly. And still he felt as if his skin were slipping his body half the time and that his people were beginning to wonder whether he really could deliver on this grand plan he'd offered them.

He needed to appear in public with Ana and Sophia soon, and the security risks ate at him, reminding him that grand plans had been so much easier to create when he hadn't had anything to lose.

Schools. Heaven help him, he was going to send his daughter to school; it was a life she knew and a world he was wholly unaccustomed to. He'd spent the afternoon in crisis talks with Rudolpho.

Over schools.

Ana would doubtless spend a good portion of the night trying to reassure him that schooling was a perfectly normal endeavour for a child and that his daughter would fit in just fine.

He wanted her to fit in.

But schools and the security risks that went with them. Heaven help him.

Ana and Sophia weren't in Lor's kitchen and he didn't think they'd be anywhere in the garden. His pilot had barely been able to land the helicopter, given the limited visibility. Only the latest navigation system had allowed them down safely, and even then his pilot had been cursing.

They weren't in the Queen's quarters or the sunroom Ana had claimed as her office.

They weren't in the bathhouse.

They weren't in the library.

Ten minutes later he got the sinking feeling they weren't in the fortress at all, especially once Lor told him Ana had been going to take Sophia for walk.

By the time his guards had checked the aviary, the stables, the gardens and every other outbuilding in existence, his unease was evident. Every last member of staff had been accounted for. Not a security guard or groundsman was missing.

Ana and Sophia were the only ones missing. 'Search the fortress again from top to bottom. Every room, every passageway, every goddamn cupboard!'

'They were going for a walk,' Lor said, and not for the first time, only not one of his guards had seen them venture beyond the walls.

'They were headed for the stables,' added Tomas.

'Which would be of help if they were still in the stables. Which they're *not*. Search the grounds again. *Now*.' People nodded and refused to catch his eye as they melted from sight.

He never roared. In all his years Casimir had never roared. Until now.

He wondered, with an increasing sense of being out

of control, whether he should release the wolfhounds. The dogs would scent their trail. One would, at any rate. The dog and his daughter were damn near inseparable. 'Where's Jelly?'

'In the kitchen with her puppies,' said Lor.

The big wolfhound was happy to see him and seemed to know what he wanted when he put one of Sophia's shoes to her nose. She led him to the stables and scratched at the door that led to the bridle path, so he saddled the big black stallion he usually rode while Tomas saddled a nearby mare.

Members of his security team were already fanning out beyond the walls, although what good they were if they could let a six-year-old girl and her mother *slip through their fingers…*

'I've seen them follow the bridle path before,' Tomas said in a voice tight with worry as they followed the loping wolfhound out and onto the bridle path. 'Following butterflies. Picking flowers. They do that.'

That was all Claudia had been doing too, when they'd taken her. She'd been inside the garden walls and supposedly well protected.

And then she'd been gone.

'I stirred up the northerners.' Out here, with a man he'd known since childhood, Casimir could finally voice his greatest fear. 'I've been pushing them.'

'No.' This time his falconer's voice came firm and hard. 'You're giving them a chance to sit at the negotiating table again. They won't refuse that. They won't make old mistakes again.'

'You don't know that. *I* don't know that.'

'I know there are no strangers about. There's no one lying in wait for the opportunity to take Sophia and Ana away from you. I flew falcons today. Falcons trained to circle at the presence of humans. *They* would have known.'

'You trust falcons?'

'More than I trust people,' said Tomas.

They headed in the direction of the mountain pass, the dog confident in her direction. This was the bridle path that wove through the outer pastures before joining the road. A tempting walk for a woman and child. He hoped.

He called for them at intervals, Ana's name, and then Sophia's, and he could hear the fear in his voice and so smothered it with anger.

No one had taken them. He *had* to believe that.

History could not repeat itself.

They were just lost.

They were sitting on a rock beside the bridle path, singing, when he and Tomas finally reached them. Jelly had led them straight to them. He could give the dog a medal later. Name a valley after her. He reined the stallion in and slid to the ground, his fury barely contained.

'See?' Ana said by way of greeting. 'I told you someone would find us if we sang.'

'Do you have any idea how many people are looking for you?' he began.

'Er—'

'Everyone! Everyone is looking for you.'

'We just—'

'Don't you dare say you went for a walk.'

'Not even if it's the truth?'

'Where is your guide?'

'I didn't think—'

'Indeed you did *not*.'

Ana's beautiful, beloved features took on a mutinous slant.

'We weren't going far. We can see the fortress from here!'

'Oh, you can, can you?' he snarled, heavy on the sarcasm. 'Because no one at the fortress can see *you*.'

'Well, we could,' said Ana. 'And when we couldn't we sat and waited and here you are.' She tried a tentative smile and lit Casimir's fury to new heights. 'No harm done.'

'You don't know these mountains,' he said.

'We've been gone twenty minutes.'

'Do you even wear at watch?' He couldn't see one.

'An hour at the most,' she amended.

An hour too long. 'You could have been killed. Or taken.' Or worse.

'Now you're projecting.'

'I have the right. *Get up.*'

Sophia was already up, staring at the furious man in front of her with wide eyes. He crouched down and ran a hand through his hair. He was scaring them; he knew he was. 'Hey,' he said gruffly. 'I was worried about you.'

'Me too,' Sophia whispered, and then stepped closer and put cold hands to his cheeks as she studied his face. 'Are you crying?'

'It's just moisture from the clouds.' The hell it was. 'Jelly found you,' he said and gathered her close and held tight. This child. How had she found her way into his heart so fast? 'And my horse is going to take you home.'

Her arms tightened around his neck. 'That's the cranky horse. Tomas said we couldn't ride him.'

'Not alone, no.' Tomas was right. 'You can ride with Tomas.' He spared a glance for the man who'd ridden alongside him.

'Maman has to come too.'

'She can ride with me.' He stood, with Sophia still

clinging to him, and stared at the woman who could fill his heart with terror as easily as she could make it soar. 'I thought I'd lost you.'

She shook her head and her eyes filled with tears. 'No.'

'We were coming back,' his little girl said, with her arms tightly wrapped around his neck. 'We were always coming back to you. We just couldn't see the way.'

A very subdued Ana rode back to the fortress behind Casimir. Sophia rode with Tomas, who had not long ago sounded a hunting horn. A message to those back at the fortress, signalling that Ana and Sophia had been found. Sophia had wanted him to sound the horn again but Tomas had refused her. To sound the horn again and again would be a call to arms, Tomas had told them.

This place…

It didn't take long for them to reach the stables. The fog was still rolling in but both Cas and Tomas appeared to have a homing instinct and so did the dog.

They were still on horseback when they slipped through the door and entered the stables. The doors closed behind them with an emphatic thud and the number of people waiting for them far exceeded the number of horses.

He really had had everyone out looking for them.

'I'm very sorry,' she murmured as she dismounted. 'I should have been more observant about the weather.'

Casimir's lips tightened. He didn't say a word, merely handed the horse to a groomsman.

'I should have stayed closer to home and heeded Lor's warning,' she said next, as Lor took Sophia from Tomas and hugged her close. Tomas wouldn't look at her, or at anyone else for that matter. The falconer looked pallid and drawn, as if he'd aged twenty years since she'd seen him last.

As for Casimir, he was already striding from the stables.

No one spoke. Not one person, until Tomas finally looked at her. 'The northerners aren't co-operating. He thought they'd taken you.'

Oh.

Oh.

She looked to Tomas with his white face and Lor with her pinched lips and to her daughter, who was in good hands. 'Sophia needs a bath,' she said, because of course that made sense. And then she turned and began to run towards her king.

She caught up with him at the bottom of the stairs that led to the landing overlooking the garden. He didn't slow down and she struggled to keep up, taking two steps at a time and silently cursing the sheer number of them.

'I should have told someone which way I was going,' she said when they reached the landing.

'You should have taken a guide,' he said in a tone made all the more menacing by its mildness.

'I wasn't thinking.' Too distracted by all the changes in her world to note the change of weather coming in, never mind that she'd been warned. She hadn't known what that warning *meant*. It hadn't meant to her what it meant to the people who lived here. 'I'm sorry for all the concern I caused. I know better now. It won't happen again.'

'You're right; it won't. Your chances of going anywhere ever again without a full security detail on your tail are non-existent.'

'That seems a little…extreme.' There was contrition and then there was total loss of privacy.

'You think so? I don't think so,' he said.

He looked to be heading to the library, so she followed

him and watched as he poured a drink from the decanter on the sideboard. The liquid glowed amber in the soft lamplight and he knocked it back hard and poured another. That went the same way as the first and his hand trembled.

'It won't happen again,' she said. 'No need to put people on me twenty-four hours a day. That won't be necessary. I'll be more mindful. Cas—'

'This would go so much better,' he said, 'if you didn't talk.'

She waited, but he didn't fill the silence. For a very long time she stood there while he paced and glowered and looked anywhere but at her.

'This would go so much better if you *did* talk,' she said finally. 'Casimir, I'm still here. I'm right here. And I'm listening.'

He didn't know where to begin. He couldn't find a way to cut through the immobilising fear of losing her and speak to the heart of things. Anger ruled his movements, stiff and fierce, and he couldn't look at her for fear of losing his way.

'I brought you into this,' he began. 'I know I shouldn't have but I did it anyway and if you die because of me, because of dangers I haven't made clear or because some political outsiders want revenge on me, that's on me.'

'How can you say you brought me—?'

'Damned if I brought you here to die. Don't you chase that road. Don't you do that to me!'

There it lay. His fear of losing everyone he loved, bright and shiny and finally spoken. Time to walk away now, before anger and fear got him saying all sorts of things he shouldn't, but he couldn't make himself move.

'Don't you leave me.'

He tried to turn away but she was right there beside him, raising her hand to his cheek and not to strike him but to cup it, and he closed his eyes at the sweetness.

'This fear isn't real,' she murmured fiercely. 'It's one of your shadows. Casimir, look at me.'

He couldn't. He couldn't do this love thing. 'I need you to be more careful,' he managed.

'I can be. That's what I'm telling you.' She kissed him, soothed him.

He didn't want to love this hard. He hated it. That was the biggest difference between them. She *wanted* to love wholeheartedly.

He took her lips more roughly than she'd taken his; he let passion and fear mix and burn white. When she twined her arms around his neck, he backed her against the wall and tried not to let his hunger get the better of him. He pushed her hair to one side and buried his face in her neck, tasting, trailing, finding her pulse-point with his tongue and letting its rapid beat chase away the lingering flavour of death. *Not this time. Not dead.*

Take a man who'd lost everyone he'd ever cared about and give him a family and then threaten to take it away and see how he fared.

'I'm right here,' she said quietly. 'I believe in what you're doing. What you're fighting for. I'm right here beside you, and I am not afraid to be.' She fisted her hand in his hair, licked his lips open and cut off his breath. They were both breathing hard when she released him. 'Can we have make-up sex now?'

'Yes.' Of all the things she'd asked of him, that one he could do.

CHAPTER ELEVEN

To say that security got tighter after that would be an understatement. When Cas wasn't with her—and he was with her far more than he'd ever been—Tomas would magically appear, or Silas would show up, or Lor's niece, who was now Sophia's nanny, would drop by. Ana had yet to see a roster but dammit they had one and the purpose of that roster was to make sure that Ana was never alone. She'd stake her life on it.

The sooner she made her way to the dower house and eked out some small semblance of privacy the better.

It was a week after the incident with the fog, as she preferred to call it, and the dower house wasn't ready yet and Sophia's schooling still hadn't been organised and Cas had flown to the capital to meet with Augustus.

Two weeks ago she'd been in Geneva, going about her business. These days she was thoroughly embroiled in Byzenmaach politics. If she wasn't in the library reading up on the history of the region, she was at Rudolpho to feed her more reports. She'd taken extended leave from her work for the UN.

Her call, and no one else's. There was too much to come up to speed on here.

The majority of Byzenmaach's people had rallied behind Casimir and his plans, but the northerners had yet to reveal their intentions.

And then Sophia skidded into the room, her eyes wide and her cheeks red. 'Tomas says you have to come to the tower,' she said.

'Why? Are you flying falcons today?'

'Yes, and the riders are coming.' Sophia's excitement was evident. 'A lady and a man and they're armed and Tomas is all upset and you have to come *now*.'

'Armed how?'

'They have *wolfhounds*.'

'Oh.' This world... 'Better get Silas too.'

'He's already there,' said Sophia.

Many, many grey stone steps later, Ana stood on the battlements and gazed out across the plains towards the mountain pass. Two riders were approaching, two wolfhounds, two horses. And Tomas was in a right state.

He'd flown a falcon upon their approach, he told her. A falcon with a strip of royal purple cloth around one leg instead of the traditional leather jesses. He'd flown the cloth because it was a welcome, of sorts. A message—for those who could understand it—that they were now under the king's personal protection.

'Okay. So far so good,' Ana said when the usually taciturn Tomas stopped for breath. She looked to Silas for direction but he offered no guidance. 'So the falcon flew a piece of purple cloth as a welcome. What happened next?'

'That woman got off her horse, pulled a gauntlet from her saddlebag and called my bird to her hand,' Tomas said. 'The bird now flies a white strip of cloth and *two* strips of purple. She's saying that royalty is coming, in peace.' Tomas paced, his eyes a little wild. 'It was only whimsy that made me fly the cloth. Superstition. An old, old custom. And then she had the audacity to call *my* bird straight out of the sky. Using *my* signals.'

Tomas the falconer was the calmest man Ana knew. Except for now.

'So...she's a falconer too?'

'He thinks it's Claudia,' Silas said calmly, his eyes never leaving Tomas's face.

'I didn't *say* that,' said Tomas.

'But you think it.' The older man was giving the falconer no quarter.

'Just to be clear, you're talking Claudia as in Casimir's dead sister?' Ana looked from one man to the other. 'You're serious.'

'We never got her body back,' Tomas said stubbornly.

'We got some of it back,' said Silas.

'Okay,' Ana said hurriedly. 'Six-year-old girl on the battlements. Listening.'

Tomas flushed red. Silas shut his eyes and shook his head.

'Is there any way we can get a look at the woman's face?' she asked, and Tomas handed her a set of binoculars.

'She's wearing traditional headdress. Only part of her face is showing,' he said. 'It could be her. It could be anyone.'

'But you think it's her,' said Ana.

'I don't *know*.' Tomas turned away and swore profusely, and that was another thing he never did—at least not in front of Ana and Sophia. '*She* knew about the coloured cloth instead of jesses and what they meant. It's in one of the royal falconry journals and I read that section aloud to her one day when she was helping me nurse a hawk with a broken wing. She was good with the birds. They trusted her. She knew all the call signals.'

'Why would she stay away all these years, only to return now?' asked Silas.

'Because the father who left her to rot is dead, her brother is whole and happy, Byzenmaach is moving forward and she wants to come home?' snapped Tomas. 'How should I know?'

'But you think it's her,' said Ana. 'Again, just to be clear.'

'Yes.' The word sounded as if it had been dragged from Tomas's soul.

'Then we need to tell Cas.'

'And say what?' Tomas started pacing again. 'You would have me talk of colours and hawks and then tell him I think his sister's alive? Do I tell him I can feel her on the wind, like a storm coming in? He'll think me mad. *I* think I'm mad.'

'They're heading for the bridle path,' Silas said suddenly.

'They would have heard about it in the village,' Tomas replied.

'They're taking the *old* bridle path,' Silas said, and there was a whole lot of silence after that.

'Is there another not dead dead person coming?' asked Sophia.

Ana really didn't want to say *maybe* in answer to that question. But she did. 'Maybe.'

Everyone watched the two riders and their hounds accelerate into a loping canter. 'How long before they get here?' she asked.

'Two hours, if they keep to the pace they're going,' said Silas.

'And if they push it?'

'Half that.'

* * *

Casmir sat with Augustus and a room full of advisors, trying to debate the merits of Augustus approaching the rebels to the north when an aide summoned Rudolpho from the room. That wasn't so strange in itself, but the fact that Rudolpho returned with a frown, holding a phone that he held out to Casimir was.

'Ana,' the older man said, and Casimir immediately feared the worst. Why had Rudolpho brought the phone into the meeting? Why hadn't he called Casimir out of the room to take the call? There was a protocol for the way phone calls were handled. And his head advisor wasn't following it.

He took the phone and headed for the door. 'What is it?' he asked.

'Two riders are approaching by horseback,' Ana said. 'Silas thinks they're an envoy from the north and Tomas thinks he knows one of them. You need to be here within the hour to greet them.'

'And you and Sophia need to *not* be there. Start packing.'

'Not on your life,' she said.

'You will stay away from them.' He could feel his temper rising.

'That I can do. Until you get here and then we'll see. Rudolpho says you're in an important meeting.'

'I've just stepped out.' He closed the door behind him.

'Are you alone?'

'Yes.'

'Tomas says you can fire him if he's wrong. Personally, I don't think you'll need to. He'll probably jump off a cliff if he's wrong.'

'Ana, what is it?'

'One of the envoy is a woman and there's no easy way to say this so I'm just going to say it. Tomas thinks it's Claudia.'

Forty-seven minutes later, Casimir landed in the courtyard of the winter fortress. His security team had run the faces of the riders through recognition software and the elder male had been identified as a statesman for the mountain tribes to the north. No surprises there. The woman remained unidentified but Casimir had seen the picture, black and white and grainy as it was, and Tomas could be forgiven for thinking it was her. If it wasn't her—if they'd deliberately chosen a negotiator who resembled his dead sister...

If they'd done that he would be hard pressed to negotiate at all.

'Any more information?' he asked as he fell into step alongside Silas and headed towards the door.

'They're ten minutes out, Tomas can barely speak and Sophia is wearing her best dress and shiniest shoes because her dead aunt's coming to town.'

Oh, dear God.

'Breathe,' said Silas.

'Sophia's secure?'

'In the playroom, under guard.'

'And Anastasia?'

'On the battlements with Tomas.'

Then that was where he wanted to be. He adjusted course and when he got there and Ana smiled at him he felt his world settle again into something he had a hope of controlling. He clasped Tomas's arm next and drew his childhood playmate into an embrace.

'Hell of a day,' he said. 'Let's go find out who she is.'

'They're stopping,' said Ana, and it was true. Less

than five hundred metres from the walls the two riders had stopped to dismount. The man held out his arms and slowly turned in a circle and then shed his riding cloak and then his outer tunic. He heaped them on the ground and a scimitar followed. The rifle at his back was added to the pile. A sheathed knife at his ankle got thrown on top of that. The woman did the same with her weapons, up to and including the long slender pencil-like rods in her hair.

'Hidden knives,' said Tomas.

'Well, at least she's getting rid of them. I'm sure she'll feel lighter,' said Ana, responding to Casimir's dark amusement with a shrug and open hands.

The woman's dark hair was plaited and fell to her waist. Her features were proud and her movements graceful. Casimir stared hard and tried to fit the face of a child onto the face of the woman who rode, but it was no use. Claudia or not, time had moved on and she was not the sister he remembered.

They left their belongings in two neat heaps and remounted their horses, their pace sedate as they continued their approach.

'Send someone out to pick up their belongings and tell the snipers to stand down,' he told Silas.

'Snipers?' Ana looked aghast.

'Precaution.' Time to get to the stables. 'Coming?'

'You really need to stop making that sound like a command,' she said.

'King,' he countered, and took her hand so that she could feel its tremble and know he was holding onto his composure by a thread and that he needed her close.

'I don't suppose there's a rule book for this meeting?' she asked. 'Protocol to follow? Curtseys to make?'

'No. But if I falter, step in.'

'I will. But you won't falter.' Her quiet certainty buoyed him. This was what it was like to have someone in your corner, he thought. This was what it felt like to be the recipient of someone else's strength.

He felt the warmth of it and finally, willingly, let the last of his defences fall. He wanted this with all his heart. This world in which he loved hard and was loved just as hard in return.

'I love you,' he said in Russian. 'So much. I understand now, what it feels like to stand beside the woman I love and feel loved in return. You were right. There is no place I'd rather be.'

She stumbled and would have teetered but for her hand in his.

'You pick your times,' she muttered, but her hand tightened in his. 'I can't believe that out of all the opportunities you've had of late, you're telling me this now.'

The stables weren't like any other stables Ana had ever seen. Twenty stalls capable of holding three or four horses apiece ran either side of a large central square. The square was covered in sawdust and the stable hands kept it immaculate. Huge wooden doors stood open at both ends of the square. Doors strong enough to hold invaders out more than horses in.

Ana waited alongside Cas, with Tomas on her other flank. A dozen more security people stood dotted around, all of them armed.

The male rider was the first to dismount, doing so before he reached the doors and walking his horse in. His gaze fixed on Casimir as he let his horse's reins drop and he stepped forward. 'Your Majesty,' he said. 'It's been a long time.'

Casimir nodded. 'Welcome, Lord Ildris. Who's your companion?'

Lord Ildris waited a beat before speaking, as if choosing his words with the utmost care. 'A future for a future,' he offered quietly. 'She's the negotiator you requested and speaks for the people of the north and for herself.'

The woman had dismounted but her eyes remained lowered. She strode into the stables, swift and sure, and the horse and dogs followed. Whoever she was, she didn't lack confidence. And then she raised her gaze and her eyes said it all.

The woman had eyes the same shape and colour as Casimir's. The same eyes as Sophia. The eyes of the royal family of Byzenmaach.

'Hello Casimir,' she said and her gaze flickered sideways for a moment. 'Tomas. You're the falconer here now?'

'Yes,' said Ana when Tomas appeared incapable of speech. 'He is.'

The woman smiled gently. 'I thought so.' And then her gaze returned to Casimir and her expression grew a whole lot more complex. 'Brother. It's been a long time.'

Cas too seemed incapable of movement or speech. 'Guess she's not *dead*, dead either,' Ana muttered in Russian because he needed a push and was fluent in the language and boy were they going to have words about *that* later. 'Welcome her home.'

And then Cas was striding across the sawdust and pulling his sister into an embrace that left no room for air, and if anyone could have ever doubted his love for his sister, the depth of his loss or the extent of his joy at seeing her alive, they couldn't possibly doubt it now because it was written all over his face.

'Lord Ildris,' Ana said, forcing the man's attention.

'You must be weary after your travels. We have a bathhouse here I think you'll like. And refreshments and rooms available for your use. Come.' She was beginning to understand why Casimir used that word a lot. 'Let us leave others to their reunion, shall we? We shall meet up with them again for a meal soon enough.'

She waited until he'd joined her and then headed for the fortress. The walk would take several minutes. They could chat along the way. She could wring his neck.

The four-man security detail surrounding them probably wouldn't stop her.

'I hear you have a daughter,' Lord Ildris said when they were halfway through the gardens.

'Yes, and I do hope you like wolfhound puppies because we currently have eight of them.'

'I too keep wolfhounds,' he replied easily. 'Perhaps we can arrange an exchange.'

'Exchanges do seem to be your forte.' He could take that any way he liked. She waited until they'd reached the steps that led from the garden to the patio before mounting her next offensive. 'Why now?' she asked. 'After all these years, why return her now?'

'You disapprove?'

'I'm new around here. I barely know which way is up. But I do question the motives of a man who would remove a child from her family only to produce her again twenty years later.'

'I'm afraid that's a question for Claudia to answer.'

'Are you her lover?'

'No!' His eyes snapped ice. 'Claudia has not been misused by us. Not as a child. Not as a woman. Which is more than I can say for her own family. She stayed with us because she wanted to stay and returns of her own free will. That is all I have to say on the matter.'

Protective. How very interesting.

She led him to a suite of rooms that were often used by various aides who overnighted at the fortress and opened the door for him. 'Do you or Claudia have any dietary requirements I should know about? I'd hate to poison you by accident.'

'I have no special dietary requirements and neither does Claudia.'

'Excellent. We dine at seven. I'd suggest a tour of the aviaries beforehand but my falconer's currently having a meltdown at the unexpected arrival of his long-lost childhood friend. Perhaps next time.'

'Of course,' he said. 'May I be permitted to congratulate you on your engagement?'

'Sure,' she said. 'Go right ahead.'

'A woman of humour is a rare asset for a king,' he said. 'Ms Douglas, mother of the young duchess of Sanesch, future consort to the king of Byzenmaach, it is my pleasure to make your acquaintance.'

And she'd thought the UN was a diplomatic circus. 'Rest well, Lord Ildris. The belongings you parted with earlier will be brought to your room. Some of them, at any rate. The rest will be held in safe keeping until your departure. We'll see you at dinner.'

Later, much later that evening, long after dinner had been served and dessert had been eaten, Ana stood in Casimir's bedroom and waited for him to start shedding his clothes.

'So,' he said, 'Claudia's alive.' He looked a little lost, a little low. He'd walked his sister to her guest room and clearly had plenty on his mind.

'She likes Sophia.' Casimir's sister had won a lot of ground with her unforced attention for the wide-eyed little girl with the ruby-red shoes and the blue eggshell that simply had to come from a dragon.

'Yes.' He loosened his tie. 'I asked her why she stayed away all these years.'

'Oh.' He'd speak when he was ready, or not at all.

'She said she had the opportunity to return, several times over, but that she would not go where she wasn't wanted. She said my father renounced her. That he thought she was not his and that my mother had had an affair.'

'With those eyes?' Because, seriously, if ever there was an inherited trait…

'An affair with my uncle, who had the eyes. He died in a hunting accident in the mountains. Before Claudia was born.'

'So is he *dead*, dead, or likely to arrive any minute?'

Casimir's eyes warmed just for her. 'I love what you bring to my world.'

'You're welcome.' She had a new nightgown she wanted to bring to his world too. It was ivory silk with amber ribbon bows, but now was probably not the time.

'I was three years old at the time, but I'm going to say that my uncle is dead. By all accounts his body came down from the mountain after the accident. We buried him.'

Cas began to remove his cufflinks, but he wasn't undressing to please her. His thoughts were still firmly lodged in the past. 'Claudia believes my father found out about my mother's affair and had my uncle killed. My father then claimed Claudia as his own, but changed his tune when she was kidnapped. He didn't care what her captors did with her. And my mother knew why and killed herself. It makes sense.'

Maniacal sense.

'Lord Ildris's wife took Claudia in. When she was ten they told her everything and asked if she wanted to return to the palace. She didn't. At eighteen, they asked again if Claudia wanted to return.'

'And she didn't,' Ana said quietly.

'All these years she let me think she was dead and that it was somehow my fault. I blamed myself for her death and for my mother's death and no one ever told me I was wrong to do so,' he said roughly. 'I want to be angry with all of them, and with Claudia for letting me think she was dead, but I can't. Claudia was a pawn. A child who thought no one wanted her, and when she was offered a way out she took it. Her allegiance now is to the north. Not to me.'

'And yet she returns to you, flying royal colours. Don't write her allegiances off so easily, Casimir. Wait and see. Because it seems to me you may both want the same thing. A new beginning.'

Casimir said nothing.

'Does she want to be acknowledged as your sister or your half-sister?'

'I don't know.' He rubbed at the royal ring he wore. 'We never got that far in conversation.'

'What would *you* prefer? The lie or the truth?'

He shrugged. 'Me the man or me the monarch?'

'This is our bedchamber.' Okay, *his* bedchamber, but she slept here too these days. 'Out there, at the dinner table tonight, I sat with the king in front of guests of unknown influence and responded accordingly. When we're in here I'm speaking to the man. I prefer the man. I'm really not here for the figurehead.'

The man smiled crookedly. 'The identity of Claudia's father doesn't change my feelings for her or my joy at knowing she's alive and well. She's my sister. My family. Mine to love. I don't do things by halves.'

He certainly did not. Which reminded her of his words on the battlements and that she had her own bone to pick with him.

'So,' she said mildly because she'd been patient with him all evening. She'd been patient with everyone all evening. Clearly she had the patience of a *saint*. 'You speak Russian.'

'Ah,' he said. 'Yes.'

'You let *me* speak Russian up by the watch tower.' His tie came off and then his snowy white shirt. The view of the valleys and crests of his chest was impressive but she refused to be distracted by pleasures of the flesh.

'In my defence, I really did just want to hear you speak the language. I even gave you a book to read from. You were the one who went off the page.'

'You said we had no secrets left.'

'And we don't,' he said as he unbuckled his belt.

'Trousers stay on,' she commanded. 'I'm not falling for that old trick ever again.'

'I'm very tired,' he said next.

'Coward.'

'And overwrought,' he continued doggedly. 'My sister just returned from the dead.'

'Say it again.'

'My sister just—oomph!'

Her shoe had connected with his crotch. Granted, it wasn't attached to her foot, but who needed a karate black belt when she had a good throwing arm and exceptionally good aim?

'That was below the belt,' he said.

'I have been very patient with you,' she began. 'I have put up with your autocratic ways and your tendency not to share your thoughts and feelings unless naked or pressed. I have given up my career and embraced a whole new world for you. I have born you a daughter. There is nothing I wouldn't do for you, and you know it. Now say it again.'

'I was going to have candles set out all around the room,' he said, but his eyes were alight with unholy appreciation. 'And jewellery, lots and lots of jewellery. A tiara.'

'I do like tiaras,' she said and picked up her other shoe and spun it until the stiletto heel faced him. 'I'm waiting.'

'Would you like to hear it in Russian or in French?'

She let fly with a grin and watched him double over when struck.

'King,' he wheezed. 'Crown jewels.'

'Still waiting,' she said.

'I love you.' He said it in French and she sniffed. It wasn't his mother tongue and it certainly wasn't hers.

'Again.'

'I love you.' He said it in Russian and that was much better. The words spoke to her heart but did they come from his?

'Again.'

'I love you. Beyond words, I will always love you.' He said it in his own tongue, and this time she believed him.

A deep peace settled in her heart. Claudia wasn't the only one who'd finally come home. 'I love you too. But you already knew that.'

'I'm really glad you're out of shoes,' he said. 'Nor am I as tired as I was before. I love endorphins.'

They were alone in his bedroom, and his eyes held a promise she was never going to get tired of seeing. 'Would you like me to give you something to do?' she asked.

'Yes.'

Playful Cas was back. The one who filled her heart to overflowing. 'Would you like to take the rest of your clothes off?'

'Why, yes.' Just a man, when all was said and done. A man who'd offered her his heart. 'I'd like that a lot.'

EPILOGUE

Two weeks later...

ANASTASIA DOUGLAS, FUTURE wife of King Casimir of Byzenmaach, was dressing for a ball. She wasn't doing it alone. A small would-be duchess oversaw the production, and Ana's future sister-in-law was getting dressed in the room too. Ana didn't know who was more nervous about the upcoming introduction to Byzenmaach society, her or Claudia, but there was comfort to be had from company and Ana wasn't about to say no to it.

Tailors had worked around the clock for a week in order to get the gowns ready to wear. Ana's creation was ivory silk with a beaded pearl bodice that was a slightly darker shade of ivory than the fabric. The gown was backless and the pearls curved up and over her curves to wrap lovingly around her neck in a high collar. Her hair had been styled by experts and her pearl earrings were upstaged only by the delicate pearl and diamond strands woven through her hair. The only other piece of jewellery she wore was a ring on her engagement finger. It was big, it was pink, and it had once belonged to Casimir's grandmother. It was a statement of intent.

Within a year, Anastasia Douglas was going to marry

the man she loved and who loved her back with a thoroughness and intensity that left her breathless.

It was the first time she'd worn it.

'I don't know if I'm ever going to get used to the jewels,' she said. 'They're so...'

'I know.' Beside her, Claudia lifted her hands to the tiara that sat on her head. Ana was not allowed to wear a tiara until after she was married, according to Lor, but Claudia could, and had chosen one from the vault, and hadn't that been a visit to the royal vault worth remembering. They'd taken Sophia, the Lady Serah, Rudolpho and a pile of dresses and had vowed to make the king's chief advisor crack a smile.

He'd done more than that. When his pomp and ceremony had finally shattered and he'd finally smiled, he'd also walked away to try and hide the tears in his eyes. The Lady Serah had said to let him be. She'd said that laughter had been a long time coming to these halls and that while the change was welcome, some—who had lived a lifetime in the shadows—found it overwhelming.

They'd stopped teasing him after that, and he'd put his defences back together and returned, only to have Sophia begin an animated conversation with him about whether he preferred the rings on her fingers to the ones on her toes.

He'd told her the history of each and every one of them with a sly and wicked humour, and won himself three Rudolpho fans for life.

The gown Claudia had chosen for the evening was the shimmering colour of beaten bronze and the designers had made the most of her slender form. It had a full gauzy skirt, a herringbone corsetry bodice and was strapless. With it she wore a purple and white sash denoting that she was a member of the royal family of Byzenmaach. The cross that pinned her sash low on the waist was a gift from the north, announcing her allegiance to one of their orders as well. The glittering diamond tiara on Claudia's head had belonged to her mother and her diamond necklace and earrings had come from the royal collection. She too wore her hair swept up in a style wholly flattering.

Sophia, future duchess and self-proclaimed member of the Order of the Dragon, was not going to the ball. *She* wore a white cotton nightgown with lace around the edges and a long strand of hopefully not priceless pearls draped across her thin frame and tied at the hip like a sash. She was barefoot and tousle-haired and danced around them, already in attendance at her own imaginary ball.

'I have jewels for you too,' Sophia said and opened her fist to reveal two small, smooth pebbles of mottled green. 'They're dragon stones and there's one for each of you. You have to wear them close to your heart.'

'Thank you,' said Claudia as she took one of the offered pebbles and tucked it into her bodice. 'For courage.'

'You can keep it,' said Sophia.

'I will.'

Ana took the other pebble and tucked it into her bodice too. Her daughter was in danger of becoming seriously indulged. 'How do we look?'

'Like princesses.' Sophia twirled and the pearls twirled with her. 'Papa said he was going to dance with you all night long. Both of you.'

'We should clone him,' said Ana.

'I heard that,' said a voice at the doorway and there he stood, resplendent in white tie and weighed down with medals and a sash just like Claudia's.

'Pinch me,' Ana muttered to her soon-to-be sister-in-law. 'But not somewhere people will see the bruise.'

Claudia stepped closer, smiled angelically at her brother and obligingly pinched Ana on the ass. 'That what you wanted?'

'Perfect.' She really was here and he really was real. Because sometimes she could have sworn she was living a fairy tale. 'All good.'

'Are we ready?' asked Casimir.

Sophia eyed him narrowly. 'Do you have your dragon stone?'

'Right here.' He patted the general direction of his heart.

'What's keeping it there?' Claudia asked with the lift of an elegant eyebrow, and Ana could really grow to like this woman.

'Duct tape.'

'I love you,' Ana said, because he should be told this often. The more she told him the more he lit up like Christmas morning. It was a good look on him.

'You two go ahead,' Claudia said. 'I'll stay with Sophia while you greet your guests and then I'll make my big entrance a little later in the evening, when everybody's there to appreciate it.'

'But I need back-up,' Ana protested.

'He's right there,' Claudia said. 'Indulge me. Please. I want to read to my niece and then show her the secret room that overlooks the ballroom. I want to stand her on a chair and slide the viewing panel open so we can watch you two dance.'

Casimir smiled.

'You are putty in their hands,' Ana told him.

'I'm putty in your hands as well,' he said. 'And you're

wearing my ring.' He'd left it by her bedside table earlier that evening. There was a question in his eyes.

'I am.' And she intended to keep wearing it. 'What are your thoughts on a spring wedding?'

His smile widened. 'I'm all for it.'

'Gloves,' said Claudia, and Ana clicked her fingers. She'd forgotten about the gloves. They were snowy white and slid up past her elbows. 'But if I wear the gloves, people won't be able to see the ring.'

'Does it matter?' he murmured. 'I'll know it's there.'

'Now your tiara,' said Sophia.

'I don't have a tiara. Lor says— Oh!' Because suddenly there was a tiara dangling from Casimir's fingertips and it was delicate and whimsical and made from the finest of silver wire, diamonds and pearls.

'Wear it,' said Casimir. 'It's my gift to you. It's not from the vault.'

'Pinch me again,' said Ana when the tiara was in place and she stood facing the mirror.

'It's real. *You're* real,' said Claudia. 'And the king's waiting.'

Ana took his hand and walked with him to the ballroom, where Casimir began to introduce her to his guests. He never missed a person and Ana's smile never dimmed and she never missed a name.

'Do you think Claudia and Sophia are watching us yet?' she asked some time later as the musicians tuned their instruments and Casimir led her to the centre of the dance floor and swept her into his arms.

'Yes.'

Music filled the room and Casimir's smile softened. 'I love you.' This time he said it in Latin. 'I'm planning on saying it in every language that exists, including all of the non-verbal ones.'

'You're my fairy tale,' she said. 'And I'm not talking about all the trappings. Being with you is the fairy tale. Here at your side.'

She put one hand on his shoulder and her other hand in his.

And they danced.

* * * * *

MAID FOR A MAGNATE

JULES BENNETT

A huge thanks to the Mills & Boon team for including me in this amazing continuity. And a special thanks to Janice, Kat, Katherine, Andrea and Charlene. I loved working with you all on this project.

One

JUAN CARLOS SALAZAR II TRUE HEIR
TO THRONE

Will Rowling stared at the blaring headline as he sipped his coffee and thanked every star in the sky that he'd dodged marrying into the royal family of Alma. Between the Montoro siblings and their cousin Juan Carlos, that was one seriously messed up group.

Of course his brother, James, had wedded the beautiful Bella Montoro. Will's father may have had hopes of Will and Bella joining forces, but those devious plans obviously had fallen through when James fell in love with Bella instead.

Love. Such a fickle thing that botched up nearly every best laid plan. Not that Will had ever been on board with the idea of marrying Bella. He'd rather remain single than marry just to advance his family's business interests.

The Montoros were a force to be reckoned with in Alma, now that the powerful royal family was being restored to the throne after more than seventy years in exile. And Patrick Rowling was all too eager to have his son marry into such prestige, but thankfully that son was not to be Will.

Bella's brother had been heading toward the throne, until shocking letters were discovered in an abandoned family farmhouse, calling into question the lineage of the Montoros and diverting the crown into the hands of their cousin.

Secrets, scandal, lies... Will was more than happy to turn the reins over to his twin.

And since Will was officially single, he could carry out his own devious plan in great detail—his plot didn't involve love but a whole lot of seduction.

First, though, he had to get through this meeting with his father. Fortunately, Will's main goal of taking back control of his life involved one very intriguing employee of his father's household so having this little meeting at the Rowling home in Playa del Onda instead of the Rowling Energy offices was perfectly fine with him. Now that James had married and moved out and Patrick was backing away from working as much, Patrick used his weekend home more often.

"Rather shocking news, isn't it?"

Still clutching the paper in one hand and the coffee mug in the other, Will turned to see his father breeze into the den. While Patrick leaned more toward the heavier side, Will prided himself on keeping fit. It was just another way he and his father were different though some around them felt Will was a chip off the old block.

At one time Will would've agreed with those people, but he was more than ready to show everyone, including his father, he was his own man and he was taking charge.

"This bombshell will certainly shake things up for Alma." Will tossed the newspaper onto the glossy mahogany desktop. "Think parliament will ratify his coronation?"

Patrick grunted as he sank into his leather desk chair. "It's just a different branch of the Montoro family that will be taking the throne, so it really doesn't matter."

Will clutched his coffee cup and shook his head. Anything to do with the Montoros was not his problem. He had his own battles to face, starting with his father right now.

"What did you need to see me so early about?" his father asked, leaning back so far in the chair it squeaked.

Will remained standing; he needed to keep the upper hand here, needed to stay in control. Even though he was going up against his father's wishes, Will had to take back control of his own life. Enough with worrying about what his father would say or do if Will made the wrong move.

James had never bowed to their father's wishes and Will always wondered why his twin was so against the grain. It may have taken a few years to come around, but Will was more than ready to prove himself as a formidable businessman.

Will was a master at multitasking and getting what he wanted. And since he'd kissed Cat a few weeks ago, he'd thought of little else. He wanted her…and he would have her. Their intense encounter would allow for nothing less.

But for right this moment, Will was focusing on his

new role with Rowling Energy and this meeting with his father. Conquering one milestone at a time.

"Up till now, you've had me dealing with the company's oil interests," Will stated. "I'm ready to take total control of the real estate division, too."

His father's chest puffed out as he took in a deep breath. "I've been waiting for you to come to me with this," Patrick said with a smile. "You're the obvious choice to take over. You've done a remarkable job increasing the oil profits. They're up twelve percent since you put your mark on the company."

Will intended to produce financial gains for all of the company's divisions. For years, he'd wanted to get out from under his father's thumb and take control, and now was his chance. And that was just the beginning of his plans where Rowling Energy was concerned.

Finally, now that Will was seeing clearly and standing on his own two feet, nothing would stand in his way. His father's semiretirement would just help ease the path to a beautiful life full of power and wealth… and a certain maid he'd set in his sights.

"I've already taken the liberty of contacting our main real estate clients in London," Will went on, sliding his hands into his pockets and shifting his weight. "I informed them they would be dealing with me."

Will held his father's gaze. He'd taken a risk contacting the other players, but Will figured his father would be proud and not question the move. Patrick had wanted Will to slide into the lead role of the family business for years. Slowly Will had taken over. Now he was ready to seal every deal and hold all the reins.

"Another man would think you're trying to sneak behind his back." Patrick leaned forward and laced his fingers together on the desktop. "I know better. You're taking charge and that's what I want. I'll make sure my assistant knows you will be handling the accounts from here on out. But I'm here anytime, Will. You've been focused on this for so long, your work has paid off."

Will nodded. Part one of his plan was done and had gone just as smoothly as he'd envisioned. Now he needed to start working on the second part of his plan. And both aspects involved the same tactic…trust. He needed to gain and keep the trust of both his father and Cat or everything would blow up in his face.

Will refused to tolerate failure on any level.

Especially where Cat was concerned. That kiss had spawned an onslaught of emotions he couldn't, wouldn't, ignore. Cat with her petite, curvy body that fit perfectly against his. She'd leaned into that kiss like a woman starved and he'd been all too happy to give her what she wanted.

Unfortunately, she'd dodged him ever since. He didn't take that as a sign of disinterest. Quite the opposite. If she wasn't interested, she'd act as if nothing had happened. But the way she kept avoiding him when he came to visit his father at the Playa del Onda estate only proved to Will that she was just as shaken as he was. There was no way she didn't feel something.

Just one kiss and he had her trembling. He'd use that to his advantage.

Seeing Cat was another reason he opted to come to his father's second home this morning. She couldn't avoid him if he cornered her at her workplace. She'd been the maid for his twin brother, James, but James had often been away playing football—or as the Yanks called it, soccer—so Cat hadn't been a temptation thrust right in Will's face. But now she worked directly under Patrick. Her parents had also worked for Patrick, so

Cat had grown up around Will and James. It wasn't that long ago that Will had set his sights on Cat. Just a few years ago, in fact, he'd made his move, and they'd even dated surreptitiously for a while. That had ended tragically when he'd backed down from a fight in a moment of weakness. Since their recent kiss had brought back their scorching chemistry, Will knew it was time for some action.

Will may have walked out on her four years ago, but she was about to meet the new Will...the one who fought for what he wanted. And he wanted Cat in his bed and this time he wouldn't walk away.

Will focused back on his father. "I'll let myself out," he stated, more than ready to be finished with this part of his day. "I'll be in touch once I hear back from the investors and companies I contacted."

Heading for the open double doors, Will stopped when his father called his name.

"You know, I really wanted the thing with you and Bella to work," Patrick stated, as he stared at the blaring, boldface headline.

"She found love with my brother. She and I never had any type of connection. You'd best get used to them together."

Patrick focused his attention back on Will. "Just keep your head on your shoulders and don't follow the path your brother has. Getting sidetracked isn't the way to make Rowling Energy grow and prosper. Just do what you've been doing."

Oh, he intended to do just that.

Will gave his father a brief nod before heading out into the hallway. Little did his father know, Will was fully capable of going after more than one goal at a time. He had no intention of letting the oil or real estate businesses slide. If anything, Will fully intended to expand both aspects of the business into new territory within the next year.

Will also intended to seduce Cat even sooner. Much sooner. And he would stop at nothing to see all of his desires fulfilled.

That familiar woodsy scent assaulted her…much like the man himself had when he'd kissed her a few weeks ago.

Could such a full-on assault of the senses be called something so simple as a kiss? He'd consumed her from the inside out. He'd had her body responding within seconds and left her aching and wanting more than she should.

Catalina kept her back turned, knowing full well who stood behind her. She'd managed to avoid running into him, though he visited his father more and more lately. At this point, a run-in was inevitable.

She much preferred working for James instead of Patrick, but now that James was married, he didn't stay here anymore and Patrick did. Catalina had zero tolerance for Patrick and the fact that she worked directly for him now only motivated her more to finish saving up to get out of Alma once and for all. And the only reason she was working for Patrick was because she needed the money. She knew she was well on her way to leaving, so going to work for another family for only a few months didn't seem fair.

Years ago her mother had moved on and still worked for a prestigious family in Alma. Cat prayed her time here with Patrick was coming to an end, too.

But for now, she was stuck here and she hadn't been able to stop thinking about that kiss. Will had silently taken control of her body and mind in the span of just a few heated moments, and he'd managed to thrust her directly into their past to the time when they'd dated.

Unfortunately, when he'd broken things off with her, he'd hurt her more than she cared to admit. Beyond leaving her when she hadn't even seen it coming, he'd gone so far as to say it had all been a mistake. His exact words, which had shocked her and left her wondering how she'd been so clueless. Catalina wouldn't be played for a fool and she would never be his "mistake" again. She had more pride than that…even if her heart was still bruised from the harsh rejection.

Even if her lips still tingled at the memory of their recent kiss.

Catalina continued to pick up random antique trinkets on the built-in bookshelves as she dusted. She couldn't face Will, not just yet. This was the first encounter since that night three weeks ago. She'd seen him, he'd purposely caught her eye a few times since then, but he'd not approached her until now. It was as if the man enjoyed the torture he inflicted upon her senses.

"You work too hard."

That voice. Will's low, sultry tone dripped with sex appeal. She didn't turn around. No doubt the sight of him would still give her that swift punch of lust to the gut, but she was stronger now than she used to be…or she'd been stronger before he'd weakened her defenses with one simple yet toe-curling kiss.

"Would that make you the pot or the kettle?" she asked, giving extra attention to one specific shelf because focusing on anything other than this man was all that was holding her sanity together.

His rich laughter washed over her, penetrating any

defense she'd surrounded herself with. Why did her body have to betray her? Why did she find herself drawn to the one man she shouldn't want? Because she hadn't forgotten that he'd recently been the chosen one to wed Bella Montoro. Bella's father had put out a false press release announcing their engagement, but of course Bella fell for James instead and Will ended up single. James had informed Cat that Bella and Will were never actually engaged, but still. With Will single now, and after that toe-curling kiss, Cat had to be on her guard. She had too much pride in herself to be anybody's Plan B.

"That spot is clean." His warm, solid hand slid easily onto her shoulder. "Turn around."

Pulling in a deep breath, Catalina turned, keeping her shoulders back and her chin high. She would not be intimidated by sexy good looks, flawless charm and that knowing twinkle in Will's eye. Chemistry wouldn't get her what she wanted out of life…all she'd end up with was another broken heart.

"I have a lot on my list today." She stared at his ear, trying to avoid those piercing aqua eyes. "Your dad should be in his den if you're looking for him."

"Our business is already taken care of." Will's hand dropped, but he didn't step back; if anything, he shifted closer. "Now you and I are going to talk."

"Which is just another area where we differ," she retorted, skirting around him to cross in front of the mantel and head to the other wall of built-in bookcases. "We have nothing to discuss."

Of course he was right behind her. The man had dropped her so easily four years ago yet in the past few weeks, he'd been relentless. Perhaps she just needed to be more firm, to let him know exactly where she stood.

"Listen." She spun back around, brandishing her feather duster at him. Maybe he'd start sneezing and she could make a run for it. "I've no doubt you want to talk about that kiss. We kissed. Nothing we hadn't done before."

Of course this kiss was so, so much more; it had penetrated to her very soul. Dammit.

"But I'm not the same girl you used to know," she continued, propping her hand on her hip. "I'm not looking for a relationship, I'm not looking for love. I'm not even interested in you anymore, Will."

Catalina nearly choked on that lie, but she mentally applauded herself for the firmness in her delivery and for stating all she needed to. She wasn't about to start playing whatever game Will had in mind because she knew one thing for certain…she'd lose.

Will stepped closer, took hold of her wrist and pulled her arm gently behind her back. Her body arched into his as she gripped her feather duster and tried to concentrate on the bite of the handle into her palm and not the way those mesmerizing eyes were full of passion and want.

"Not interested?" he asked with a smirk. "You may be able to lie to yourself, Cat, but you can never lie to me. I know you too well."

She swallowed. "You don't know me at all if you think I still like to be called Cat."

Will leaned in until his lips caressed the side of her ear. "I want to stand out in your mind," he whispered. "I won't call you what everyone else does because our relationship is different."

"We have nothing but a past that was a mistake." She purposely threw his words back in his face and she didn't care if that was childish or not.

Struggling against his hold only caused her body to respond even more as she rubbed against that hard, powerful build.

"You can fight this all you want," he said as he eased back just enough to look into her eyes. "You can deny you want me and you can even try to tell yourself you hate me. But know this. I'm also not the same man I used to be. I'm not going to let you get away this time."

Catalina narrowed her gaze. "I have goals, Will, and you're not on my list."

A sultry grin spread across his face an instant before he captured her lips. His body shifted so that she could feel just how much he wanted her. Catalina couldn't stop herself from opening her mouth for him and if her hands had been free, she probably would've fully embarrassed herself by gripping his hair and holding him even tighter.

Damn this man she wanted to hate, but couldn't.

He demanded her affection, demanded desire from her and she gave it. Mercy, she had no choice.

He nipped at her, their tongues tangling, before he finally, finally lifted his head and ran a thumb across her moist bottom lip.

"I have goals, too, Cat," he murmured against her mouth. "And you're on the top of *my* list."

The second he released her, she had to hurry to steady herself. By the time she'd processed that full-on arousing attack, Will was gone.

Typical of the man to get her ready for more and leave her hanging. She just wished she still wasn't tingling and aching all over for more of his touch.

Two

Will sat on his patio, staring down at his boat and contemplating another plan of action. Unfortunately his cell phone rang before he could fully appreciate the brilliant idea he'd just had.

His father's name popped up on the screen and Will knew without answering what this would be about. It looked as if Patrick Rowling had just got wind of Will's latest business actions.

"Afternoon," he greeted, purposely being more cheerful than he assumed his father was.

"What the hell are you doing with the Cortes Real Estate company?"

Will stared out onto the sparkling water and crossed his ankles as he leaned back in his cushioned patio chair. "I dropped them."

"I'm well aware of that seeing as how Dominic called me to raise hell. What were you thinking?" his father demanded. "When you steamrolled into the head position, I thought you'd make wise moves to further the family business and make it even more profitable into the next generation. I never expected you to sever ties with companies we've dealt with for decades."

"I'm not hanging on to business relationships based on tradition or some sense of loyalty," Will stated, refusing to back down. "We've not gained a thing in the past five years from the Corteses and it was time to cut our losses. If you and Dom want to be friends, then go play golf or something, but his family will no longer do business with mine. The bottom line here is money, not hurt feelings."

"You should've run this by me, Will. I won't tolerate you going behind my back."

Will came to his feet, pulled in a deep breath of ocean air and smiled because he was in charge now and his father was going to start seeing that the "good" twin wasn't always going to bend and bow to Patrick's wishes. Will was still doing the "right thing," it just so happened the decisions made were Will's version of right and not his father's.

"I'm not sneaking at all," Will replied, leaning against the scrolling wrought iron rail surrounding his deck. "I'll tell you anything you want to know, but since I'm in charge now, I'm not asking for permission, either."

"How many more phone calls can I expect like the one I got from Cortes?"

His father's sarcasm wasn't lost on Will.

"None for the time being. I only let one go, but that doesn't mean I won't cut more ties in the future if I see we aren't pulling any revenue in after a period of time."

"You run your decisions by me first."

Giving a shrug even though his father couldn't see him, Will replied, "You wanted the golden son to take over. That's exactly what I'm doing. Don't second-guess me and my decisions. I stand to gain or lose like you do and I don't intend to see our name tarnished. We'll come out on top if you stop questioning me and let me do this job the way it's meant to be done."

Patrick sighed. "I never thought you'd argue with me."

"I'm not arguing. I'm telling you how it is."

Will disconnected the call. He wasn't going to get into a verbal sparring match with his father. He didn't have time for such things and nothing would change Will's mind. He'd gone over the numbers and cross-referenced them for the past years. Though that was a job his assistant could easily do, Will wanted his eyes on every report since he was taking over. He needed to know exactly what he was dealing with and how to plan accordingly.

His gaze traveled back to his yacht nestled against his private dock. Speaking of planning accordingly, he had more personal issues to deal with right now. Issues that involved one very sexy maid.

It had taken a lifeless, arranged relationship with Bella to really wake Will up to the fact his father had his clutches so tight, Will had basically been a marionette his entire life. Now Will was severing those strings, starting with the ridiculous notion of his marrying Bella.

Will was more than ready to move forward and take all the things he'd been craving: money and Cat. A beautiful combo to start this second stage of his life.

And it would be soon, he vowed to himself as he stalked around his outdoor seating area and headed inside. Very soon he would add to his millions, secure his place as head of the family business by cementing its leading position in the oil and real estate industries and have Cat right where he wanted her...begging.

Catalina couldn't wait to finish this day. So many things had come up that hadn't been on her regular schedule...just another perk of working for the Rowling patriarch. She had her sights set on getting home, taking off her ugly, sensible work shoes and digging into another sewing project that would give her hope, get her one step closer to her ultimate goal.

This next piece she'd designed late last night would be a brilliant, classy, yet fun outfit to add to her private collection. A collection she fully intended to take with her when she left Alma very soon.

Her own secret goal of becoming a fashion designer had her smiling. Maybe one day she could wear her own stylish clothes to work instead of boring black cotton pants and button-down shirt with hideous shoes. Other than her mother, nobody knew of Catalina's real dream, and she had every intention of keeping things that way. The last thing she needed was anyone trying to dissuade her from pursuing her ambitions or telling her that the odds were against her. She was fully aware of the odds and she intended to leap over them and claim her dream no matter how long it took. Determination was a hell of a motivator.

She came to work for the Rowlings and did her job—and that was about all the human contact she had lately. She'd been too wrapped up in materials, designs and fantasies of runway shows with her clothing draped on models who could fully do her stylish fashions justice.

Not that Catalina hated how she looked, but she

wasn't blind. She knew her curvy yet petite frame wasn't going to get her clothing noticed. She merely wanted to be behind the scenes. She didn't need all the limelight on her because she just wanted to design, no more.

As opposed to the Rowling men who seemed to crave the attention and thrive on the publicity and hoopla.

Adjusting the fresh arrangement of lilacs and white calla lilies in the tall, slender crystal vase, Catalina placed the beautiful display on the foyer table in the center of the open entryway. There were certain areas where Patrick didn't mind her doing her own thing, such as choosing the flowers for all the arrangements. She tended to lean toward the classy and elegant…which was the total opposite of the man she worked for.

James on the other hand had more fun with her working here and he actually acknowledged her presence. Patrick only summoned her when he wanted to demand something. She hated thinking how much Will was turning into his father, how business was ruling him and consuming his entire life.

Will wasn't in her personal life anymore, no matter how much she still daydreamed about their kisses. And Patrick would only be her employer for a short time longer. She was hoping to be able to leave Alma soon, leave behind this life of being a maid for a man she didn't care for. At least James was pleasant and a joy to work for. Granted, James hadn't betrayed Cat's mother the way Patrick had. And that was just another reason she wanted out of here, away from Patrick and the secret Cat knew about him.

Catalina shoved those thoughts aside. Thinking of all the sins from Patrick's past wouldn't help her mood.

Patrick had been deceitful many years ago and Catalina couldn't ignore her mother's warning about the Rowling men. Even if Will had no clue how his father had behaved, it was something Catalina would never forget. She was only glad she'd found out before she did something foolish like fall completely in love with Will.

Apparently the womanizing started with Patrick and trickled down to his sons. James had been a notorious player before Bella entered his life. After all, there was nothing like stealing your twin brother's girl, which is what James had done to Will. But all had worked out in the end because Bella and James truly did love each other even if the way they got there was hardly normal. Leave it to the Rowlings and the Montoros to keep life in Alma interesting.

Catalina just wished those recent kisses from Will weren't overriding her mother's sound advice and obvious common sense.

Once the arrangement was to her liking—because perfection was everything whether you were a maid or a CEO—Catalina made her way up the wide, curved staircase to the second floor. The arrangements upstairs most likely needed to be changed out. At the very least, she'd freshen them up with water and remove the wilting stems.

As she neared the closed door of the library, she heard the distinct sound of a woman sobbing. Catalina had no clue who was visiting. No women lived here, and she'd been in the back of the house most of the morning and hadn't seen anyone come in.

The nosy side of her wanted to know what was going on, but the employee side of her said she needed to mind her own business. She'd been around the Rowling family enough to know to keep her head down, do her job and remember she was only the help.

Inwardly she groaned. She hated that term. Yes, she was a maid, but she was damn good at her job. She took pride in what she did. No, cleaning toilets and washing sheets wasn't the most glam of jobs, but she knew what she did was important. Besides, the structure and discipline of her work was only training her for the dream job she hoped to have someday.

The rumble of male voices blended in with the female's weeping. Whatever was going on, it was something major. Catalina approached the circular table in the middle of the wide hall. As she plucked out wilted buds here and there, the door to the library creaked open. Catalina focused on the task at hand, though she was dying to turn to see who came from the room.

"Cat."

She cringed at the familiar voice. Well, part of her curiosity was answered, but suddenly she didn't care what was going on in that room. She didn't care who Will had in there, though Catalina already felt sorry for the poor woman. She herself had shed many tears over Will when he'd played her for a fool, getting her to think they could ignore their class differences and have a relationship. "I need to see you for a minute."

Of course he hadn't asked. Will Rowling didn't ask... he demanded.

Stiffening her back, she expected to see him standing close, but when she turned to face him, she noted he was holding onto the library door, with only the top half of his body peeking out of the room.

"I'm working," she informed him, making no move to go see whatever lover's spat he was having with the unknown woman.

"You need to talk to Bella."

Bella? Suddenly Catalina found herself moving down

the hall, but Will stepped out, blocking her entry into the library. Catalina glanced down to his hand gripping her bicep.

"Her aunt Isabella passed away in the middle of the night," he whispered.

Isabella Montoro was the grand matriarch of the entire Montoro clan. The woman had been around forever. Between Juan Carlos being named the true heir to the throne and now Isabella's death, the poor family was being dealt one blow after another.

Will rubbed his thumb back and forth over Catalina's arm. "You know Bella enough through James and I figured she'd want another woman to talk to. Plus, I thought she could relate to you because…"

Swallowing, she nodded. When she and Will had dated briefly, Catalina had just lost her grandmother, a woman who had been like a second mother to her. Will had seen her struggle with the loss…maybe the timing of the loss explained why she'd been so naïve to think she and Will could have a future together. For that moment in time, Catalina had clung to any hope of happiness and Will had shown her so much…but it had all been built on lies.

Catalina started to move by him, but his grip tightened. "I don't want to bring up bad memories for you." Those aqua eyes held her in place. "As much as Bella is hurting, I won't sacrifice you, so tell me if you can't go in there."

Catalina swallowed as she looked back into those eyes that held something other than lust. For once he wasn't staring at her as if he wanted to rip her clothes off. He genuinely cared or at least he was playing the part rather well. Then again, he'd played a rather impressive role four years ago pretending to be the doting boyfriend.

Catalina couldn't afford to let her guard down. Not again with this man who still had the power to cripple her. That kiss weeks ago only proved the control he still had and she'd never, ever let him in on that fact. She could never allow Will to know just how much she still ached for his touch.

"I'll be fine," she replied, pulling her arm back. "I'd like to be alone with her, though."

Will opened his mouth as if to argue, but finally closed it and nodded.

As soon as Catalina stepped inside, her heart broke. Bella sat in a wingback chair. James rested his hip on the arm and Bella was curled into his side sobbing.

"James." Will motioned for his twin to follow him out.

Leaning down, James muttered something to Bella. Dabbing her eyes with a tissue, Bella looked up and saw she had company.

Catalina crossed to the beautiful woman who had always been known for her wild side. Right now she was hurting over losing a woman who was as close as a mother to her.

The fact that Will thought Catalina could offer comfort, the fact that he cared enough to seek her out, shouldn't warm her heart. She couldn't let his moment of sweetness hinder her judgment of the man. Bella was the woman he'd been in a relationship with only a month ago. How could Catalina forget that? No matter the reasons behind the relationship, Catalina couldn't let go of the fact that Will would've said *I do* to Bella had James not come along.

Will had an agenda, he always did. Catalina had no

clue what he was up to now, but she had a feeling his newfound plans included her. After all this time, was he seriously going to pursue her? Did he honestly think they'd start over or pick up where they'd left off?

Catalina knew deep down he was only after one thing…and she truly feared if she wasn't careful, she'd end up giving in.

Three

Will lifted the bottle of scotch from the bar in the living room, waving it back and forth slightly in a silent invitation to his brother.

James blew out a breath. "Yeah. I could use a drink."

Neither mentioned the early time. Sometimes life's crises called for an emergency drink to take the edge off. And since they'd recently started building their relationship back up, Will wanted to be here for his brother because even though Bella was the one who'd suffered the loss, James was no doubt feeling helpless.

"Smart thinking asking Catalina to help." James took the tumbler with the amber liquid and eased back on the leather sofa. "Something going on there you want to talk about?"

Will remained standing, leaning an elbow back against the bar. "Nothing going on at all."

Not to say there wouldn't be something going on very

soon if he had his way about it. Those heated kisses only motivated him even more...not to mention the fact that his father would hate knowing "the good twin" had gone after what he wanted, which was the total opposite of Patrick's wishes.

James swirled the drink as he stared down into the glass. "I know Isabella has been sick for a while, but still, her death came as a shock. Knowing how strong-willed she was, I'd say she hung on until Juan Carlos was announced the rightful heir to the throne."

Will nodded, thankful they were off the topic of Cat. She was his and he wasn't willing to share her with anyone right now. Only a month ago, Bella had caught Will and Cat kissing, but at the time she'd thought it was James locking lips with the maid. The slight misunderstanding had nearly cost James the love of his life. "How is Bella dealing with the fact her brother was knocked off the throne before he could fully take control?"

The Montoro family was being restored to the Alma monarchy after decades of harsh dictatorship. First Rafael Montoro IV and then, when he abdicated, his brother Gabriel were thought to be the rightful heirs. However, their sister, Bella, had then uncovered damning letters in an old family farmhouse, indicating that because of a paternity secret going back to before World War II, Juan Carlos's line of the family were the only legitimate heirs.

"I don't think that title ever appealed to Gabriel or Bella, to be honest." James crossed his ankle over his knee and held onto his glass as he rested it on the arm of the sofa. "Personally, I'm glad the focus is on Juan Carlos right now. Bella and I have enough media attention as it is."

In addition to the fact that James had married a member of Alma's royal family, he was also a star football player who drew a lot of scrutiny from the tabloids. The newlyweds no doubt wanted some privacy to start building their life together, especially since James had also recently taken custody of his infant baby, Maisey—a child from a previous relationship.

"Isabella's passing will have the media all over the Montoros and Juan Carlos. I'm probably going to take Bella and Maisey back to the farmhouse to avoid the spotlight. The renovations aren't done yet, but we need the break."

"What can I do to help?" Will asked.

James tipped back the last of the scotch, and then leaned forward and set the empty tumbler on the coffee table. "Give me back that watch," he said with a half smile and a nod toward Will's wrist.

"Nah, I won this fair and square," Will joked. "I told you that you wouldn't be able to resist putting a ring on Bella's finger."

James had inherited the coveted watch from their English grandfather and wore it all the time. It was the way people told the twins apart. But Will had wanted the piece and had finally won it in a bet that James would fall for Bella and propose. Ironically, it had almost ended James and Bella's relationship because Will had been wearing the watch that night he'd kissed Cat in the gazebo. Bella had mistaken him for James and jumped to conclusions.

"Besides the watch, what else can I do?" Will asked.

"I have no idea." James shook his head and blew out a sigh. "Right now keeping Dad out of my business would be great."

Will laughed. "I don't think that will be a problem.

He's up in arms about some business decisions I've made, so the heat is off you for now."

"Are you saying the good twin is taking charge?"

"I'm saying I'm controlling my own life and this is only the first step in my plan."

Leaning forward, James placed his elbows on his knees. "Sounds like you may need my help. I am the black sheep, after all. Let me fill you in on all the ways to defy our father."

"I'm pretty sure I'm defying him all on my own." Will pushed off the bar and shoved his hands in his pockets. "I'll let you know if I need any tips."

James leveled his gaze at Will. "Why do I have a feeling this new plan of yours has something to do with the beautiful maid?"

Will shrugged, refusing to rise to the bait.

"You were kissing her a few weeks ago," James reminded him. "That little escapade nearly cost me Bella."

The entire night had been a mess, but thankfully things ultimately worked out the way they should have.

"So Catalina…"

Will sighed. "You won't drop it, will you?"

"We practically grew up together with her, you dated before, you were kissing a few weeks ago. I'm sure dear old Dad is about to explode if you are making business decisions that he isn't on board with and if you're seducing his maid."

"I'm not seducing anyone." Yet. "And what I do with my personal life is none of his concern."

"He'll say different once he knows you're after the maid. He'll not see her as an appropriate match for you," James countered, coming to his feet and glancing toward the ceiling as if he could figure out what was going on upstairs between the women. "What's taking them so long? Think it's safe to go back?"

Will nodded. "Let's go see. Hopefully Cat was able to calm Bella down."

"Cat, huh?" James smiled as he headed toward the foyer and the staircase. "You called her that years ago and she hated it. You still going with that?"

Will patted his brother on the shoulder. "I am going for whatever the hell I want lately."

And he was. From this point on, if he wanted it, he was taking it…that went for his business and his bedroom.

The fact that the maid was consoling a member of the royal family probably looked strange from the outside, and honestly it felt a bit weird. But Catalina had been around Bella enough to know how down-to-earth James's wife was. Bella never treated Catalina like a member of the staff. Not that they were friends by any means, but Catalina was comfortable with Bella and part of her was glad Will had asked her to come console Bella over the loss of her aunt.

"You're so sweet to come in here," Bella said with a sniff.

Catalina fought to keep her own emotions inside as she hugged Bella. Even though years had passed, Catalina still missed her grandmother every single day. Some days were just more of a struggle than others.

"I'm here anytime." Catalina squeezed the petite woman, knowing what just a simple touch could do to help ease a bit of the pain, to know you weren't alone in your grief. "There will be times memories sneak up on you and crush you all over again and there will be days you are just fine. Don't try to hide your emotions.

Everyone grieves differently so whatever your outlet is, it's normal."

Bella shifted back and patted her damp cheeks. "Thank you. I didn't mean to cry all over you and bring up a bad time in your life."

Pushing her own memories aside, Catalina offered a smile. "You didn't do anything but need a shoulder to cry on. I just hope I helped in some small way to ease the hurt and I'm glad I was here."

"Bella."

The sound of James's voice had Catalina stepping back as he came in to stand beside his wife. Tucking her short hair behind her ears, Catalina offered the couple a brief smile. James hugged Bella to his side and glanced at Catalina.

"I didn't want to interrupt, but I know you need to work, too," James said. "We really appreciate you."

Those striking Rowling eyes held hers. This man was a star athlete, wanted by women all over the world. Yet Catalina felt nothing. He looked exactly like Will, but in Catalina's heart...

No. Her heart wasn't involved. Her hormones were a jumbled mess, but her heart was sealed off and impenetrable...at least where Will was concerned. Maybe when she left Alma she'd settle somewhere new and find the man she was meant to be with, the man who wouldn't consider her a mistake.

Those damning words always seemed to be in the forefront of her mind.

"I'm here all day through the week," Catalina told Bella. "You can always call me, too. I'm happy to help any way I can."

"Thank you." Bella sniffed. She dabbed her eyes again and turned into James's embrace.

Catalina left the couple alone and pulled the door shut behind her. She leaned against the panel, closed her eyes and tipped her head back. Even though Catalina still had her mother, she missed her grandmother. There was just something special about a woman who enters your life in such a bold way that leaves a lasting impression.

Catalina knew Bella was hurting over the loss of her aunt, there was no way to avoid the pain. But Bella had a great support team and James would stay by her side.

A stab of remorse hit her. Bella's and Catalina's situations were so similar, yet so different. Will had comforted her over her loss when they'd first started dating and Catalina had taken his concern as a sign of pure interest. Unfortunately, her moments of weakness had led her to her first broken heart.

The only good thing to come out of it was that she hadn't given him her innocence. But she'd certainly been tempted on more than one occasion. The man still tempted her, but she was smarter now, less naïve, and she had her eyes wide open.

Pushing off the door, she shoved aside the thoughts of Will and their past relationship. She'd jumped from one mistake to another after he broke things off with her. Two unfortunate relationships were more than enough for her. Focusing on turning her hobby and passion for making clothes into a possible career had kept her head on straight and her life pointed in the right direction. She didn't have time for obstacles…no matter how sexy.

She made her way down the hall toward the main bathroom on the second floor. This bathroom was nearly the size of her little flat across town. She could afford something bigger, but she'd opted to keep her place small because she lived alone and she'd rather save her money for fabrics, new sewing machines, investing in her future and ultimately her move. One day that nest egg she'd set aside would come in handy and she couldn't wait to leave Alma and see how far her dreams could take her. Another couple months and she truly believed she would be ready. She still couldn't pinpoint her exact destination, though. Milan was by far the hot spot for fashion and she could head there and aim straight for the top. New York was also an option, or Paris.

Catalina smiled at the possibilities as she reached beneath the sink and pulled out fresh white hand towels. Just as she turned, she collided with a very hard, very familiar chest.

Will gripped her arms to steady her, but she wasn't going anywhere, not when she was wedged between his solid frame and the vanity biting into her back.

"Excuse me," she said, gripping the terrycloth next to her chest and tipping her chin up. "I'm running behind."

"Then a few more minutes won't matter." He didn't let up on his hold, but instead leaned back and kicked the door shut with his foot. "You're avoiding me."

Hadn't she thought this bathroom was spacious just moments ago? Because now it seemed even smaller than the closet in her bedroom.

"Your ego is getting in the way of common sense," she countered. "I'm working. Why are you always here lately anyway? Don't you have an office to run on the other side of town?"

The edge of his mouth kicked up in a cocky half smile. "You've noticed. I was beginning to think you were immune."

"I've been vaccinated."

Will's rich laugh washed over her and she cursed the goose bumps that covered her skin. Between his touch, his masculine scent and feeling his warm breath on her, her defenses were slipping. She couldn't get sucked back into his spell, not when she was so close to breaking free once and for all.

"Come to dinner with me," he told her, smile still in place as if he truly thought she'd jump at the chance. "Your choice of places."

Now Catalina laughed. "You're delusional. I'm not going anywhere with you."

His eyes darkened as they slid to her lips. "You will."

Catalina pushed against him, surprised when he released her and stepped back. She busied herself with changing out the hand towels on the heated rack. Why wouldn't he leave? Did he not take a hint? Why suddenly was he so interested in her when a few years ago she'd been "a mistake"? Plus, a month ago he'd almost been engaged to another woman.

Being a backup plan for anybody was never an option. She'd rather be alone.

Taking more care than normal, Catalina focused on making sure the edges of the towels were perfectly lined up. She needed to keep her shaking hands busy.

"You can't avoid this forever." Will's bold words sliced through the tension. "I want you, Cat. I think you know me well enough to realize I get what I want."

Anger rolled through her as she spun around to face him. "For once in your life, you're not going to be able to have something just because you say so. I'm not just a possession, Will. You can't buy me or even work your charm on me. I've told you I'm not the same naïve girl I used to be."

In two swift steps, he'd closed the gap between them

and had her backed against the wall. His hands settled on her hips, gripping them and pulling them flush with his. This time she didn't have the towels to form a barrier and his chest molded with hers. Catalina forced herself to look up into his eyes, gritted her teeth and prayed for strength.

Leaning in close, Will whispered, "I'm not the man I used to be, either."

A shiver rippled through her. No, no he wasn't. Now he was all take-charge and demanding. He hadn't been like this before. He also hadn't been as broad, as hard. He'd definitely bulked up in all the right ways…not that she cared.

"What would your father say if he knew you were hiding in the bathroom with the maid?" she asked, hoping the words would penetrate through his hormones. He'd always been yanked around by Daddy's wishes… hence their breakup, she had no doubt.

Will shifted his face so his lips were a breath away from hers as his hands slid up to her waist, his thumbs barely brushing the underside of her breasts. "My father is smart enough to know what I'd be doing behind a closed door with a sexy woman."

Oh, man. Why did she have to find his arrogance so appealing? Hadn't she learned her lesson the first time? Wanting Will was a mistake, one she may never recover from if she jumped in again.

"Are you saying you're not bowing down to your father's commands anymore? How very grown up of you."

Why was she goading him? She needed to get out of here because the more he leaned against her, the longer he spoke with that kissable mouth so close to hers, the harder he was making her life. Taunting her, making her ache for things she could never have.

"I told you, I'm a different man." His lips grazed hers as he murmured, "But I still want you and nobody is going to stand in my way."

Why did her hormones and need for his touch override common sense? Letting Will kiss her again was a bad, bad idea. But she couldn't stop herself and she'd nearly arched her body into his just as he stepped back. The heat in his eyes did nothing to suppress the tremors racing through her, but he was easing backward toward the closed door.

"You're leaving?" she asked. "What is this, Will? A game? Corner the staff and see how far she'll let me take things?"

He froze. "This isn't a game, Cat. I'm aching for you, to strip you down and show you exactly what I want. But I need you to literally hurt for wanting me and I want you to be ready. Because the second I think we're on the same level, you're mine."

And with that, he turned and walked out, leaving the door open.

Catalina released a breath she hadn't realized she'd been holding. How dare he disrupt her work and get her all hot and bothered? Did he truly think she'd run to him begging to whisk her off to bed?

As much as her body craved his touch, she wouldn't fall into his bed simply because he turned on the sex appeal. If he wanted her, then that was his problem.

Unfortunately, he'd just made his wants her problem as well because now she couldn't think of anything else but how amazing he felt pressed against her.

Catalina cursed herself as she gathered the dirty towels. If he was set on playing games, he'd chosen the wrong opponent.

Four

Catalina lived for her weekends. Two full days for her to devote to her true love of designing and sewing. There was nothing like creating your own masterpieces from scratch. Her thick portfolio binder overflowed with ideas from the past four years. She'd sketched designs for every season, some sexy, some conservative, but everything was timeless and classy in her opinion.

She supposed something more than just heartache and angst had come from Will's exiting her life so harshly. She'd woken up, finally figured out what she truly wanted and opted to put herself, her dreams as top priority. And once she started achieving her career goals, she'd work on her personal dreams of a family. All of those were things she couldn't find in Alma. This place had nothing for her anymore other than her mother, who worked for another family. But her mother had already said she'd follow Catalina wherever she decided to go.

Glancing around, Catalina couldn't remember where she put that lacy fabric she'd picked up in town a few weeks ago. She'd seen it on the clearance table and had nothing in mind for it at the time, but she couldn't pass up the bargain.

Now she knew exactly what she'd use the material for. She had the perfect wrap-style dress in mind. Something light and comfortable, yet sexy and alluring with a lace overlay. The time would come when Catalina would be able to wear things like that every single day. She could ditch her drab black button-down shirt and plain black pants. When she dressed for work every morning, she always felt she was preparing for a funeral.

And those shoes? She couldn't wait to burn those hideous things.

Catalina moved around the edge of the small sofa and thumbed through the stack of folded materials on the makeshift shelving against the wall. She'd transformed this spare room into her sewing room just last year and since then she'd spent nearly all of her spare time in the cramped space. One day, though… One day she'd have a glorious sewing room with all the top-notch equipment and she would bask in the happiness of her creations.

As she scanned the colorful materials folded neatly on the shelves, her cell rang. Catalina glanced at the arm of the sofa where her phone lay. Her mother's name lit up the screen.

Lunging across the mess of fabrics on the cushions, Catalina grabbed her phone and came back to her feet as she answered.

"Hey, Mum."

"Sweetheart. I'm sorry I didn't call earlier. I went out to breakfast with a friend."

Catalina stepped from her bedroom and into the cozy

living area. "No problem. I've been sewing all morning and lost track of time."

"New designs?" her mother asked.

"Of course." Catalina sank down onto her cushy sofa and curled her feet beneath her. "I actually have a new summery beach theme I'm working on. Trying to stay tropical and classy at the same time has proven to be more challenging than I thought."

"Well, I know you can do it," her mother said. "I wore that navy-and-gray-print skirt you made for me to breakfast this morning and my friend absolutely loved it. I was so proud to be wearing your design, darling."

Catalina sat up straighter. "You didn't tell her—"

"I did not," her mother confirmed. "But I may have said it was from a new up-and-coming designer. I couldn't help it, honey. I'm just so proud of you and I know you'll take the fashion world by storm once you leave Alma."

Just the thought of venturing out on her own, taking her secret designs and her life dream and putting herself out there had a smile spreading across her face as nerves danced in her belly. The thought of someone looking over her designs with a critical eye nearly crippled her, but she wouldn't be wielding toilet wands for the rest of her life.

"I really think I'll be ready in a couple of months," Catalina stated, crossing back to survey her inventory on the shelves. "Saying a timeframe out loud makes this seem so real."

Her mother laughed. "This is your dream, baby girl. You go after it and I'll support you all the way. You know I want you out from under the Rowlings' thumb."

Catalina swallowed as she zeroed in on the lace and

pulled it from the pile. "I know. Don't dwell on that, though. I'm closer to leaving every day."

"Not soon enough for me," her mother muttered.

Catalina knew her mother hated Patrick Rowling. Their affair years ago was still a secret and the only reason Catalina knew was because when she'd been dumped by Will and was sobbing like an adolescent schoolgirl, her mother had confessed. Maria Iberra was a proud woman and Catalina knew it had taken courage to disclose the affair, but Maria was dead set on her daughter truly understanding that the Rowling men were only after one thing and they were ruthless heartbreakers. Feelings didn't exist for those men, save for James, who seemed to be truly in love and determined to make Bella happy.

But Patrick was ruthless in everything and Will had followed suit. So why was he still pursuing her? She just wanted a straight answer. If he just wanted sex, she'd almost wish he'd just come out and say it. She'd take honesty over adult games any day.

Before she could respond to her mother, Catalina's doorbell rang. "Mum, I'll call you back. Someone is at my door."

She disconnected the call and pocketed her cell in her smock pocket. She'd taken to wearing a smock around her waist to keep pins, thread, tiny scissors and random sewing items easily accessible. Peeking through the peephole, Catalina only saw a vibrant display of flowers.

Flicking the deadbolt, she eased the door open slightly. "Yes?"

"Catalina Iberra?"

"That's me."

The young boy held onto the crystal vase with two hands and extended it toward her. "Delivery for you."

Opening the door fully, she took the bouquet and soon realized why this boy had two hands on it. This thing was massive and heavy.

"Hold on," she called around the obscene arrangement. "Let me give you a tip."

"Thank you, ma'am, but that was already taken care of. You have a nice day."

Catalina stepped back into her apartment, kicked the door shut with her foot and crossed the space to put the vase on her coffee table. She stood back and checked out various shades and types of flowers. Every color seemed to be represented in the beautiful arrangement. Catalina couldn't even imagine what this cost. The vase alone, made of thick, etched glass, appeared to be rather precious.

A white envelope hung from a perfectly tied ribbon around the top of the vase. She tugged on the ribbon until it fell free and then slid the small envelope off. Pulling the card out and reading it, her heart literally leapt up into her throat. *Think of me. W.*

Catalina stared at the card, and then back at the flowers. Suddenly they weren't as pretty as they'd been two minutes ago. Did he seriously think she'd fall for something as cliché as flowers? Please. And that arrogant message on the card was utterly ridiculous.

Think of him? Lately she'd done little else, but she'd certainly never tell him that. What an ego he'd grown since they were last together. And she thought it had been inflated then.

But because no one was around to see her, she bent down and buried her face in the fresh lilacs. They smelled so wonderful and in two days they would still look amazing.

A smile spread across her face as her plan took shape. Will had no idea who he was up against if he thought an expensive floral arrangement was going to get her to drop her panties or common sense.

As much as she was confused and a bit hurt by his newfound interest in her now that he wasn't involved with Bella, she had to admit, toying with him was going to be fun. Only one person could win this battle…she just prayed her strength held out and she didn't go down in the first round.

Will slid his cell back into his pocket and leaned against the window seat in his father's office at his Playa del Onda home. "We've got them."

Patrick blinked once, twice, and then a wide smile spread across his face. "I didn't think you could do it."

Will shrugged. "I didn't have a doubt."

"I've been trying to sign with the Cherringtons for over a year." Patrick shook his head and pushed off the top of his desk to come to his feet. "You're really making a mark here, Will. I wondered how things would fair after Bella, but business is definitely your area of expertise."

Will didn't tell his father that Mrs. Cherrington had tried to make a pass at Will at a charity event a few months back. Blackmail in business was sometimes not a bad thing. It seemed that Mrs. Cherrington would do anything to keep her husband from learning she'd had too much to drink and gotten a little frisky. She apparently went so far as to talk him into doing business with the Rowlings, but considering both families would prosper, Will would keep her little secret.

In Will's defense, he didn't let her advances go far. Even if she weren't old enough to be his mother and if she hadn't smelled as if she bathed in a distillery, she was married. He may not want any part of marriage for himself, but that didn't mean he was going to home in on anybody else's, either.

Before he could say anything further, Cat appeared in the doorway with an enormous bouquet. The arrangement reminded him of the gift he'd sent her. He'd wondered all weekend what she'd thought of the arrangement. Had she smiled? Had she thought about calling him?

He'd end this meeting with his father and make sure to track her down before he headed back to the Rowling Energy offices for an afternoon meeting. He had an ache that wasn't going away anytime soon and he was starting to schedule his work around opportunities to see Cat. His control and priorities were becoming skewed.

"I'm sorry to interrupt," she stated, not glancing Will's way even for a second. "I thought I'd freshen up your office."

Patrick glanced down at some papers on his desk and motioned her in without a word. Will kept his eyes on Cat, on her petite, curvy frame tucked so neatly into her black button-down shirt and hip-hugging dress pants. His hands ached to run over her, *sans* clothing.

She was sporting quite a smirk, though. She was up to something, which only put him on full alert.

"I don't always keep flowers in here, but I thought this bouquet was lovely." She set it on the accent table nestled between two leather wingback chairs against the far wall. "I received these the other day and they just did a number on my allergies. I thought about trashing them, but then realized that you may want something fresh for your office, Mr. Rowling."

Will stood straight up. She'd received those the other day? She'd brought his bouquet into his father's office and was giving it away?

Apparently his little Cat had gotten feisty.

"I didn't realize you had allergies," Will stated, drawing her attention to him.

She tucked her short black hair behind her ears and smiled. "And why should you?" she countered with a bit more sass than he was used to from her. "I'll leave you two to talk."

As she breezed out just as quickly as she'd come, Will looked at his father, who was staring right back at him with a narrowed gaze. Why did Will feel as if he'd been caught doing something wrong?

"Keep your hands off my staff," his father warned. "You already tried that once. I hesitated keeping her on, but James swore she was the best worker he'd ever had. Her mother had been a hard worker, too, so don't make me regret that decision."

No way in hell was he letting his father, or anybody else for that matter, dictate what he could and couldn't do with Cat. Listening to his father's instructions about his personal life was what got Will into this mess in the first place.

"Once we've officially signed with the Cherringtons, I'll be sure to send them a nice vintage wine with a personalized note."

Patrick came to his feet, rested his hands on his desk and leaned forward. "You're changing the subject."

"The subject of your staff or my personal life has no relevance in this meeting," Will countered. "I'll be sure to keep you updated if anything changes, but my assistant should have all the proper paperwork emailed by the end of the day."

Will started to head out the door, but turned to glance over his shoulder. "Oh, and the next time Cat talks to you, I suggest you are polite in return and at least look her in the eye."

Leaving his father with his mouth wide open, Will turned and left the office. Perhaps he shouldn't have added that last bit, but Will wasn't going to stand by and watch his father dismiss Cat like that. She was a person, too—just because she cleaned for Patrick and he signed her checks didn't mean he was more important than she. Will had no doubt that when Cat worked for James, he at least treated her with respect.

Dammit. Why was he getting so defensive? He should be pissed she'd dumped his flowers onto his father. There was a twisted irony in there somewhere, but Will was too keyed up to figure it out. What was it about her blatantly throwing his gift back in his face that had him so turned on?

Will searched the entire first and second floors, but Cat was nowhere to be found. Granted, the house was twelve thousand square feet, but there weren't that many people on staff. How could one petite woman go missing?

Will went back to the first floor and into the back of the house where the utility room was. The door was closed and when he tried to turn the knob, he found it locked. That was odd. Why lock a door to the laundry? He heard movement, so someone was in there.

He tapped his knuckles on the thick wood door and waited. Finally the click of a lock sounded and the door eased open. Cat's dark eyes met his.

"What do you want?" she asked.

"Can I come in?"

"This isn't a good time."

He didn't care if this was good or bad. He was here and she was going to talk to him. He had to get to another meeting and wasn't wasting time playing games.

Will pushed the door, causing her to step back. Squeezing in, he shut the door behind him and flicked the lock into place.

Cat had her back to him, her shoulders hunched. "What do you want, Will?"

"You didn't like the flowers?" he asked, crossing his arms over his chest and leaning against the door.

"I love flowers. I don't like your clichéd way of getting my attention or trying to buy me."

He reached out, grabbed her shoulder and spun her around. "Look at me, dammit."

In an instant he realized why she'd been turned away. She was clutching her shirt together, but the swell of her breasts and the hint of a red lacy bra had him stunned speechless.

"I was trying to carry a small shelf into the storage area and it got caught on my shirt," she explained, looking anywhere but at his face as she continued to hold her shirt. "I ran in here because I knew there was a sewing kit or maybe even another shirt."

Everything he'd wanted to say to her vanished from his mind. He couldn't form a coherent thought at this point, not when she was failing at keeping her creamy skin covered.

"I'd appreciate it if you'd stop staring," she told him, her eyes narrowing. "I don't have time for games or a pep talk or whatever else you came to confront me about. I have work to do and boobs to cover."

Her snarky joke was most likely meant to lighten the mood, but he'd wanted her for too long to let anything deter him. He took a step forward, then another, until he'd backed her up against the opposite wall. With her hands holding tight onto her shirt, her eyes wide and her cheeks flushed, there was something so wanton yet innocent about her.

"What do you like?" he asked.

Cat licked her lips. "What?" she whispered.

Will placed a hand on the wall, just beside her head, and leaned in slightly. "You don't like flowers. What do you like?"

"Actually, I love flowers. I just took you for someone who didn't fall into clichés." She offered a slight smile, overriding the fear he'd seen flash through her eyes moments ago. "But you're trying to seduce the maid, so maybe a cliché is all we are."

Will slid his other hand across her cheek and into her hair as he brought his mouth closer. "I don't care if you're the queen or the maid or the homeless person on the corner. I know what I want and I want you, Cat."

She turned her palms to his chest, pushing slightly, but not enough for him to think she really meant for him to step back...not when she was breathless and her eyes were on his mouth.

"I'm not for sale," she argued with little heat behind her words.

He rubbed his lips across hers in a featherlight touch that instantly caused her to tremble. That had to be her body, no way would he admit those tremors were from him.

"Maybe I'll just sample, then."

Fully covering her mouth, Will kept his hand fisted in her hair as he angled her head just where he wanted it. If she didn't want him at all, why did she instantly open for him?

The sweetest taste he'd ever had was Cat. No woman compared to this one. As much as he wanted to strip her naked right here, he wanted to savor this moment and simply savor her. He wanted that familiar taste only Cat could provide, he wanted to reacquaint himself with every minute sexy detail.

Delicate hands slid up his chest and gripped his shoulders, which meant she had to have released her hold on her shirt. Will removed his hand from the wall and gripped her waist as he slid his hand beneath the hem of her shirt and encountered smooth, warm skin. His thumb caressed back and forth beneath the lacy bra.

Cat arched into him with a slight moan. Her words may have told him she wasn't interested, but her body had something else in mind…something much more in tune with what he wanted.

Will shifted his body back just enough to finish unbuttoning her shirt. He parted the material with both hands and took hold of her breasts. The lace slid beneath his palm and set something off in him. His Cat may be sweet, somewhat innocent, but she loved the sexy lingerie. Good to know.

Reluctantly breaking the kiss, Will ached to explore other areas. He moved down the column of her throat and continued to the swell of her breasts. Her hands slid into his hair as if she were holding him in place. He sure as hell wasn't going anywhere.

Will had wanted this, wanted her, four years ago. He'd wanted her with a need that had only grown over the years. She'd been a virgin then; he'd known it and respected her for her decisions. He would've waited for her because she'd been so special to him.

Then his father had issued an ultimatum and Will had made the wrong choice. He didn't fight for what he wanted and he'd damn well never make that mistake again.

Now Cat was in his arms again and he'd let absolutely nothing stand in the way of his claiming her.

"Tell me you want this," he muttered against her heated skin. "Tell me."

His hands encircled her waist as he tugged her harder against his body. Will lifted his head long enough to catch the heat in her eyes, the passion.

A jiggling of the door handle broke the spell. Will stepped back as Cat blinked, glanced down and yanked her shirt together.

"Is someone in there?" a male voice called.

Cat cleared her throat. "I got something on my shirt," she called back. "Just changing. I'll be out shortly, Raul."

Will stared down at her. "Raul?" he whispered.

Cat jerked her shirt off and stalked across the room. Yanking open a floor-to-ceiling cabinet, she snagged another black shirt and slid into it. As she secured the buttons, she spun back around.

"He's a new employee, not that it's any of your business." When she was done with the last button, she crossed her arms over her chest. "What just happened here, as well as in the bathroom the other day, will not happen again. You can't come in to where I work and manhandle me. I don't care if I work for your family. That just makes this even more wrong."

Will couldn't suppress the grin. "From the moaning, I'd say you liked being manhandled."

He started to take a step forward but she held up her hand. "Don't come closer. You can't just toy with me, Will. I am not interested in a replay of four years ago. I have no idea what your agenda is, but I won't be part of it."

"Who says I have an agenda?"

Her eyes narrowed. "You're a Rowling. You all have agendas."

So she was a bit feistier than before. He always loved a challenge—it was impossible to resist.

"Are you still a virgin?"

Cat gasped, her face flushed. "How dare you. You have no right to ask."

"Considering I'm going to take you to bed, I have every right."

Cat moved around him, flicked the lock and jerked the door open. "Get the hell out. I don't care if this is your father's house. I'm working and we are finished. For good."

Will glanced out the door at a wide-eyed Raul. Before he passed, he stopped directly in front of Cat. "We're not finished. We've barely gotten started."

Crossing into the hall, Will met Raul's questioning stare. "You saw and heard nothing. Are we clear?"

Will waited until the other man silently nodded before walking away. No way in hell did he need his father knowing he'd been caught making out in the damn laundry room with the maid.

Next time, and there would be a next time, Will vowed she'd be in his bed. She was a willing participant every time he'd kissed her. Hell, if the knock hadn't interrupted them, they'd probably both be a lot happier right now.

Regardless of what Cat had just said, he knew full well she wanted him. Her body wasn't lying. What kind of man would he be if he ignored her needs? Because he sure as hell wasn't going to sit back and wait for another man to come along and explore that sexual side.

She was his.

Five

Alma was a beautiful country. Catalina was going to miss the island's beautiful water and white sandy beaches when she left. Swimming was her first love. Being one with the water, letting loose and not caring about anything was the best source of therapy.

And tonight she needed the release.

For three days she'd managed to dodge Will. He had come to Patrick's house every morning, holed himself up in the office with his father and then left, assumedly to head into the Rowling Energy offices.

Will may say he'd changed, but to her he still looked as if he was playing the perfect son, dead set on taking over the family business. Apparently he thought he could take her over as well. But she wasn't a business deal to close and she certainly wouldn't lose her mind again and let him devour her so thoroughly no matter how much she enjoyed it.

Lust was something that would only get her into trouble. The repercussions of lust would last a lifetime; a few moments of pleasure wouldn't be worth the inevitable heartache in the end.

Catalina sliced her arms through the water, cursing herself for allowing thoughts of Will to infringe on her downtime when she only wanted to relax. The man wanted to control her and she was letting him because she had no clue how to stop this emotional roller coaster he'd strapped her into.

Heading toward the shoreline, Catalina pushed herself the last few feet until she could stand. Shoving her short hair back from her face, she took deep breaths as she sloshed through the water. With the sun starting to sink behind her, she crossed the sand and scooped up her towel to mop her face.

He'd seriously crossed the line when he'd asked about her virginity. Yes, she'd gotten carried away with him, even if she did enjoy those stolen moments, but her sexual past was none of his concern because she had no intention of letting him have any more power over her. And she sure as hell didn't want to know about all of his trysts since they'd been together.

Cat wrapped the towel around her body and tucked the edge in to secure the cloth in place. This small stretch of beach wasn't far from her apartment, only a five-minute walk, and rarely had many visitors in the evening. Most people came during the day or on weekends. On occasion, Catalina would see families playing together. Her heart would always seize up a bit then. She longed for the day when she could have a family of her own, but for now, she had her sights set on fashion.

Giving up one dream for another wasn't an option. Who said she couldn't have it all? She could have her ideal career and then her family. She was still young. At twenty-four some women were already married and had children, but she wasn't like most women.

And if Will Rowling thought he could deter her from going after what she wanted, he was delusional. And sexy. Mercy, was the man ever sexy.

No, no, no.

Will and his sexiness had no room in her life, especially her bed, which he'd work his way into if she wasn't on guard constantly.

Catalina pulled out her tank-style sundress and exchanged the towel for the modest coverup. After shoving the towel into her bag, she slid into her sandals and started her walk home. The soft ocean breeze always made her smile. Wherever she moved, she was going to need to be close to water or at least close enough that she could make weekend trips.

This was the only form of exercise she enjoyed, and being so short, every pound really showed. Not that she worried about her weight, but she wanted to feel good about herself and she felt her best when she'd been swimming and her muscles were burning from the strain. She wanted to be able to throw on anything in her closet and have confidence. For her, confidence came with a healthy body.

Catalina crossed the street to her apartment building and smiled at a little girl clutching her mother's hand. Once she reached the stoop leading up to her flat, she dug into her bag for her keys. A movement from the corner of her eye caught her attention. She knew who was there before she fully turned, though.

"What are you doing here, Will?"

She didn't look over her shoulder, but she knew he

followed her. Arguing that he wasn't invited was a moot point; the man did whatever he wanted anyway.

"I came to see you."

When she got to the second floor, she stopped outside her door and slid her key into the lock. "I figured you'd given up."

His rich laughter washed over her chilled skin. Between the warm water and the breezy air, she was going to have to get some clothes on to get warm.

"When have you known me to give up?" he asked.

Throwing a glance over her shoulder, she raised a brow. "Four years ago. You chose your career over a relationship. Seeing me was the big mistake. Ring any bells?"

Will's bright aqua-blue eyes narrowed. "I didn't give up. I'm here now, aren't I?"

"Oh, so I was just put on hold until you were ready," she mocked. "How silly of me not to realize."

"Can I come in?" he asked. "I promise I'll only be a couple minutes."

"You can do a lot of damage in a couple minutes," she muttered, but figured the sooner she let him in, the sooner he'd leave…she hoped.

Catalina pushed the door open and started toward her bedroom. Thankfully the door to the spare room was closed. The last thing she needed was for Will to see everything she'd been working on. Her personal life was none of his concern.

"I'm changing and you're staying out here."

She slammed her bedroom door, hoping he'd get the hint he wasn't welcome. What was he doing here? Did he think she'd love how he came to her turf? Did he think she'd be more comfortable and melt into a puddle at his feet, and then invite him into her bed?

Oh, that man was infuriating. Catalina jerked off

her wet clothes and draped them over her shower rod in her bathroom. Quickly she threw on a bra, panties and another sundress, one of her own designs she liked to wear out. It was simple, but it was hers, and her confidence was always lifted when she wore her own pieces.

Her damp hair wasn't an issue right now. All she wanted to know was why he was here. If he only came for another make-out scene that was going to leave her frustrated and angry, she wanted no part of it. She smoothed back a headband to keep her hair from her face. It was so short it would be air-dried in less than an hour.

Padding barefoot back into her living room, she found Will standing near the door where she'd left him. He held a small package in his hands that she hadn't noticed before. Granted she'd had her back to him most of the time because she didn't want to face him.

"Come bearing gifts?" she asked. "Didn't you learn your lesson after the flowers?"

Will's smile spread across his face. "Thought I'd try a different tactic."

On a sigh, Catalina crossed the room and sank into her favorite cushy chair. "Why try at all? Honestly. Is this just a game to see if you can get the one who got away? Are you trying to prove to yourself that you can conquer me? Is it a slumming thing? What is it, Will? I'm trying to understand this."

He set the box on the coffee table next to a stack of the latest fashion magazines. After taking a seat on her couch, Will rested his elbows on his knees and leaned forward.

Silence enveloped them and the longer he sat there, the more Catalina wondered what was going through his mind. Was he planning on lying? Was he trying to figure out how to tell her the truth? Or perhaps he was second-guessing himself.

She studied him—his strong jawline, his broad frame taking up so much space in her tiny apartment. She'd never brought a man here. Not that she'd purposely brought Will here, but having such a powerful man in her living room was a new experience for her.

Maybe she was out of her league. Maybe she couldn't fight a force like Will Rowling. But she was sure as hell going to try because she couldn't stand to have her heart crushed so easily again.

Catalina curled her feet beside her in the spacious chair as Will met her gaze. Those piercing aqua eyes forced her to go still.

"What if I'm here because I've never gotten over you?"

Dammit. Why did he let that out? He wasn't here to make some grand declaration. He was here to soften her, to get her to let down that guard a little more because he was not giving up. He'd jump through whatever hoop she threw in front of him, but Cat would be his for a while. A steamy affair that no one knew about was exactly what they needed whether she wanted to admit it or not.

When he'd been given the ultimatum by his father to give up Cat or lose his place in Rowling Energy, Will hadn't had much choice. Oh, and his father had also stated that he'd make sure Catalina Iberra would never work anywhere in Alma again if Will didn't let her go.

He'd had to protect her, even though she hated him at the time. He'd do it all over again. But he didn't want to tell her what had happened. He didn't want her to feel guilty or to pity him. Will would win her back just as he'd won her the first time. He'd be charming and wouldn't take no for an answer.

His quiet, almost vulnerable question still hung heavy in the space between them as he waited for her response. She hadn't kicked him out of her flat, so he was making progress. Granted, he'd been making progress since that spur-of-the-moment kiss a month ago, but he'd rather speed things along. A man only had so much control over his emotions.

"You can have any woman you want." Catalina toyed with the edge of the hem on her dress, not making eye contact. "You let me go, you called me a mistake."

He'd regret those words until he died. To know he'd made Cat feel less than valuable to him was not what he'd wanted to leave her with, but once the damning words were out, he couldn't take them back. Anything he said after that point would have been moot. The damage had been done and he'd moved on…or tried to. He'd said hurtful things to get her to back away from him; he'd needed her to stay away at the time because he couldn't afford to let her in, not when his father had such a heavy hand.

Will had been devastated when she'd started dating another man. What had he expected? Did he think a beautiful, vibrant woman was just going to sit at home and sulk about being single? Obviously she had taken the breakup better than he had. And how sick was that, that he wished she'd been more upset? He wanted her to be happy…he just wanted it to be with him.

"I can't have any woman," he countered. "You're still avoiding me."

She lifted her dark eyes, framed by even darker lashes, and focused on him. Every time she looked at him, Will felt that punch to the gut. Lust. It had to be lust because he wouldn't even contemplate anything else. They'd been apart too long for any other emotion to have settled in. They were two different people now and he just wanted to get to know her all over again, to prove himself to her. She deserved everything he had to give.

Will came to his feet. He couldn't stay here because the longer he was around her, the more he wanted her. Cat was going to be a tough opponent and he knew all too well that the best things came from patience and outlasting your opponent. Hadn't it taken him four years to best his father? And he was still in the process of doing that.

"Where are you going?" she asked, looking up at him.

"You want me to stay?" He stepped forward, easing closer to the chair she sat in. "Because if I stay, I'm going to want more than just talking."

"Did you just come to see where I lived? Did you need this reminder of how opposite we are? How I'm just—"

Will put his hand over her mouth. Leaning down, he gripped the arm of her chair and rested his weight there. He eased in closer until he could see the black rim around her dark eyes.

"We've been over this. I don't care what you are. I know what I want, what I need, and that's you."

Her eyes remained locked on his. Slowly he drew his hand away and trailed his fingertips along the thin tan line coming down from behind her neck.

"You're getting red here," he murmured, watching her shiver beneath his touch. "I haven't seen you out of work clothes in years. You need to take better care of your skin."

Cat reached up, grabbed his hand and halted his movements. "Don't do this, Will. There's nothing for you here and I have nothing to give. Even if I gave you my body, I'd regret it because you wouldn't give me any more and I deserve so much. I see that now and I won't lose sight of my goals just because we have amazing chemistry."

Her pleading tone had him easing back. She wanted him. He'd broken her down enough for her to fully admit it.

What goals was she referring to? He wanted to know what her plans were because he wouldn't let this go. He'd waited too long for this second chance and to finally have her, to finally show his father he was in control now, was his ultimate goal.

"I'm not about to give up, Cat." Will stood straight up and kept his eyes on hers. "You have your goals, I have mine."

As he turned and started walking toward the door, he glanced back and nodded toward the package on the table. "You didn't like flowers. This may be more practical for you."

Before she could say a word, he let himself out. Leaving her flat was one of the hardest things he'd done. He knew if he'd hung around a bit longer she would give in to his advances, but he wanted her to come to him. He wanted her to be aching for him, not reluctant.

Cat would come around. They had too much of a history and a physical connection now for her to ignore her body. He had plenty to keep him occupied until she decided to come to him.

Starting with dropping another bomb on his father where their investments and loyalties lay.

Six

Damn that man.

Catalina resisted the urge to march into the Rowling Energy offices and throw Will's gift back in his face.

But she'd used the thing all weekend. Now she was back at the Playa del Onda estate cleaning for his father. Same old thing, different day.

Still, the fact that Will had brought her a sewing kit, a really nice, really expensive sewing kit, had her smiling. She didn't want to smile at his gestures. She wanted to be grouchy and hate them. The flowers had been easy to cast aside, but something as personal as the sewing kit was much harder to ignore.

Will had no idea about her love of sewing, he'd merely gotten the present because of the shirt she'd ripped the other day. Even though he had no clue of her true passion, he thought outside the proverbial box and took the time to find something to catch her attention… as if he hadn't been on her radar already.

Catalina shoved a curtain rod through the grommets and slid it back into place on the hook. She'd long put off laundering the curtains in the glass-enclosed patio room. She'd been too distracted since that initial kiss nearly a month ago.

Why, after four years, why did Will have to reawaken those feelings? Why did he have to be so bold, so powerful, making her face those desires that had never fully disappeared?

The cell in her pocket vibrated. Pulling the phone out, she glanced down to see Patrick's name on the screen. She wasn't afraid of her boss, but she never liked getting a call from him. Either she'd done something wrong or he was about to unload a project on her. He'd been so much more demanding than James had. Granted James had traveled all over the world for football and had rarely been home, but even when he was, he treated Catalina with respect.

Patrick acted as if the dirt on his shoe had a higher position in the social order than she did.

But she needed every dime she could save so that she could leave once she'd finished all her designs. She made a good income for a maid, but she had no idea how much she'd need to start over in a new country and get by until she got her big break.

"Hello?" she answered.

"Come to my office."

She stared at the phone as he hung up. So demanding, so controlling...much like his son.

Catalina made her way through the house and down the wide hall toward Patrick's office. Was Will here today? She didn't want to pry or ask, but she had a feeling Patrick was handing over the reins to the twin he'd groomed for the position.

The office door stood slightly ajar, so Catalina tapped her knuckles against the thick wood before entering.

"Sir," she said, coming to stand in front of Patrick's wide mahogany desk.

The floral arrangement she'd brought a few days ago still sat on the edge. Catalina had to suppress her grin at the fact that the gift a billionaire purchased for a maid now sat on said billionaire's father's desk.

When Patrick glanced up at her, she swallowed. Why did he always make her feel as if she was in the principal's office? She'd done nothing wrong and had no reason to worry.

Oh, wait. She'd made out with his son in the laundry room and there had been a witness outside the door. There was that minor hiccup in her performance.

"I'm going to have the Montoro family over for a dinner," Patrick stated without preamble. "With the passing of Isabella, it's fitting we extend our condolences and reach out to them during this difficult time."

Catalina nodded. "Of course. Tell me what we need."

"The funeral will be Wednesday and I know they will have their own gathering. I'd like to have the dinner Friday night."

Catalina pulled out her cell and started typing in the notes as he rattled off the details. Only the Montoros and the Rowlings would be in attendance. Patrick expected her to work that day preparing the house and that evening cleaning up after the party... Long days like that were a killer for her back and feet. But the double time pay more than made up for the aches and pains.

"Is that all?" she asked when he stopped talking.

He nodded. "There is one more thing."

Catalina swallowed, slid her phone into her pocket and clasped her hands in front of her body. "Yes, sir?"

"If you have a notion of vying for my son's attention, it's best you stop." Patrick eased back in his chair as if he had all the power and not a worry in the world. "He may not be marrying Bella as I'd hoped, but that doesn't mean he's on the market for you. Will is a billionaire. He's handling multimillion dollar deals on a daily basis and the last thing he has time for is to get tangled up in the charms of my maid."

The threat hung between them. Patrick wasn't stupid; he knew exactly what was going on with his own son. Catalina wasn't going to be a pawn in their little family feud. She had a job to do. She'd do it and be on her way in just a few months. Patrick and Will would still be bringing in money and she'd be long forgotten.

"I have no claim on your son, Mr. Rowling," she stated, thankful her voice was calm and not shaky. "I apologize if you think I do. We dated years ago but that's over."

Patrick nodded. "Let's make sure it stays that way. You have a place here and it's not in Will's life."

Even though he spoke the truth, a piece of her heart cracked a bit more over the fact.

"I'll get to work on these arrangements right away," she told Patrick, purposely dropping the topic of his son.

Catalina escaped the office, making it out to the hall before she leaned back against the wall and closed her eyes. Deep breaths in and out. She forced herself to remain calm.

If Patrick had known what happened in the laundry room days ago, he would've outright said so. He wasn't a man known for mincing words. But he knew something was up, which was all the more reason for her to stay clear of Will and his potent touch, his hypnotizing kisses and his spellbinding aqua eyes.

Pushing off the wall, Catalina made her way to the kitchen to speak to the head chef. They had a dinner to discuss and Catalina needed to focus on work, not the man who had the ability to destroy her heart for a second time.

He'd watched her bustle around for the past hour. She moved like a woman on a mission and she hadn't given him one passing glance.

Will wouldn't tolerate being ignored, especially by a woman he was so wrapped up in.

Slipping from the open living area where Cat was rearranging seating and helping the florist with new arrangements, Will snuck into the hallway and pulled his phone from his pocket. Shooting off a quick text, he stood in a doorway to the library and waited for a reply.

And waited. And waited.

Finally after nearly ten minutes, his phone vibrated in his hand. Cat hadn't dismissed him completely, but she wasn't accepting his offer of a private talk. What the hell? She was just outright saying no?

Unacceptable.

He sent another message.

Meet me once the guests arrive. You'll have a few minutes to spare once you're done setting up.

Will read over his message and quickly typed another. I'll be in the library.

Since he hadn't seen his father yet, Will shot his dad a message stating he may be a few minutes late. There was no way he could let another opportunity pass him by to be alone with Cat.

He'd worked like a madman these past few days and

hadn't even had a chance to stop by for a brief glimpse of her. He knew his desires ran deep, but he hadn't realized how deep until he had to go this long without seeing her, touching her, kissing her.

In the past two days Will had severed longstanding ties with another company that wasn't producing the results he wanted. Again he'd faced the wrath of his father, but yet again, Will didn't care. This was his time to reign over Rowling Energy and he was doing so by pushing forward, hard and fast. He wasn't tied to these companies the way his father was and Will intended to see the real estate division double its revenues in the next year.

But right now, he didn't want to think about finances, investments, real estate or oil. He wanted to focus on how fast he could get Cat in his arms once she entered the room. His body responded to the thought.

She wasn't even in the same room and he was aching for her.

Will had plans for the weekend, plans that involved her. He wanted to take her away somewhere she wouldn't expect, somewhere they could be alone and stop tiptoeing around the chemistry. Stolen kisses here and there were getting old. He felt like a horny teenager sneaking around his father's house copping a feel of his girl.

Will took a seat on the leather sofa near the floor-to-ceiling windows. He kept the lights off, save for a small lamp on the table near the entryway. That soft glow was enough; he didn't want to alert anyone who might be wandering outside that there was a rendezvous going on in here.

Finally after he felt as if he'd waited for an hour,

the door clicked softly and Cat appeared. She shut the door at her back, but didn't step farther into the room.

"I don't have much time," she told him.

He didn't need much…yet. Right now all he needed was one touch, just something to last until he could execute his weekend plans.

Will stood and crossed the spacious room, keeping his eyes locked on hers the entire time. With her back to the door, he placed a hand on either side of her face and leaned in.

His lips grazed over hers softly. "I've missed kissing you."

Cat's body trembled. When her hands came up to his chest, he thought she'd take the initiative and kiss him, but she pushed him away.

"I know I've given mixed signals," she whispered. "But this has to end. No matter how much I enjoy kissing you, no matter how I want you, I don't have the energy for this and I can't lose my j—"

Cat put a hand over her mouth, shook her head and glanced away.

"Your job?" he asked, taking hold of her wrist and prying her hand from her lips. "You think you're going to lose your job over what we have going?"

Her deep eyes jerked back to his. "We have nothing going, Will. Don't you get that? You can afford to mess around. You have nothing at stake here."

He had more than she realized.

"I need to get back to the guests. Bella and James just arrived."

He gripped her elbow before she could turn from him. "Stop. Give me two minutes."

Tucking her hair behind her ears, she nodded. "No more."

Will slid his thumb beneath her eyes. "You're exhausted. I don't like you working so hard, Cat."

"Some of us don't have a choice."

If she were his woman, she'd never work a day in her life.

Wait. What was he saying? She wasn't his woman and he wasn't looking to make her his lifelong partner, either. Marriage or any type of committed relationship was sure as hell not something he was ready to get into. Yes, he wanted her and wanted to spend time with her, but anything beyond that wasn't on his radar just yet.

Gliding his hands over her shoulders, he started to massage the tense muscles. His thumbs grazed the sides of her neck. Cat let out a soft moan as she let her head fall back against the door.

"What are you doing to me?" she groaned.

"Giving you the break you've needed."

Will couldn't tear his gaze from her parted lips, couldn't stop himself from fantasizing how she would look when he made love to her...when, not if.

"I really need to get back." Cat lifted her head and her lids fluttered open. "But this feels so good."

Will kept massaging. "I want to make you feel better," he muttered against her lips. "Let me take you home tonight, Cat."

On a sigh, she shook her head and reached up to squeeze his hands, halting his movements. "You have to know your father thinks something is going on with us."

Will stilled. "Did he say something to you?"

Her eyes darted away. "It doesn't matter. What matters is I'm a maid. You're a billionaire ready to take on the world. We have different goals, Will."

Yeah, and the object of his main goal was plastered against his body.

Will gripped her face between his palms and forced her to look straight at him. "What did he say?"

"I'm just fully aware of my role in this family and it's not as your mistress."

Fury bubbled through Will. "Patrick Rowling does not dictate my sex life and he sure as hell doesn't have a clue what's going on with us."

The sheen in her eyes only made Will that much angrier. How dare his father say anything? He'd done that years ago when Will had let him steamroll over his happiness before. Not again.

"There's nothing going on between us," she whispered.

Will lightened his touch, stroked her bottom lip with the pads of his thumbs. "Not yet, but there will be."

Capturing her lips beneath his, Will relaxed when Cat sighed into his mouth. Will pulled back because if he kept kissing her, he was going to want more and he'd be damned if he had Cat for the first time in his father's library.

When he took Cat to bed, it would be nowhere near Patrick Rowling or his house.

"Get back to work," he muttered against her lips. "We'll talk later."

"Will—"

"Later," he promised with another kiss. "I'm not done with you, Cat. I told you once, I've barely started."

He released her and let her leave while he stayed behind.

If he walked out now, people would know he'd been hiding with Cat. The last thing he ever intended was to get her in trouble or risk her job. He knew she took pride in what she did and the fact she was a perfectionist only made Will respect her more. She was so much more, though. She was loyal and determined. Qualities he admired.

Well, he was just as determined and his father would never interfere with his personal life again. They'd gone that round once before and Patrick had won. This time, Will intended to come out, not only on top, but with Rowling Energy and Cat both belonging to him.

Seven

Will stared over the rim of his tumbler as he sipped his scotch. The way Cat worked the room was something he'd seen in the past, but he hadn't fully appreciated the charm she portrayed toward others during such a difficult time.

There were moments where she'd been stealthy as she slipped in and out of the room, removing empty glasses and keeping the hors d'oeuvre trays filled. Will was positive others hadn't even noticed her, but he did. He noticed every single thing about her.

The dinner was due to be served in thirty minutes and the guests had mostly arrived. Bella stood off to the side with her brother Gabriel, his arm wrapped around her shoulders.

"Your maid is going to get a complex if you keep drilling holes into her."

Will stiffened at James's words. His brother came to stand beside him, holding his own tumbler of scotch.

"I'm not drilling holes," Will replied, tossing back the last of his drink. He welcomed the burn and turned to set the glass on the accent table. "I'm making sure she's okay."

James's brief laugh had Will gritting his teeth to remain quiet and to prevent himself from spewing more defensive reasons as to why he'd been staring at Cat.

"She's used to working, Will. I'd say she's just fine."

Will turned to face his twin. "Did you come over here to hassle me or did you actually want to say something important?"

James's smile spread across his face. Will knew that smile, dammit. He'd thrown it James's way when he'd been in knots over Bella.

"Shut up," Will said as he turned back to watch Cat.

If his brother already had that knowing grin, then Will's watching Cat wouldn't matter at this point. She was working too damn hard. She'd been here all day to make sure the house was perfect for the Montoros and she was still busting her butt to make everyone happy. The chef was really busting it, too, behind the scenes. Cat was definitely due for a much needed relaxing day away from all of this.

"You appear to be plotting," James commented. "But right now I want to discuss what Dad is in such a mood about."

Will threw his brother a glance. "He's Patrick Rowling. Does he need a reason?"

"Not necessarily, but he was a bit gruffer than usual when I spoke with him earlier."

Will watched his father across the room as the man approached Bella and Gabriel. As they all spoke, Will knew his father was diplomatic enough to put on a front of being compassionate. He wouldn't be his stiff, grouchy self with those two.

"I may have made some business decisions he wasn't happy with," Will stated simply.

"Business? Yeah, that will do it." James sighed and finished his scotch. "He put you in charge, so he can't expect you to run every decision by him."

"That's what I told him. I'm not one of his employees, I'm his son and I'm the CEO of Rowling Energy now."

"Plus you're trying to seduce his maid," James added with a chuckle. "You're going to get grounded."

Will couldn't help but smile. "You're such an ass."

"It's fun to see the tables turned and you squirming over a woman for once."

"I'm not squirming, dammit," Will muttered.

But he wouldn't deny he was using Cat as another jab at his father. Yes, he wanted Cat and always had, but if being with her still irritated the old man, so much the better.

Part of him felt guilty for the lack of respect for his father, but that went both ways and the moment Patrick had issued his ultimatum years ago, Will had vowed then and there to gain back everything he deserved, no matter what the cost to his relationship with his father.

Bella's oldest brother, Rafe, and his very pregnant wife, Emily, crossed the room, heading for Will and James. Since he'd abdicated, Rafe and Emily had lived in Key West. But they'd traveled back to be with the family during this difficult time.

"This was a really nice thing for Patrick to do," Rafe stated as he wrapped an arm around his wife's waist. "Losing Isabella has been hard."

"I'm sorry for your loss," Will said. "She was definitely a fighter and Alma is a better place because of her."

"She was quite stubborn," Emily chimed in with a smile. "But we'll get through this because the Montoros are strong."

Will didn't think this was the appropriate time to bring up the subject of Rafe resigning from his duties before his coronation. It was the proverbial elephant in the room.

"I'm going to save my wife from my father," James told them. "Excuse me."

Rafe and Emily were talking about the funeral—how many people had turned out and how supportive the country was in respecting their time of mourning. But Will was only half listening. Cat glanced his way once and that's all it took for his heart to kick up and his body to respond. She didn't smile, she merely locked those dark eyes on him as if she knew his every thought.

Tension crackled between them and everyone else in the room disappeared from his world. Nobody existed but Cat and he knew without a doubt she would agree to his proposal.

He wouldn't accept no for an answer.

Her feet were absolutely screaming. Her back wasn't faring much better. The Montoros lingered longer than she'd expected and Catalina had stuck around an hour after the guests had left.

This fourteen-hour workday would certainly yield a nice chunk of change, but right now all Catalina could think of was her bed, which she hoped to fall into the moment she got home. She may not even take the time to peel out of her clothes.

Catalina nearly wept as she walked toward her car.

She'd parked in the back of the estate near the detached garage where Patrick kept his sporty cars that he only brought out on special occasions. The motion light popped on as she approached her vehicle.

Instantly she spotted Will sitting on a decorative bench along the garage wall. Catalina stopped and couldn't help but smile.

"Are you hiding?" she asked as she started forward again.

"Waiting." He unfolded that tall, broad frame and started coming toward her. "I know you're exhausted, but I just wanted to ask something."

Catalina crossed her arms and stared up at him. "You could've called or texted me your question."

"I could've," he agreed with a slight nod. "But you could say no too easily. I figure if you're looking me in the eye—"

"You think I can't resist you?" she laughed.

Exhaustion might have been consuming her and clouding her judgment, but there was still something so irresistible and charming about this overbearing man...and something calculating as well. He'd purposely waited for her, to catch her at a weak moment. He must really want something major.

"I'm hoping." He reached out, tucking her hair behind her ears before his fingertips trailed down her jawline. "I want to take you somewhere tomorrow afternoon. Just us, on my yacht for a day out."

Catalina wanted to give in to him, she wanted to forget all the reasons they shouldn't be together in any way. She wished her head and her heart would get on the same page where Will Rowling was concerned. She had goals, she had a job she needed to keep in order to reach those goals...yet everything about Will made her want to entertain the idea of letting him in, even if just for one night.

"I even have the perfect spot chosen for a swim," he added, resting his hands on her shoulders. Squeezing her tense muscles, Will smiled. "I'll be a total gentleman."

"A total gentleman?" Catalina couldn't help but laugh. "Then why are you so eager to go?"

"Maybe I think it's time someone gives back to you." His hands stilled as he held her gaze and she realized he wasn't joking at all. "And maybe it's time you see that I'm a changed man."

Her heart tumbled in her chest. "I'm so tired, Will. I'm pretty sure I'm going to spend the next two days sleeping."

"You won't have to do a thing," he promised. "I'll bring the food. All you have to do is wear a swimsuit. I promise this will be a day of total relaxation and pampering."

Catalina sighed. "Will, your father—"

"He's not invited."

She laughed again. "I'm serious."

"I am, too."

Will backed her up to her car and towered over her with such an intense gaze, Catalina knew she was fighting a losing battle.

"This has nothing to do with my father, your job or our differences." His strong jaw set firm, he pressed his gloriously hard body against hers as he stared into her eyes. "I want to spend time with you, Cat. I've finally got my sights set on what is important to me and I'm not letting you get away again. Not without a fight."

"That's what scares me." She whispered the confession.

"There's nothing to be afraid of."

"Said the big bad wolf."

Will smiled, dropped his hands and eased back. "No pressure, Cat. I want to spend time with you, but if you're not ready, I understand. I'm not going anywhere."

The man knew exactly what to say and his delivery was flawless. In his line of work, Will was a master at getting people to see things his way, to ensure he got what he wanted at the end of the day.

No matter what common sense tried to tell her, Catalina wasn't about to start in on a battle she had no chance of winning.

"I'll go," she told him.

The smile that spread across his face was half shadowed by the slant of the motion lights, but she knew all too well how beautiful and sexy the gesture was.

"I'll pick you up at your apartment around noon," he told her. "Now, go home. I'm going to follow you to make sure you get there safely since you're so tired."

"That's not necessary."

Will shrugged. "Maybe not, but I wasn't kidding when I said someone needed to take care of you and pamper you for a change. I'm not coming in. I'll just follow, and then be on my way home."

"I live in the opposite direction from your house," she argued.

"We could've been halfway to your flat by now." He slid his arm around her and tugged on her door handle. "Get in, stop fighting me and let's just save time. You know I'll win in the end anyway."

That's precisely what she feared the most. Will having a win over her could prove more damaging than the last time she'd let him in, but she wanted to see this new side of him. She wanted to take a day and do absolutely nothing but be catered to.

Catalina eased behind the wheel and let Will shut her door. Tomorrow would tell her one of two things: either she was ready to move on and just be his friend or she wanted more with him than stolen kisses behind closed doors.

Worry and panic flooded Catalina as she realized she already knew what tomorrow would bring.

Will had been meaning to see his niece, Maisey, and this morning he was making her his top priority. Before he went to pick up Cat for their outing, he wanted to surprise his adorable niece with a gift…the first of many. He had a feeling this little girl was going to be spoiled, which was better than a child being ignored.

Maisey Rowling would want for nothing. Will's brother had given up being a playboy and was growing into his family-man role rather nicely, and Bella was the perfect stepmother to the infant. Will figured since he and his twin were growing closer, he'd stop in and offer support to James. This complete one-eighty in lifestyles had to be a rough transition for James, but he had Bella and the two were completely in love. And they both loved sweet Maisey.

A slight twinge of jealousy speared through Will, but not over the fact that his brother had married Bella. There had been no chemistry between Will and Bella. She was sweet and stunning, but Will only had eyes for one woman.

The jealousy stemmed from the thought of his brother settling down with his own family. Will hadn't given much thought to family before. He'd been raised to focus solely on taking over Rowling Energy one day.

Will tapped on the etched glass front door to James and Bella's temporary home. They were living here until they knew for sure where they wanted to be permanently. They were in the middle of renovating the old farmhouse that belonged to the Montoros and James had mentioned that they'd probably end up there.

But for now, this house was ideal. It was near the beach, near the park and near Bella's family. Family was important to the Montoros…and yet Will was still thrilled he'd dodged that clan.

The door swung open and Bella greeted him with a smile. "Will, this is a surprise. Come on in."

Clutching the doll he'd brought as a present, Will stepped over the threshold. "I should've called, but I really thought of this last-minute."

Bella smoothed her blond hair behind her shoulders. "This is fine. Maisey and James are in the living room. They just finished breakfast and they're watching a movie."

Her blue eyes darted down to his hands. "I'm assuming that's for Maisey?"

Will nodded. "I haven't played the good uncle yet. Figured it was time I started spoiling her."

Bella's smile lit up her face. "She's going to love it."

The thought of being married to this woman did nothing for Will. Yes, she was stunning, but he'd never felt the stirrings of lust or need when he'd been around her. Their fathers never should have attempted to arrange their engagement, but thankfully everything had worked out for the best…at least where Bella and James were concerned. They were a unified family now.

The thought of his black sheep, playboy brother snuggling up with a baby girl and watching some kid flick was nearly laughable. But Will also knew that once James had learned he had a child, his entire life had changed and his priorities had taken on a whole new order, Maisey being at the top.

Bella led Will through a wide, open-arched doorway to a spacious living room. Two pale yellow sofas sat facing each other with a squat, oversized table between them. An array of coloring books and crayons were scattered over the top of the glossy surface.

James sat on one of the sofas, legs sprawled out before him with Maisey on his lap. James's short hair was all in disarray. He still wore his pajama bottoms and no shirt, and Maisey had a little pink nightgown on; it was obvious they were enjoying a morning of laziness.

As Will stepped farther into the room, James glanced over and smiled. "Hey, brother. What brings you out?"

Bella sat at the end of the couch at her husband's feet. Maisey crawled over her father's legs and settled herself onto Bella's lap. Will looked at his niece and found himself staring into those signature Rowling aqua eyes. No denying who this baby's father was.

"I brought something for Maisey." Will crossed the room and sat on the edge of the coffee table. "Hey, sweetheart. Do you like dolls?"

What if she didn't like it? What if she didn't like him? Dammit. He should've planned better and called to see what Maisey actually played with. He'd just assumed a little girl would like a tiny stuffed doll.

"Her dress matches your nightgown," Bella said softly to the little girl.

Maisey kept her eyes on him as she reached for the toy. Instantly the blond hair went into Maisey's mouth.

"She likes it." James laughed. "Everything goes into her mouth these days."

Will continued to stare at his niece. Children were

one area where he had no clue, but if James said Maisey liked it, then Will had to assume she did.

James swung his legs to the floor and leaned forward. "You hungry?" he asked. "We still have some pancakes and bacon in the kitchen."

"No, I'm good. I'm getting ready to pick up Cat, so I can't stay anyway."

James's brows lifted as he shot Bella a look. "Is this a date?"

Will hadn't intended on telling anyone, but in growing closer with James over the past couple months, he realized he wanted this bond with his twin. Besides, after their conversation last night, James pretty much knew exactly where Will stood in regards to Cat.

He trusted James, that had never been an issue. The issue they'd had wedged between them stemmed from their father always doting on one brother, molding him into a disciple, while ostracizing the other one.

"I'm taking her out on my yacht," Will told him. "We're headed to one of the islands for the day. I'm hoping for total seclusion. Most tourists don't know about them."

There was a small cluster of islands off the coast of Alma. He planned on taking her to Isla de Descanso. The island's name literally meant Island of Relaxation. Cat deserved to be properly pampered and he was going to be the man to give her all of her needs…every single one.

"Sounds romantic." Bella shifted Maisey on her lap as she stared at Will. "I wasn't aware you and Catalina were getting more serious."

James laughed. "I think they've been sneaking."

"We're not serious and we're not sneaking," Will

defended himself. "Okay, fine. We were sneaking, but she's private and she's still leery of me."

"You can't blame her," James added.

Will nodded. "I don't, which is why we need this time away from everything. Plus she's working like crazy for Dad and she's never appreciated."

James snorted. "He barely appreciates his sons. You think he appreciates a maid? I was worried when he moved into my old house. I tried to warn her, but she said she could handle it and she needed the job."

Will hated the thought of her having to work. Hated how much she pushed herself for little to no praise and recognition.

"Well, I appreciate her," Bella chimed in. "I saw how hard she worked the dinner last night. I can't imagine the prep that she and the cooks went through, plus the cleanup after. Catalina is a dedicated, hard worker."

"She won't stay forever," James stated as he leaned over and ruffled Maisey's hair.

Will sat up straighter. "What do you mean?"

His brother's eyes came back to meet his. "I'm just saying someone who is such a perfectionist and self-disciplined surely has a long-term goal in mind. I can't imagine she'll want to play maid until she's old and gray. She hinted a few times when she worked for me that she hoped to one day leave Alma."

Leave Alma? The thought hadn't even crossed Will's mind. Would Cat really go somewhere else? Surely not. Her mother still worked here. She used to work for Patrick, but years ago she had suddenly quit and gone to work for another prominent family. Cat had been with the Rowlings for five years, but James was right. Someone as vibrant as Cat wouldn't want to dust and wash sheets her entire life. He'd already seen the toll her endless hours were taking on her.

Will came to his feet, suddenly more eager than ever to see her, to be alone with her. "I better get going. I just wanted to stop by and see Maisey before I headed out."

James stood as well. "I'll walk you to the door."

Bidding a goodbye to Bella and Maisey, Will followed his brother to the foyer.

"Don't say a word about Cat and me," Will said.

Gripping the doorknob, James nodded. "I'm not saying a word. I already know Dad would hate the idea and he's interfered enough in our personal lives lately. And I'm not judging you and Catalina. I actually think you two are a good match."

"Thanks, man, but don't let this happily-ever-after stuff you have going on filter into my world. I'm just spending time with Cat. That's all." Will gave his brother a one-armed man hug. "I'll talk to you next week."

Will headed toward his car, more than ready to pick up Cat and get this afternoon started. He planned to be in complete control, but he'd let her set the tone. As much as he wanted her, he wasn't going to pressure her and he wasn't going to deceive her.

Yes, there was the obvious appeal of the fact that his father would hate Will bedding the maid, but he wouldn't risk her job that way even to get petty revenge on his domineering father.

Besides, Cat was so much more than a romp. He couldn't figure out exactly what she was…and that irritated him.

But now he had another worry. What was Cat's ultimate goal in life? Would she leave Alma and pursue something more meaningful? And why did he care? He wasn't looking for a ring on his finger and he wasn't about to place one on hers, either.

Still, the fact that she could leave bothered him more than he cared to admit.

Will pushed those thoughts aside. Right now, for today, all he was concerned with was Cat and being alone with her. All other world problems would have to wait.

Eight
<u></u>

Nerves kicked around in Catalina's belly as she boarded the yacht. Which seemed like such a simple word for this pristine, massive floating vessel. The fact that the Rowlings had money was an understatement, but to think that Will could own something this amazing…it boggled her mind. She knew he would make a name for himself, knew he'd climb to the top of Rowling Energy. There was never any doubt which twin Patrick was grooming for the position.

But she wasn't focusing on or even thinking of Patrick today. Will wanted her to relax, wanted her to enjoy her day off, and she was going to take full advantage.

Turning toward Will, Catalina laughed as he stepped on board. "I'm pretty sure my entire flat would fit on this deck."

Near the bow, she surveyed the wide, curved outdoor seating complete with plush white pillows. There was even a hot tub off to the side. Catalina couldn't even imagine soaking in that warm water out under the stars. This yacht screamed money, relaxation...and seduction.

She'd voluntarily walked right into the lion's den.

"Let me show you around." Will took hold of her elbow and led her to the set of steps that went below deck. "The living quarters are even more impressive."

Catalina clutched her bag and stepped down as Will gestured for her to go first. The amount of space in the open floor plan below was shocking. It was even grander than she'd envisioned. A large king-sized bed sat in the distance and faced a wall of curved windows that overlooked the sparkling water. Waking up to a sunrise every morning would be heavenly. Waking up with your lover beside you would simply be the proverbial icing on the cake.

No. She couldn't think of Will as her lover or icing on her cake. She was here for a restful day and nothing else. Nookie could not play a part in this because she had no doubt the second he got her out of her clothes, she'd have no defense against him. She needed to stay on guard.

A deep, glossy mahogany bar with high stools separated the kitchen from a living area. The living area had a mounted flat-screen television and leather chairs that looked wide enough for at least two people.

The glossy fixtures and lighting only added to the perfection of the yacht. It all screamed bachelor and money...perfect for Will Rowling.

"You've done well for yourself," she told him as she placed her tote bag on a barstool. "I'm impressed."

Will's sidelong smile kicked up her heart rate. They hadn't even pulled away from the dock and he was already getting to her. This was going to be a day full of her willpower battling her emotions and she didn't know if she'd have the strength to fight off Will's advances.

Who was she kidding? Catalina already knew that if Will tried anything she would succumb to his charms. She'd known this the moment she'd accepted his invitation. But that didn't mean she'd drop her wall of defenses so easily. He'd seriously hurt her before and if he wanted to show her what a changed man he was now, she was going to make him work for it.

"Did you think I was taking you out in a canoe for the day?"

"I guess I hadn't given much thought to the actual boat," she replied, resting her arm on the smooth, curved edge of the bar. "I was too worried about your actions."

"Worried you'd enjoy them too much?" he asked with a naughty grin.

"More like concerned I'd have to deflate your ego," she countered with a matching smile. "You're not seriously going to start putting the moves on me now, are you?"

Will placed a hand over his heart. "You wound me, Cat. I'm at least going to get this boat on course before I rip your clothes off."

Catalina's breath caught in her throat.

Will turned and mounted the steps to go above deck, and then froze and threw a sexy grin over his shoulder. "Relax, Cat. I won't do anything you don't want."

The playful banter had just taken a turn, a sharp turn that sent shivers racing through her entire body. Was she prepared for sex with this man? That's what everything leading up to this moment boiled down to.

Cat would be lying to herself if she tried to say she

didn't want Will physically. That had been proven each time he'd kissed her recently.

I won't do anything you don't want, he'd said.

And that was precisely what scared her the most.

With the ocean breeze sliding across his face, Will welcomed the spittle of spray, the taste of salt on his lips. He needed to get a damn grip. He hadn't meant to be so teasing with Cat.

Okay, he had, but he hadn't meant for her to get that panicked look on her face. He knew full well she was battling with herself where he was concerned. There wasn't a doubt in his mind she wanted him physically and that was easy to obtain. But there was part of Will that wanted her to see that he wasn't at all the same man he used to be.

She would get to see that side of him today. He intended to do everything for her, to prove to her just how appreciated she was and how valued. Will had fully stocked the yacht when he'd had this idea a couple days ago. He'd known he would take her out at some point, but it wasn't until he saw her working the crowd, with circles under her eyes and a smile on her face at the dinner last night, that he decided to invite her right away.

With all of the recent upheaval in Alma—the Montoro monarchy drama and Isabella's passing, not to mention Will's taking the reins of Rowling Energy—there was just too much life getting in the way of what he wanted. Too many distractions interfering with his main goal…and his goal was to have Cat.

He may be the good son, the twin who was raised to follow the rules and not question authority. But Will wasn't about to make the same mistake with Cat as he had in the past. The moment he'd let her walk away years ago, he'd already started plotting to get her back. Then the whole debacle with Bella had happened and Will knew more than ever that it was time to make his move with Rowling Energy and Cat.

Spending the day together on his yacht, however, was something totally unrelated to everything else that had happened in their past. Today was all about them and nothing or nobody else. Everything that happened with Cat from here on out was going to be her call…he may just silently nudge and steer her in the right direction. Those initial kisses had reignited the spark they'd left burning long ago and he knew without a doubt that she felt just as passionate as he did.

He didn't blame her one bit for being leery. He'd done some major damage before and she wouldn't let him forget it anytime soon. Not that he could. He'd never forget that look on her face when he'd told her they'd been a mistake and then walked away. That moment had played over and over in his mind for the past several years. Knowing he'd purposely hurt Cat wasn't something he was likely to ever forget.

Still, if she ever discovered the truth, would she see that he'd done it for her? He'd best keep that secret to himself and just stay on course with his plan now. At least she was here, she was talking and she was coming around. The last thing Will wanted to do was rehash the past when they could be spending their time concentrating on the here and now.

Will steered the yacht toward the private island not too far from Alma. In just under an hour he'd have Cat on a beach with a picnic. He wondered when the last time was that she'd had someone do something like that for her, but quickly dismissed the thought. If another man had pampered her, Will sure as hell didn't want to know.

Of course, there was no man in her life now. Will was the one kissing her, touching her. She was his for at least today so he needed to make the most of every moment they were alone. He truly hoped the tiny island was deserted. He'd come here a few times to think, to get away from all the pressure and stress. Only once had he run into other people.

Cat stayed below for the duration of the trip. Perhaps she was trying to gather her own thoughts as well. Maybe she was avoiding him because she thought that taking her out to a private island for sex was so cliché, so easy to read into.

But for reasons Will didn't want to admit or even think about, this day was so much more than sex. *Cat* was more than sex. Yes, he wanted her in the fiercest way imaginable, but he also wanted more from her… he just didn't know what.

No, that was wrong. The first thing he wanted was for her to see him in a different light. He wanted her to see the good in him she'd seen when they'd grown up together, when they'd laughed and shared secrets with each other. He wanted her to see that he wasn't the monster who had ripped her heart out and diminished their relationship into ashes with just a few damning words.

Perhaps this outing wasn't just about him proving to her what a changed man he was, but for him to try to figure out what the hell to do next and how far he wanted to take things with her once they got back to reality.

When he finally pulled up to the dock and secured the yacht, he went below deck. He hoped the last forty-five minutes had given Cat enough time to see that he wasn't going to literally jump her. The playful banter had taken a sexual turn, but he wasn't sorry. He was only sorry Cat hadn't come up once to see him. This initial space was probably for the best. After all, today was the first time they'd been fully alone and not sneaking into the bathroom or laundry area of his father's home for a make-out session.

Yeah, his seduction techniques needed a bit of work to say the least. But he'd had four years to get control over just how he wanted to approach things once he finally got his Cat alone. And now he was ready.

As he stepped below, Will braced his hands on the trim overhead and froze on the last step. Cat lay sideways, curled into a ball on his bed. The innocent pose shouldn't have his body responding, but…well, he was a guy and this woman had had him tied in knots for years.

Will had wanted Cat in his bed for too long. All his fantasies involved the bed in his house, but the yacht would do. At this point he sure as hell wasn't going to be picky. He'd waited too damn long for this and he was going to take each moment he could get, no matter the surroundings.

And the fact that she was comfortable enough to rest here spoke volumes for how far they'd come. Just a few weeks ago he'd kissed her as if she was his next breath and she'd run away angry. Though Will was smart enough to know her anger stemmed from arousal.

Passion and hate…there was such a fine line between the two.

Slowly, Will crossed the open area and pulled a small throw from the narrow linen closet. Gently placing the thin blanket over her bare legs and settling it around her waist, Will watched the calm rise and fall of her chest. She was so peaceful, so relaxed and not on her guard.

For the first time in a long time, Will was finally seeing the woman he knew years ago, the woman who was more trusting, less cautious.

Of course, he'd helped shape her into the vigilant person she was today. Had he not made such bad choices when they'd been together the first time, perhaps she wouldn't have to feel so guarded all the time. Perhaps she'd smile more and laugh the way she used to.

Cat shifted, let out a throaty moan and blinked up at Will. Then her eyes widened as she sat straight up.

"Oh my. Was I asleep?"

Will laughed, crossing his arms over his chest. "Or you were playing dead."

Cat smoothed her short hair away from her face and glanced toward the wall of windows. "I was watching the water. I was so tired, so I thought I'd just lie here and enjoy the scenery."

"That was the whole point in having my bed right there. It's a breathtaking view."

When she turned her attention back to him, she gasped. That's right, he hadn't been discussing the water. The view of the woman was much more enticing.

"Why don't you use the restroom to freshen up and change into your suit?" he suggested. "I'll get our lunch set up."

The bright smile spreading across her face had something unfamiliar tugging on his heart. He may not be able to label what was going on between them, but he couldn't afford to be emotional about it.

Dammit. He didn't even know what to feel, how to act anymore. He wanted her, but he wasn't thinking of forever. He wanted now. He needed her to see he was a different man, yet he was more than ready to throw this relationship into his father's face.

Sticking to business would have been best; at least he knew exactly what he was getting into with real estate and oil. With Cat, he had no clue and the fact that she had him so tied in knots without even trying was terrifying.

Once his mission had been clear—to win back Cat to prove he could and to show his father who was in charge. But then, somewhere along the way, Will had shifted into needing Cat to see the true person he'd come to be, the man who still had feelings for her and cared for her on a level even he couldn't understand.

Cat came to her feet and started folding the throw. "I'm sorry I fell asleep on you."

Stepping forward and closing the space between them, Will pulled the blanket from her hands, wadded it up and threw it into the corner. "You aren't cleaning. You aren't folding, dusting, doing dishes. Your only job is to relax. If you want a nap, take a nap. The day is yours. The cleaning is up to me. Got it?"

Her eyes widened as she glanced at the crumpled blanket. "Are you just going to leave that there?"

Will took her chin between his thumb and finger, forcing her to look only at him. "You didn't answer my question."

Her wide, dark eyes drew him in as she merely nodded. "I can't promise, but I'll try."

Unable to help himself, Will smacked a kiss on her lips and pulled back as a grin spread across his face. "Go freshen up and meet me on the top deck."

Will watched as Cat grabbed her bag off the barstool and crossed to the bathroom. Once the door clicked shut, he let out a breath.

He'd sworn nobody would ever control him or hold any power over him again. Yet here was a petite, doe-eyed maid who had more power over him than any business magnate or his father ever could.

Will raked a hand through his hair. He'd promised Cat a day of relaxation and he intended to deliver just that. If she wasn't ready for more, then he'd have to pull all of his self-control to the surface and honor her wishes.

What had he gotten himself into?

Nine

Maybe bringing this particular swimsuit had been a bad idea. When she'd grabbed the two-piece black bikini, Catalina had figured she'd make Will suffer a little. But, by wearing so little and having him so close, she was the one suffering.

Catalina pulled on a simple red wrap dress from her own collection and slipped on her silver flip-flops.

One glance in the mirror and she laughed. The bikini would at least draw attention away from the haggard lines beneath her eyes and the pallor of her skin. Over the past few months, if she wasn't working for James or Patrick, she was working for herself getting her stock ready to showcase when the opportunity presented itself. She believed in being prepared and the moment she saw an opening with any fashion design firm, she was going to be beating down their doors and promoting her unique styles.

Catalina tossed her discarded clothes back into her tote and looked around to make sure she hadn't left anything lying around in the bathroom. Could such a magnificent room be a simple, mundane bathroom?

With the polished silver fixtures, the glass wall shower and sparkling white tile throughout, Catalina had taken a moment to appreciate all the beauty before she'd started changing. The space screamed dominance...male dominance.

Will was pulling out all the stops today. He'd purposely invited her aboard his yacht because he knew that given her love of water she'd never be able to say no. He was right. Anything that got her away from her daily life and into the refreshing ocean was a no-brainer.

Exiting the bathroom, Catalina dropped her bag next to the door and headed up to the top deck. The sun warmed her skin instantly as she turned and spotted Will in a pair of khaki board shorts and a navy shirt he'd left completely unbuttoned. The man wasn't playing fair...which she assumed was his whole plan from the start.

Fine. She had a bikini and boobs. Catalina figured she'd already won this battle before it began. Men were the simplest of creatures.

Will had transformed the seating area into a picnic. A red throw covered the floor, a bucket with ice and wine sat to one side and Will was pulling fruit from a basket.

"Wow. You really know how to set the stage."

He threw her a smile. "Depends on the audience."

"It's just me, so no need to go to all the trouble." She edged around the curving seats and stood just to the side of the blanket. "I'd be happy with a simple salad."

"There is a need to go to all this trouble," he corrected her as he continued to pull more food from the basket. "Have a seat. The strawberries are fresh, the wine is chilled and I have some amazing dishes for us."

Catalina couldn't turn down an invitation like that. She eased down onto the thick blanket and reached for a strawberry. She'd eaten three by the time Will came to sit beside her.

With his back resting against the sofa, he lifted his knee and wrapped his arm around it. "I have a variety of cheese, salmon, baguettes, a tangy salad my chef makes that will make you weep and for dessert…"

He reached over and pulled the silver lid from the dish. "Your favorite."

Catalina gasped as she stared at the pineapple upside-down cheesecake. "You remembered?"

"Of course I did." He set the lid back down. "There's not a detail about you that I've forgotten, Cat."

When she glanced over at him, she found his eyes locked on hers and a small smile dancing around his lips. "I remembered how much you love strawberries and that you will always pick a fruity dessert over a chocolate one. I also recall how much you love salmon, so I tried to incorporate all of your favorites into this lunch."

Strawberry in hand, she froze. "But you just asked me last night. How did you get all of this together?"

Will shrugged and made up a plate for her. "I knew I wanted to take you out on my yacht at some point. I was hoping for soon, but it wasn't until yesterday that I realized how hard you've been working."

He passed her the plate with a napkin. "You need this break and I want to be the one to give it to you. Besides, there's a lot I can do with a few hours and the right connections."

Catalina smiled as she picked up a cube of cheese.

"I'm sure your chef was making the cheesecake before the crack of dawn this morning."

Will shrugged. "Maybe. He did have nearly everything else done by the time I headed out to James and Bella's house this morning."

"You visited James already, too?"

Will settled back with his own plate and forked up a bite of salmon before answering. "I wanted to see Maisey before James heads back out on the road for football. I haven't really bonded with her much, especially with the strain on my relationship with James. But we're getting there and I wanted to see my niece. I'm sure she and Bella will accompany James on the road when they can."

Something inside Catalina warmed at the image of Will playing the doting, spoiling uncle. A family was definitely in her future plans, but knowing Will was taking an active part in little Maisey's life awakened something in her she hadn't yet uncovered.

But no. Will couldn't be father material. He wasn't even husband material. No matter how much, at one time, she'd wished he was. Will was a career-minded, power-driven man who valued family, but he didn't scream minivan and family portraits.

"How did the bonding go?" she asked, trying to concentrate on her food and not the fact that the image had been placed in her head of Will with a baby. Was there anything sexier than a big, powerful man holding an innocent child?

"She seemed to like the doll I brought her."

Of course he'd brought a doll. Now his "aww" level just exploded. Why did the man have to be so appealing on every single level? She didn't want to find him even more irresistible. She couldn't afford to let her heart get tangled up with him again.

Catalina couldn't handle the struggle within her. "You took her a doll? Did your assistant or someone on your staff go buy it?"

Will glanced at her, brows drawn in. "No, I bought it the other day when I was out and just got the chance to take it to her this morning. Why?"

The man was gaining ground and scaling that wall of defenses she'd so carefully erected. And in unexpected ways. He'd wanted to have a special moment with his niece, which had nothing to do with Catalina. Yet here she sat, on his boat, eating her favorite foods that he'd remembered while listening to him talk of his love for his baby niece.

Why was she keeping him at a distance again?

Oh, yeah. That broken heart four years ago.

They ate the rest of their lunch in silence, except when she groaned like a starved woman as she inhaled her piece of cheesecake. As promised, Will cleaned up the mess and took everything back down to the galley. Once he returned, he extended his hand to her.

"Ready to go for a walk?" he asked.

Catalina placed her hand in his, allowing him to pull her up. "I'm not sure I can walk after that, but I can waddle. I'm pretty stuffed."

Will laughed as he led her from the boat. Once they stepped off the wooden dock, Catalina slipped out of her sandals to walk on the warm, sandy beach. The sand wasn't too hot to burn her feet and as the soft grains shifted beneath her, she found herself smiling. She couldn't remember the last time she'd done absolutely nothing by way of working in one form or another.

"I hope that smile has something to do with me,"

Will stated, again slipping his hand into hers as they walked along the shoreline.

"I'm just happy today. I needed a break and I guess I didn't realize it."

"From one workaholic to another, I recognized the signs."

His confession had her focusing on the words and not how powerful and wonderful his fingers felt laced with hers.

"I never thought you took a break," she replied.

Catalina looked at all the tiny seashells lining the shore and made a mental note to find some beautiful ones to take back with her.

"I've had breaks," he replied. "Not many, mind you, but I know when I need to step back so I don't get burnt out."

Catalina turned her face toward the ocean. She'd been burnt out on cleaning since she started. But sewing and designing, she could never imagine falling out of love with her passion.

They walked along in silence and Catalina let her thoughts run wild. What would've happened between them had Will not succumbed to his father's demands that he drop her? Would they have these romantic moments often? Would he make her take breaks from life and put work on hold for her?

She really couldn't see any of that, to be honest. Will was still under his father's thumb, whether he admitted it or not. He'd been at the house most mornings going over Rowling Energy stuff, which Catalina assumed was really just Will checking in.

"Why did you give up on us before?" she asked before she could think better of it.

Will stopped, causing Catalina to stop as well. She dropped his hand and turned to fully face him.

"Never mind," she said, shaking her head. "It doesn't matter now."

The muscle in Will's jaw ticked as he stared back at her. "It does matter. Our breakup damaged both of us."

Catalina pushed her hair behind her ears, which was useless as the wind kept whipping it out. "I'm pretty sure you weren't damaged, seeing as how ending our relationship was your decision."

When she started to walk on, Will gripped her elbow. "You think seeing you move on and dating another man wasn't crushing to me? You think knowing you were in another man's arms, maybe even in his bed, didn't tear me up?"

She'd tried not to think about Will when she threw herself into another relationship to mask the hurt. From the angst in his tone and the fire in his eyes, though... *had* Will been hurt over the breakup? How could that be when he was the one who had ultimately ended things? Did he not want the split? Was he doing it to appease his father? If that was the case then she was doubly angry that he hadn't fought for them.

"You thought I'd sit around and cry myself to sleep over you?" she retorted, refusing to feel guilt over a decision he'd made for both of them.

And so what if she'd shed tears over him? Many tears, in fact, but there was no way she'd admit such a thing. As far as he knew she was made of steel and stronger than her emotions.

"Besides, you had moved on quite nicely. You ended up in a relationship with a Montoro princess."

Dammit. She hadn't meant for that little green monster to slip out. Catalina knew just how much Bella and

James loved each other, yet there was that sliver of jealousy at the fact that Will had been all ready to put a ring on Bella's finger first.

Will laughed. "That fake engagement was a mistake from all angles. James and Bella have found something she never would've had with me."

"But you would've married her."

And that fact still bothered Catalina. She hated the jealousy she'd experienced when she'd discovered Will was engaged. Not that she ever thought she stood a chance, but how could anyone compete with someone as beautiful and sexy as Bella Montoro? She was not only royalty, she was a humanitarian with a good heart.

On a sigh, Catalina started walking again, concentrating on the shells lining the shore. "It doesn't matter, honestly. I shouldn't have brought it up."

She reached down to pick up an iridescent shell, smoothing her finger over the surface to swipe away the wet sand. Catalina slid the shell into the small hidden pocket on the side of her dress and kept walking, very much aware of Will at her side. He was a smart man not to deny her last statement. They both knew he would've married Bella because that's what his father had wanted. Joining the fortunes of the two dynamic families was Patrick's dream…the wrong son had fallen for the beauty, though.

They walked a good bit down the deserted beach. Catalina had no idea how Will had managed to find such a perfect place with total privacy, but he had no doubt planned this for a while. On occasion he would stop and find a shell for her, wordlessly handing it to her as they walked on. The tension was heavier now that she'd opened up the can of worms. She wished she'd kept her feelings to herself.

What did it matter if he was going to marry Bella? What man wouldn't want to spend his life with her? Not only that, had Catalina truly thought Will would remain single? Had she believed he was so exclusively focused on work that he wouldn't want to settle down and start the next generation of Rowling heirs?

The warm sun disappeared behind a dark cloud as the wind kicked into high gear. Catalina looked up and suppressed a groan. Of course a dark cloud would hover over her. The ominous sky was starting to match her mood.

"Should we head back to the yacht?" she asked, trying to tuck her wayward strands of hair behind her ears as she fought against the wind.

"I don't think it's going to do anything major. The forecast didn't show rain."

That nasty cloud seemed to indicate otherwise, but she wasn't going to argue. They already had enough on their plate.

Catalina glanced through the foliage, squinting as something caught her eye. "What's that?"

Will stopped and looked in the direction she'd indicated. "Looks like a cabin of sorts. I've not come this far inland before. Let's check it out."

Without waiting for her, Will took off toward the small building. Catalina followed, stepping over a piece of driftwood and trailing through the lush plants that had nearly overtaken the property.

"I wonder who had this cabin built," he muttered as he examined the old wood shack. "The island belongs to Alma from what I could tell when I first started coming here."

The covered porch leaned to one side, the old tin roof had certainly seen better days and some of the wood around the door and single window had warped. But the place had charm and someone had once cared enough to put it here. A private getaway for a couple in love? A hideout for someone seeking refuge from life? There was a story behind this place.

Will pushed on the door and eased inside. Catalina couldn't resist following him. The musty smell wasn't as bad as she'd expected, but the place was rather dusty. Only a bit of light from outside crept in through the single window, but even that wasn't bright because of the dark cloud covering.

"Careful," he cautioned when she stepped in. "Some of those boards feel loose."

There was enough dim light coming in the front window for them to see a few tarps, buckets and one old chair sitting against the wall.

"Looks like someone was working on this and it was forgotten," Catalina said as she walked around the room. "It's actually quite cozy."

Will laughed. "If you like the rustic, no-indoor-plumbing feel."

Crossing her arms over her chest, she turned around. "Some of us don't need to be pampered with amenities. I personally enjoy the basics."

"This is basic," he muttered, glancing around.

The sudden sound of rain splattering on the tin roof had Catalina freezing in place. "So much for that forecast."

Will offered her a wide smile. "Looks like you get to enjoy the basics a bit longer unless you want to run back to the yacht in the rain."

Crossing the room, Catalina sank down onto the old, sheet-covered chair. "I'm good right here. Will you be able to handle it?"

His aqua eyes raked over her, heating her skin just as effectively as if he'd touched her with his bare hands. "Oh, baby, I can handle it."

Maybe running back to the yacht was the better option after all. How long would she be stranded in an old shack with Will while waiting out this storm?

Catalina wasn't naïve. She knew full well there were only so many things they could talk about and nearly every topic between them circled back to the sexual tension that had seemed to envelop them and bind them together for the past several weeks.

Her body trembled as she kept her gaze locked onto his.

There was only one way this day would end.

Ten

Will stared out the window at the sheets of rain coming down. He didn't need to look, though; the pounding on the roof told him how intense this storm was.

So much for that flawless forecast.

Still, staying across the room from Cat was best for now. He didn't need another invisible push in her direction. He glanced over his shoulder toward the woman he ached for. She sat as casual as you please with her legs crossed, one foot bouncing to a silent beat as her flip-flop dangled off her toes. Those bare legs mocked him. The strings of her bikini top peeking out of her dress mocked him as well. Every damn thing about this entire situation mocked him.

What had he been thinking, inviting her for a day out? Why purposely resurrect all of those old, unresolved feelings? They'd gone four years without bringing up their past, but Will had reached his breaking point. He needed to know if they had a chance at… what? What exactly did he want from her?

He had no clue, but he did know the need for Cat had never lessened. If anything, the emptiness had grown without her in his life. He'd let her go once to save her, but he should've fought for them, fought for what he wanted and found another way to keep her safe. He'd been a coward. As humiliating as that was to admit, there was no sugarcoating the truth of the boy he used to be.

"You might as well have a seat," she told him, meeting his gaze. "The way you're standing across the room is only making the tension worse. You're making me twitchy."

Will laughed. Leave it to Cat to call him on his actions, though he didn't think the tension could get worse.

He crossed the room and took a seat on the floor in front of the chair.

"This reminds me of that time James, you and I were playing hide-and-seek when it started raining," she said. "You guys were home from school on break and I had come in to work with my mum."

Will smiled as the memory flooded his mind. "We were around eight or nine, weren't we?"

Cat nodded. "James kept trying to hold my hand when we both ran into the garage to hide and get dry."

Will sat up straighter. "You never told me that."

"Seriously?" she asked, quirking a brow. "You're going to get grouchy over the actions of a nine-year-old?"

"I'm not grouchy. Surprised, but not grouchy."

"James was only doing it because he knew I had a thing for you."

The corner of Will's mouth kicked up. "You had a thing for me when you were that young?"

Cat shrugged, toying with the edge of her dress. "You were an older man. Practically worldly in all of your knowledge."

"It was the Spanish, wasn't it?" he asked with a grin.

Cat rolled her eyes and laughed. "James was fluent in Spanish as well. You two both had the same hoity-toity schooling."

Will lifted his knee and rested his arm on it as he returned her smile. "Nah. I was better. We would sometimes swap out in class because the teacher couldn't tell us apart. She just knew a quiet blond boy sat in the back. As long as one of us showed up, she didn't pay much attention to the fact there were really supposed to be two."

"Sneaky boys. But, I bet if I asked James about the Spanish speaking skills he'd say he was better," she countered.

"He'd be wrong."

Cat tipped her head, shifting in her seat, which only brought her bare legs within touching distance. "You tricked your teachers and got away with it. Makes me wonder how many times you two swapped out when it came to women."

Will shook his head. "I'm not answering that."

"Well, I know that watch nearly cost James the love of his life," Cat said, nodding toward the gold timepiece on his wrist.

"It was unfortunate Bella saw you and me kissing. I truly thought we were secluded." Will sighed and shifted on the wood floor. "She had every right to think James was kissing someone else because she had no clue about the bet."

The rain beat against the window as the wind kicked up. Cat tensed and her eyes widened.

"Hope this old place holds up," she said. "Maybe running back to the yacht would have been a better idea."

"Too late now." Will reached over, laying his hand on her knee. "We're fine. It's just a pop-up storm. You know these things pass fast."

With a subtle nod, she settled deeper into the seat and rested her head on the back cushion. Guilt rolled through Will. He'd planned a day for her, and had been hopeful that seduction would be the outcome. Yet here they sat in some abandoned old shack waiting out some freak storm. Even Mother Nature was mocking him.

But there was a reason they were here right now, during this storm, and Will wasn't going to turn this chance away. He planned on taking full advantage and letting Cat know just how much he wanted her.

Shifting closer to her chair, Will took Cat's foot and slid her shoe off. He picked up her other foot and did the same, all while knowing she had those dark, intoxicating eyes focused on his actions. It was her exotic eyes that hypnotized him.

Taking one of her delicate feet between his hands, Will started to massage, stroking his thumb up her arch.

"I'll give you ten minutes to stop that," she told him with a smile.

The radiant smile on her face was something he hadn't realized he'd missed so much. Right now, all relaxed and calm, even with the storm raging outside, Cat looked like the girl he once knew…the girl he'd wanted something more with.

But they were different people now. They had different goals. Well, he did; her goals were still unclear to him. He suddenly found himself wanting to know about those dreams of hers, and the fact that she'd hinted to James that she wouldn't stay in Alma forever.

But all of those questions could come later. Right now, Cat's comfort and happiness were all that mattered. Tomorrow's worries, issues and questions could be dealt with later. He planned on enjoying Cat for as long as she would allow.

Damn. When had this petite woman taken control over him? When had he allowed it? There wasn't one moment he could pinpoint, but there were several tiny instances where he could see in hindsight the stealthy buildup of her power over him.

Cat laughed as she slid down a bit further in the chair and gazed down at him beneath heavy lids. "If your father could see you on the floor rubbing his maid's feet, you'd lose your prestigious position at Rowling Energy."

Will froze, holding her gaze. It may have been a lighthearted joke, but there was so much truth to her statement about how angry this would make his father. But Will had already set in motion his plan to freeze his father out of the company.

Besides, right now, Will didn't care about Patrick or Rowling Energy. What he did care about was the woman who was literally turning to putty in his hands. Finally, he was going to show her exactly what they could be together and anticipation had his heart beating faster than ever.

"Does this feel good?" he asked.

Her reply was a throaty moan, sexy enough to have his body responding.

"Then all of the other stuff outside of this cabin doesn't matter."

Blinking down at him, Cat replied, "Not to me, but I bet if your father made you choose, you'd be singing a different tune."

Just like last time.

The unspoken words were so deafening, they actually drowned out the beating of the rain and the wind against the small shelter.

Will's best option was to keep any answer to himself. He could deny the fact, but he'd be lying. He'd worked too hard to get where he was to just throw it all away because of hormones.

At the same time, he planned on working equally as hard to win over Cat. There was no reason he had to give up anything.

His hand glided up to her ankle, then her calf. She said nothing as her eyes continued to hold his. He purposely watched her face, waiting for a sign of retreat, but all that was staring back at him was desire.

There was a silent message bouncing between them, that things were about to get very intimate, very fast.

The old cabin creaked and groaned against the wind's force. Cat tensed beneath him.

"You're safe," he assured her softly, not wanting to break this moment of trust she'd settled into with him. "This place is so old. I know it has withstood hurricanes. This little storm won't harm the cabin or us."

And there weren't any huge trees around, just thick bushes and flowers, so they weren't at risk for anything falling on them.

Right now, the only thing he needed to be doing was pushing through that line of defense Cat had built up. And from her sultry grin and heavy lids, he'd say he was doing a damn fine job.

Catalina should tell him to stop. Well, the common sense side of her told her she should. But the female side, the side that hadn't been touched or treasured in more time than she cared to admit, told her common sense to shut up.

Will had quite the touch. She had no idea the nerves in your feet could be so tied into all the girly parts. She certainly knew it now. Every part of her was zipping with ache and need. If he commanded her to strip and dance around the room naked, she would. The power he held over her was all-consuming and she was dying to know when he was going to do more.

She'd walked straight into this with her eyes wide open. So if she was having doubts or regrets already, she had no one to blame but herself. Though Catalina wasn't doubting or regretting. She was aching, on the verge of begging him to take this to the next level.

Catalina's head fell back against the chair as his hands moved to her other calf, quickly traveling up to her knee, then her thigh. She wanted to inch down further and part her legs just a tad, but that would be a silent invitation she wasn't quite brave enough for.

Yet.

"I've wanted to touch you for so long," he muttered, barely loud enough for her to hear over the storm. "I've watched you for the past four years, wondering if you ever thought of me. Wondering if you ever fantasized about me the way I did you."

Every. Single. Night.

Which was a confession she wasn't ready to share. The ball was in his court for now and she planned on just waiting to see how this played out.

He massaged her muscles with the tips of his fingers and the room became hotter with each stroke. If the man could have such power over her with something so simple as a foot massage, how would her body react once Will really started showing her affection?

"Do you remember that time your mother caught us making out?" he asked with a half laugh.

At the time, Catalina had been mortified that her mother caught them. But it wasn't until after the breakup that she realized why her mother had been so disappointed.

Patrick Rowling had really done a number on Catalina's mum. And it was those thoughts that could quickly put a bucket of cold water on this encounter, but she refused to allow Patrick to steal one more moment of happiness from her life…he'd already taken enough from her.

Will may not be down on his knees proposing marriage, but he was down on his knees showing her affection. And maybe she hoped that would be a stepping-stone to something more… But right now, that was all she wanted. She'd fought this pull toward him for too long. She hadn't wanted to let herself believe they could be more, but now she couldn't deny herself. She couldn't avoid the inevitable…she was falling for Will all over again.

"She didn't even know we were dating," Catalina murmured, her euphoric state suddenly overtaking her ability to speak coherently.

"Not many people did. That's when I realized I didn't want to keep us a secret anymore."

And that had been the start of their spiral toward the heartbreak she'd barely recovered from.

Once they were an "official" item, Patrick had intervened and put a stop to his good son turning to the maid. Shocking, since turning to the staff for pleasure certainly hadn't been below Patrick at one time. Not that what Catalina and Will shared had been anything like that. But the idea that Patrick could act as if he were so far above people was absolutely absurd.

"Don't tense on me now," Will warned. "You're supposed to be relaxing."

Catalina blew out a breath. "I'm trying. It's just hard when I'm stuck between the past and whatever is happening to us now."

Will came up to his knees, easing his way between her parted legs, his hands resting on the tops of her thighs, his fingertips brushing just beneath the hem of her dress.

"It's two different times. We're two different people. There's nothing to compare. Focus on now."

She stared down at those bright blue eyes, the wide open shirt and something dark against his chest. Was that…

"Do you have a tattoo?" she asked, reaching to pull back the shirt.

He said nothing as she eased the material aside. The glimpse she got wasn't enough. Catalina didn't ask, she merely gripped the shirt and pushed it off his shoulders. Will shifted until it fell to the floor.

Sure enough, black ink swirled over the left side of his chest and over his shoulder. She had no idea what the design was. All she knew was that it was sexy.

Without asking, she reached out and traced a thin line over his heart, then on up. The line thickened as it curled around his shoulder. Taut muscles tensed beneath her featherlight touch.

Catalina brought her gaze up to Will's. The intensity of his stare made her breath catch in her throat and stilled her hand.

"Don't stop," he whispered through clenched teeth. "Will…"

His hand came up to cover hers. "Touch me, Cat."

He'd just handed her the reins.

With just enough pressure, he flattened her hand between his palm and his shoulder. The warmth of his skin penetrated her own, the heat sliding through her entire body.

"I—I want to but—"

She shook her head, killing the rest of her fears before they could be released and never taken back.

"But what?" he muttered, pushing her hair behind her ear, letting his fingertips trail over her cheek, her jawline and down her neck until she trembled.

"I'm not sure I can go any farther than that," she confessed. "I don't want to tease you."

"I've fantasized about you touching me like this for years. You're not teasing, you're fulfilling a fantasy."

Catalina stared into those aqua eyes and knew without a doubt he was serious. The fact that he'd been dreaming of her for this long confused her further, brought on even more questions than answers.

"Don't go there," he warned as if he knew where her thoughts were headed. "Keep touching me, Cat. Whatever happens here is about you and me and right this moment. Don't let past memories rob us of this time together."

Catalina opened her mouth, but Will placed one finger over her lips. "I have no expectations. Close your eyes."

Even though her heart beat out of control from anticipation and a slither of fear of the unknown, she did as he commanded.

"Now touch me. Just feel me, feel this moment and nothing else."

His tone might have been soft, but everything about

his words demanded that she obey. Not that he had to do much convincing. With her eyes closed, she wasn't forced to look at the face of the man who'd broken her heart. She wanted this chance to touch him, to ignore all the reasons why this was such a bad idea. But she couldn't look into those eyes and pretend that this was normal, that they were just two regular people stranded in an old shack.

With her eyes closed she actually felt as if they were regular people. She could pretend this was just a man she ached for, not a man who was a billionaire with more power than she'd ever see.

With her eyes closed she could pretend he wanted her for who she was and not just because she was a challenge.

Catalina brought her other hand up and over his chest. If she was given the green light to explore, she sure as hell wanted both hands doing the job. Just as she smoothed her palms up and over his shoulders, over his thick biceps, she felt the knot on her wrap dress loosen at her side.

Her eyes flew open. "What are you doing?"

"Feeling the moment."

The dress parted, leaving her torso fully exposed. "You don't play fair."

The heat in his eyes was more powerful than any passion she'd ever seen. "I never will when it comes to something I want."

"You said—"

"I'd never force you," he interrupted, gliding his fingertips over the straps of her bikini that stretched from behind her neck to the slopes of her breasts. "But that doesn't mean I won't try to persuade you."

As the rain continued to beat against the side of the

shack, Catalina actually found herself happy that she was stuck here. Perhaps this was the push she needed to follow through with what she truly wanted. No, she wasn't looking for happily-ever-after, she'd never be that naïve again where Will was concerned. But she was older now, was going into this with both eyes wide open.

And within the next couple months, hopefully she'd be out of Alma and starting her new life. So why not take the plunge now with a man she'd always wanted? Because he was right. This was all about them, here and now. Everything else could wait outside that door.

For now, Catalina was taking what she'd wanted for years.

Eleven

Catalina came to her feet. From here on out she was taking charge of what she'd been deprived of and what she wanted…and she wanted Will. Whatever doubts she had about sleeping with him wouldn't be near as consuming as the regret she'd have if she moved away and ignored this opportunity.

The moment she stood before him, Will sank back down on the floor and stared up at her as her dress fell into a puddle around her feet. As she stepped away and kicked the garment aside, his eyes roamed over her, taking in the sight of the bikini and nothing else.

The image of him sitting at her feet was enough to give her a sense of control, a sense of dominance. The one time when it counted most, she didn't feel inferior.

Will could've immediately taken over, he could've stood before her and taken charge, but he'd given her the reins.

"That bikini does some sinful things to your body." He reached out, trailed his fingertips over the sensitive area behind her knee and on up to her thigh. "Your curves are stunning, Cat. Your body was made to be uncovered."

"How long have you wanted me, Will?" she asked, needing to know this much. "Did you want me when we were together before?"

"More than anything," he rasped out, still sliding his fingers up and down the backs of her legs. "But I knew you were a virgin and I respected you."

"What if I were a virgin now?" she asked, getting off track. "Would you still respect me?"

"I've always respected you." He came up to his knees, putting his face level with her stomach. He placed a kiss just above her bikini bottoms before glancing up at her. "And I don't want to discuss if there's been another man in your bed."

With a move she hadn't expected, he tossed her back into the chair and stood over her, his hands resting on either side of her head. "Because I'm the only man you're going to be thinking of right now."

"I've only been with one other, but you're the only man I've ever wanted in my bed," she admitted. "I need you to know that."

Maybe she was naïve for letting him in on that little piece of information she'd kept locked in her heart for so long, but right now, something more than desire was sparking between them. He was too possessive for this to just be something quick and easy.

They weren't just scratching an itch, but she had no clue what label to put on what was about to happen. Which was why she planned on not thinking and just feeling. This bond that was forming here was something she'd have to figure out later...much later.

"All I need to know is that you want this as much as I do," he told her. "That you're ready for anything that happens because I can't promise soft and gentle. I've wanted you too long."

A shiver of arousal speared through her. "I don't need gentle, Will. I just need you."

In an instant his lips crushed hers. She didn't know when things had shifted, but in the span of about two minutes, she'd gone from questioning sex with Will to nearly ripping his shorts off so she could have him.

Will's strong hands gripped her hips as he shifted the angle of his head for a deeper kiss. Cat arched her body, needing to feel as much of him as possible. There still didn't seem to be enough contact. She wanted more... she wanted it all. The need to have everything she'd deprived herself of was now an all-consuming ache.

"Keep moaning like that, sweetheart," he muttered against her lips. "You're all mine."

She hadn't even realized she'd moaned, which just proved how much control this man had over her actions.

Gripping his shoulders, she tried to pull him down further, but he eased back. With his eyes locked onto hers, he hooked his thumbs in the waistband of his board shorts and shoved them to the floor. Stepping out of them he reached down, took her hand and pulled her to her feet.

Keeping her eyes on his, she reached behind her neck and untied her top. It fell forward as she worked on the knot. Soon they'd flung the entire scrap of fabric across the room. Will's eyes widened and his nostrils flared.

Excitement and anticipation roiled through her as she shoved her bottoms down without a care. She had no clue who reached for whom first, but the next second she was in his arms, skin to skin from torso to knees and she'd never felt anything better in her entire life.

Will's arms wrapped around her waist, his hands splaying across her bare back. He spun her around and sank down into the chair, pulling her down with him. Instinctively her legs straddled his hips. Catalina fisted her fingers in his hair as his lips trailed down her throat.

"So sexy," he murmured against her heated skin. "So mine."

Yes. She was his for now…maybe she always had been.

When his mouth found her breast, his hands encircled her hips. She waited, aching with need.

"Will," she panted, not recognizing her own voice. "Protection."

With his hair mussed, his lids heavy, he looked up. "I don't have any with me. Dammit, they're on the yacht. I didn't expect to get caught out here like this." Cursing beneath his breath, he shook his head. "I'm clean. I swear I wouldn't lie about something like that. I haven't been with a woman in…too long, and I recently had a physical."

"I know I'm clean and I'm on birth control."

He gave her a look, silently asking what she wanted to do. Without another word she slowly sank down onto him, so that they were finally, fully joined after years of wanting, years of fantasizing.

Their sighs and groans filled the small room. Wind continued to beat against the window as rain pelted the tin roof. Everything about this scenario was perfect. Even if they were in a rundown shed, she didn't care. The ambiance was amazingly right. The storm that had swept through them over the years only matched Mother

Nature's fury outside the door. This was the moment they were supposed to be together, this was what they'd both waited for so long.

"Look at me," he demanded, his fingertips pressing into her hips.

Catalina hadn't realized she'd closed her eyes, but she opened them and found herself looking into Will's bright, expressive aqua eyes. He may be able to hold back his words, but those eyes told her so much. Like the fact that he cared for her. This was sex, but there was so much more going on...so much more they'd discuss later.

As her hips rocked back and forth against his, Will continued to watch her face. Catalina leaned down, resting her hands on his shoulders. The need inside her built so fast, she dropped her forehead against his.

"No," he stated. "Keep watching me. I want to see your face."

As she looked back into his eyes, her body responded to every touch, every kiss, every heated glance. Tremors raced through her at the same time his body stilled, the cords in his neck tightened and his fingertips dug even further into her hips.

His body stiffened against hers, his lips thinned as his own climax took control. Catalina couldn't look away. She wanted to see him come undone, knowing she caused this powerful man to fall at the mercy of her touch.

Once their bodies eased out of the euphoric state, Catalina leaned down, rested her head on his shoulder and tried to regain some sense of normal breathing. She didn't know what to say now, how to act. They'd taken this awkward, broken relationship and put another speed bump in it. Now all they had to do was figure out how to maneuver over this new hurdle since they'd moved to a whole new, unfamiliar level.

Will trailed his hand up and down Cat's back, which was smooth and damp with sweat. Damn, she was sexier than he'd ever, *ever* imagined. She'd taken him without a second thought and with such confidence. Yet she'd been so tight…had she not slept with anyone? How had that not happened? Surely she wasn't still a virgin.

Had Cat kept her sexuality penned up all this time? For completely selfish reasons, this thought pleased him.

As much as Will wanted to know, he didn't want to say a word, didn't want to break the silence with anything that would kill the mood. The storm raged on outside, the cabin creaked and continued to groan under the pressure, but Cat was in his arms, her heart beating against his chest, and nothing could pull him from this moment.

The fact that he was concentrating on her heartbeat was a bit disconcerting. He didn't want to be in tune with her heart, he couldn't get that caught up with her, no matter how strong this invisible force was that was tugging him to her. Having her in his arms, finally making love to her was enough.

So why did he feel as if there was more to be had?

Because when he'd originally been thinking of the here and now, he'd somehow started falling into the zone of wanting more than this moment. He wanted Cat much longer than this day, this week, even. Will wanted more and now he had to figure out just how the hell that would work.

"Tell me I wasn't a substitute for Bella."

Will jerked beneath her, forcing her to sit up and meet his gaze. "What?"

Cat shook her head, smoothing her short hair away from her face. "Nothing," she said, coming to her feet. "That was stupid of me to say. We had sex. I'm not expecting you to give me anything more."

As she rummaged around the small space searching for her bikini and dress, Will sat there dumbfounded. So much for not letting words break the beauty of the moment.

What was that about Bella? Seriously? Did Cat honestly think that Will had had a thing for his brother's fiancée?

"Look at me," he demanded, waiting until Cat spun around, gripping her clothing to her chest. "Bella is married to James. I have no claim to her."

"It's none of my business."

Will watched as she tied her top on and slid the bikini bottoms up her toned legs. "It is your business after what we just did. I don't sleep with one woman and think of another."

Cat's dark eyes came up to his. A lock of her inky black hair fell over her forehead and slashed across her cheek.

"You owe me no explanations, Will." Hands on her hips, she blew the rogue strand from her face. "I know this wasn't a declaration of anything to come. I'm grown up now and I have no delusions that things will be any different than what they are. We slept together, it's over."

Okay, that had originally been his mindset when he'd gone into this, but when the cold words came from her mouth, Will suddenly didn't like the sound of it. She wasn't seeing how he'd changed at all and that was his fault. She still believed he was a jerk who had no cares at all for her feelings. But he did care...too damn much.

"I know you saw me as a challenge," she went on as she yanked the ties together to secure her dress. "A conquest, if you will. It's fine, really. I could've stopped you, but I was selfish and wanted you. So, thanks for—"

"Do not say another word." Pushing to his feet, Will jerked his shorts from the floor and tugged them on before crossing to her. "You can't lie to me, Cat. I know you too well. Whatever defense mechanism you're using here with ugly words isn't you. You're afraid of what you just felt, of what just happened. This wasn't just sex and you damn well know it."

Her eyes widened, her lips parted, but she immediately shut down any emotion he'd just seen flash across her face. No doubt about it, she was trying to cut him off before he did anything to hurt her...again. He should have seen this coming.

Guilt slammed into him. Not over sleeping with her just now, but for how she felt she had to handle the situation to avoid any more heartache.

"Will, I'm the maid," she said softly. "While I'm not ashamed of my position, I also know that this was just a onetime thing. A man like you would never think twice about a woman like me for anything more than sex."

Will gripped her arms, giving her a slight shake. "Why are you putting yourself into this demeaning little package and delivering it to me? I've told you more than once I don't care if you're a maid or a damn CEO. What just happened has nothing to do with anything other than us and what we feel."

"There is no us," she corrected him.

"There sure as hell was just a minute ago."

Why was he so dead set on correcting her? Here he

stood arguing with her when she was saying the same exact thing he'd been thinking earlier.

"And I have no clue why you're bringing Bella into this," he added.

Cat lifted her chin in a defiant gesture. "I'm a woman. Sometimes my insecurities come out."

"Why are you insecure about her?"

Cat laughed and broke free from his hold, taking a step back. "You were with one of the most beautiful women I've ever seen. Suddenly when that relationship is severed, you turn to me. You haven't given me any attention in nearly four years, Will. Forgive me if suddenly I feel like leftovers."

"Don't downgrade what just happened between us," he demanded. "Just because I didn't seek you out in the past few years doesn't mean I didn't want you. I wanted the hell out of you. And I was fighting my way back to you, dammit."

He eased closer, watching as her eyes widened when he closed the gap and loomed over her. "Seeing you all the time, being within touching distance but knowing I had no right was hell."

"You put yourself there."

As if he needed the reminder of the fool he'd been.

Will smoothed her hair back from her forehead, allowing his hand to linger on her jawline. "I can admit when I was wrong, stubborn and a jerk. I can also admit that I have no clue what just happened between us because it was much more than just sex. You felt it, I felt it, and if we deny that fact we'd just be lying to ourselves. Let's get past that. Honesty is all we can have here. We deserve more than something cheap, Cat."

Cat closed her eyes and sighed. When her lids lifted,

she glanced toward the window. "The rain has let up. We should head back to the yacht."

Without another word, without caring that he was standing here more vulnerable than he'd ever been, Cat turned, opened the door and walked out.

Nobody walked out on Will Rowling and he sure as hell wasn't going to let the woman he was so wrapped up in and had just made love to be the first.

Twelve

Catalina had known going into this day that they'd most likely end up naked and finally giving into desires from years ago.

And she hadn't been able to stop herself.

No matter what she felt now, no matter what insecurities crept up, she didn't regret sleeping with Will.

This was a one and done thing—it had to be. She couldn't afford to fall any harder for this man whom she couldn't have. She was planning on leaving Alma anyway, so best to cut ties now and start gearing up for her fresh start. Letting her heart interfere with the dreams she'd had for so long would only have her working backward. She was so close, she'd mentally geared up for the break from Alma, from Will…but that was before she'd given herself to him.

But what had just transpired between them was only closure. Yes, that was the term she'd been looking for.

Closure. Nothing else could come from their intimacy and finally getting each other out of their systems was the right thing to do...wasn't it?

While the rain hadn't fully stopped, Catalina welcomed the refreshing mist hitting her face. She had no clue of the amount of time that had passed while they'd been inside the cabin lost in each other. An hour? Three hours?

The sand shifted beneath her bare feet as she marched down the shore toward the dock. Sandals in her hand, she kept her focus on the yacht in the distance and not the sound of Will running behind her. She should've known he'd come chasing after her, and not just because he wanted to get back to the yacht.

She'd left no room for argument when she'd walked out, and Will Rowling wouldn't put up with that. Too bad. She was done talking. It was time to move on.

Too bad her body was still humming a happy tune and tingling in all the areas he'd touched, tasted.

Figuring he'd grab her when he caught up to her, Catalina turned, ready to face down whatever he threw her way. Will took a few more steps, stopping just in front of her. He was clutching his wadded up shirt at his side. Catalina couldn't help but stare at his bare chest and the mesmerizing tattoo as he pulled in deep breaths.

"You think we're done?" he asked as he stared her down. "Like we're just heading back to the yacht, setting off to Alma and that's it? You think this topic is actually closed? That I would accept this?"

Shrugging, Catalina forced herself to meet his angry gaze. "You brought me here to seduce me. Wasn't that the whole plan for getting me alone? Well, mission accomplished. The storm has passed and it'll start getting dark in a couple hours. Why wait to head back?"

"Maybe because I want to spend more time with you," he shouted. "Maybe because I want more here than something cheap and easy."

As the misty rain continued to hit her face, Catalina wanted to let that sliver of hope into her heart, but she couldn't allow it…not just yet. "And what do you want, Will? An encore performance? Maybe in your bed on the yacht so you can have a more pampered experience?"

His lips thinned, the muscle in his jaw tightened. "What made you so harsh, Cat? You weren't like this before."

Before when she'd been naïve, before when she'd actually thought he may love her and choose her over his career. And before she discovered a secret that he still knew nothing about.

Beyond all of that, she was angry with herself for allowing her emotions to get so caught up in this moment. She should've known better. She'd never been someone to sleep around, but she thought for sure she could let herself go with Will and then walk away. She'd been wrong and now because of her roller coaster of emotions, she was taking her anger out on him.

Shaking her head, Catalina turned. Before she could take a step, she tripped over a piece of driftwood she hadn't seen earlier. Landing hard in the sand, she hated how the instant humiliation took over.

Before she could become too mortified, a spearing pain shot through her ankle. She gasped just as Will crouched down by her side.

"Where are you hurt?" he asked, his eyes raking over her body.

"My ankle," she muttered, sitting up so she could look at her injury.

"Anywhere else?" Will asked.

Catalina shook her head as she tried to wiggle her ankle back and forth. Bad idea. She was positive it wasn't broken—she'd broken her arm as a little girl and that pain had been much worse—but she was also sure she wouldn't be able to apply any pressure on it and walk. The piercing pain shot up her leg and had her wincing. She hoped she didn't burst into tears and look even more pathetic.

So much for her storming off in her dramatic fit of anger.

Will laid his shirt on her stomach.

"What—?"

Before she could finish her question, he'd scooped her up in his arms and set off across the sand. Catalina hated how she instantly melted against his warm, bare chest. Hated how the image of them in her mind seemed way more romantic than what it was, with Will's muscles straining as he carried her in his arms—yeah, they no doubt looked like something straight out of a movie.

"You can't carry me all the way to the yacht," she argued. "This sand is hard enough to walk in without my added weight."

"Your weight is perfect." He threw her a glance, silently leaving her no room for argument. "Relax and we'll see what we're dealing with once I can get you on the bed in the cabin."

Those words sent a shiver of arousal through her that she seriously did not want. Hadn't she learned from the last set of shivers? Hadn't she told herself that after they slept together she'd cut ties? She had no other choice, not if she wanted to maintain any dignity and sanity on her way out of his life for good.

As they neared the dock, Will was breathing hard,

but he didn't say a word as he trudged forward. Her ankle throbbed, which should have helped shift her focus, but being wrapped in Will's strong arms pretty much overrode any other emotion.

Catalina had a sinking feeling that in all her pep talks to herself, she'd overlooked the silent power Will had over her. She may have wanted to have this sexcapade with him and then move on, but she'd seriously underestimated how involved her heart would become.

And this hero routine he was pulling was flat-out sexy...as if she needed another reason to pull her toward him.

Will quickly crossed toward the dock, picking up his pace now that he was on even ground. When he muttered a curse, Catalina lifted her head to see what the problem was. Quickly she noted the damage to the yacht and the dock. Apparently the two had not played nice during the freak storm.

"Oh, Will," she whispered.

He slowed his pace as he carefully tested the weight of the dock. Once his footing was secure, and it was clear that the planks would hold them, he cautiously stepped forward.

"I need to set you down for a second to climb on board, but just keep pressure off that ankle and hold onto my shoulders."

She did as he asked and tried not to consider just what this damage meant for their return trip home. When Will was on deck, he reached out, proceeded to scoop her up again and lifted her onto the yacht.

"I can get down the steps," she told him, really having no clue if she could or not. But there was no way they could both fit through that narrow doorway to get below deck. "Go figure out what happened."

He kept his hold firm. "I'm going to get you settled, assess your ankle and then go see what damage was done to the yacht."

Somehow he managed to get her down the steps and onto the bed without bumping her sore, now swollen ankle along the way. As he adjusted the pillows behind her, she slid back to lean against the fluffy backdrop. Will took a spare pillow and carefully lifted her leg to elevate her injury.

"It's pretty swollen," he muttered as he stalked toward the galley kitchen and returned with a baggie full of ice wrapped in a towel. "Keep this on it and I'll go see if I can find some pain reliever."

"Really, it'll be fine," she lied. The pain was bad, but she wanted him to check on the damage so they could get back to Alma... She prayed they could safely get back. "Go see how bad the destruction is. I'm not going anywhere."

Will's brows drew in. With his hands on his hips, that sexy black ink scrolling over his bare chest and the taut muscles, he personified sex appeal.

"Staring at my ankle won't make it any better," she told him, suddenly feeling uncomfortable.

His unique blue eyes shifted and held her gaze. "I hate that I hurt you," he muttered.

So much could be read from such a simple statement. Was he referring to four years ago? Did he mean the sexual encounter they'd just had or was he referencing her fall?

No matter what he was talking about, Catalina didn't want to get into another discussion that would only take them in circles again. They were truly getting nowhere...well, they'd ended up naked, but other than that, they'd gotten nowhere.

"Go on," she insisted. "Don't worry about me."

He looked as if he wanted to argue, but ended up nodding. "I'll be right back. If you need something, just yell for me. I'll hear you."

Catalina watched as he ascended the steps back up to the deck. Closing her eyes, she dropped her head against the pillows and pulled in a deep breath. If the storm had done too much damage to the yacht, she was stuck. Stuck on a glamorous yacht with an injured ankle with the last person she should be locked down with.

The groan escaped before she could stop it. Then laughter followed. Uncontrollable laughter, because could they be anymore clichéd? The maid and the millionaire, stranded on a desert island. Yeah, they had the makings for a really ridiculous story or some skewed reality show.

Once upon a time she would've loved to have been stranded with Will. To know that nothing would interrupt them. They could be who they wanted to be without pretenses. Just Will and Catalina, two people who l—

No. They didn't love each other. That was absurd to even think. Years ago she had thought they were in love, but they couldn't have been. If they'd truly been in love, wouldn't he have fought for everything they'd discussed and dreamed of?

Maybe he'd been playing her the entire time. A twenty-year-old boy moving up the ladder of success really didn't have much use for a poor staff member. She was a virgin and an easy target. Maybe that's all he'd been after.

But she really didn't think so. She'd grown up around Will and James. James was the player, not Will. Will had always been more on the straight and narrow, the rule follower.

And he'd followed those rules right to the point of breaking her heart. She should have seen it coming, really. After their mother passed away, Will did every single thing he could to please his father, as if overcompensating for the loss of a parent.

Yet there was that little girl fantasy in her that had held out hope that Will would see her as more, that he would fall in love with her and they could live happily ever after.

Catalina sighed. That was long ago; they were different people now and the past couldn't be redone...and all those other stupid sayings that really didn't help in the grand scheme of things.

And it was because she was still so tied up in knots over this man that she needed to escape Alma, fulfill her own dreams and forget her life here. She was damn good at designing and she couldn't wait to burn her uniforms and sensible shoes, roast a marshmallow over them and move on.

"We're not going anywhere for a while."

Catalina jerked her head around. Will was standing on the bottom step, his hands braced above him on the doorframe. The muscles in his biceps flexed, drawing her attention to his raw masculinity. No matter how much the inner turmoil was caused by their rocky relationship, Catalina couldn't deny that the sight of his body turned her on like no other man had ever been able to do.

"There's some major damage to the starboard side. I thought maybe I could get it moving, but the mechanics are fried. I can only assume the boat was hit by lightning as well as banging into the dock repeatedly."

Catalina gripped the plush comforter beneath her palms. "How long will we be stuck here?"

"I have no clue."

He stepped farther into the room and raked a hand over his messy hair. Will always had perfectly placed hair, but something about that rumpled state made her hotter for him.

"The radio isn't working, either," he added as he sank down on the edge of the bed, facing her. "Are you ready for some pain medicine since we're going to be here awhile?"

She was going to need something a lot stronger if she was going to be forced to stick this out with him for too long. Hours? Days? How long would she have to keep her willpower on high alert?

"I probably better," she admitted. "My ankle's throbbing pretty good now."

Will went to the bathroom. She heard him rummaging around in a cabinet, then the faucet. When he strode back across the open room, Catalina couldn't keep her eyes off his bare chest. Why did he have to be so beautiful and enticing? She wanted to be over her attraction for this man. Anything beyond what happened in that cabin would only lead to more heartache because Will would never choose anyone over his father and Rowling Energy and she sure as hell wasn't staying in Alma to clean toilets the rest of her life waiting to gain his attention.

Catalina took the pills and the small paper cup of water he offered. Hoping the medicine kicked in soon, she swallowed it as Will eased back down beside her on the bed.

"Dammit," he muttered, placing his hand on the shin of her good leg. "If we hadn't been arguing—"

"We've argued for weeks," she told him with a half smile. "It was an accident. If anyone is to blame it's me for not watching where I was going and for trying to stomp off in a fit."

"Were you throwing a fit?" he asked. "I don't remember."

Catalina lifted an eyebrow. "You're mocking me now."

Shaking his head, he slid his hand up and down her shin. "Not at all. I just remember thinking how sexy you looked when you were angry. You have this red tint to your cheeks. Or it could've been the great sex. Either way, you looked hot."

"Was that before or after I was sprawled face first in the sand?" she joked, trying to lighten the mood.

"You can't kill sexy, Cat, even if you're eating sand."

The slight grin he offered her eased her worry. Maybe they could spend the day here and actually be civil without worrying about the sexual tension consuming them. Maybe they had taken the edge off and could move on.

Well, they could obviously move on, but would this feeling of want ever go away? Because if anything, since they'd been intimate, Catalina craved him even more.

So now what could she do? There was nowhere to hide and definitely nowhere to run in her current state.

As she looked into Will's mesmerizing eyes, her worry spiked once again because he stared back at her like a man starved…and she was the main course.

Thirteen

Thankfully the kitchen was fully stocked and the electricity that fed the appliances hadn't been fried because right now Will needed to concentrate on something other than how perfect Cat looked in his bed.

He'd come to the kitchen a while ago to figure out what they should do for dinner. Apparently the pain pills had kicked in because Cat was resting peacefully, even letting out soft moans every now and then as she slept.

It was those damn moans that had his shorts growing tighter and his teeth grinding as he attempted to control himself. He'd heard those groans earlier, up close and personal in his ear as she'd wrapped her body around his.

The experience was one he would never forget.

Will put together the chicken and rice casserole that his mother used to make. Yes, they'd had a chef when he was a child, but James and Will had always loved this dish and every now and then, Will threw it together just to remember his mother. He still missed her, but it was the little things that would remind him of her and make him smile.

Setting the timer on the oven, Will glanced back to the sleeping beauty in his bed. His mother would have loved Cat. She wouldn't have cared if she was the maid or—

What the hell? How did that thought sneak right in without his realizing the path his mind was taking? It didn't matter what his mother would have thought of Cat. He wasn't getting down on one knee and asking her into the family.

He needed to get a grip because his hormones and his mind were jumbling up all together and he was damn confused. Sleeping with Cat should have satisfied this urge to claim her, but instead of passing, the longing only grew.

With the casserole baking for a good bit, Will opted to grab a shower. He smelled like sex, sand and sweat. Maybe a cold shower would help wake him up to the reality that he'd let Cat go once. Just because they slept together didn't mean she was ready to give this a go again. And was that what he wanted? In all honesty did he want to try for this once more and risk hurting her, hurting himself, further?

He was making a damn casserole for pity's sake. What type of man had he become? He'd turned into some warped version of a homemaker and, even worse, he was perfectly okay with this feeling.

Before he went to the shower, he wanted to try the radio one more time. There had to be a way to communicate back to the mainland. Unfortunately, no matter which knobs he turned, which buttons he hit, nothing sparked to life. Resigned to the fact they were indeed stuck, Will went to his master suite bathroom.

As he stripped from his shorts and stepped into the spacious, open shower, he wondered if maybe being stranded with Cat wasn't some type of sign. Maybe they were supposed to be together with no outside forces hindering their feelings or judgment.

And honestly, Will wanted to see what happened with Cat. He wanted to give this another chance because they were completely different people than they were before and he was in total control of his life. She was that sliver of happiness that kept him smiling and their verbal sparring never failed to get him worked up.

No other woman matched him the way she did and he was going to take this opportunity of being stranded and use every minute to his advantage. He'd prove to her he was different because just telling her he was really wouldn't convince her. He needed to show her, to let her see for herself that he valued her, that he wanted her. He'd never stopped wanting her.

While he may want to use this private time to seduce the hell out of her, Will knew those hormones were going to have to take a back seat because Cat was worth more and they were long overdue for some relaxing, laid back time. And then maybe they could discuss just what the hell was happening between them.

Whatever that smell was, Catalina really hoped she wasn't just dreaming about it. As soon as she opened her eyes, she was greeted with a beautiful orange glow across the horizon. The sun was setting, and lying in this bed, Will's bed, watching such beauty was a moment she wanted to lock in her mind forever.

She rolled over, wincing as the pain in her ankle reminded her she was injured. The ice bag had melted and slid off the pillow she'd propped it on. As soon as she sat up, she examined her injury, pleased to see the swelling had gone down some.

"Oh, good. Dinner is almost ready."

Catalina smoothed her hair away from her face and smiled as Will scooped up something from a glass pan.

"I tried the radio again," he told her. "It didn't work. The whole system is fried."

Catalina sighed. As much as she wanted to get back home, she couldn't deny the pleasure she'd experienced here, despite the injury. She had a feeling she was seeing the true Will, the man who wasn't all business and power trips, but a man who cared for her whether he was ready to admit it or not.

"Someone will come for us," she told him. "Besides, with you cooking and letting me nap, you're spoiling me. Dinner smells a lot like that chicken dish you made me for our first date."

Will grinned back at her and winked. *Winked.* What had she woken to? Will in the kitchen cooking and actually relaxed enough to wink and smile as if he hadn't a care in the world.

"It is," he confirmed. "I'll bring it to you so don't worry about getting up."

"I actually need to go to the restroom."

In seconds, Will was at her side helping her up. When he went to lift her in his arms, she pushed against him.

"Just let me lean on you, okay? No need to carry me."

Wrapping an arm around her waist, Will helped her stand. "How's the ankle feeling?"

"Really sore, but better than it was." She tested it, pulling back when the sharp throbbing started again.

"Putting weight on it still isn't a smart move, but hopefully it will be much better by tomorrow."

Will assisted her across the room, but when they reached the bathroom doorway, she placed a hand on his chest. "I can take it from here."

No way was he assisting her in the bathroom. She'd like to hold onto some shred of dignity. Besides, she needed a few moments to herself to regain mental footing since she was stuck playing house with the only man she'd ever envisioned spending forever with.

"I'll wait right here in case you need something," he told her. "Don't lock the door."

With a mock salute, Catalina hobbled into the bathroom and closed the door. The scent of some kind of masculine soap assaulted her senses. A damp towel hung over the bar near the shower. He'd made use of the time she'd been asleep. Her eyes darted to the bathtub that looked as if it could seat about four people. What she wouldn't give to crawl into that and relax in some hot water, with maybe a good book or a glass of wine. When was the last time she'd indulged in such utterly selfish desires?

Oh, yeah, when she'd stripped Will naked and had her way with him in the old cabin earlier today.

A tap on the door jerked her from her thoughts. "Are you okay?"

"Yeah. Give me a minute."

A girl couldn't even fantasize in peace around here. She still needed time to process what their intimacy meant and the new, unexpected path their relationship had taken. Will had most likely thought of what happened the entire time she'd been asleep. Of course he was a man, so he probably wasn't giving their encounter the amount of mind space she would.

Minutes later, Catalina opened the door to find Will leaning against the frame. Once again he wrapped an arm around her and steered her toward the bed.

"I can eat at the table." She hated leaning on him, touching him when her nerves were still a jumbled up mess. "I'm already up. That bed is too beautiful to eat on."

In no time he'd placed their plates on the table with two glasses of wine…again, her favorite. A red Riesling.

"If I didn't know better, I'd say you stocked this kitchen just for me," she joked as she took her first sip and knew it wasn't the cheap stuff she kept stocked in her fridge.

"I did buy a lot of things I knew you liked." His fork froze midway to his mouth as he looked up at her. "At least, you liked this stuff four years ago."

For a split second, he seemed unsure. Will was always confident in everything, but when discussing her tastes, he suddenly doubted himself. Why did she find that so adorable?

She felt a shiver travel up her spine. She didn't have time for these adorable moments and couldn't allow them to influence her where this man was concerned. That clean break she wanted couldn't happen if she let herself be charmed like that.

They ate in silence, but Catalina was surprised the strain wasn't there. Everything seemed…normal. Something was up. He wasn't trying to seduce her, he wasn't bringing up the past or any other hot topic.

What had happened while she'd been asleep? Will had suddenly transformed into some sort of caretaker with husbandlike qualities.

But after a while she couldn't take the silence anymore. Catalina dropped her fork to her empty plate.

"That was amazing. Now, tell me what's going through your mind."

Will drained his glass before setting it back down and focusing on her. "Right now I'm thinking I could use dessert."

"I mean why are you so quiet?"

Shrugging, he picked up their plates and put them in the kitchen. When he brought back the wine bottle, she put a hand over hers to stop him from filling her glass back up.

"If I need more pain pills later, it's best I don't have any more even though I only took a half pill."

Nodding, he set the bottle on the table and sat across from her again.

"Don't ignore the question."

A smile kicked up at the corners of his mouth. "I'm plotting."

Catalina eased back in her seat, crossing her arms over her chest. "You're always plotting. I take it I'm still in the crosshairs?"

His eyes narrowed in that sexy, toe-curling way that demanded a woman take notice. "You've never been anywhere else."

Her heart beat faster. When he said those things she wanted to believe him. She wanted to be the object of his every desire and fantasy. And when he looked at her as if nothing else in the world mattered, she wanted to stay in that line of sight forever, though she knew all of that was a very naïve way of thinking.

"I only set out to seduce you," he went on, toying with the stem on his glass. "I wanted you in my bed more than anything. And now that I've had you…"

Catalina wished she'd had that second glass of wine after all. "What are you saying?"

His intense stare locked onto her. "We're different people. Maybe we're at a stage where we can learn from the past and see…"

It took every ounce of her willpower not to lean forward in anticipation as his words trailed off yet again. "And see what?" she finally asked.

"Maybe I want to see where we could go."

Catalina gasped. "You're not serious."

Those heavy-lidded eyes locked onto her. "I can't let you go now that I know how right we are together."

Her eyes shifted away and focused on the posh living space while she tried to process all he was saying.

Her mother's words of warning from years ago echoed in Catalina's mind. How could she fall for this man with his smooth words and irresistible charm? Hadn't her mother done the same thing with Patrick?

No. Will wasn't Patrick and Catalina was not her mother.

To her knowledge, Will, even to this day, had absolutely no idea what had transpired when he'd been a young boy right around the time of his mother's death. That hollow pit in Catalina's stomach deepened. Had the affair been the catalyst in Mrs. Rowling's death?

"Why now?" she asked, turning back to face him. "Why should I let you in now after all this time? Is it because I'm convenient? Because I'm still single or because you're settling?"

Why was fate dangling this right in front of her face when she'd finally decided to move on? It had taken her years to get up the nerve to really move forward with her dream and now that she'd decided to take a chance, Will wanted back in?

"Trust me, you're anything but convenient," he laughed.

"I've busted my butt trying to think of ways to get your attention."

Catalina swallowed. "But why?"

"Because you want this just as much as I do," he whispered.

Catalina stared down at her hands clasped in her lap. "We're at the age now that our wants don't always matter." Letting her attention drift back up, she locked her eyes on him. "We both have different goals, Will. In the end, nothing has really changed."

"On that we can agree." Will came to his feet, crossed to her side of the table and loomed over her. His hands came to rest on the back of her chair on either side of her shoulders. "In the end, I'll still want you and you'll still want me. The rest can be figured out later."

Before she could say anything, he'd scooped her up in his arms. "Don't say a word," he chided. "I want to carry you, so just let me. Enjoy this moment, that's all I'm asking. Don't think about who we are away from here. Let me care for you the way you deserve."

His warm breath washed over her face as she stared back at him. He didn't move, he just waited for her reply.

What could she say? He was right. They both wanted each other, but was that all this boiled down to? There were so many other outside factors driving a wedge between them. Did she honestly believe that just because he said so things would be different?

Catalina stared into those eyes and for once she saw hope; she saw a need that had nothing to do with sex.

Resting her head on his shoulder, Catalina whispered, "One of us is going to get hurt."

Fourteen

Catalina leaned back against Will's chest as they settled onto the oversized plush sofa on the top deck. The full moon provided enough light and just the perfect ambiance; even Will couldn't have planned it better.

Granted he didn't like that the yacht was damaged or that Catalina had been injured, but the feel of her wrapped in his arms, their legs intertwined, even as he was careful of her ankle, was everything he'd wanted since he let her walk away so long ago.

Will laced his hands over her stomach and smiled when she laid her hands atop his.

"It's so quiet and peaceful," she murmured. "The stars are so vibrant here. I guess I never pay much attention in Alma."

"One of these days you're going to have your own maid, your own staff," he stated firmly. "You deserve to be pampered for all the hours you work without asking for anything in return. You work too hard."

"I do," she agreed. "I have so many things I want to do with my life and working is what keeps me motivated."

A strand of her hair danced in the breeze, tickling his cheek, but he didn't mind. Any way he could touch her and be closer was fine with him. She wasn't trying to ignore this pull and she'd actually relaxed fully against him. This is what they needed. The simplicity, the privacy.

"What are your goals, Cat?"

"I'd love a family someday."

The wistfulness in her tone had him wanting to fulfill those wishes. Will knew he'd never be able to sit back and watch her be with someone else, make a life and a family with another man.

"What else?" he urged. "I want to know all of your dreams."

She stiffened in his arms. Will stroked her fingers with his, wanting to keep her relaxed, keep her locked into this euphoric moment.

"It's just me, Cat." He purposely softened his tone. "Once upon a time we shared everything with each other."

"We did. I'm just more cautious now."

Because of him. He knew he'd damaged that innocence in her, he knew full well that she was a totally different woman because of his selfish actions. And that fact was something he'd have to live with for the rest of his life. All he could do was try to make things better now and move forward.

"I shouldn't have let you go," he muttered before he could think.

"Everything happens for a reason."

Will didn't miss the hint of pain in her tone. "Maybe so, but I should've fought for you, for us."

"Family has always been your top priority, Will. You've been that way since your mother passed. You threw yourself into pleasing your father and James ran wild. Everyone grieves differently and it's affected your relationships over the years."

Will shouldn't have been surprised that she'd analyzed him and his brother so well. Cat had always been so in tune with other people's feelings. Had he ever done that for her? Had he ever thought of her feelings if they didn't coincide with his own wants and needs?

"I never wanted you hurt." Yet he'd killed her spirit anyway. "I have no excuse for what I did. Nothing I say can reverse time or knock sense into the man I was four years ago."

"Everything that happened made me a better person." She shifted a bit and lifted her ankle to resettle it over the edge of the sofa. "I poured myself into new things, found out who I really am on my own. I never would've done that had I been with you."

Will squeezed her tighter. "I wouldn't have let you lose yourself, Cat. Had you been with me I would've pushed you to do whatever you wanted."

She tipped her head back and met his gaze. "You wouldn't have let me work. You would've wanted the perfect, doting wife."

There was a ring of truth to her words. He most likely would have tried to push her into doing what he thought was best.

"I wasn't good to you." He swallowed. "You were better off without me, but it killed me to let you go, knowing you'd be fine once you moved on."

Silence settled heavily around them before she finally said, "I wasn't fine."

"You were dating a man two months after we broke up."

Cat turned back around, facing the water. "I needed to date, I needed to move on in any way that I could and try to forget you. When I was alone my mind would wander and I'd start to remember how happy I was with you. I needed to fill that void in any way I possibly could."

Will swallowed. He'd hated seeing her with another man, hated knowing he was the one who drove her into another's arms.

"I slept with him."

Her words cut through the darkness and straight to his heart. "I don't want—"

"I slept with him because I was trying to forget you," she went on as if he hadn't said a word. "I was ready to give myself to you, then you chose to obey your father once again at my expense. When I started dating Bryce, I mistook his affection for love. I knew I was on the rebound, but I wanted so badly to be with someone who valued me, who wanted to be with me and put me first."

Those raw, heartfelt words crippled him. He'd had no idea just how much damage he'd caused. All this time, she'd been searching for anyone to put her at the top of their priority list when he'd shoved her to the bottom of his.

"Afterward I cried," she whispered. "I hated that I'd given away something so precious and I hated even more that I still wished I'd given it to you."

Her honesty gutted him. Will wished more than anything he could go back and make changes, wished he could go back and be the man she needed him to be.

But he could be honest now, he could open up. She'd shared such a deep, personal secret, he knew she deserved to know why he'd let her go so easily.

"I had to let you go."

"I know, your father—"

"No." Will adjusted himself in the seat so he could face her better. "I need you to know this, I need you to listen to what I'm saying. I let you go because of my father, but not for the reasons you think."

The moon cast enough of a glow for Will to see Cat's dark eyes widen. "What?"

"I let you go to save you. My father's threats…" Will shook his head, still angry over the way he'd let his father manipulate him. "As soon as I let you go, I was plotting to get you back, to put my father in his place. I didn't care how long it took, didn't care what I had to do."

Cat stared back at him, and he desperately wanted to know what was swirling around in her head. There was so much hurt between them, so many questions and years of resentment. Will hated his father for putting him in this position, but he hated even more the way Cat had been the victim in all of this.

"Your father threatened me, didn't he?" Cat asked, her voice low, yet firm. "He held me over your head? Is that why you let me go?"

Swallowing the lump of guilt, Will nodded.

Cat sat up, swung her feet over the side and braced her hands on either side of her hips. Will lifted his leg out of her way and brought his knee up to give her enough room to sit. He waited while she stared down at the deck. Silence and moonlight surrounded them, bathing them in a peace that he knew neither of them felt.

"Talk to me." He couldn't handle the uncertainty. "I don't want you going through this alone."

A soft laugh escaped her as she kept her gaze averted. "But you didn't care that I went through this alone four years ago."

"Dammit, Cat. I couldn't let you get hurt. He had the ability to ruin you and I wasn't going to put my needs ahead of yours."

When she threw him a glance over her shoulder, Will's gut tightened at the moisture gathered in her eyes. "You didn't put my needs first at all. You didn't give me a chance to fight for us and you took the easy way out."

Raking a hand over his hair, Will blew out a breath. "I didn't take the easy way," he retorted. "I took the hardest way straight through hell to keep you safe and to work on getting you back."

She continued to stare, saying nothing. Moments later her eyes widened. "Wait," she whispered. "How did Bella come into play?"

"You know I never would've married her. That was all a farce to begin with." Will shifted closer, reaching out to smooth her hair back behind her ear. "And once I kissed you, I knew exactly who I wanted, who I needed."

Cat started to stand, winced and sat back down. Will said nothing as he pushed his leg around her, once again straddling her from behind. He pulled her back against his chest and leaned on the plush cushions. Even though she remained rigid, he knew the only way to get her to soften was for him to be patient. He'd waited four years; he was the epitome of patient.

Wrapping his arms around her, he whispered in her ear. "I messed up," he admitted. "I only wanted to protect you and went about it the wrong way. Don't shut me out now, Cat. We have too much between us. This goes so much deeper than either of us realizes and I won't let my father continue to ruin what we have."

Dammit, somewhere along the way to a heated affair Will had developed stronger feelings, a deeper bond with Cat than he'd anticipated. And now that he knew he wanted more from her, he was close to losing it all.

"And what do we have, Will?" Her words came out on a choked sob.

"What do you want?"

What do you want?

Catalina couldn't hold in the tension another second. There was only so much one person could handle and Will's simple question absolutely deflated her. Melting back against his body once more, she swallowed the emotion burning her throat.

"I want..." Catalina shut her eyes, trying to figure out all the thoughts fighting for head space. "I don't know now. Yesterday I knew exactly what I wanted. I was ready to leave Alma to get it."

Will's fingertips slid up and down her bare arms, causing her body to tremble beneath his delicate touch. "And now? What do you want now, Cat?"

Everything.

"I don't want to make things harder for you," he went on. "But I'm not backing down. Not this time."

And there was a portion of her heart that didn't want him to. How could she be so torn? How could two dreams be pulling her in completely different directions?

Because the harder she'd tried to distance herself from him, the more she was being pulled back in.

"I'm afraid," she whispered. "I can't make promises and I'm not ready to accept them from you, either."

His hands stilled for the briefest of moments before he kissed the top of her head. Catalina turned her cheek to rest against his chest, relishing the warmth of his body, the strong steady heartbeat beneath her. Part of her wanted to hate him for his actions years ago, the other part of her wanted to cry for the injustice of it all.

But a good portion of her wanted to forgive him, to believe him when he said that he'd sacrificed himself to keep her safe. Why did he have to be so damn noble and why hadn't he told her to begin with? He didn't have to fight that battle all on his own. Maybe she could have saved him, too.

Catalina closed her eyes as the yacht rocked steadily to the soothing rhythm of the waves. She wanted to lock this moment in time and live here forever. Where there were no outside forces trying to throw obstacles in their way and the raw honesty...

No. She still carried a secret that he didn't know and how could she ever tell him? How could she ever reveal the fact that his father had had an affair with her mother? Would he hate her for knowing?

"Will, I need—"

"We're done talking. I just want to hold you. Nothing else matters right now."

Turning a bit more in his arms, Catalina looked up into those vibrant eyes that had haunted her dreams for years. "Make love to me, Will. I don't care about anything else. Not when I can be with you."

In one swift, powerful move, he had her straddling his lap. Catalina hissed a breath when her ankle bumped his thigh.

"Dammit. Sorry, Cat."

She offered him a smile, stroking the pad of her thumb along the worry lines between his brows. "I'm fine," she assured him as she slid the ties at the side of her dress free. "I don't want to think about my injury, why we're stuck here or what's waiting for us when we get back. All I want is to feel you against me."

Will took in the sight of her as she continued to work out of her clothing. When his hands spanned her waist, she arched against his touch.

He leaned forward, resting his forehead against her chest as he whispered, "You're more than I deserve and everything I've ever wanted."

Framing his face with her hands, Catalina lifted his head until she could look him in the eyes. "No more talking," she reminded him with a soft kiss to his lips. "No more talking tonight."

Tomorrow, or whenever they were able to get off this island, she'd tell him about his father. But for now, she'd take this gift she'd been given and worry about the ugly truth, and how they would handle it, later.

Fifteen

By the second day, Catalina still hadn't told Will the truth. How could she reveal such a harsh reality when they'd been living in passionate bliss on a beautiful island in some fantasy?

They'd both fiddled with the radio and tried their cell phones from various spots on the island, but nothing was going through. She wasn't going to panic quite yet. They had plenty of food and for a bit, she could pretend this was a dream vacation with the man she'd fallen in love with.

Will rolled over in bed, wrapping his arm around her and settling against her back. "I'd like to say I can't wait to get off this island, but waking up with you in my arms is something I could get used to."

His husky tone filled her ear. The coarse hair on his chest tickled her back, but she didn't mind. She loved the feel of Will next to her.

"I'm getting pretty spoiled, too." She snuggled deeper into his embrace. "I'm never going to want to leave."

"Maybe that's how I want you to be," he replied, nipping her shoulder.

"We can't stay here forever," she laughed.

"As long as you don't leave Alma, I'm okay with going back."

A sliver of reality crept back in. Catalina shifted so that she could roll over in his arms and face him.

"I don't plan on working as a maid forever," she informed him, staring into his eyes. "And after what you told me about your father, I think it's best if I don't work there anymore. I can't work for a man who completely altered my future. I stayed with James because I adore him and I moved on to Patrick because I needed the job, but now that I know the full truth, I can't stay there."

Will propped himself up on his elbow and peered down at her. "I understand, but stay in Alma. Stay with me."

"And do what?" she asked, already knowing this conversation was going to divide them. "I have goals, Will. Goals that I can't ignore simply because we're… I don't even know what this is between us right now."

"Do you need a label?" he asked.

Part of her wanted to call this something. Maybe then she could justify her feelings for a man who'd let her go so easily before.

She had no idea what she was going to do once she got back to Alma. Working for Patrick was not going to happen. She'd put up with his arrogance for too long. Thankfully she'd only worked for him a short time because up until recently, James had been the one occupying the Playa del Onda home. Catalina had had a hard enough time working for Patrick knowing what she did about her mother, but now knowing he'd manipulated his son and crushed their relationship, Catalina couldn't go back there. Never again.

So where did that leave her? She didn't think she was quite ready to head out with her designs and start pursuing her goal. She had a few more things she'd like to complete before she made that leap.

"What's going through your mind?" Will asked, studying her face.

"You know the sewing set you got me?"

Will nodded.

"You have no idea how much that touched me." Catalina raked her hand through his blond hair and trailed her fingertips down his jaw, his neck. "I've been sewing in my spare time. Making things for myself, for my mother. It's been such a great escape and when I saw what you'd gotten me, I…"

Catalina shook her head and fell back against the bed. She stared up at the ceiling and wished she could find the right words to tell him how much she appreciated the gift.

"So you're saying it was a step up from the flowers?" he joked.

Shifting her gaze to him, her heart tightened at his playful smile. "I may have cried," she confessed. "That was the sweetest gift ever."

Will settled over her, his hands resting on either side of her head. "It was meant more as a joke," he said with a teasing smile. "And maybe I wanted to remind you of what we did in the utility room."

Cat smacked his chest. "As if I could've forgotten. That's all I could think about and you know it."

He gave her a quick kiss before he eased back. "It's all I could think of, too, if that helps."

Catalina wrapped her arms around his neck, threading her fingers through his hair. "What are we going to do when we get back?"

"We're going to take this one day at a time because I'm not screwing this up again."

"We can't seem to function in normal life."

Will's forehead rested against hers as he let out a sigh. "Trust me, Cat. I've fought too hard to get you back. I'm going to fight just as hard to keep you."

Catalina prayed that was true, because all too soon she was going to have to reveal the final secret between them if she wanted a future with this man.

Cat lay on the deck sunbathing in that skimpy bikini, which was positively driving him out of his mind. Right now he didn't give a damn that the radio was beyond repair or that their phones weren't getting a signal. For two days they'd made love, stayed in bed and talked, spending nearly every single moment together.

Perhaps that's why he was in such agony. He knew exactly what that lush body felt like against his own. He knew how amazingly they fit together with no barriers between them.

Will couldn't recall the last time he'd taken this much time away from work. Surprisingly he wasn't getting twitchy. He'd set his plan into motion a couple months ago for Rowling Energy and it shouldn't be too much longer before everything he'd ever wanted clicked into place like a perfectly, methodically plotted puzzle.

Will folded his arms behind his head and relaxed on the seat opposite Cat. But just as he closed his eyes, the soft hum of an engine had him jumping to his feet.

"Do you hear that?" he asked, glancing toward the horizon.

Cat sat up, her hand shielding her eyes as she glanced in the same direction. "Oh, there's another boat."

Will knew that boat and he knew who would be on board. Good thing his brother hadn't left to go back to training for football yet because that meant he could come to their rescue. Which was what he was doing right now.

"Looks like our fairy tale is over," Catalina muttered.

He glanced her way. "It's not over," he corrected. "It's just beginning."

As James's yacht closed the distance between them, Will slid his shoes back on. "Stay here. I'll wave James to the other side of the dock where the damage isn't as bad. And I'll carry you on board once we're secure."

Cat rolled her eyes and reached for her wrap draped across the back of the white sofa. "I can walk, Will. My ankle is sore, but it's much better than it was."

Will wasn't going to argue. He'd win in the end regardless.

As soon as James was near enough, Will hopped up onto the dock and made his way toward the other end. By the time James came to a stop, Bella was at his side, a worried look etched across her face.

"Coast guard has arrived," James said, coming up behind his wife.

"I figured you'd come along sooner or later," Will replied.

James took in the damage to the dock and the yacht. "Damn, you've got a mess. That must've been one hell of a storm. It rained and there was some thunder and wind in Alma, but no damage."

"Let me go get our things," Will told his brother. "I need to carry Cat, too. She's hurt."

"Oh no," Bella cried. "What happened?"

"I fell."

Will turned to see Cat leaning over the side of the yacht. "You're supposed to be sitting down," he called back.

"I'm fine. I will need some help off this thing, but I can walk if I go slow."

Will shook his head. "I'll carry her," he told his brother. "Give me a few minutes to get our personal stuff gathered."

Once they transferred everything Will and Cat needed to his brother's yacht and Will carried a disgruntled Cat on board, they were ready to head out. The trip back to Alma was filled with questions from Bella and James. Their worry was touching and Will actually found himself loving this newfound bond he and his brother shared. This is what he'd been missing for years. This is what their grief had torn apart after their mother had died. But now they were slowly making their way back to each other.

"I wasn't quite sure which island you went to," James said as they drew nearer to Alma's coastline. "I went to two last night and had to start again today when I couldn't find you."

"Did you tell anyone what was going on?" Will asked.

"No." James maneuvered the boat and pulled back on the throttle. "Bella and I are the only ones who know where you were."

Will was relieved nobody else knew. He didn't want to share Cat or their relationship with anyone just yet. He wanted to bask in their privacy for a bit longer.

"Dammit," James muttered as they neared what was supposed to be a private dock where Alma's rich and famous kept their boats. "The damn press is here."

"What for?" Cat asked, her eyes widening.

"There were a few reporters here when I left earlier,"

James stated as he steered the yacht in. "They were speculating because Will's yacht had been missing for a few days and they knew a storm had come through. They asked me where you were and I ignored them."

Will groaned. So much for that privacy he'd been clinging to. "Don't they have anything better to cover? Like the fact Juan Carlos is going to be crowned king in a few weeks? Do they seriously have to focus on me?"

Cat's eyes remained fixed on the throng of reporters and cameras turning in their direction.

Will crouched down before her seat and smoothed her hair back from her face. "Ignore them. No matter what they say, do not make a comment. They'll forget about this by tomorrow and we can move on."

Her eyes sought his and she offered him a smile. "Ignore them. That I can do."

Will stood back up and offered her his hand. "I'm going to at least put my arm around you so you can put some of your weight on me. Anyone looking will just think I'm helping you."

"I'll carry her bag," Bella offered. "I'll go first. Maybe they'll focus on James and me. I can always just start discussing my upcoming fund-raiser for my foundation next weekend. I'm okay with yanking the reporters' chains, too."

Will couldn't help but laugh at Bella's spunk. She was the perfect match for his brother.

As they made their way down the dock, Will kept his arm secured around Cat's waist. James and Bella took the lead, holding hands as they wedged through the sea of nosy people.

The reporters seemed to all start shouting at once.

"Where have you been for three days?"

"Was your yacht damaged by the storm?"

"Were you stranded somewhere?"

"Who is with you, Will?"

The questions kept coming as Will tried to shield Cat from the press. The whispers and murmurs infuriated him. Seriously? Wasn't there other newsworthy stuff happening in Alma right now? Dammit, this was one major drawback to being a wealthy, well-known businessman. And if he thought for a second he could have any privacy with Cat now that they were back, he was living in a fantasy.

When he heard someone say the word "staff" he clenched his jaw. He wouldn't respond. That's what they wanted: some type of reaction. He heard his father's name and for reasons unbeknownst to Will, the gossipmongers were starting to piece things together rather quickly. Where the hell would they have seen Cat? On occasion his father would allow a few press members to attend certain parties thrown by the Rowlings if there was a charity involved. Cat had been James's maid, too, though.

Will groaned as he kept his sights on his brother's back as the foursome pushed through to the waiting car in the distance. They couldn't get there fast enough for Will.

"Is your mistress a member of your family's staff, Mr. Rowling?"

The rude question had Cat stiffening at his side. "Keep going," he murmured. "Almost there."

"Wasn't she working for your brother?"

"Is she on Patrick's staff?"

"How long have you been seeing your father's maid?"

"Weren't you just engaged to your brother's wife?"

"What does your father think about you and his maid?"

Will snapped. "This isn't like that. You're all making a mistake."

Catalina's gasp had him jerking his gaze toward her. "Dammit," he muttered beneath his breath. "You know that's not what I mean."

Those damn words echoed from the last time he'd said them to her. And this time they were just as damaging when taken out of context.

Easing back from his side, Cat kept her eyes on his. "I'm not sure, Will. Because only moments ago you said ignore them and you said we'd take this one day at a time. We've only been back in Alma five minutes and you're already referring to me as a mistake."

Will raked a hand through his hair. From the corner of his eye he spotted James and Bella standing close. For once the reporters weren't saying a word. They waited, no doubt hoping to really get something juicy for their headlines.

"Marry me."

Okay, he hadn't meant to blurt that out there, but now that the words hovered between them, he wasn't sorry. Maybe Cat would see just how serious he was about them.

"Marry you?" she asked, her brows drawn in. "You're not serious."

He stepped forward and took her hand. "We are not a mistake, Cat. You know we're perfect together. Why wouldn't you?"

Cat stared back at him, and then shook her head and let out a soft laugh. "This is ridiculous. You don't mean this proposal so why would you do this to me? Why would you ask that in front of all these people? To prove them wrong? Because you got caught with the maid and you're trying to glamorize it?"

"Dammit, Cat, this has nothing to do with anyone else. We can talk later, in private."

He didn't want to hash this out here in front of the press. And he sure as hell didn't want to sound as if he was backpedaling because he'd chosen the worst possible time to blurt out a proposal.

Crossing her arms over her chest, she tipped her chin up just a notch, but enough for him to know she was good and pissed. "Would you have proposed to me if all of these people hadn't been around? Later tonight when we were alone, would you have asked me to marry you?"

Will gritted his teeth, clenched his fists at his side and honestly had no reply. He had absolutely no idea what to say. He didn't want to have such an intimate talk in front of the whole country, because that's exactly what was happening. The press would no doubt splash this all over the headlines.

"That's what I thought." Cat's soft tone was full of hurt. "I'd say it's officially over between us."

When she turned, she winced, but just as Will reached to help her, Bella stepped forward and slowly ushered Cat to the car. James moved in next to Will and ordered the press away. Will didn't hear much, didn't comprehend what was going on because in the span of just a few minutes, he'd gone from deliriously happy and planning his future, to seeing that future walk away from him after he'd hurt her, called her a mistake, once again.

This time, he knew there would be no winning her back.

Sixteen

"What the hell is this?"

Will turned away from his office view to face his father, who stood on the other side of his desk with a folder in his hand. Will had been waiting for this moment. But he hadn't expected to feel this enormous pit of emptiness inside.

"I see you received the notice regarding your shares in Rowling Energy." Will folded his arms across his chest and leveled his father's gaze. "Your votes in the company are no longer valid. I held an emergency meeting with the other stockholders and we came to the decision."

Patrick's face reddened. "How dare you. What kind of son did I raise that he would turn around and treat his father like this?"

"You raised the son who fought for what he wanted." Will's blood pressure soared as he thought of all he'd lost and all he was still fighting for. "You raised a son who watched his father put business first, above family, and to hell with the rest of the world. I'm taking Rowling Energy into new territory and I need sole control. I'm done being jerked around by you."

Patrick rested his palms on the desk and leaned in. "No, you'd rather be jerked around by my maid. You two made quite a scene yesterday—it made headlines. You're becoming an embarrassment and tarnishing the Rowling name."

Will laughed. "What I do in my personal life is not your concern. You poked your nose in years ago when you threatened to dismiss Catalina if I didn't dump her. I won't be manipulated ever again and you will leave Cat alone. If I even think you've tried to—"

"Knock off the threats," his father shouted as he pushed off the desk. "Your little maid quit on me and has really left me in a bind. If you were smart, you'd stay away from her. You two get cozy and she quits. I don't believe in coincidences. Those Iberra women are nothing but gold diggers."

Will stood up straighter, dropped his arms to his sides. "What did you say?"

Patrick waved a hand in the air, shaking his head. "Forget it."

"No. You said 'those Iberra women.' What did you mean?"

Will knew Cat's mother had worked for Patrick years ago. Maria had been around when James and Will had been young, when their mother was still alive.

"What did Maria do that you would call her a gold digger?" Will asked when his father remained silent.

Still, Patrick said nothing.

Realization dawned on Will. "No. Tell me you didn't have an affair with Maria."

"Every man has a moment of weakness," Patrick stated simply. "I expect this past weekend was yours."

Rage boiled to the surface. Will clenched his fists. "You slept with Cat's mother while my mother was still alive? Did Mum know about the affair?"

The thought of his sweet, caring mother being betrayed tore through Will's heart. Part of him prayed she never knew the ugly acts his father had committed.

"She found out the day she died." Patrick let out a sigh, his eyes darting to the ground. "We were arguing about it when she left that night."

For once the great Patrick Rowling looked defeated. Which was nothing less than he deserved. Will's heart was absolutely crushed. He reached out, gripped the back of his desk chair and tried to think rationally here. Finding out your father had an affair with the mother of a woman you had fallen for was shocking enough. But to add to the intensity, his mother had died as a result of the affair.

Dread settled deep in Will's his gut. Did Cat know of this affair? Surely not. Surely she would have told him or at least hinted at the knowledge. Would this crush her, too?

"Get out," Will said in a low, powerful tone as he kept his eyes on the blotter on his desk. "Get the hell out of my office and be glad my freezing your voting rights in this company is all I'm doing to you."

Patrick didn't move. Will brought his gaze up and glared at the man he'd once trusted.

"You have one minute to be out of this building or I'll call security."

"I never thought you'd turn on me," his father replied.

"I turned on you four years ago when you threatened the woman I love."

Will hadn't meant to declare his love for Cat, but it felt good to finally let the words out. And now more than ever he wasn't giving up. He was going to move heaven and earth to win her back because he did love her. He'd always loved her if he was honest with himself. And he wanted a life with her now more than ever.

Bella was having a fund-raiser this coming weekend and Will knew he was going to need reinforcements. He wasn't letting Cat go. Not this time. Never again.

"I figured you'd be at work today." James sank down onto the chaise longue on his patio as Maisey played in her sandbox. "You look like hell, man."

Will shoved his hands in his pockets and glanced toward the ocean. "I feel like hell. Thanks for pointing it out."

"You still haven't talked to Catalina?"

Maisey squealed, threw her toy shovel and started burying her legs beneath the sand. Will watched his niece and wondered if there could ever be a family for Cat and him. She wanted a family and the more he thought of a life with her, the more he wanted the same thing.

"No, I haven't seen her." Will shifted his focus to his brother and took a seat on the edge of a chair opposite him. "Bella's fund-raiser is going to be at the Playa del Onda house this weekend, right?"

"Yes. Dad will be out of town and that house is perfect for entertaining. Why?"

"I want you to ask Cat to help with the staff there." Will held up a hand before his brother could cut him off. "I have my reasons, but I need your help in order to make this work."

James shook his head and stared down at his daughter for a minute before he looked back at Will. "This could blow up in your face."

Will nodded. "It's a risk I'm willing to take."

"What's in it for me?" James asked with a smirk.

Will laughed. Without even thinking twice, he unfastened the watch on his wrist and held it up. "This."

James's eyes widened. "I was joking."

"I'm not." Will reached out and placed the watch on the arm of his brother's chair. "You deserve it back. This has nothing to do with you helping me with Cat. The watch is rightfully yours."

James picked it up and gripped it in his hand. "We've really come a long way," he muttered.

Will had one more piece of business to take care of and he was not looking forward to this discussion at all. There was no way James knew of the affair or he definitely would've said something. Will really hated to crush his brother with the news, but James deserved to know.

"I need to tell you something." Will glanced at Maisey. "Is your nanny here or is Bella busy?"

James sat up in his seat, slid his watch on and swung his legs around to the deck. "Bella was answering emails, but she can watch Maisey. Is everything okay?"

Will shook his head. "Not really."

Worry and concern crossed James's face as he nodded. After taking Maisey inside, he returned moments later, closing the patio doors behind him.

"This must really be something if it has you this upset." James sat back down on the edge of his chair. "What's going on?"

Will took in a deep breath, blew it out and raked a hand through his hair. "This is harder than I thought," he said on a sigh. "Do you remember the night Mum died? Dad woke us and said she'd been in an accident?"

James nodded. "I heard them arguing earlier that evening. I was heading downstairs to get some water and heard them fighting so I went back upstairs."

Will straightened. "You heard them arguing?"

James nodded. "Dad raised his voice, and then Mum was crying and Dad was saying something else but in a lower tone. I didn't hear what all he said."

Will closed his eyes and wished like hell he could go back and...what? What could he have done differently? He'd been a kid. Even if James had gone downstairs and interrupted the fight, most likely their mother still would've walked out to get away from their father.

"What is it?" James prodded. "What aren't you telling me?"

Will opened his eyes and focused on his brother. "Dad had an affair. They were arguing about that."

"What?" James muttered a curse. "Has that man ever valued his family at all?"

"There's more." Will hesitated a moment, swallowed and pushed forward. "The affair was with Maria. Cat's mum."

Will started to wonder if James had heard him, but suddenly his brother jumped to his feet and let out a chain of curses that even had Will wincing. James kicked the leg of the chair, propped his hands on his hips and dropped his head between his shoulders.

"If I'd have gone downstairs that night..." he muttered.

"Mum still would've left," Will said softly. "We can't go back in time and you're not to blame. Our dad is the one whose selfish needs stole our mother. He crushed her. She would've done anything for him and he threw it all away."

James turned. "Does Cat know this?"

Shaking his head, Will came to his feet. "I doubt it. She's never said a word to me."

"Do you think once she knows the truth she'll take you back?"

Yeah, the odds were more than stacked against him, but he refused to back down. Nobody would steal his life again. And Cat was his entire life.

"I don't even know what to say about this," James said, staring out to the ocean. "I never had much respect for Dad, but right now I hate that man."

"I've made his life hell." Will was actually pleased with the timing. "As CEO of Rowling Energy, I've frozen his shares. He can no longer vote on any company matters that come before the board."

James smiled. "If this action were directed to an enemy, dear old Dad would be proud of your business tactics."

"Yeah," Will agreed, returning the grin. "He's not too proud right now, though. But I have more pressing matters to tend to."

James reached out, patted Will on the back. "I'll do what I can where Cat is concerned. I know what this is like to be so torn over a woman."

Torn wasn't even the word.

"I never thought either of us would fall this hard." Will pulled in a deep breath. "Now we need Bella to convince Cat to work the party. I can take it from there. I just need you guys to get her there."

Seventeen

If Catalina didn't adore Bella and her valiant efforts to raise money for the Alma Wildlife Conservation Society which she'd recently founded, Catalina wouldn't have stepped foot back into this house.

But Patrick was out of town and Bella and James had caught Catalina at a weak moment, offering her an insane amount of money to help set up for the event.

In the past week since she'd last seen Will, she'd not heard one word from him. Apparently she wasn't worth fighting for after all. Not that she would have forgiven him, but a girl likes to at least know she's worth something other than a few amazing sexual encounters.

Catalina hurried through the house, hoping to get everything set up perfectly before the first guests arrived.

Okay, fine. There was only one person on the guest list she was trying like hell to avoid.

She'd spent this past week furiously working on her

final designs. She didn't have the amount of money saved up that she wanted before she left Alma, but it would just have to be enough. Alma had nothing left to offer her. Not anymore.

Catalina took a final walkthrough, adjusting one more floral arrangement on the foyer table before she was satisfied with everything. She'd already double-checked with the kitchen to make sure the food was ready and would be served according to the set schedule. She'd also told Bella she would be back around midnight to clean up. There was just no way she could stay during the party. That had been her only condition for working tonight, and thankfully Bella had agreed.

Catalina checked her watch. Only thirty minutes until guests were due to arrive. Time to head out. She'd opted to park near the side entrance off the utility room. Just as she turned into the room to grab her purse and keys, she ran straight into a very hard, very familiar chest.

Closing her eyes, she tried like hell not to breathe in, but Will's masculine aroma enveloped her just as his strong arms came around to steady her.

"Running away?" he whispered in her ear.

Knowing she'd never get out without talking, Catalina shored up all of her courage and lifted her gaze to his. "I'm not the one who usually runs."

Keeping his aqua eyes on her, Will reached around, slammed the door and flicked the lock. "Neither of us is getting out of here until we talk."

"I don't need you to hold onto me," she told him, refusing to glance away. No way was he keeping the upper hand here just because her heart was in her throat.

"I want to make sure you'll stay put."

He dropped his hands but didn't step back. The

warmth from his body had hers responding. She wished she didn't fall so easily into the memories of their lovemaking, wished she didn't get swept away by such intriguing eyes. Even through their rocky moments, Catalina couldn't deny that all the good trumped the bad…at least in her heart.

"I'll stay." She stepped back until she was flat against the door. "If I don't listen now, I know you'll show up at my apartment. Might as well get this over with."

Why couldn't he be haggard or have dark circles beneath his eyes? Had he not been losing sleep over the fact he'd been a jerk? Why did he have to be so damn sexy all the time and why couldn't she turn off her hormones around this man who constantly hurt her?

"There's so much I want to say," he muttered as he ran a hand over his freshly shaven jaw. "I don't know where to start."

Catalina tapped her watch. "Better hurry. The party starts soon."

"I don't give a damn about that party. I already gave Bella a check for the foundation."

"Of course you did," she muttered. "What do you want from me, Will?"

He stepped forward until her body was firmly trapped between his and the door. Placing a hand on either side of her head, he replied, "Everything."

Oh, mercy. She wasn't going to be able to keep up this courage much longer if he kept looking at her like that, if he touched her or used those charming words.

"You can't have everything." She licked her lips and stared up at him. "You can't treat everything like a business deal, only giving of yourself when it's convenient for you or makes you look good in the public eye."

Will smoothed her hair away from her face and she

simply couldn't take it anymore. She placed her hands on his chest and shoved him back, slipping past him to get some breathing room before she lost her mind and clung to him.

"I'm actually glad you cornered me," she went on, whirling around to face him. "I didn't want to run into you tonight, but we both need closure. I don't want to leave Alma with such awkwardness between us."

"Leave Alma," he repeated. "You're not leaving Alma."

Catalina laughed. "You know you can't control everyone, right? I am leaving. In two weeks, actually. My mother and I have tickets and we're heading to Milan."

"What's in Milan?"

Catalina tucked her hair behind her ears and crossed her arms. "My new life. I've been working for nearly four years and I'm finally ready to take my clothing designs and see what I can do in the world. I may not get far, but I'm going to try."

Will's brows drew in as he listened. Catalina actually liked the fact that she'd caught him off guard. He'd been knocking the air out of her lungs for a good while now and it was only appropriate she return the favor.

"I know you're angry with me for blurting out the proposal in front of such an audience, but you have to listen to me now."

"I'll listen, but you're wasting your time if you're trying to convince me of anything. We're not meant to be, Will. We've tried, and we weren't successful either time. I don't want to keep fighting a losing battle."

"I've never lost a battle in my life," he informed her as he took a step closer. "I don't intend to lose this one."

"You already lost," she whispered. "On the island we were so happy and for that time I really thought we could come back here and build on that. But once again, I was naïve where you were concerned. As soon as we stepped foot back in Alma, you turned into that take-charge man who didn't want to look like a fool in front of the cameras. You were embarrassed to be seen with the maid, and then when you realized just how much of a jerk you were being, you opted to propose? Did you honestly think I'd accept that?"

Will was close enough to touch, but he kept his hands propped on his hips. "I reacted without thinking. Dammit, Cat we'd just had the best few days together and I was scared, all right? Everything about us terrifies me to the point I can't think straight. I've never wanted anything or anyone the way I want you and I've never been this afraid of losing what I love forever."

Catalina gasped. He didn't just say... No, he didn't love her. He was using those pretty words to control her, to trick her into...

What? What was his end game here?

"You don't love me, Will." Oh, how she wished he did, but that was still the naïve side of her dreaming. "You love power."

"I won't deny power is important to me. But that also means I can use that power to channel some pretty damn intense emotions." He leaned in, close enough for her to feel his breath on her face, yet he still didn't touch her. "And I love you more than any business deal, more than any merger or sale. I love you, Catalina."

She didn't want to hear this. He'd used her full name so she knew he was serious, or as serious as he could be.

"I don't want this," she murmured, trying to look away, but trapped by the piercing gaze. "I have plans, Will, and I can't hinge my entire life around a man who may or may not put me above his career."

And even if she could give in and let him have her heart, she carried this secret inside of her that would surely drive another sizeable wedge between them.

"Listen to me." He eased back, but reached out and placed his hands on either side of her face. "Hear every single word I'm about to tell you. For the past four years I've fought to get you back. At first I'll admit it was because my father wanted something else for my life and I was being spiteful, but the longer you and I were apart, the more I realized there was an empty ache inside of me that couldn't be filled. I poured myself into work, knowing the day would come when I'd take over Rowling Energy. Even through all of that, I was plotting to get you back."

He stared at her, his thumb stroking back and forth along the length of her jawline as if he was putting her into some type of trance.

"Just the thought of you with another man was crushing, but I knew if I didn't fight for you, for us, then you'd settle down and I'd lose you forever. I've always put you first, Cat. Always. Even when we weren't together, I was working my way back to you."

When she started to glance away, he tipped her head up, forcing her to keep her eyes on his. "You think I was working this long to win you back just to have sex with you? I want the intimacy, I want the verbal sparring matches we get into, I want to help you pick up those little seashells along the beach and I want to wake up with you beside me every day for the rest of my life. Rowling Energy and all I have there mean nothing in the grand scheme of things. I want the money and the power, but I want you more than any of that."

Catalina chewed on her bottom lip, trying to force her chin to stop quivering. She was on the verge of losing it and once the dam burst on her tears, she might never regain control.

"Before you decide, I don't want anything coming between us again," he went on. "I need to tell you something that is quite shocking and I just discovered myself."

Catalina reached up, gripped his wrists and eased his hands away from her face. She kept hold of him, but remained still. "What is it?"

"There's no easy way to tell you this without just saying it."

Fear pumped through her as her heart kicked up the pace. What on earth was he going to reveal? Whatever it was, it was a big deal. And once he told her his shocking news, she had a bombshell of her own to drop because she also couldn't move forward, with or without him, and still keep this secret.

"I found out that my father and your mother had an affair."

When Catalina stared at him for a moment, his eyes widened and he stepped back. She said nothing, but the look on his face told her all she needed to know.

"You already knew?" he asked in a whisper. "Didn't you?"

Cat nodded. Will's heart tightened. How had she known? How could she keep something so important from him?

"You've known awhile," he said, keeping his eyes on her unsurprised face. "How long?"

Cat blinked back the moisture that had gathered in her dark eyes. "Four years."

Rubbing the back of his neck, Will glanced down at

the floor. He couldn't look at her. Couldn't believe she'd keep such a monumental secret from him.

"I didn't know when we were together," she told him. "My mom told me after we broke up. I was so upset and she kept telling me how the Rowling men... Never mind. It's not important."

Everything about this was important, yet the affair really had nothing to do with how he felt for Cat. The sins of their parents didn't have to trickle down to them and ruin their happiness.

"I still can't believe you didn't say anything."

Cat turned, walked to the door and stared out into the backyard. Will took in her narrow shoulders, the exposed nape of her neck. She wasn't wearing her typical black shirt and pants. Right now she had on a pair of flat sandals, a floral skirt and some type of fitted shirt that sat right at the edge of her shoulders. She looked amazing and she was just out of his reach, physically and emotionally.

"I wanted to tell you on the island," she said, keeping her back to him. "I tried once, but we got sidetracked. That's an excuse. I should've made you listen, but we were so happy and there was no such thing as reality during those few days. I just wanted to stay in that euphoric moment."

He couldn't fault her for that because he'd felt the exact same way.

"There's just so much against us, Will." She turned back around and the lone tear on her cheek gutted him. "Sometimes people can love each other and still not be together. Sometimes love isn't enough and people just need to go their own way."

Will heard what she was saying, but how could he not hone in on the one main point to her farewell speech?

"You love me?" He couldn't help but smile as he crossed to her. "Say it, Cat. I want to hear the words."

She shook her head. "It doesn't mean anything."

"Say it." His hands settled around her waist as he pulled her flush against him. "Now."

"I love you, Will, but—"

He crushed his lips to hers. Nothing else mattered after those life-altering words. Nothing she could say would erase the fact that she loved him and he loved her, and he'd be damn it if he would ever let her walk away.

Her body melted against his as her fingers curled around his biceps. Will lifted his mouth from hers, barely.

"Don't leave, Cat," he murmured against her lips. "Don't leave Alma. Don't leave me."

"I can't give up who I am, Will." She closed her eyes and sighed. "No matter how much I love you, I can't give up everything I've worked for and I wouldn't expect you to give up your work for me. We have different goals in different directions."

The fear of losing her, the reality that if he didn't lay it all on the line, then she would be out of his life for good hit him hard.

"I'm coming with you."

Cat's eyes flew open as Will tipped his head back to see her face better. "What?"

"I meant what I said. I won't give you up and you're more to me than any business. But I can work from anywhere and I can fly to Alma when I need to."

"You can't be serious." Panic flooded her face. "This is rushed. You can't expect me to just say okay and we'll be on our way to happily-ever-after. It's too fast."

Will laughed. "I've known you since you were a little girl. I dated you four years ago and last weekend you spent nearly three days in my bed. You said you love me and I love the hell out of you and you think this is too fast? If we move any slower we'll be in a nursing home by the time you wear my ring on your finger."

"I can't think." Once again she pushed him aside and moved past him. "I can't take all this in. I mean, your dad and my mom…all of the things that have kept us apart. And then you corner me in a laundry room of all places to tell me you want me forever."

"So we don't do things the traditional way." He came up behind her, gripped her shoulders and kissed the top of her head. "I'm done with being by the book and boring. I want adventure, I want to be on a deserted island with the only woman in the world who can make me angry, laugh and love the way you do. I want to take care of you, I want to wear out the words *I love you* and I want to have no regrets from here on out where we are concerned."

Cat eased back against him, her head on his shoulder. "I want to believe all of that is possible. I want to hold on to the hope that I can still fulfill my dreams and I can have you. But I won't give up myself, no matter how much I love you, Will."

Wrapping his arms around her waist, he leaned his cheek on her head. "I wouldn't ask you to give up anything. I just didn't want you leaving Alma without me. We can live wherever you want. I have a jet, I have a yacht…well, I'll have a new one soon. I can travel where I need to be for work and I can take you where you need to go in order to fulfill this goal of yours. I want to be with you every step of your journey."

"I want to do it on my own," she stated, sliding her hands over his.

"I wouldn't dream of interfering," he replied. "I'll

support you in any way you need. I'll be the silent financial backer or I'll be the man keeping your bed warm at night and staying out of the business entirely. The choice is yours."

Cat turned in his arms, laced her hands behind his neck and stared up at him. "Tell me this is real. Tell me you don't hate me for keeping the secret and that you will always make me first in your life."

"It's real." He kissed her forehead. "I could never hate you." He kissed her nose. "And you'll never question again whether you're first in my life."

He slid his mouth across hers, gliding his hands down her body to the hem of her shirt. Easing the hem up, he smoothed his palms up over her bare skin, pleased when she shivered beneath his touch.

"Are you seriously trying to seduce me in a laundry room all while your sister-in-law is throwing a party to raise money for her foundation a few feet away?"

Will laughed as his lips traveled down the column of her throat. "I'm not trying. I'm about to succeed."

Cat's body arched back as her fingers threaded through his hair. "I hope no partygoers take a stroll through the backyard and glance in the window of the door," she panted when his hands brushed the underside of her breasts.

"We already made headlines." He jerked the shirt up and over her head, flinging it to the side without a care. "Another one won't matter at this point."

"What will your brother think if you don't show at the party?"

Will shrugged. "James is pretty smart. I'd say he'll know exactly where I am."

Cat started working on the buttons of his shirt and

soon sent the shirt and his jacket to the floor. "We still don't have a solid plan for our future."

Hoisting her up, Will sat her on the counter and settled between her legs. "I know how the next several minutes are going to play out. Beyond that I don't care so long as you're with me."

Will kissed her once more and eased back. "But I already have the perfect wedding present for you."

Cat laughed as her arms draped over his shoulders. "And what's that?"

"A maid. You'll not lift a finger for me ever. I want you to concentrate on your design career and the babies we're going to have in the future."

When Cat's smile widened and she tightened her hold on him, Will knew the four years he'd worked on getting back to her were worth it. Everything he'd sacrificed with his father and personal life was worth this moment, knowing he was building a future with the only woman he'd ever loved.

* * * * *

THE SCANDAL THAT MADE HER HIS QUEEN

CAITLIN CREWS

For Nina Pépin, because she asked.

CHAPTER ONE

CASTLES AND PALACES and all such trappings of royalty, Nina Graine reflected dryly, were much better in theory than in practice.

She would know, having had far too much of that practice.

In theory, castles were all about fairy tales. She'd thought so herself while growing up in the orphanage. Think of castles and it was all happy, merry songs dancing gracefully on a sweet breeze. Happy-ever-afters sounding from on high, possibly with the help of fleets of cantering unicorns.

Nina was pretty sure she'd had that dream at least a thousand times.

But then she'd learned the truth.

In practice, castles were dark and drafty old things. Most of them had been fortresses first and were therefore built in places where ransacking armies and the odd barbarian could be turned away with a minimum of fuss. They were filled with musty tapestries and bristling with trophies of battles past. No matter how modernized they claimed to be, there were always too many ghosts in the fortified walls.

Palaces, meanwhile, were less about defense and more about drama. *Look at me*, a palace cried. *I'm better than everything and especially you.*

Like the one she was currently visiting in the island kingdom of Theosia, sitting pretty in the Mediterranean Sea. The Kings of Theosia had called this place the Palace of the Gods, clearly not suffering from any form of impostor syndrome.

She *almost* started thinking about the palace's current occupants, the unwell, old King Cronos and his only son and heir, the wicked, scandalous, upsettingly beautiful Prince Zeus. *Almost.*

But there would be time enough for that.

Instead, Nina focused her attention on the stuffy little room she'd been left in. It could have been in any palace, an afterthought of a space tucked away in the administrative wing where royal feet seldom trod. Nina had been marched here after she'd pleaded her case to a succession of palace guards, starting with the ones at the looming gate. They had finally transferred her into the care of the palace staff and she had been brought here by the sniffiest, most disdainful butler she had ever encountered.

But that was par for the course in the underbelly of a royal household. Nina tried to make herself comfortable on a settee that had likely been built for the express purpose of making interlopers squirm. No wonder it was down here in the basement, the domain of all manner of petty cruelties and intense jockeying for position. Down here—and it was always the same, no matter what kingdom or huffy principality—it was really more the palace of gorgons than gods.

Because the royals were bad enough. Kings and queens with their reigns and their wars and their commandments were all very well, though they did tend to litter princes and princesses about—all primed by lives of excess to behave as atrociously as possible.

They almost couldn't help themselves, what with all that blue blood making them so constitutionally obnoxious.

It was the people who trailed about after royalty, obsequious and scheming, that Nina truly couldn't stand. The palace courtiers and uppity staff. They *could* have helped themselves but chose not to. However subservient they were when faced with the royalty they served, that was exactly how cutthroat they were behind the scenes. It might as well still be the Dark Ages, when the wrong whisper in the right ear led straight to beheadings.

There might not be too many beheadings with a blade these days, because monarchies were ever more concerned with their images. These days, beheadings were performed in the press, reputations were slashed with a single headline, and on and on the courtiers whispered gleefully, as if actual lives weren't ruined because of their games.

Why swing a blade when you could gossip to the same end?

Nina knew all of this entirely too well, and too personally. She'd been the primary lady-in-waiting to Her Royal Highness, Princess Isabeau of Haught Montagne, a small kingdom high in the Alps, since the day before her sixteenth birthday. A role she had not wanted, had not liked, and should have been overjoyed to lose six months ago.

Alas, her exit had been…complicated.

She was brooding about those complications as she fidgeted in her uncomfortable seat. The palace guards had confiscated her personal effects, so she couldn't distract herself from what she was doing. No mobile. No snacks.

It really was torture.

And then her baby kicked inside her, no doubt as cranky without a snack as Nina was—but the sensation made her smile. She smoothed her hands over her belly, murmuring a little to soothe them both.

Soon enough, someone would come and get her. And then, at some point or another, she would be face-to-face with the creature responsible for the state she was in—a state that required, once again, that she concern herself with the doings of royalty when that was the last thing she wanted.

Some people went their whole lives without encountering a person of royal blood. Nina couldn't seem to stop tripping over them. Though tripping was not how she would describe her last encounter with the arrogantly named Zeus.

Prince Zeus.

Even thinking that name made her…determined.

Nina clung to that word. She was determined, that was all. To see this through. To acquit herself appropriately. To handle this situation as well as possible, for the sake of her child.

To do the right thing—without going down the rabbit hole of blame. She was determined, and that was enough. Because she didn't like any of the other words she could have chosen to describe her current state.

She sighed and returned her attention to this palace and her officious little waiting room. All the furnishings here were too big, too formal, for a palace made all in glorious white—the better to beckon the sea, the guidebooks simpered.

When, once upon a time, the always overconfident Theosian monarchs had been far more concerned with commanding the sea than beckoning it.

The original Theosian castle lay in ruins at the far end of the island that made up the kingdom. Nina had seen it out her window as she'd flown in today from Athens. The parts that were still standing looked suitably cramped and dark, unlike the high ceilings and open archways that made the Palace of the Gods such a pageant of neoclassical eighteenth-century drama.

She'd spent the past few months studying this place as she'd slowly come to terms with what she was going to have to do. And that it was inevitable that she would actually have to come here. Sometimes she'd managed to lose herself a little in the studying, the way she had when she'd first found herself with Isabeau—and would have given anything to escape.

Nina had not had the opportunity to go off to university. Had Isabeau not chosen Nina on her desperate orphanage campaign—the Princess's attempt to show that she was benevolent in the wake of one of her many scandals—Nina would have woken up the next day released from the hold of the state at last. She would have gone out into the world, found her own way, and been marvelously free—but likely would not have studied anything. She'd always tried to remind herself of that.

Isabeau could not have cared less about the private tutoring sessions her father insisted she take. Half the time she hadn't bothered to turn up.

That had left Nina with the very finest tutors in Europe at her disposal. She'd loved every moment of her education, and she'd taken the overarching lesson with her through the years since. If she was to be forced to trail about after Isabeau, she might as well make something of the experience. She'd studied, therefore, every castle, palace, private island, and other such glorious place she found herself, dragged along with Isabeau's catty entourage wherever the Princess went. She'd studied the places and all the contents therein as if she expected she might have to sit an exam on the material.

What Nina really loved was the art all these noble-blooded people tended to hoard. Museums were lovely, but the real collections were in the private homes of collectors with bloodlines—and fortunes—that soared back through the ages. Nina had loved nothing more than sneaking away while Isabeau was entertaining one of her many lovers to take a turn about the gallery of whatever stately place they were trysting in.

That was how she knew that the painting that took up most of the wall opposite her, rather ferociously, was a satirical take on a courtier type some three hundred years ago. And it was comforting, almost, to think that those sorts had always been appalling. It made sense. As long as there were kings, courtiers swarmed.

She was telling her unborn baby about the history of Theosia—ancient Macedonians this, ancient Venetians that—when, finally, the door to her chamber opened.

Nina braced herself, but, of course, it wasn't Prince Zeus who stood there. She doubted the Prince knew this part of the palace existed. Instead, it was the starchy-looking butler who managed to give her the impression that he was curling his thin lip at her without actually moving a single muscle in his face.

It was impressive, Nina thought. Truly.

"Were you speaking with someone?" he asked, each syllable dripping with scorn. He had introduced himself the same way when he'd brought her here. *I am Thaddeus*, he had intoned.

"Yes," Nina said. They stared at each other, and she patted her bump. With, admittedly, some theatrical flair. "The royal child currently occupying my womb, of course."

She might have drawn out the word *womb*.

And it was worth it, because she had the very great pleasure of sitting there, smiling serenely, as the man battled to conceal his distaste. Not because he was trying to spare her feelings, she knew. But because it had no doubt occurred to him that said occupant of her womb might, in fact, turn out to be the heir to the kingdom, and a good servant never burned a bridge if he could help it.

She was all too aware of how these people thought.

After all, she'd been one of them. Not quite staff, not quite a courtier, and therefore condescended to on all sides.

Nina had not missed it.

"If you'll follow me, miss," said the man, all cool disdain and not-quite-repressed horror. Not to mention a subtle emphasis on *miss*, to remind her she had no title or people or, in his view, any reason whatsoever to be here. *I have seen a great many tarts*, his tone assured her, *and vanquished them all*. "His Royal Highness has deigned to grant you an audience after all."

Nina had been told repeatedly that it would not be possible to see the Prince. If indeed Zeus was even here, which perhaps he was not, none could say—despite the standard that flew today, high above the palace, which was how the Prince informed his people he was in residence. She had only smiled calmly, explained and reexplained the situation, and waited.

And, when necessary, shared both her unmistakable belly as well as photographic evidence of the fact that, yes, she knew the Prince. Yes, in *that* way.

Because while it was probably not helpful to any palace staff to ask them to think back to a scandal six months ago—given how many scandals Prince Zeus was involved in on a daily basis—not all of them had been splashed about in all the international papers. Apparently, she really was special.

Nina ignored the little tug of an emotion she did not care to recognize, smiling the sharp little smile she'd learned in the Haught Montagne court.

"How gracious of the Prince to attend to his mistakes," she murmured. "How accommodating."

Then she took her time standing up, a basic sort of movement she had never given any thought to before. But it was different at six months pregnant.

Everything was different at six months pregnant.

She found she rather enjoyed seeing the faintest hint of a crack in the butler's facade as he watched her ungainly attempts to rise. More ungainly than necessary, to be sure, but she was the pregnant woman here. They were treating her like she'd done it to herself.

When she most certainly had not—but it would help no one, least of all her child, if she let herself get lost in images that served no one. She already knew how little it served *her*, because she dreamed about that night all the time already, and always woke alone and too hot and riddled with that *longing*—

Stop it, Nina ordered herself crossly.

She kept her expression placid with the aid of years of practice, having had to hide herself in the orphanage and Princess Isabeau's entourage alike. Then she followed the snooty butler out of the antechamber, up from the bowels of the palace, and through the hushed, gleaming halls that were all about airiness and timeless glory, as if gods truly did walk here.

Nina was impressed despite herself.

She kept catching sight of herself in this or that gleaming surface. As ever, she was taken aback by the fact that her belly preceded her. But she was perfectly well acquainted with the rest of the package. *Here comes our Dumpy!* Isabeau would trill, pretending that it was an affectionate nickname. *Hurry, little hen*, she would say as Nina trailed along behind her, forced to keep a smile on her face and her thoughts on such nicknames to herself.

Isabeau had believed that she was being hurtful. And given that being hurtful was one of the main joys in Princess Isabeau's pampered life, it had taken everything Nina had to keep the fact that she was in no way hurt to herself. Snide remarks from a royal princess really didn't hold a candle to daily life in the orphanage, but Isabeau didn't have to know that.

But Isabeau saw her as a hen, so a hen Nina became. She dressed as frumpily as possible, because it annoyed the Princess, herself a fashion icon. Not only were the clothes she chose not quite right, she made sure they never fit her correctly. She made a grand mess of her hair and pretended she didn't understand what was the matter with it.

And she took particular pleasure in forever eating sweets and cakes *at* Isabeau, whose strident dedication to her figure bordered on fanatical.

Nina found she rather liked the hennishness of it all today, though. There were many ways she could have dressed for this encounter, but she'd chosen the maternity outfit that most made her look like the side of a barn. She could have done her hair, or at least brushed it. Instead, she'd opted to let it do as it would, frizzing about of its own accord. Like a rather unkempt blond halo, she thought, pleased, when she saw herself in the polished surface of an ancient mask—hanging there on the wall in bronze disapproval.

Thaddeus was striding forth briskly, clearly trying to hasten their pace, so she slowed her walk to an ungainly waddle. Then only smiled blandly when the man tried to hurry her along. And went even slower.

She was determined to do what was right, or she wouldn't have come here.

But that didn't mean she couldn't enjoy herself in the process.

That had been her philosophy throughout her indentured servitude to the Princess. She was the little orphan girl plucked from obscurity and expected to live in perpetual cringing gratitude for every scrap thrown her way, when she would have been perfectly happy to be left to her own devices in her gutter, thank you. She had perfected the downcast look, with an unreadable curve of her lips that fell somewhere between possible sainthood and the expected servility. Depending on who was looking at her.

But she made her own fun all the same. Her clothes. Her constant sweet and cake consumption, leaving her forever covered in crumbs, which had sent Isabeau into rages. She'd often pretended not to understand the things Isabeau asked of her, forcing her to ask repeatedly. And she had been known to affect deafness when most likely to make the Princess go spare.

A subject of the house of Haught Montagne could not openly defy her Princess, of course. That was unthinkable.

But there were always ways.

Nina reminded herself that she'd found those ways once and could do it again, as she walked through another set of gilded arches. More gilded than before, in fact. Her hands crept over her belly, where the baby was moving around, making itself known. She had not actually intended for this last, final act of rebellion, she could admit, if only to herself. She'd thought that she was perfectly all right with the consequences as they were.

But that was when the consequences were being ejected from Isabeau's service and called a national disgrace, among a great many other, less polite names, in an endless slew of articles that were always sourced from unnamed people in Isabeau's circle—the curse of the courtiers.

These consequences were a bit different than a bit of scandal and being called mean names by terrible people, she thought, leaving one hand on her belly as she walked.

And that same fierce, mad love blazed through her again, the way it did so often these days. Maybe she hadn't planned this baby, but she wanted it. She had never loved anything the way she loved the tiny human inside her. The little gift she couldn't wait to meet.

She reminded herself that today was all about determination. Nothing more.

Thaddeus flung open a suitably impressive set of doors with all attendant fanfare, then led Nina inside.

"Your Royal Highness," he intoned, "may I present Miss Nina Graine. Your...guest."

Nina blinked as she looked around, and it took her a moment to get her bearings. She found herself in a vast room flooded with light that poured in from exquisitely arched openings on three sides. They were not so much windows as graceful doors that let in all that Mediterranean blue, the boundless sun, and the far-off call of wheeling seabirds. There was the hint of riotous bougainvillea on the terrace outside, and the breeze brought in the scent of honeysuckle and jasmine.

She knew she was standing in a room in the palace

—very likely the royal version of a lounge—but it seemed more like some kind of temple.

And as if summoned by that thought alone, there was suddenly a far brighter gleam where the sun was brightest, until it detached itself from such lesser light and became a man.

Not just any man.

Zeus.

Bathed in light as if he'd conjured it and wearing nothing but a pair of flowing white trousers that clung low on his hips.

Nina hated herself, but that didn't stop the way the sight of him rolled through her, like a song from on high. Except this song came with heat and licked over her. Her breasts. Her belly. The softness between her legs.

Focus, she ordered herself. He was magnificent, but as a person saddled with the name Zeus, he would have to be. He had clearly taken his name as a lifelong challenge.

A challenge he had met, if not exceeded.

And Nina couldn't help but remember, with an unhelpful vividness, that she knew every inch of him.

Zeus moved closer, somehow looking regal and glorious when he was barefoot and wearing the princely version of pajama bottoms. She tried her best to find him ridiculous, with that dark blond hair that looked forever tousled and the half smile that appeared welded to his lips, but she couldn't quite get there. Instead, she was struck by the similarity between him and that bronze mask she'd seen out in the palace halls.

He looked ancient. Almost forbidding, so severely

drawn were his features. If she hadn't known better, she would have sworn that he could only have been carved from stone or forged from metal. There was no possibility he could be a man of flesh and blood.

But Nina knew better.

Still he came toward her, until she could see the green of his wicked eyes. And then, sure enough, that slow, edgy curve of his sculpted lips.

She braced herself for that inescapable magnetism of his that she had always thought ought to be bottled, so it could be used as a weapon. It was that fierce. That intense. It seemed to fill the room, closing around her so it was impossible to pretend that she was anything but captivated, no matter how little she wished to be. Her pulse was a racket inside her veins. Her heart thudded.

Even her baby stopped kicking, as if awed.

But far more concerning was the melting sensation that swept over her, making the fire in her burn hotter. Brighter.

As if she hadn't already gotten into enough trouble with this man.

Prince Zeus of Theosia did not say a word. He put his hands on his lean hips, still with that half smile, as if this was all deeply entertaining, and took a long, slow circle around her. Studying her like she was a cow on a market block in the kind of medieval keeps this man's relatives had ruled over when the earth was young.

When he made it back around to her front, his face was transformed with laughter.

Her heart stopped. Then kicked back into gear, so hard it was painful.

Nina had prepared a brief, informative little speech so she could get the practicalities out of the way and then get back to her life. And she would have told anyone who asked—though no one ever had—that she was not the least bit intimidated by royalty of any stripe. In her case, familiarity really had bred contempt. She wanted no part of hereditary laziness, ceremonial scepters in place of any hint of kindness, or too many thrones instead of thoughtfulness.

And yet she couldn't seem to make her mouth work the way it should.

"I remember you," Zeus said after a long moment of that face of his, far too beautiful for any mortal man.

But he said it as if that surprised him. That it was not that she was in any way memorable, but it was deeply amusing to him that he should recognize her.

As if it was a great compliment to a woman who stood before him, her reason for being here clear enough, as she was swollen with his child.

Nina was sick to death of these royals.

"Are you certain?" she asked crisply, ignoring all that stunning male beauty. Not to mention her memories and the chaos inside. She also ignored the way his brows rose at her tone. "You've had more than a legion or two, I imagine, and there's no telling how many have turned up with claims like mine. Easy to get them all mixed up. You should take a closer look, surely. I could be anyone."

CHAPTER TWO

THE LITTLE BROWN hen clucking at him was…unexpected.

Yet unexpected was not boring.

And His Royal Highness, Crown Prince Zeus of Theosia, had been bored beyond all reason for entirely too long. Since the last time he'd seen her, not that he cared to think too closely about his curious reactions to that night. He'd put them aside and had quickly returned to his usual state of tedium. That was the trouble with declaring oneself rebellious at a young age and then pursuing each and every potential rebellion that arose thereafter with intensity and commitment.

It turned out that a man could not live on sin alone.

Zeus had certainly tried.

"A legion or two, perhaps," he agreed, moving toward the bizarre apparition in the vague shape of a woman who had somehow braved the palace gates and found her way here. A task many had tried, but most had failed. Resoundingly. He received weekly reports on the women who attempted to skirt security and chase him down. That she had succeeded was…

not boring at all. "A gentleman does not count such things."

"No need when the tabloids count for you."

He stopped before her, taking in this strange little creature who had scurried around in the wake of Princess Isabeau for all these years. She looked much as she had during the years of his irksome arranged engagement. Dressed to accentuate every possible flaw on her body. Her hair an obvious afterthought. Isabeau had always cultivated glamour, and yet in the background of too many of her photos had lurked her little pet.

Impervious to criticism. Unmoved by commentary.

Zeus had come to see Miss Nina Graine as a kind of symbol. Perhaps, particularly last summer, he had ascribed to her a great many motivations and inner thoughts she did not possess. He had spent more time than he liked to admit conjuring her into an unlikely heroine, the better to suit his schemes.

Then he'd discovered the truth. Beneath all the stories he'd told himself and more, beneath each and every one of the masks she'd ever worn. And the truth had nearly burned him alive.

He didn't like to think about that too much.

Or the fact that her disappearance after their night together had...bothered him.

Zeus allowed himself a smile now as he gazed down at her, returned to all her frumpy splendor. "Most women who claw their way past the palace guard for an audience with me are of a certain stripe. They are not you, however. They do not *actually* convince poor Thaddeus to bring them before me."

Isabeau's hen did not smile. She did not flutter, as women so often did in his presence, like so many small and hapless birds in need of a strong hand to perch upon. She only gripped her enormous, pregnant belly—a development Zeus doubted very much was unrelated to her appearance in his rooms, yet did not wish to consider too closely just yet—and glared at him.

Glared, when he was used to obliging sighs and simpering calf's eyes.

How novel.

"Is that meant to be flattering?" Nina demanded.

When, as a rule, no one dared make demands of him. Unless they were his perpetually unamused father, who never did anything but. And was eternally disappointed at Zeus's refusal to meet them.

His fondest rebellion yet.

"Your memory losses are your own business," Nina was saying in that same distinctly unsimpering manner. "But you must have me confused for one of those women you can't remember if you think I'd find your inability to recall the faces of the women you've slept with to be anything but sad. For you."

Zeus was unrepentant. "I always remember *some* part of the women gracious enough to share themselves with me. It is not always their faces, I grant you. Shall I tell you what I recall of you?"

"I think not. My memory is not clouded with excess. *I* know what happened that night."

She did not exactly *thrust* her belly at him, but Zeus eyed it like it was a weapon all the same. Still, he wasn't ready to go there. He was intrigued for the first time in as long as he could remember—*six months, perhaps*, a voice in him suggested slyly—and besides, he was perfectly capable of plotting his next move while appearing to be nothing more than the sybaritic fool he'd been playing too well for too long.

He lived in that space. Owned it, even.

Zeus shoved his hands in his trouser pockets and endeavored to look as if, given the faintest push, he might actually lounge about in midair.

"If you mean you did me a great service, I certainly remember that," he said lazily. "Have you gone to all this trouble so that I might thank you? Perhaps an investiture of some kind? I do wish I'd known to dig out the ceremonial swords."

"I shouldn't be at all surprised that you've rewritten what happened to suit yourself." She rolled her eyes—another gesture that Zeus did not usually see before him. Who would dare? No matter how little he seemed to stand upon ceremony, he was still the Crown Prince of Theosia. "I think we both know that you used me."

"I?" Zeus laughed then. He had wanted something novel, something more than this morbid waiting game he had no choice but to be mired in. He hadn't thought to specify what it was he wanted, and lo, she had appeared. "*I* used *you*? I was under the impression it was the other way around. I have long felt that my primary function is to provide scandals on command, the better for a certain kind of woman to be forced to leave a life she secretly never liked in the first place."

The creature before him scowled, her wild blond hair bobbing slightly from where it was inadequately knotted atop her head. "That is not a *function*. You say it like you've made toying with sad women your own cottage industry."

"I do what I can," Zeus murmured, as if attempting to be humble. A state of being he did not recognize, personally. What purpose could it serve? "No, no, your gratitude alone is my reward."

"Don't be ridiculous," huffed the little brown hen. "I was nothing but a servant. You, on the other hand, were not only a royal prince, destined for a throne—"

"Not just any throne," he added helpfully. "The humbly named Throne of Ages. It's right down the hall if you want to take a peek. Maybe snap a few pictures? I hear that's all the rage."

"You were also engaged," Nina continued doggedly. "To be married. Since the very day of her birth, if I remember it rightly, as set up by your fathers in an agreement that all of Europe knows inside and out. Given how many times it's been trotted out in the tabloids while one or the other of you was caught entertaining someone outside the bonds of your arrangement."

"Such busybodies, fathers," Zeus murmured. "Don't you think? Forever arranging things on their own and then acting surprised that no one wishes to be an *arrangement*."

"I wouldn't know," she replied coolly. Censoriously, even. "My father died when I was five, and the only arrangements that were ever made for me involved orphanages or princesses."

"Neither of which you liked all that much, if memory serves."

"We have already established that you have pervasive memory issues," she shot back, her chin tilting up. "I will remind you that you were not only the Crown Prince of Theosia that night. You were not only engaged. You were engaged *to my mistress*."

That had rather been the point.

Though, admittedly, Zeus had gotten sidetracked. How could he have known that Isabeau's little hen was hiding the curves of a goddess beneath the outlandish and unflattering things she wore?

And Zeus was, at heart, a connoisseur of the female form.

He had spent six months assuring himself that was all he was, especially when it came to her.

"Darling Isabeau, the most poisonous viper in all of Europe," he said now with a sigh, fairly certain that Nina would not care for any rhapsodizing about her charms. She looked as if she might bite him. "Such a tender union that would have been."

The fact that Isabeau was fake and unpleasant, at best, had not been the reason Zeus hadn't wanted to marry her. Zeus didn't want to marry anyone. He had been making his sentiments known for years and had questioned the arrangement he'd had no hand in making—but his royal fiancée had been nothing if not ambitious. Her kingdom was little more than an uppity ski slope, and that wasn't enough for Isabeau. She'd had big dreams of what it would mean to be the Theosian Queen.

Fidelity hadn't factored in.

Zeus had needed to find a way to make her break things off before her thirtieth birthday, as stipulated in the contracts his father had signed a lifetime ago. It was that or pay outrageous penalties. Like ransoming off one of the outlying Theosian islands, which even Zeus, for all his game playing, could not justify. Or countenance.

His ancestors would have risen from the dead in protest. And really, his father was quite enough. Zeus couldn't imagine having more family around to shout at him about bloodlines and duties and the debt he owed to history.

The perfect solution had come to him in a blast of inspiration during a deathly boring dinner engagement on one of his trips to Haught Montagne—the trips he put off as long as possible, until Isabeau's father began to make threats of violence. Which in their world could lead to war—whether in the markets or the streets. Neither was acceptable, for obvious reasons.

Or so Zeus had been constantly told by his father for the whole of his life.

Though Zeus had been entertaining himself by imagining otherwise at that dinner. Then he'd spied Isabeau's pet and his plotting had gone off in an entirely different direction. Zeus had been deeply pleased with himself.

But that night had not gone according to plan.

He was blessed with the ability to see the beauty in any woman he encountered. And so he did, and had. Yet what he had not anticipated was that Nina was wholly unlike the other courtiers and ladies who circled his unwanted bride-to-be. Her innocence had awed him. Her enthusiasm had left a permanent mark.

And it turned out a man did not have to look hard

for the beauty in Nina. She was hiding it. Deliberately. But he'd found her out.

The truth he did not intend to share was that he, Zeus of Theosia, had actually thought about her in the months since that night.

More than once.

And at the start, he had done more than *think* about her—

But he barely admitted that to himself.

"You are welcome, Your Royal Highness," Nina was saying in that sharp way he remembered from that evening in Haught Montagne, when he'd found his way beneath all those layers she wore. So deliciously sharp up close when she seemed so soft from a distance. "What a pleasure it was to break off your engagement for you, since you were apparently unable to do it yourself."

But Zeus could not be shamed. Many had attempted it. All had fallen short. He merely lifted a shoulder. "If I had broken it myself, there would have been too many unpleasant consequences. Monies to be paid. Kings to placate. Wars to avert. Far better all round to make Isabeau break it herself." He inclined his head in her direction. "You, apparently, were the bridge too far."

Nina made a noise of frustration. He found it cute. Yes. *Cute*.

More unforeseen reactions. Zeus hardly knew what to do with himself.

"Your assorted scandals never bothered her." Nina scowled up at him. "Why should they? She always enjoyed her own fun. It was that it was me, her dumpy charity case that she was saddled with because the palace worried she seemed too unlikable. But then, you know this. It's why you chose me."

"Surely lightning struck us both. That is how I recall it."

"It was a clear night in summer." She shook her head. "We were not engaged in the same enterprise, I think."

"Little hen," he chided her. "You break my heart, which is nothing, as anyone will tell you. It is but a cheap little trinket. But you also poke at my pride. A dangerous game. I am not only certain that we were, both of us, very much engaged in the same glorious enterprise that night. But that you enjoyed yourself thoroughly."

Zeus remembered more about that night than he wanted to. He remembered the heat, the unexpected longing, the blast of unconquerable desire. He remembered the way his lips had moved over hers and the responses he had coaxed from her.

How it had all become need and flame—then burned out of control. So bright and greedy that instead of the happy, carefree seduction he'd intended, all charm and release, he'd had no choice but to throw himself into it.

Headfirst.

And he might have spent the past six months telling himself he remembered very little about that night, but that was a lie.

He remembered everything.

Her taste. Her scent.

The small sounds she'd made in the back of her throat.

"I'm afraid the night dims a bit in my memory," she said now, her brown eyes glittering. And she was lying. He could see that she was lying, but in a way, that was more fascinating. "Given what happened the next morning."

She looked at him as if she expected he might collapse in paroxysms of shame at that. Sadly for her, he was still…himself.

"Desperate times," he said, with the grin that had gotten him out of more scrapes than he could count.

And he could see that she was not unaffected.

But she did not giggle or melt. She frowned.

"I'm embarrassed to say that it took me some time to work out what had actually happened," she said. Without the faintest hint of a giggle. "Then I realized. You called them. You *personally invited* the paparazzi in that morning."

"I am devastated to discover that you were so misled in your assessment of my character." Zeus enjoyed watching her brow furrow all the more. "Were you truly under the impression that I was or am a good man?"

Though he remembered, little as he might wish to, that making love to this woman had made him wish he was. If only because the gift of her sweet innocence had demanded it.

But it had been too late.

"I have never thought you were anything but you." And that was what made her smile at last, edgy as that smile was. At least it looked like a real one. "If anything, understanding the role you played in this has helped make my course of action clear."

She looked down at the belly between them. He did the same.

But luckily, he'd now had some time to think about the opportunity she presented.

Zeus always had liked an opportunity.

Especially if it helped stick the knife in deeper.

"I do hate to be indelicate," he began. She let out a laugh, and he grinned. "You're quite right. I don't. But you must know that there's almost no purpose to this confrontation scene you have planned, all tears and recriminations followed swiftly by demands—"

"You've had this conversation often, have you?"

He offered her a bland smile. "A great many women assume they must be carrying my child, simply because they wish it to be so."

Her brows lifted. "You being such a paragon of fatherhood and all."

"I'm sure that's the draw." He inclined his head. "Unless and until a DNA test proves that you're carrying my child, this can only be a theoretical conversation. A parade of what-ifs, all destined to end in nothing." Zeus shrugged with a wholly unaffected lack of concern. "I have always enjoyed these things."

She eyed him. "How many children do you have, then?"

"Theoretical children any number of distraught women have claimed must be mine? Pick a number, then multiply it. Real children? Not a one." He allowed himself a smile, perhaps a little more real than necessary. When he usually preferred to hide anything real. There was something about this woman—but he brushed that off. "Perhaps that has something to do with the fact that I do not partake in unprotected sex."

Yet even as he said that, hadn't he gotten a little too enthusiastic with Nina? He remembered that he had been…a little too intense. All of that fire had been such an unexpected wallop. There had been a little too much bathing in it. A little too much wishing that he hadn't already set the wheels in motion that would end their encounter with a shower of flashbulbs.

Something in him seemed to roll over, then hum.

Almost like…anticipation.

He hardly recognized it.

"You may give me any tests you like," she was saying with a dismissive wave of her hand. No tears. No caterwauling. None of the performance of pregnancy that he'd come to expect from this scene. "I've come to inform you of your impending fatherhood, and you may do with that information anything you wish. Summon your doctors and lab technicians at will. Oh, and congratulations."

Zeus wondered if his mask had slipped a little when she paused a moment, that dent between her brows returning. He made sure to look as bored as possible until she cleared her throat and carried on.

"I'll catch you up on what happened after you invited the tabloids in." She paused as if waiting for him to toss in an apology. He didn't, of course. But something in him almost wanted to, and that was unnerving enough. "I was cast out of all royal circles. As this was, in fact, the goal I've been striving toward since

Isabeau first took it upon herself to force me under her wing, I was quite pleased. Until…"

She only lifted a hand, indicating her belly. "I thought I was ill. Or perhaps detoxing from too long in Isabeau's presence. Either way, it took me quite some time to understand what had happened to me. And even longer to accept it."

"So long that any other alternatives were no longer available to you," he said, smoothly enough, though he found—to his great surprise—that he had a certain distaste for the notion, as it involved this woman and this baby.

But Nina jerked back as if he'd slapped her.

"I'm an orphan," she said matter-of-factly, though he could see far more emotion in her brown gaze, gone as dark as the bitterest coffee now. His favorite. "This baby is the only family I have."

Something seemed to roar inside him then, shocking Zeus. And he had not been shocked by anything in…six long months. It reminded him a little too closely of that night they'd shared, the shock of all that heat where he'd expected an easy, forgettable pleasure.

Nina had come out of nowhere with a sucker punch yet again.

"I can't say I had any particular intention of sharing this news with you," Nina was saying. "I thought that perhaps I could simply live my life, as I always wanted, with no royal nonsense to consider." She shrugged. "I'm afraid I know too much."

"About royalty?" He nodded sagely. "A tragedy indeed."

"One does not require a great deal of knowledge

about royalty," she shot back at him. "They rule things. The end. Everything you need to know about your average, run-of-the-mill member of any royal family can be summed up like so. It's what makes them so presumptuous."

Zeus could not deny that. What astounded him was that…he wanted to.

But Nina was still speaking. "No, what I know too much about is the tabloids. The paparazzi. Just because I've enjoyed six months to myself doesn't mean my solitude will continue. Sooner or later, someone will remember me. Then they'll all find me. And worse, my baby."

She rubbed that belly of hers again, currently housed in a dress he suspected might possibly have been used as a circus tent. When he knew that her actual figure was so sweet and ripe that he found himself hungry even now. For he could see—what little of her he could truly see—that this pregnancy had ripened her further.

Zeus had the blistering notion that he actually *wanted* her to be carrying his child. He *wanted* this ripeness to be his. All his.

He shoved that aside.

Because he couldn't believe such a notion could cross his mind, much less bloom the way it seemed to be doing.

"Are you saying that the paparazzi have already found you?" he managed to ask past what amounted to a full-scale riot inside of him.

A riot her ripeness, so close to him, did not help.

"I don't think they have, but who can say where a

photographer with a nasty telephoto lens might lurk?" Again, that edgy smile. "The more my pregnancy shows, the more likely someone is to do the math. It will be worse once the baby comes."

"I see. You thought you'd come to me and try to get ahead of mathematics."

"No, it occurred to me that the math being what it is, I can expect that whether I wanted to involve you or not, you would end up involved." She sniffed. "Now or later. I decided to come ahead of the inevitable exposé to let you know what my demands are."

"See? I told you there would be demands." He smiled benevolently at her and found it delightful when she gritted her teeth in response. Far easier to deal with that sort of thing than any *ripening*. Much less his response to it. He was going to have to sort himself out. Later. "There are always demands. It's almost as if demands are the point of these little scenes."

"I've researched Theosian law," she said, without any indication she'd heard his comments. And Zeus was not used to being so soundly and repeatedly ignored. He couldn't tell if he hated it…or if his reaction was a bit more intense. And was something more like admiration. "Apparently, one of your ancestors so enjoyed spreading himself about that it was written into law that all royal bastards must be given a certain stipend from the crown. To keep them in an appropriate style, though not under the same roof, as that might offend any given queen."

Zeus laughed out loud. Of all the things he'd imagined she might say, it wasn't that.

"Ah, yes, the bastard clause." The clause that every

young royal Theosian man was lectured about extensively as he set to head out into the world and misbehave. He hadn't heard it mentioned by anyone outside the palace staff in ages—no doubt because he was considered such a lost cause. "It may surprise you to learn that the clause originated from the betrayed Queen in question, because she preferred to make public her husband's indiscretions. I think you'll find we haven't used it here in generations."

"Then I suppose I've come to ask for the usual amount of support," Nina replied easily enough, though her chin notched higher. "I'm not one for charity. I've already spent a lifetime being force-fed it while being told how grateful I should be for each and every sour bite. If it were up to me, you would never have seen me again. I would have made my own way in this world, and happily. That was my intention."

"So you have now stated twice." Zeus sighed. "I do hope you're not going to get boring on me. That would be a tragedy indeed."

She did not look like she agreed. And the Theosian sun made love to her as she stood there, facing off with him. It danced over the spun straw of her hair and the sensual bow of her lips. It was the sort of light that most women of his acquaintance avoided, and for good reason.

But it only made Nina that much more beautiful.

Inarguably lovely.

You need to remember who you are, a stern voice within him piped up then.

"I found a perfectly decent situation in England," she told him. "It would be hard, of course, but I'm not afraid of hard. I believed I could do it. I began to think I *would* do it, damn it…" Nina smiled a little ruefully. "Until it occurred to me that this baby is neither an orphan nor a prince. He or she should not have to pay for the sins of either."

Zeus heard a swift intake of breath. It took him a moment to realize it was his.

Nina straightened her shoulders. "Just as this baby doesn't deserve the lengths I'm willing to go to for freedom, it also doesn't deserve to be cut off from the kind of life it could have, just because its father is you."

An uncomfortable sensation worked its way through Zeus then, though it took him far too long to recognize it. Much less name it.

But he was fairly certain it was temper. When he had learned, so very long ago, that his own temper was useless and it was far better to poke and prod and play games, so that others could experience theirs and lose control.

He'd learned how to be very, very good at that.

And he had come to think of temper as weakness. Because what was it but emotion, twisted around and easily manipulated by men like him? He allowed himself none of that, either. Yet there was no mistaking it. The curl of a kind of smoke winding around inside him was very clearly temper.

How…astonishing.

"So, like every other woman who has ever pursued me," he said, drawling out the words and making sure no hint of temper leaked through, because he didn't know why it should. He refused to feel such things. Or any things. "You are after me for my money."

And he watched, too fascinated for his own good, as Nina's pretty brown eyes flashed. This orphan, this little brown hen, had never been what she seemed. He did not know how he had suffered through any number of interactions with Isabeau before he'd come to understand that.

But once he'd begun to see her, all too plainly, he couldn't unsee her.

He only saw *more* of her.

She had pride, this creature. And if he wasn't mistaken, a healthy dose of a burning need for retribution about her.

In other words, she was perfect.

"Yes," she said, as if she knew the direction his thoughts had gone. "I want your money. I see no reason this baby shouldn't be raised like the child of a prince it is."

"Then I have some deliciously good news for you," Zeus informed her with a little bow, because he couldn't resist a flourish. Not when his endgame had just altered completely. "Assuming this isn't all an elaborate ruse that will be uncovered shortly by the palace's medical staff, allow me to be the first to congratulate you."

"Why?" she asked, suspicion stamped all over her. "For what?"

Zeus only gazed down at her, that temper still curling around and around inside him, though he was happy to discover it did not inhibit his enjoyment. That would have been a tragedy.

"On your nuptials," he told her.

"My...what?"

"Oh, happy day," Zeus said, letting his voice carry and rebound back from the pristine walls like so much dizzy heat. "We are to be married, little hen. You lucky thing. Women have been jostling for that position since before I was born."

"Not me!" She looked almost insultingly horrified. "I don't want to marry *you*!"

Which, he could admit, was another reason she was perfect. Zeus could not have tolerated any of the women who did actually want to marry him, and quite desperately. They longed for either the man they thought he was or the throne he would take, and either way, it wasn't him.

Only this woman, only Nina, would do.

"I am afraid that what you want does not signify," he said, only the pulse he could feel hammering away in his neck indicating that he was perhaps not as calm as he was pretending. "You should have done more research. If you had, you might have found that here on Theosian soil, the heir to the kingdom belongs to the crown."

Her eyes widened. Almost comically. "That can't possibly mean what I think it does."

Zeus rocked back on his heels, all the strange emotions and memories of this encounter washing over him. But he concentrated on her dismay instead.

"I am the Crown Prince. If you are carrying my heir, I have every right to do with you what I will." He allowed himself a smile then, one that in no way hid the truth of him, and enjoyed it when her eyes widened farther still. "Welcome to Theosia. I hope you like our little island. You will one day reign as Queen."

Nina cemented her place here by looking ill at the very idea. Not triumphant. Not thrilled. *Ill*. "That will never, ever happen. Never."

"Oh, but it will, my little hen," Zeus replied, something perilously close to happy, for once. He told himself it was because the pieces of this last part of his plan were coming together so beautifully. And for no other reason. Because there could not possibly be another reason. Zeus would not allow there to be. "You can depend on it."

CHAPTER THREE

EVERYTHING HAPPENED A little too quickly then.

So quickly that Nina found herself perilously close to dizzy.

Zeus moved across the vast room, striding like a man with purpose instead of the monument to idleness he usually appeared to be in all things. He swung open the doors to his chamber, said two words, and half the palace staff seemed to flow in. He barked out orders, and for all that he lounged about Europe—acting as if he was too lazy to lift his finger when he could find any number of willing women to lift it for him—it was clear that his staff knew this version of him well. Peremptory in the extreme.

Princely, something in her whispered. *A man who is not only used to command, but infinitely comfortable in it.*

That made her head spin enough, because that wasn't Zeus. Not the Zeus the world knew entirely too well.

But the voice within her wasn't done.

Just like that night, it murmured, so that more of that wild heat charged through her, setting her aflame.

The way it had when she'd seen him again. And when he'd called her *little hen*.

Because the Zeus he'd become that night had been…intense. Demanding.

Different.

But she didn't have any time to take any of that in as she was marched from his rooms by a phalanx of aides. Who, at least, acted more polite and solicitous than the initial butler and the whole of the palace guard had. They swept her through the halls of the palace, climbing from one fairy-tale level to the next, one of them talking in a low voice into her mobile as they moved.

They arrived at their destination, another suite of graceful, expertly appointed rooms that looked, on the one hand, like every suite of rooms she had ever stayed in at places like this—though she'd never stayed in one quite as lovely. For this was the Palace of the Gods, so everything was that much brighter and inlaid with gold and silver. As if the light filling every room was not the weather, but a part of the planned decor. She was taken to a small salon, dappled with light that poured in from a shaded balcony outside.

"You will wait here," said the aide with the phone, who Nina suspected was the one in charge. Though the older woman managed to make the very clear command sound as if, maybe, it had been Nina's idea and she was only confirming it.

"I would love to wait," Nina replied as she lowered herself down to a settee that was so much more comfortable than the one she'd been sitting on before that she rather thought they shouldn't share the same name. She sat and smiled up at the woman. "But I'm afraid the baby won't. If I don't eat soon, neither one of us is going to be very happy."

The older woman looked at her moment, then snapped her fingers. Confirming that she was, indeed, in charge of this particular set of staff—and also setting one of her underlings running from the room.

"Then, of course, you shall eat," she said.

Nina was almost too grateful to bear it. "If you know where my personal belongings are, I can feed myself. I have snacks in my bag."

"Your personal belongings are being looked over by the palace guard," her aide said, sounding sorrowful. Though her eyes remained shrewd. "Security will do as they like, you know. But not to worry, we'll have something from the kitchens shortly."

And Nina could not have been more surprised when, not five minutes later, the underling reappeared. He was trailed by another staff member pushing a cart, who then began to lay out the makings of a hearty afternoon tea. But in Theosian style, with dishes of grilled fish to go along with finger sandwiches, mountains of vegetables and fresh fruits, hard cheeses, pots of herbed butter, and loaves of fragrant baked bread.

By the time another set of people appeared before her, she felt better than she had all day.

Which was maybe why, when one of the new people introduced herself as a doctor and announced that she was there to check on Nina's health—and the paternity of the baby she carried while they were at it—she was less outraged than she might otherwise have been. Because, as ever, she was a realist. She had known before she came here, no matter how grudgingly, that there was no possibility anyone would simply take her word for it. That was not how powerful men operated, whether they had their own palaces or not.

She followed the doctor and her cheerful, efficient team into the next room, a small study with stacks of books on whitewashed shelves and bright blue flowers in handcrafted vases. And there submitted to all necessary tests. Whatever it took to make her case in a place where her word wouldn't do.

The story of her life, really.

"You must be tired," said the aide from before, coming in to collect her once her exam was done. "After all the traveling, and then such a long day in the palace. Perhaps it would be best if you rested, no? Do feel free to ring should you require anything. Shall we say, a light supper later this evening? The kitchen will bring it up at the hour of your choice."

"I appreciate the concern for my feelings," Nina said dryly. "But I'm not the least bit tired."

"I feel certain you must be," replied the other woman, implacably.

"You could simply say that I'm to be locked in these quarters until such time as the paternity of my baby can be determined," Nina said. Then smiled. "I think we'd both respect each other more, don't you?"

The other woman inclined her head, but her shrewd gaze warmed. "Indeed, miss."

"You may call me Nina." And Nina had the strangest sense of vertigo, because she couldn't recall the last time she'd been the one to offer her first name. She had always been the one who had to mind her manners constantly around her betters.

"I am Daphne," the woman replied. Her mouth curved. "And I will let you know when you're free to move about the palace."

"See?" Nina asked. "Isn't that better?"

Daphne smiled wider, then clapped her hands and emptied the suite, leaving Nina alone.

For a while, she stayed where she was, staring at pretty blue flowers in small earthenware vases while inside of her everything was... Zeus.

That night six months ago was all tangled up in today, a temple of light and all his dark-honeyed glory, as if baklava had taken human form and called itself a prince.

Nina let out a long, shuddery breath.

She got up, then went out of the study into the atrium that took the place of any central hall. She could see into the first salon and was pleased to find they'd left her the remains of her tea, which made her smile despite herself. Because if she needed to, she would have thrown open these doors and stormed the palace kitchens if she was hungry.

Clearly, Daphne knew that and had removed the temptation to leave here.

She walked into the center of the atrium, where a fountain gurgled sedately, appreciating the glass ceiling and the greenery everywhere. Slowly, she turned in a circle. She could see the bedroom beyond two blue doors, a massive four-poster bed set against a wall done in mosaic. There were several other rooms, but their doors were shut, so she could only guess what was behind them. Some of these palatial guest quarters had screening rooms and bowling alleys, their own elevators and private pools. Boardrooms and full offices for government and business-minded guests. Palaces these days were equipped to cater to the needs of visiting royalty and all of their expectations on the high end, and questionable guests like Nina in more self-contained units like this.

And then she laughed at herself, because the atrium alone was larger than any place she'd lived in the last six months. Maybe she'd have been happier if she didn't know it was the sort of smallish suite Princess Isabeau would have sneered at—but deemed good enough for Nina.

She shook off memories of the wretched Isabeau and followed the light. Through the bedroom and out onto the wide balcony that she found waiting for her, wrapping around the side of the corner suite she occupied.

There was a shaded part of the balcony and then a far sunnier bit. Nina went out and stood in the sun for as long as she could, letting the heat sink into her bones and chase away the lingering cold after her last couple of months in England, then she made her way back into the shade. She found the chaise with the best view, straight out into the sea, and settled herself there.

And then, listening to the waves and staring at all that deep blue, she found herself getting drowsy. Despite her claims. She told herself it was all the food she'd just eaten. It had nothing to do with the day she'd had here.

Nina wasn't getting *soft*.

And as she drifted off into sleep, all she could see was that bright, impossible light growing even brighter, and then Zeus stepping out of it, shining far hotter than the lot.

So it wasn't as much of a shock as it might otherwise have been when she woke to find Zeus standing over her once again.

She was glad she'd worn her most hideous skirt, wide like a tent. Because it functioned like bedding, and she knew without having to look that she was properly covered. And then laughed at herself. The man had already seen her naked. That was why she was here in the first place.

Nina rubbed her hands over her eyes, then over the rest of her face, mostly to check to see if she had been caught drooling.

Then she tried to focus on Zeus, standing so still in the kind of dark bespoke suit that she associated with his inevitable presence across all the capitals of Europe. Cut to make him seem even taller, even broader, even more perfectly shaped. A love letter to his perfect body. The sky behind him was turning a deep blue, smudged with orange and pink, from a sun just set, as if it had prettied itself just for him.

And Nina felt breathless, as if the whole world was holding its breath when really, that was just her. She tried to force herself to breathe normally again. She assured herself it had nothing at all to do with the man standing at the foot of her chaise. She was pregnant. Surely she could blame any odd physical sensations on that.

Not on Zeus and the sunset all around him that made him look even more ancient and unworldly.

"I take it you've learned that you're the father of my baby," Nina said.

She blamed the rasp in her voice on her nap.

Zeus only looked at her a long while. The sky continued to put on a show behind him. "It seems we are to be parents, little hen."

And Nina had never minded that nickname from Isabeau. She hadn't liked it, but it hadn't *bothered* her. Isabeau had imagined it held more weight than it did.

But it was very different the way Zeus said it. And he *kept* saying it.

She had tried to ignore, earlier, the way his mouth moved over those words and, worse, the echo of them inside her. But his little hen was in danger of burning alive.

"At least we've established that I'm not a liar," she said before she immolated where she sat. She smoothed her hair back from her face, then remembered that she'd deliberately left it wild. So she dropped her hands again and folded them the only place they folded now, up above her belly. "But I have no intention of marrying you."

"I already told you that your intentions cannot matter in such a case." He waved a hand when she started to protest. "I have avoided matrimony the entirety of my life, Nina. I will require sustenance if I'm to discuss such a drastic change in my dissipated lifestyle any further."

Nina sat up straighter as lights appeared, and it took her a moment to work out it was from the lanterns hung on all the overhangs. And then she couldn't think about *lanterns*, because Zeus was beside her, leaning down—

And for a moment, she thought, *Yes, please, again—*

But all he did was lift her to her feet. With an economy of movement that reminded her, with a rush of sensation, of the way he'd tossed her this way and that six months ago.

She did not need the reminder.

Because it was easy to dismiss Prince Zeus. A playboy, a reprobate, a deeply unserious man who prided himself on being wicked to the core. It was easy to dismiss his beauty and make salty remarks about the fact he didn't have anything better to do with his time *but* work on that abdomen. She'd heard all of those things from snippy aristocrats in balls and palaces and had thought many of them herself.

But no matter why or how he came by his physicality, he certainly knew how to use it.

She knew that firsthand.

Nina didn't like that. Just as she didn't like the way everything inside her had leaned into that *yes*. And she *really* didn't like the fact it was only in Zeus's arms that she felt like her old self again. Graceful. Lithe.

She pushed away from him, hoping her feet would hold her. Then she felt a bit sad when they did—which was unacceptable. She shouldn't *want* him to hold her. "I'm not sure that stuffing yourself full of food is going to garner you the results that you want. I don't need to eat to know that I'm against marrying you. I don't even need a lifetime of dissipation to know it."

"My dear Nina," he said as he indicated she should

walk with him down the length of the balcony toward the corner. "The food is for me. I'm very hungry. I'm given to understand that my tea went astray."

Nina felt as if she'd betrayed herself, because she had the strangest urge to laugh at the look he swept her from beneath lashes that no man should be allowed to possess. She shouldn't find him *amusing*. What was the matter with her?

"How could the Crown Prince's tea go anywhere?" she asked. "I would have thought that, given your station, every chef in the kitchen would drop everything for the privilege of serving you any snack you desired."

"You're missing the point of the comment," he said, walking beside her with all the dignity of the prince he was. And yet still, she was certain she could detect something wilder beneath it. There was that sort of roll to the way he moved. As if the reality of him was caged somewhere deep within. *Stop telling yourself fairy tales*, she snapped at herself. "I'm attempting to make small talk. I understand that is the basis of any marriage."

"Funnily enough, I thought a good marriage was based on respect," Nina replied. She couldn't remember her parents or their marriage, but she was sure theirs had been a good one. Because it had to have been. She knew it did. "Friendship. Support of each other. Little things like that."

"Please tell me people don't sit around all day discussing their supportive impulses." Zeus shuddered. "That sounds markedly tedious."

"Best to avoid the institution, then," Nina said tartly.

And then wondered what she was playing at, because the way his mouth curved made her glad. When it shouldn't. Nothing about him should make her *glad*.

They turned the corner, and Nina's breath caught against her will. On this side of her rooms, the balcony was much wider. There was a small pool and a hot tub some distance farther down. But closer in, a dinner for two had been set up at a cozy round table. There were lights strewn on wires above, making everything seem magical. And with every step, the dark seemed to get thicker and the lights brighter.

Like a fairy tale, whispered a voice inside her with entirely too much wonder.

She ignored it. The way she always did.

Nina wanted to tell him that she wasn't hungry, and that even if she was, she didn't want to eat a private dinner with him. Anything to put the distance between them that should have been there automatically, given how their night together had ended. But as she drew close to the table, she could see the spread awaiting them. And she suddenly realized she was starving.

Again. Always.

And clearly the baby agreed, because it kicked her, hard.

Zeus helped her sit with an exaggerated courtesy that Nina had last seen him display toward the elderly Queen of a tiny northern country. She wanted to snap at that gesture, too, but she didn't dare.

Because she was afraid that if she opened her mouth, things she shouldn't say might come out.

Instead of sitting across the little table, Zeus pulled the chair around to settle himself next to her, only smiling blandly as the staff appeared and rearranged the table until it looked as if there had never been any choice at all for him to sit anywhere but there.

What must that be like, Nina wondered. That certainty. That knowledge that no matter what, his choices would always be supported and celebrated. And it was more than that. *His* every choice was a command.

"I hope you do not find dinner with me too much of a trial," he said as the staff retreated and left them to their own devices. "Many do, I fear."

He did not look as if he feared anything. Nina tried not to look at him and took in the feast before them instead. There were serving dishes taking up all the available space on the table, filled with all manner of savory delights. And to her astonishment, Zeus served himself, and her, with the same innate grace he did everything.

She did mean everything.

Stop that, she ordered herself, frowning at her own…idiocy.

"When is a trial too much?" she managed to ask. "I don't know how I would begin to measure."

"Did you learn this kind of wit in the orphanage?" Zeus's voice was mild, and yet still a caress. "I know you didn't learn it while at the mercy of Isabeau the humorless."

"It's a natural talent," Nina found herself saying. "Not everyone can be born into a royal family. Some of us really do have to rely on our wits."

He was toying with his food almost absently, but his gaze was intent. And on her. "What warms my heart is the notion that we will be having this conversation for the rest of our lives."

She felt that same surge of instant denial rush through her, but she caught herself.

This was Zeus of Theosia. He lived to be provoking. Letting him succeed in provoking her was letting him win. And she might have been carrying his child, but she had no intention of letting him win anything. Not if she could help it.

She was determined that she could.

"You're going to have to explain your reasoning to me." She lowered her gaze to her plate and took up a forkful of rice laden with spices. "Six months ago you engineered a ridiculous French farce of a setup to get out of one marriage. Why would you want to jump into another?"

"I consider myself several steps above a French farce, thank you," he said reproachfully. But his green eyes were gleaming, brighter than any lantern or string of lights. "Perhaps I have finally seen the error of my ways."

"I doubt that very much."

"I do rather like the error of my ways, now that you mention it," he said. "It could be that as my father grows ever more frail, I am filled with a sudden burst of filial devotion and wish to give him what he's always wanted—a wife and a child. One-stop shopping."

"That's almost sweet." Nina smiled at him. Sharply. "Which is how I know that's not your motivation."

"I shall have the palace's legal team deliver the relevant proclamations to your bedchamber," he told her. "I think you should find them interesting reading. The crux of the matter, I'm afraid, is that I don't have to offer you any explanation at all."

"Very well," Nina said and shrugged. She returned her attention to her food.

And, because she'd been raised in a harder school than this, she proceeded to ignore him as she tasted all the various dishes he'd arranged on her plate. The flavors were as bright as the lights above her, but she could hardly take them in.

Because Zeus lounged there beside her, simmering with intensity and entirely too male. She couldn't pretend she wasn't aware of him. At least not to herself. She was hardly aware of anything else. Still, she ate her dinner as if she was entirely on her own, gazing out over the sea as a tender moon began to rise.

And she would have carried on in the same vein, because he was apparently prepared to sit there in brooding silence for as long as she could maintain hers, but the baby began kicking again. Extra hard, so that she had to stop and press her hand against the point of impact.

She didn't even mean to look at Zeus while she did it, but she couldn't seem to help herself. And she found an arrested sort of expression in those deep green eyes.

"The baby's kicking," she told him, though she immediately questioned why she was telling him anything. It would have been far easier to say nothing and keep on doing what she was doing. Far less intimate, anyway. Because though she would have told a stranger on the bus that the baby was kicking, it was something else again to tell the man who'd helped make that baby.

Or maybe it was just that the man was him.

It was something about how green his eyes were, perhaps. Or how, just for a moment, she got a glimpse of the man she thought she'd seen that long-ago night.

Nina didn't like to think about that night in such detail. She'd been confused, that was all. That was the sort of thing that happened when a person accidentally fell into the arms of a notoriously wicked prince, proceeded to give him her virginity, and then stayed up the rest of the night—very nearly every moment of it—compounding the error.

Repeatedly.

And in between those rounds of experiencing so much pleasure that she couldn't believe she'd lived this long without it, they'd talked, too. The way people talked when they never expected to see each other again, she understood now.

She hadn't understood it then. *Then* she'd been wonderstruck at finally—*finally*—being seen. For herself. Her real, true self.

Nina definitely didn't like to remember that.

Now she was carrying the baby they'd made that night. And she was sitting high up on a magical balcony in a palace dedicated to gods, looking at the closest example to one she had ever seen on earth.

For a moment she thought he'd smirk, make a droll remark, do his *Zeus* thing.

Maybe that would be better.

Instead, the ancient mask seemed to crumble as she watched. Zeus leaned forward, suddenly looking nothing like that lounging, lazy creature who all the world thought they knew so well because he was always performing for them.

He wasn't performing now. She was sure of it.

"Here?" His voice was gruff and low, his hand hovering over her belly.

Nina told herself she was being efficient, that was all, as she took his hand in hers and guided it to the spot where the baby he'd helped make was using her ribs as a drum.

She'd felt the baby kick for some time now, and still, it felt miraculous. Every time. She could still remember the very first time, the sudden quickening that had changed everything. Because the baby had kicked and she'd known, beyond any of the doubts that might have chased her through those first few months when she'd worried about how her life would change, that they were in it together. Her child and her. Forever. She'd started preparing to come to Theosia the very next day.

But Nina had done all that alone.

This was something else again. Taking the hand of the man who'd fathered her baby and placing it on her body, and then watching as that hard, starkly sensual face of his lit up with wonder.

Something inside of her seemed to shatter, though it wasn't a breaking. It was a kind of shattering that went on and on, too thick and too hot.

And it seemed to take a very long while for Zeus to pull his hand away again.

Nina felt…changed. There was that shattering inside her, and now there was the imprint where his hand had been. She could feel the heat of it, charging through her. It kicked up feelings she thought had only ever been fleeting, only that one night, and never to be repeated.

It made her feel…fragile, somehow, that she'd been wrong.

Zeus sat back in his chair, and his gaze was inscrutable. "Why don't you want to marry me? It's very disconcerting, given women usually fling wedding rings at my feet and beg for the privilege. Are you only saying it to distinguish yourself from the masses?"

That didn't entirely break the spell, but it went a long way toward it. Nina laughed. "I have absolutely no wish to distinguish myself in your eyes."

She thought he might take offense to that—really, she'd *meant* him to take offense to it—but instead, he only smiled lazily.

"One of the things I like most about you," he told her, gaze and voice as dark as the night around them, "is what a liar you are."

"Strange. That sounds like a compliment. And yet."

"Oh, it is."

He moved forward and took her hand in his, and every single instinct she had screamed at her to snatch it back. *Now.* Or he'd know. Or he'd see it, that shattering in place of who she'd been only moments ago. Or the way that all that glimmering within her turned quickly into a molten fire when he touched her.

But then, when his gaze found hers and glinted with wickedness again, she suspected he already knew.

Nina didn't snatch her hand away the way she wanted to, and badly. She left it in his, painstakingly aware of the way his fingers moved over hers, kicking up storms of sensation everywhere he touched. And she had never considered a palm particularly sensitive before. It was functional. Useful. She'd scrubbed too many floors for her to believe anything else.

But with her hand in his, she found she could feel… everything. As if her palm was the center of all possible pleasure, and only he knew how to make it all ignite. And more—every place he touched seemed connected to the strings of fire already lighting her up inside.

And the more he moved his fingers this way and that, almost as if he didn't know what he was doing when she knew he did, the more she burned.

Oh, how she burned, and she couldn't seem to make herself stop.

"What I'd like to know," Zeus said, after a very long while—or possibly only a very few moments, she couldn't tell past the need and longing clashing about inside her—"is what exactly you are hiding."

She made herself sit up straighter.

"I have nothing to hide," she replied. As placidly as she used to respond to the vile insults and occasional shoes Isabeau had lobbed at her head. "I never had much of a personal life to begin with, and what little I did have was sold out to the paparazzi so you could avoid your existing commitments. There's nothing to find except this baby. And nothing to hide—the world is already well aware of how it was made."

She didn't say, *You saw to that, Zeus.* Why bother? He knew what he'd done.

"And yet you go to such lengths to hide yourself," he murmured, still playing with her hand. "Why would anyone do such a thing? Unless there was something hidden away in there they didn't want the rest of the world to see."

"Maybe I resented forever being on display," Nina retorted before she thought better of it.

And if he'd smirked at her the way he did so often, she would have collected herself. It would have served as a dose of much-needed cold water over the head and restored her to herself. She would have gone off on a different tangent, hopefully chastened. Or she would simply have pulled her hand from his and returned to the exquisitely prepared food waiting for her. As serenely as possible.

But he didn't smirk at her. He only waited, the force of his bronze tension moving in her like the beat of her own heart.

And that beat was hard. Deep. It almost knocked her out of her seat.

"I went into the orphanage when I was five." Nina asked herself what on earth she was doing even as she spoke. But then again, none of this was a secret. It was only that no one had ever asked. "My parents were killed in an accident. A slick road in winter. No one's fault, these things happen, and so on. All the same, they died and I went into care. And then, every Sunday for the next ten years, I was trotted out to sell myself to potential buyers." She laughed, but only a little. "Excuse me. I mean, to *charm* potential adoptive *parents*."

He looked at her, frowning slightly. "Surely a cute five-year-old girl should have gone in a snap."

"You would think so. And I did. But they always brought me back."

"You can return a child?" Zeus asked in what looked like astonishment.

Laced with disbelief.

She had never liked him more than she did at the sight of that untutored reaction, but she couldn't dwell on it. Not now.

"It turns out that you can return a defective one," she said quietly. "I had night terrors and no one could deal with it. So after I got to be about ten, they started telling the prospective parents I had emotional problems. That way they didn't bother to take me for a test run only to come back the next morning, complaining of how difficult it had been and how spooky I was. And how that wasn't what they were looking for in a child."

His grip on her hand tightened. "I'm sorry," he said.

And that, too, struck her as alarmingly real.

She didn't want to deal with how the notion of Prince Zeus *being serious* tumbled through her. The things she wanted it to mean that she knew it didn't.

Because he'd showed her who he was. She needed to believe him.

"No need to be sorry. I much preferred not going off into strangers' homes, knowing perfectly well that it wasn't going to work and then being returned like faulty merchandise."

He looked as if he was going to say something, and it was suddenly clear to Nina that if he offered her any pity—if he even looked like he might—she would break into pieces.

She hurried on before he could put that to the test. "But I still had to stand there every Sunday, on display. I was counting the days until I turned sixteen and would be set free. Instead, on the day before that happened, Isabeau's publicity team felt that in light of her recent spate of scandals that year, she ought to make a grand gesture. And I was it."

"I remember," Zeus said.

And it was amazing, truly, how much Nina wanted to ask *what* he remembered… Was it the stories that had been plastered everywhere on her sixteenth birthday? Her personal pain exploited so a spoiled princess could play at looking merciful and good? Or was it the times he'd seen her over the years after that, trailing around after the same spoiled princess who loathed her forced benevolence, hated that she couldn't rid herself of Nina without a good reason to feed to her public, and had gone out of her way to be cruel?

Or was it possible that he remembered that night and the things they'd talked about when they weren't turning each other inside out? The same as she did?

But she kept her questions to herself.

"Living with Isabeau was like living in a glass bowl," she said, though she still wasn't sure why she was telling him this. Because he was the father of her child and he was *here*. Because he was beautiful. Because his hand was wrapped tight around hers, and she couldn't seem to stop herself. "There's the world forever looking at her and everyone around her, but that's not the worst of it. Even in private, every moment is watched. All the people who lurk about the palace, everywhere, like little spies. Reporting back anything and everything they can to gain favor. Currying goodwill and leverage with their reports. Isabeau herself, always there to criticize, cackle, and cut everyone down to size. But especially me, because she didn't actually choose me. Her people did. Something she wanted to make sure I knew. She wanted to be *very* sure I was never under the impression she'd wanted me anywhere near her."

It didn't hurt her to think of these things. Nina was only ashamed that there had ever been a part of her that had wished she and Isabeau could have been closer.

"You decided you would hide your real self away where no one would find you, no matter how hard they looked," Zeus said in his dark, rich voice. "Is that it?"

It was so tempting to lean closer. To thread her fingers with his, then see if he would do what he did last time and lean across what separated them to fit his lips to hers as if that had been their destiny all along—

Nina tugged her hand from his. "This isn't going to work."

Zeus stayed where he was, his elbows on the table, all of his attention focused on her. She saw the way his gaze darkened. "I don't know what you mean."

"You do."

His mouth curved into what she would have said, on someone else, was a self-deprecating sort of smile. But this was Zeus of Theosia.

Still, she couldn't seem to breathe properly when he reached out a hand and toyed with a bit of her dress between his finger and thumb. Then he moved that finger and thumb to trace his way over the swell of her belly.

Where their baby was curled up between them. And would be a person, in the world, in a few short months.

Linking them together no matter what. Like it or not.

No matter what either one of them might be hiding.

"The trouble is," Zeus said when he looked up again, his gaze pinning her to her seat, "I've seen the real you, Nina. I know the difference."

CHAPTER FOUR

ZEUS EXPECTED HER to pull away, and she did. Nina sat back so quickly that the chair scraped loudly against the stone, and he knew that if she hadn't been hampered by her newly rounded body, she would likely have stood up and stormed away.

He could see that she was considering it, even now, no matter that it might take her a moment to rise.

But then, as he watched, her face took on that studied blankness he recognized too well. It was the particular expression she had always worn in court. The very expression that—coupled with her pointed inability to dress in any kind of fashionable manner, no matter how objectively chic the garments she was butchering—had first caught his attention.

Because it was so odd. And the longer he looked, the less sense it made.

"I don't think you should read quite so much into that night," she told him now.

In a tone it took him a moment to place. She sounded as if she felt sorry for him. As if *she* pitied *him*.

He nearly laughed out loud but contained himself. "I'm not sure any reading is required, little hen. You appear to be blooming with the consequences of our choices that night. I believe the book is written."

One expression after the next moved through her brown eyes, though none appeared on her face. He had spent a long time perfecting his own public face, and he knew precisely how difficult it was. And more, what kind of dedication it took.

She was a puzzle, this commoner who would become his Queen, and he was going to enjoy solving her. Piece by delectable piece.

"I will admit that I took a certain satisfaction in making myself…unpalatable. It was my own private rebellion against Isabeau." Her chin lifted then, and Zeus didn't know what it was about her that made his chest so tight. Maybe it was this. This hurling herself at windmills when even Don Quixote would have called it hopeless. But not Nina. "You know you're a good-looking man, Zeus. Usually you're the first to say so. I merely took the opportunity to taste what the many crowds before me have tasted."

"Another lie. How intriguing."

"I'm sorry that you no longer rate your charms as highly as you used to do."

He smiled. "You were an innocent, Nina. Beneath all that bravado. Believe me, I remember it."

What he didn't want to say to her was that whether she'd been hiding or not, it was as if the alchemy of that sudden blast of fire between them—mixed with her unexpected untouched state—had changed him, too.

Because he still didn't care to accept that change.

But he'd never had a night like that.

Not ever.

Zeus had never planned to admit that. To anyone, least of all himself. And he wouldn't have. He would have taken his strange reaction to her—and to what they'd shared, and to what he'd done—to his grave.

That had been his intent.

Had she not shown up today, even more beautiful than he remembered.

He remembered too well. That was the trouble. It was those curves, certainly. But it was also the slow laughter in her gaze that always seemed to be there, at the ready. It was the way she'd matched wits with him and had actually succeeded. It was her sheer delight in each and every new thing he'd taught her. The things her body could do. The things he could make her feel.

The things she had made *him* feel. It was that part that haunted him.

And now there was a child.

His child.

And Zeus might not have wanted the things his father was so determined he should. He might, in fact, have made it his life's work to make sure that where he was concerned, his father never got the slightest bit of satisfaction.

Because he'd made a promise. And he couldn't go back on it now. His mother had never had anyone but him, he had adored her, and even he hadn't been able to save her.

This was all he could do. Accordingly, he'd been doing it for years, letting the world think what they would about him—just so long as his father thought the same, and despaired.

He would keep playing this game as long as necessary.

One thing that was true about Zeus was that he was committed.

But he had known the moment he saw her that his plans could use some changing up, here at the end, and she was the perfect pièce de résistance.

"I'm not innocent anymore," she was saying in that same way, as if she thought this was a fair fight. When she had no idea what games he was playing here. But that didn't make her any less appealing. He wondered idly if anything could. "You've seen to that, and thoroughly."

He was delighted by that, and the hint of pink that rose in her cheeks. *"Thoroughly,"* he echoed. "That is one way to put it."

The pink in her cheeks got brighter. "Right. So. No need to talk about it, I think."

"What I wonder is what would happen if you no longer hid yourself away," he said. "Even now you dress to hide. You put your hair in this mess. Did you do this in your orphanage? Is this the real reason no one chose you?" He could see from the mutinous look on her face that she had done exactly this. He smiled. "What if, for once, you stopped concealing yourself in plain sight?"

And for a moment, he thought she might let her defenses down. Her pretty face softened, and he almost forgot that he was asking her to marry him because it fit so nicely into his endgame where his father was concerned. He almost forgot about the vow he'd made to punish the man who had ruined his mother's life. He almost thought—

But that was madness.

"There is no hidden part of me that wants to marry you, Zeus." And then she seemed to hear herself, out here where there was only the moon and the sea as witness. She shifted in her chair. "I have no intention of marrying anyone. I will have this child and we will be a family. That is more than enough for me."

Zeus didn't think Nina had the slightest idea what *enough* was. And what he wanted to do was pick her up, carry her inside, and prove it. Over and over, the way he had six months ago, ruining them both.

But he didn't.

Because he only played the part of a man unable to control himself.

"You understand that this is Theosia, do you not?" he asked.

"I could hardly forget it while staring at its most overexposed advertisement, could I?" she retorted.

And Zeus's trouble was that he liked that this woman, who should have been the most in awe of him—the most tongue-tied, the most intimidated to find herself once again in his presence—was none of those things. Not then, not now.

She was as unafraid of him as she was unimpressed with him. And what did it say about him that he liked it? That he liked *her*?

"Then you must know that your options are limited here," he told her. Instead of all the other things he could have told her. "I do not require your consent to wed you, Nina. Know this now and spare yourself a fight you will not win."

Nina vibrated in her chair. "Is that a threat?"

He laughed. "Of course it is a threat. What else would it be?"

"But why?" She sounded more desperate than before. "Why do you want this? Because I know you don't want me. And I've already indicated that I intended the baby should know its father, or I wouldn't have come here at all. Why isn't that enough?"

And Zeus had the strangest urge to tell her. Even though he knew better. For what woman would wish to hear that she could be yet another game piece in this endless war with his father? What man would confess it?

He wanted to tell her all the same. And not because he thought she might understand. Since when had he required understanding? But because she was different. She always had been. And he was the only one who had always known that she was beautiful, there beneath the clown show she'd put on. He had seen things in her she'd never shown anyone else.

Maybe Zeus wanted to see if it was at all possible that someone could see such things in him—

But that was his weakness talking.

And he'd chosen his path a long time ago.

He would not lose his way now, no matter the temptation.

"The child, Nina," he told her, with enough severity that he almost believed it was the whole of his reason to marry her. And then, as the words sat there, he understood they were not a lie. Not quite. "That is why.

Whatever else I might be, I am also a Prince of Theosia. No child of mine will be born out of wedlock."

Her mouth moved, but no sound came forth.

And Zeus shook his head as he gazed at her. "I might not care much for my father, but I believe that every child should have one. If at all possible."

She held his gaze for what seemed like an age, then dropped it.

"What did your father do to you?" she asked softly.

"It is what he didn't do." But he would not speak of this. He refused.

Zeus rose then, gazing down at this woman who had already upended his world. He thought that perhaps he should have taken against that, but the truth was, he liked it.

She was not boring, this hen of his, and he would have liked her for that alone.

But there was a child to consider. And to his great astonishment, he hadn't been lying when he'd said those things to her about wedlock and fatherhood. Even if, were he to be scrupulously honest, he hadn't actually known he had such traditional notions knocking around inside him.

Until now.

"We will be married," he said, and though he knew he sounded severe instead of his usual lackadaisical self, he did nothing to temper his voice. "Soon. I suggest you come to terms with it. If you do not, nothing will change, I should not like to see you so needlessly unhappy, Nina."

Her eyes narrowed. "You are all heart," she murmured.

Zeus left her there, out on the balcony with the sea all around, to think over her choices. And because if he didn't walk away from her, he wouldn't, and he couldn't indulge that kind of need. Not when it was nothing so simple as a forgettable pleasure.

It was harder to leave her rooms than it should have been.

Zeus tried to distract himself from the greedy longing storming around in him by imagining what form of rebellion she would take on now. Would she still try to look a mess, as it seemed she had in both previous parts of her life? Would she fashion herself Princess Pigsty?

He thought that sounded entertaining.

But it wasn't her little rebellions that kept him up that night. It was the touch of her hand to his. The press of her belly beneath his palm. The way she'd tried to hide the way she was breathing when he'd toyed with her fingers.

That flame. That need.

The night he told himself he could barely remember, yet had never forgotten.

He was thin-tempered the next morning when his butler let her in again, leading her out to the morning room.

And yet, one look at her and he felt fully restored.

Because Nina had clearly chosen her next rebellion. Sheer perfection.

She stood before him looking nothing short of edible, no sign of the clownish buffoon she'd played in Haught Montagne to be seen.

Her blond hair was woven into a crown of braids

atop her head, showing off her slender neck and wide mouth. And instead of yesterday's tent, she wore something clingy enough that he could see her generous breasts and that marvelous bump, but all the rest of her, too. Her delicate shoulders, her lovely legs.

She was beautiful. She always had been, but today it was on display.

"Did you find a hairbrush in your bathroom suite?" he asked mildly.

Nina glared at him but straightened her shoulders. "I might as well marry you as not, I suppose."

"I'm touched," he said. "Deeply."

He did not rise from the small table where he took his breakfast. The expansive windows let the sun in, and he liked to bask in it while he sipped at an espresso and tracked various items of interest in the financial pages. Only after this ritual did he venture into his actual office, where he spent more and more of his time since his father's decline these last months had forced the reluctant Cronos to shift the bulk of his duties to his son. Zeus had gone to great lengths to make himself seem ineffectual—as if the kingdom ran itself. If anyone outside the palace even knew he had an office, they assumed it was a PR affair kept on hand for no other purpose than to clean up the messes he made.

He had one of those, too. But that wasn't what he did all day.

Another thing he did not intend to share.

Zeus waved Nina into the seat opposite him and then leaned back to give off his usual impression of an indolent little princeling. The one she already thought he was. So she could truly contemplate the step she was taking.

Nina took her time sitting down, and he couldn't tell if her discomfort came from him—or the fact that she'd proven his point by effectively unveiling herself. And he liked his games, it was true. But it was untenable that she should sit with him in *discomfort*.

"The first time I noticed you was at an opera some years ago," he said, though he would have sworn he had no such memory. That she had been there, like wallpaper, until he'd decided to use her as a weapon to effect his escape. Yet it seemed he could remember that night in Vienna with perfect clarity. "You sat just behind me, and I did not hear a note. All I could think was that you smelled of strawberries."

"That's because I was eating them," Nina replied in that bland way of hers. Her lips twitched. "Dipped in chocolate, naturally, or what's the point? Perhaps you were hungry."

He lifted his espresso to his lips and took a sip. "It fascinates me that you will not take a compliment."

"While it fascinates me that you're so determined to give them." She lifted a shoulder. "I don't need to be complimented by you, Zeus. The fact of the matter is that if I were choosing husbands, I would not choose you, either."

"I'm devastated. And you are still trapped. My condolences on the life of hardship that awaits you here."

But she'd settled into her chair, despite his sardonic tone. And was clearly leaning into this topic. "You're selfish. Your behavior is atrocious. That's on a good day. As far as anyone can tell, the main purpose of your existence appears to be racking up as many sexual encounters as you can and flaunting them in the tabloids."

"You say that like it's a bad thing."

Nina sighed. "As far as I'm aware, marriages like these survive because certain understandings are put in place from the start."

She was more correct than she knew, but Zeus did not let himself react. He bit back the automatic response that leaped in him. And waited until he was calm enough to shrug.

With all expected indolence.

"I cannot say I have concerned myself overmuch with the state of marriages, royal or otherwise," he said.

Across from him, Nina shifted in her chair. "I know that Isabeau had every intention of continuing her usual exploits while married to you. She talked about it all the time. All she needed to do was pop out an heir and then, duty done, she could return to doing what she truly enjoyed. The expectation was that you would do the same. And that neither of you would care."

"And am I to expect the same understanding with you?" he asked. "Or are you worried that's what I want?"

He forced himself to sound bored when he was… not. He unclenched his jaw. And his fist. And did not allow himself to contemplate this woman with other lovers. The very idea made everything in him…burn.

Not that Nina noticed.

"Oh, no, you misunderstand," she said airily. "I already know my part."

Everything in Zeus went still. Dangerously still.

Alarmingly still, even. Had he been paying attention to anything but her, he might have heeded those alarms.

"I beg your pardon. Do you have some lover you feel you cannot give up?"

Because if she did, he would rip the man apart. And then the world.

He opted not to ask himself why he, who had always professed he could not begin to understand the notion of jealousy or possession, felt both here. To a disturbing degree.

"It's not about *me*," Nina said, frowning at him. "It's for you. I want you to go out there and do whatever it is you do so that I don't have to worry about it."

There was no answer she could have given that would have stunned him more.

"So you don't…have to *worry* about it?" He could do little more than blink in astonishment.

She nodded enthusiastically. "It's a perfect solution. I'm sure your sexual demands are very… Well. *Demanding*. And I certainly couldn't keep up with all that." Nina waved a hand. "You should go out there and keep spreading it around, the way you always have. You have my blessing."

And that strange temper kicked through him all over again. Laced through with what he could only assume was outrage that this woman who would be his wife was offering him carte blanche to carry on as if he were to remain single.

It felt blistering. Life-altering.

Yet the strangest part was, he knew that what she

was suggesting should have thrilled him. Zeus had never been any particular fan of monogamy. He had often advanced the theory that it didn't truly exist. That it was only fear masquerading as all the pledging of troths and other such horrors.

He should have been delighted with this, and yet he was not.

Not at all.

"This way, everyone's happy," she was saying brightly. *Happily.* "You can do what you do best. And I—"

"What is it, pray, that you do best?" Zeus growled. "I shudder to think."

Nina cast a look his way that suggested he was being strange. "I don't know what I do best. I've never had the opportunity to find out." But she studied him for moment, tilting her head to one side. "I thought you'd be thrilled. You do not look thrilled."

"You're awfully quick to forgo the pleasures of the flesh, Nina."

She laughed, which was somehow the most insulting thing yet. "I think I'll survive."

"Will you?"

And he didn't mean to move. Zeus would have sworn that he'd had no intention of doing anything of the sort.

But then, as if he had no part in it, his hand was reaching out. And then he was leaning across the small table until he could hook his palm around her neck.

And then pull her face to his.

He could taste her startled exhalation. He could see the shock in those warm, pretty brown eyes.

And everything about her was sweet. Soft.

But he kissed her like a drowning man, all the same.

Hot and hard, like he was setting a fire, then throwing gasoline on the blaze.

And it was like the six months that he knew had existed between that night with her and now simply... disappeared. As if they'd been shadows that he'd traveled through and nothing more.

Because this, finally, was vivid.

It was *right*.

It was the opposite of boring.

Without lifting his mouth from hers, Zeus moved from his seat, rounding the small table so he could lift her up and pull her into his arms. And she fit differently, with that beautiful belly between them, but somehow that only made it hotter.

They had made a child, and he could feel the solid weight of the baby between them, and still she kissed him with all of that passion, all of that need, that had haunted him for half a year.

Maybe it had haunted her, too.

He kissed her and he kissed her, deeper and wilder with every stroke, until he got his answer.

Then he kept on kissing her, until he'd almost forgotten that he was marrying her for any reason but this.

This slick perfection. This unnerving sense that he was home at last.

That thought sobered him too quickly. This was about a narrative, that was all, and he needed to be in control of it. He needed to make sure she was seen the way he wanted her seen. The same way he made sure he was seen in only one way outside his office. *Home* had nothing to do with this. Zeus didn't know what the word meant.

He pulled back so he could rest his forehead on hers, letting one hand move down to stroke the belly between them at last.

Because he knew every other part of her. He remembered it all. In extraordinary detail.

Her eyes were closed, and she was breathing heavily. It took her a long time to look at him again, and when she did, she looked dazed.

"That can't happen again," she told him, very distinctly.

But all he could do was stand there, sharing breath with her while his sex shouted at him and every part of him urged him to get closer. To keep going. To do whatever was necessary to have her naked and beneath him, sobbing out her joy as they found each other again—

"Zeus." Her voice cracked a little on his name. "This *can't* happen again. Ever."

"Somehow, little hen," he murmured, reaching up to slide his hand along her pink-tinged cheek and brush his thumb over her lips, "I think that it will."

When she pulled away, he let her. Just as he let her rush from out of the room. But he could taste her on his mouth again. At last. He could feel the press of her body against his, like she'd marked him.

And he found himself smiling long after she'd gone.

CHAPTER FIVE

THAT KISS COMPLICATED EVERYTHING.

It was bad enough that Nina had agreed to marry him. She'd lain awake that first night, staring at the ornate ceiling that arched high above her. She'd listened to the sound of the sea outside. And she'd asked herself what on earth she thought she was doing here.

But came back, always, to her baby.

How could she reasonably refuse to marry her baby's father? She'd argued with herself all night. Because certainly, she had her issues with royals in general. This child would be a crown prince or princess. Nina had never met one of those she didn't have deep suspicions about in one way or another, but that didn't mean there couldn't be a perfectly lovely version.

Was that good enough reason to deny her child its birthright?

The fact of the matter was, she wasn't romantic, despite the odd daydream. Not really. She had congratulated herself on that, lying in that vast bed in her guest bedchamber, running her fingers up and down her sides and over her belly as she tried to get used to sleeping on one side or the other.

I can make decisions based on what's good for you, she told her baby. *Not silly little fairy tales of true love.*

She might have dreamed of romance and other such things when she was with Isabeau, but that was only because the Haught Montagne court had been devoid of any such tender notions. And because she'd been sixteen when she'd first gotten there and might have been foolish enough to think *what if* in those first few months. Before Isabeau had stopped pretending and had showed her true colors. When Nina had let herself imagine that there might be a place she belonged.

Her years at Isabeau's side had cured her of such foolishness. And watching Isabeau's many passionate entanglements—all while she was so determined to marry Zeus—had soured Nina on romance completely. Zeus's own exploits, extensively covered in the press, had suggested to her that love was nothing more than a cynical bid to sell more column space in greedy magazines.

Nina had always told herself that when she was finally set free, she would go out into the world and follow her heart wherever it led without involving the tabloids at all.

But what she'd discovered was that she liked following her heart well enough—but only in terms of the many destinations she could finally explore on her own terms. She'd never had any interest in following her heart to *people*. Not once in her first two months of travel, before she'd started to feel so wretched, had it even occurred to her to try out a *passionate entanglement* of her own. Maybe she should have.

She'd loved what little part she'd taken in the happy

nights in the various hostels where she'd stayed. It had seemed like such a different world, all these heedless young people, dancing and drinking without a care—night after night, as if no one was watching them. Because no one *was* watching them.

But she'd never followed through on any of the invitations, spoken or unspoken, that had come her way.

A romantic would have, surely. A romantic would have wondered *what if*.

That had been what decided her. If she was the kind of woman who intended to hold out for love, that would have been one thing. But she wasn't. She was practical. A realist. Love was for silly girls in skimpy dresses, filled with wonder and maybes. Not grown, weathered women who knew better, who'd already been called a horrid disgrace in at least ten languages. And if she wasn't the sort who was going to hold out for romantic love, she might as well marry the Prince, who had his own, likely nefarious, reasons for marrying her—but what did that matter?

It was about her child in the end.

That was the only love that mattered.

She'd marched off to find him that morning, filled with a sense of purpose and even pleasure that she could secure her child's future like this. Almost as if, finally, she'd relegated her memories of her own cold, hard childhood to the dustbin.

Then Zeus had kissed her and ruined everything.

Because now she was forced to lie in her bed, night after night, and wonder if the reason she hadn't used her travel time to experiment in all the ways everyone else did was not because she was so practical and *above it all*.

She was terribly afraid it had been because of him.

After all, she'd only started on that adventure in the first place because of her night in Prince Zeus's arms. And once the scandal had broken, she had happily left Haught Montagne. Then marched out into the world, telling herself with every step that she barely remembered a thing, because all that really mattered was that she was free of Isabeau at last.

But even if that were true—and it wasn't—his kiss brought it all back.

Because the man tasted like sunshine and the darkest nights, sin and sweet surrender, and she remembered every single thing she'd ever done with him. Every last detail of that long, languorous night. Almost as if his betrayal of her come morning didn't matter.

Now she was more than six months pregnant, trapped in the Palace of the Gods with the only man she'd ever met who could reasonably suggest he might earn that title in the modern world. And Prince Zeus, the wickedest man alive, was insisting she marry him.

Nina couldn't come up with a good enough reason why she shouldn't.

But she'd regretted it the moment she said she would.

Not just because he'd kissed her—and she'd betrayed herself entirely by kissing him back like a desperate woman, a shocking truth she was still struggling to come to terms with—but because the palace staff descended upon her soon after, the inevitable Theosian courtiers in their wake.

And as they began to play their little games around her, it occurred to Nina that she hadn't even thought to have *this* nightmare.

"I can't have a staff and all those horrible aristocratic groupies," she told Zeus one night at another one of the dinners he insisted upon. Tonight he wore a crisp linen affair that would have melted into a tragedy of wrinkles on anyone else in this climate. On Zeus, it did not dare.

It seemed at odds with the man she'd glimpsed in his offices earlier that same day, when she'd been wandering about on one of her art walks, looking… focused and somber as he spoke in low tones with his ministers, none of them the least bit groupie-ish. Almost as if he took his job seriously when no one was watching him.

She didn't know where to put that. Particularly when he showed up looking every inch his rakish, playboy self.

"Some of the aristocratic groupies you disdain are my cousins, Nina," he replied, genially enough. But she was sure she could see behind that mask of his. Maybe more than she should.

"They are a pit of snakes, waiting to strike."

Zeus laughed. "Fair enough. But you cannot hate a snake for merely following its nature."

"I can choose not to put myself in striking distance." He only gazed at her, and she blew out a breath. "The last thing in the world I want is a set of my own courtiers. They're already circling around me, looking for a head to bite off."

"They are no match for you, little hen."

Another ecstatic sunset was stretched out behind him, framing him in deep pinks and oranges. And Nina's pulse was too quick, another betrayal, suggesting as it did that she was *afraid* when she was not. Why should she be afraid? What were a pack of status-hungry aristocrats to her?

But her pulse carried on making her a liar.

"Perhaps it is not the sad reality of palace courtiers that you dislike," Zeus said, almost as if he was addressing the sunset instead of her. "Here they do not creep about the palace at all hours, as in Haught Montagne. They are only allowed in at my discretion. Perhaps what you cannot fathom is facing them without your usual armor."

"I don't know what you mean," Nina threw back at him.

Even as her stomach dropped and her pulse picked up again. Because she did know. One of the reasons she hadn't minded all those terrible articles about her was because…they weren't about her, really. They were about the character she'd played to annoy Isabeau. Or even, in some cases, about the ungainly orphan girl no one had ever wanted. That was also not her, because she'd wanted her own parents, not new ones. After a certain point, she'd taken pleasure in being overlooked.

She'd hidden herself her whole life, but not here.

Here, she dressed as if she considered herself just as pretty as any idle aristocratic courtier whose job it was to look lovely at all times. She did her hair and took care with her appearance for the first time in her life. And yes, she was doing it because Zeus had challenged her. Because he'd suggested she couldn't handle showing herself.

But she hadn't expected how much she would hate the fact that the sort of people she disliked most could see her, too.

"Nina."

She only kept herself from jolting by the barest thread. And that was before he reached over and took her hand, sending that rush of heat and longing shooting through her, lighting her up. Everywhere.

His gaze was intent. "Hiding in the way you have may have amused you, but it also gave them ammunition. Imagine if you denied them even that. It is possible to keep a boundary around what is private, what is yours, without playing at dress-up."

"Is that what you do?" she managed to ask.

And she knew she'd scored a point when that gaze of his shuttered. Behind him, the winter sun dipped below the horizon. Zeus let go of her hand.

Nina had the distinct thought that, perhaps, she was tired of point scoring.

But that felt far too much like an admission of something she refused to accept, so she swept it aside and attended to yet another spectacular feast laid out before her.

"Whatever you think of courtiers, you must choose a staff," Zeus said after a moment or two. In his usual manner, all ease and male grace and that wickedness beneath. "Not for your personal needs, as I am sure you will tell me you can take care of yourself, but because you will be Queen one day. And there will be a great many considerations it is better a staff handles. I think you know this."

Her hand was still branded by his touch. Her body was still reacting to that jolt of its favorite source of heat. And Nina wanted to argue, or maybe succumb to the pressure inside her that felt too much like a sob—but Zeus had that look in those gleaming green eyes of his again. That wicked, knowing light when she was determined that no more kissing would occur.

Because when he kissed her, she couldn't think straight.

Nina couldn't have that. She was a practical, rational, capable woman. She would not allow *kisses* to sidetrack her.

Even if kissing Zeus again was all she thought about some days.

To her eternal shame.

Zeus made himself scarce at certain hours of the day. And now and again she saw him as he apparently tended to the actual business of running his country, which was clearly a secret. Maybe the biggest secret, certainly outside the palace walls, and one she clearly didn't know how to process. Nina decided that instead of processing any of these things about him that didn't fit—or picking courtiers she didn't want or staff she didn't trust—she would dedicate herself to what she did best, instead.

That meant she hid in the palace library and reveled not only in the books but in the fact that no one questioned her right to sit around and read as much as she liked about whatever she liked. Or to sit in a window seat and daydream. No one came to lecture her.

No one demanded she attend them. No one punished her if she wandered off by herself for hours.

Daphne learned quickly to track her down in the stacks, where Nina could always be found sitting with her feet up, a book open in her lap.

If she didn't look too closely at her situation, she almost felt free.

Or at least off on the sort of holiday she'd always longed to take after she finished seeing the world.

But on the first morning of her second week in Theosia, Daphne hurried her through her breakfast, then told her there would be no library time today.

"Library time is the only thing keeping me sane," Nina told her aide—who she had made the head of her staff. They had both stared at each other, then nodded, and that had been that. Painless, really.

"I have faith in your sanity," Daphne replied. "In or out of the palace library."

And then delivered her to the airfield, where liveried servants waited to escort her onto a waiting plane. Zeus was already there, reclining in a leather seat as if it was a throne. Or as if he wanted her to think it was.

"Where are we going?" she asked as she sat down in one of the bucket seats, aiming a smile at the hovering air steward. She declined refreshment, her gaze on the man across from her. And the way he looked at her, all that dark green heat.

"I've spent the week planning how we will reveal ourselves to the world," he said when the steward was gone.

"Reveal ourselves?" Nina didn't like the sound of that at all. "I don't know what you mean. You are over-revealed as it is, surely. There was a swimsuit edition of you only last month."

"I do look fantastic in a swimsuit," he said, as if she'd been lavishing him with praise.

Nina could only roll her eyes. Because he was right. He did.

"Come now," Zeus chided her, his mouth curving. He propped up his head and all that dark blond hair with one hand. "You cannot possibly imagine that you can turn up out of the blue, hugely pregnant with the child of a prince, and reveal nothing about how you came to find yourself in this state. Especially when that prince is me. And then, of course, we have decided to marry. It will need announcing."

"I don't see why."

He only smiled. "You do. You don't want to see why, but you do. It will be reported on either way. Better to attempt to control the narrative."

"Alternatively, we could try just going about our lives," Nina said dryly. "I think the world would catch on, narrative or no narrative."

"You worked for Isabeau for far too long not to know how this works," Zeus said, too much laughter in his gaze. Mocking laughter, she thought. "You know this game as well as I do. Why are you pretending you don't know how to play?"

She tried to ignore the way her pulse rocketed around, because it had nothing to do with anything. It was proximity, that was all. Maybe it was biology. Maybe a pregnant woman couldn't help herself from feeling this way in the presence of her child's father. Maybe the need to want him was in her bones.

But that didn't mean she planned to surrender to it, either.

She tried to think strategically, the way she would if she had a little more distance from the scenario. The scenario being a wicked prince who looked at her as if he wanted nothing more than to taste her. If she were Zeus, what would she do? And why would it require a trip?

And he was right. She did know.

"You're staging some kind of engagement scene," she said after a moment or two. "You want to start them all talking about us again."

She almost said *on your terms*, but she remembered herself. The last time they'd been talked about had been on his terms, too. The only difference this time was that he was telling her what he was doing in advance.

Nina was tempted to feel a bit of outrage about that but couldn't. Because the way his smile broke across his face felt like a reward, and it made everything in her…shift. Then roll.

Then keep right on rolling until it became a molten, hot brand between her legs.

"Very good, little hen," he said.

And God, the way he said that. *Little hen.* It shouldn't be allowed.

Her breasts seemed to press against the fabric of her dress. She had to tell herself, sternly, not to squirm in her seat. It would only make things worse.

"I don't know what makes you think you can call me that," she said, because she was reeling. And because she was desperate for some hint of equilibrium.

"You do know that Isabeau called me that as an insult, don't you?"

"It's different when I say it."

It wasn't as if there was ever a moment in Zeus's presence when his arrogance didn't seem to take over the room. Or the taxiing plane, in this case. But every now and again, it seemed to boil inside of her. "How is it different?"

"Because you like it when I say it, Nina."

And suddenly, it was as if he had gripped her between his hands and was squeezing tight, forcing all the breath from her body.

All she could think about was kissing him. Hurling herself from her seat and finding his mouth with hers. The wild longing seemed to expand within her, crowding out any possibility of anything else, even breath—

You need to stop, she ordered herself. *Now*.

Nina made a little show of rubbing her belly and murmuring to the baby, who was fast asleep inside her. And then wondered if that was the kind of mother she was going to be. The kind who shamelessly used her own child to get out of awkward moments of her own creation.

"Why do you look sad?" Zeus demanded, still lounging there as the plane began to gather steam along the runway. "Surely you cannot be so distraught over the use of a nickname."

"First, I can be distraught about anything I wish," Nina retorted. "Whether you like it or not. But I was thinking about motherhood."

Their gazes seemed to tangle then, and suddenly everything seemed…stark. Stripped down in ways she wasn't sure they had ever been before—not since that night. Not since they stayed awake as the hours grew narrower and told each other things that could only belong in moments like that.

Stolen. Illicit. Never to be repeated.

She had no doubt, as the plane leaped from the earth, that Zeus was remembering the very same thing.

Are you lonely? she had dared to whisper, there in his vast guest rooms in the old Haught Montagne castle. A far cry from where she lived, down in the servants' quarters.

He had held her beside him, pulled fast to his side because they had not let each other go all night, but he did not laugh. The look he gave her was...quizzical.

What would make you ask such a thing of me? I'm forever surrounded by people. I could not be lonely if I tried.

An orphanage is filled with people, she'd replied. *And yet it is the loneliest place on earth.*

He had looked at her for a long time, still not smiling, so she had no choice but to notice how truly beautiful he really was. All those sculpted lines. That heartbreakingly sensual mouth. *Princes do not believe in loneliness*, he had said.

She had traced his cheek, his jaw, with her fingers. She had wanted to remember this, remember him, with everything she was. *I don't think it works that way.*

He had rolled her over to her back, setting himself over her again, and already she had been soft and ready for him. It was as if, after that first impossible kiss, he had made her body his.

And she had loved it.

Yes, he had whispered harshly. His green eyes glittered. *I am always lonely.*

And then he had thrust deep inside her, and she had stopped doing anything so difficult as forming words.

Now, Nina was glad they were on a plane. And that takeoff was a distraction. And that she could fuss around with the new maternity outfit she wore, one of the many items of clothing that had appeared in her bedchamber over the last week. She'd gone and looked for the clothes she'd come with, only to find them missing.

I will be certain to take it up with the palace laundry, my lady, Daphne had said mildly enough. *But who can say when I'll be able to speak to them? You had better wear these things in the meantime.*

Nina hadn't had any doubt whose order it was to dress her differently, but still. She thought she ought to protest. She ought to put up *some* resistance, surely. But the look of pleasure and heat in Zeus's gaze the next time he saw her in something that accentuated her new curves…did something to her.

A bit of acid stomach, perhaps, she told herself tartly as the plane hit cruising altitude and the man across from her was still lounging there as if propped up by indolence instead of his own arm.

And she thought, with great clarity, that discussing the moment they'd had at takeoff might actually kill her.

"What is it you do when you disappear all day?" she asked instead, though she suspected she knew. As impossible as it was to imagine this man doing anything virtuous—or even vaguely responsible. "I would have thought debauching virgins was something you had down to a science, requiring very little time. And more to the point, I did think most of your trysts occurred at night."

He treated her to one of those smiles of his, wolfish and edgy, a perfect match for the heat in his green gaze and the echoing blast of fire deep inside her.

"I don't think you really want to know."

"You don't have to tell me, of course," Nina said with a shrug. "After all, ours will be two very separate lives."

She didn't think she was imagining the way his jaw tightened at that. "I don't know that either one of us has the faintest idea what our lives will be like. But we were speaking of motherhood, were we not?"

"Indeed we were." She felt as if she'd dodged a hard punch there, or maybe caught it, because her breath seemed to come a little quicker. "I don't remember my mother, you see. Not really. I have vague impressions of a kind voice, a hand on my cheek. Though I can't say that those are actual memories. They might just as easily be things I thought I ought to imagine. Some of the kids at the orphanage could remember everything, back to when they were in a cot, staring up at their parents. But not me. You lost your mother, too, did you not?"

He was still lounging, but somehow, he looked more like a predator set to pounce than he did relaxed in any way. "I did. I was eleven."

Nina nodded. "Then you remember more."

Still, he didn't move. "I do."

The prickle of some kind of warning moved over her then, though she couldn't have said what it was. She looked down at her bump instead, smoothing her hands over the soft, stretchy material that somehow managed to both emphasize her pregnancy and make her look more delicate at the same time. It shocked her how much she liked it, when she'd spent so many years concealing anything real about herself—loath as she was to admit it. Not only choosing the most unflattering clothes, but wearing them two sizes too big, or too small, so she always looked misshapen. All for the reward of hearing Isabeau's shriek of fury every time she walked in the room.

I cannot bear the sight of you! the Princess would scream. Which meant Nina could retreat and have an afternoon to herself.

But she hadn't simply gotten used to the subterfuge—she'd liked it. And yes, maybe hid there, too. Because she hadn't changed the way she'd dressed when she'd gone traveling. She'd continued to do nothing with her appearance except make herself look worse.

This was the first time she'd tried to look pretty. And somehow, it felt important that it was with Zeus.

"I hope that I do all right," she said after a moment. "With mothering. I have no examples to look up to."

"You will be an excellent mother," he said, his voice something like rough.

And Nina didn't realize how badly she'd needed to hear those words until he said them. How she'd longed to hear someone say that to her. "I hope so," she whispered. "But it seems such a complicated thing, to raise a child. I was raised by a committee of disinterested matrons. Who knows what harm a single person might do?"

Zeus got an odd look on his beautiful face. As if she had somehow disarmed him.

"My mother was lovely," he said, his voice gruffer than she'd ever heard it before. "Being a small child in a palace is not, perhaps, the laugh riot you might imagine. But she made it fun. Everything was an adventure. We were always playing games, and looking back, that's probably because she was closer in age to me than to my father. The courtiers you hate so much were not kind to her. But that was just as well, as it meant we spent more time together. I would say that in terms of mothering, she taught me that it doesn't matter what you do as long as you make sure to do it with intention. I have lived by that ever since."

And she could tell by the look on his face that he had never said such things to another. She would be surprised if he'd ever said such a thing out loud before. Maybe because she knew he hadn't, she had the strangest urge to go to him. To move across the little space between their seats and put her hands on him. Hold him, somehow. This hard, bronze statue of a man.

But she did not dare.

He might not let her. Or worse, he would—and she would not know how to stop.

"I will do my best," she told him instead, feeling that starkness between them again. As if there was no artifice, no masks. Just the two of them.

She pressed her palms against her belly, as if already

holding their child. The way she hoped she would, with love and wisdom, as long as she lived. And was surprised to discover that she was blinking back tears.

"Before we confront our deficiencies as parents," Zeus said in a low voice, "which in my case will be epic indeed, I am certain, there is the little matter of our wedding."

She didn't want to look at him. It felt too fraught with peril. She blinked a few more times. "I already agreed."

"Your agreement was unnecessary, yet still appreciated." He only smiled, faintly, when she glared at him. "Before our wedding, we must turn our attention to presenting our relationship to the world. Our adoring public, if you will."

Nina sighed. "They will all find out soon enough. I'm sure you'll see to that personally."

Zeus made a tsking sound. "I think you know that's not quite how it works. Scandals are much easier to sort out than brand-new story lines, drip fed into the world to create a new impression of existing characters."

Nina made a low noise and directed her attention out the window, where everything was bright blue and sunny. This high above the clouds, surely no one should have to concern themselves with these concocted displays—the lives the public thought people in Zeus's position ought to be living, not the lives men like him actually lived.

"I hate all this," she said, more to the window than to him. "Constantly having to come up with these stories. Pretending to be whatever *character* it is the papers have decided I ought to play. I can see it now. *Queen Hen, clucking her way across Theosia.*"

And with her not hidden at all, but out here looking like *her*.

She shuddered.

"Nina. Please. No one will call you *hen* but me."

She looked back at him, and as ever, Zeus looked at his ease. She told herself that it was annoying, but somehow, she felt a little bit less…fluttery.

He waved a languid hand. "I only spend time with beautiful women, as you know. Therefore, it follows that the woman I marry must be the most beautiful of all."

"I think you're forgetting something," Nina said. He lifted his magnificent brows. "We already created one scandal. They already think I'm a mercenary gold digger. That was when I simply slept with my mistress's fiancé. What do you suppose they'll call me now?"

"Whatever I ask them to," he said, as if the matter was already settled, the articles already written.

She could feel the dubious look on her face. "Is that how it works? You think you're in control of the tabloid cesspool?"

But Zeus only laughed. "Nina. We're going to tell them a love story. Don't you know? All is always forgiven with love."

CHAPTER SIX

ZEUS DIDN'T KNOW what was worse. Nina's look of outright horror at his use of the word *love*. Or the fact that he'd actually spoken of his mother.

Of his own accord.

He spent the rest of the flight to Paris being outrageous and needlessly provoking to make up for it.

Because he would rather have her looking at him the way she normally did. As if he required extreme forbearance.

It wouldn't change the fact that he wanted his father—and the rest of the world—to think that the most notorious prince in the world was head over heels in love with what was considered his worst scandal yet.

Once in the City of Light, a waiting car swept them off to his favorite hotel, a discreet affair on the Left Bank that suited both his sense of luxury and his need for discretion—but only sometimes.

"I'm surprised that the Theosian crown doesn't have property in Paris," Nina said once he told her where they were staying. When any other woman he knew would simply have sat there quietly, possibly murmured a few superlatives about both him and his choice of lodging, and tried to look appealing. Then again, Nina didn't have to *try*. "Haught Montagne maintains residences in most major cities. I thought everyone did."

"The kingdom has several residences here, in fact." He thrust his legs out before him in the back of the spacious car, slumping down a bit in his seat so he'd look as rumpled as possible. "I do not always wish to have my every move dissected by the palace."

She nodded briskly. "Because they're evil."

Zeus only sighed. "I like an enemy as much as the next person, but there's something you must remember about palace staff." He turned toward her so he could hold her gaze with his. "We are the product, and they are responsible for keeping that product in as pristine condition as they can manage. Yet the product also has all the power. So what are they meant to do?"

Her gaze was steady on his. "You think of yourself as a product?"

And he kept finding himself in moments like these with her. Perilously close to being his real self around this woman when he liked to pretend he couldn't even recall that he'd ever had a real self to begin with.

"I know exactly who I am," he replied.

Possibly with a touch too much heat.

"But—" Nina began, frowning.

"I cannot speak for other palaces, but I know that I give my own nothing but trouble. And yet they manage it all magnificently." He lifted a brow. "I'm surprised that a woman elevated from the orphanage, and with such a chip on her shoulder to match, would not care for the plight of honest, hardworking servants."

She let out a small sound and looked down at her belly. Then rubbed it the way she did when she was avoiding him. He found it more fascinating every time he saw her do it. And adorable.

Because he was impossible to ignore.

"I don't really think it fair that you are utterly shameless yet think you can go about shaming others," Nina said after a moment.

He bit back a smile. "Courtiers, on the other hand. Truly the dregs of humanity. I fully agree."

"You have more courtiers than a picnic has ants."

"They like to froth about me, it's true," he said. He had always liked it that way. He had always liked to go about in a jostling, happy crowd, the more loud and obnoxious the better. Back in his university days, he'd had the company of his best friends, Vincenzo, Rafael, and Jag. He sometimes thought those days in Oxford were a dream, because they had been the easiest of his life. Good friends. The time to hang about in pubs, heedless and young and magnificently rich.

But that was the trouble with a load of princes as best friends. They did, sooner or later, have to head back to their kingdoms to handle the responsibilities.

Even him.

And now he had a great many more people who liked to call him a friend, yet only the same three real ones. He'd replaced quality with quantity, and he could not say his life was richer for it. But it helped him play his part.

For the first time, he found himself wondering if it was worth it.

The question shook him.

"You're an interesting case," Nina said, looking at him as if to study him as they slid down Parisian streets and past iconic cafés. And Zeus shoved aside that odd feeling inside—because he'd made a vow. That made all this worth it, full stop. "You've never met a crowd you didn't like. And yet you wander around your own palace quite alone."

"The palace calls for gods, not courtiers, Nina. It's in the name. I can only obey."

"I'm almost tempted to suggest that everyone's favorite wicked prince has a public *and* private side. Yet you go to great lengths to pretend otherwise." He could feel her gaze on him. "Why?"

He sent a lazy look her way and tried not to think about the picture she presented. Sitting next to him in the back of a car, her long legs visible now and crossed at the ankles. The rest of her was almost dainty, small and narrow-shouldered, with a belly so big it shouldn't have been possible for such a small woman to walk around with it.

And yet she did. Seemingly without complaint.

Already the perfect mother, he thought.

And when the usual surge of something too much like emotion crested in him, he shoved it away again. The way he always did.

It was already bad enough that he'd mentioned his mother and started questioning the vow he had made over her grave. He could not start thinking of himself as a father. Or of his own father. Because everything he'd said about his mother was true. She had been a bright light in every respect. But she had been very young and too silly for Cronos, who had dimmed a little more of her light each day until it was extinguished.

And so, with his endless criticism and neglect, King Cronos had taken the only thing that mattered to his son.

Leaving Zeus to return the favor.

By making sure that the only things that mattered to Cronos—his throne, his pure Theosian blood, and the line of succession that would carry forth his bloodline into the future—would be publicly, repeatedly, comprehensively bruised. If not stained beyond redemption.

The truth was, Zeus had never planned to have an heir. He had gone to great lengths to ensure he could not possibly father one. But now, in his bitter old father's waning days, he would present the dying King with something even better than no heir.

An heir from a bloodline his father would despise, when there was nothing he could do about it.

He could not have planned it better if he'd tried.

When Zeus was out of Nina's presence, he thought the plan was divine. He had not intended to impregnate her, but he was delighted he had. Everything fell into place with this particular woman carrying the heir to the throne of Theosia.

It was only when he was with her and she aimed that secret, tender smile down at her belly, or when she spoke of things like her fears of motherhood, that he wondered what, exactly, he was doing.

But only for a moment.

Because Zeus had lost his soul long ago. When he

was eleven, in fact, and his heart along with it. There was no getting them back now.

He told himself he hardly noticed the void.

His Parisian getaway was the two top stories of the quietly opulent hotel, far away from any other guests or nosy photographers. As soon as they arrived in the expansive suite, he had food brought in, because he knew by now that Nina was always hungry.

And as she sat in the living room and helped herself to the small yet epic tea provided, he welcomed in a smiling, diffident man with a briefcase connected to his body with a chain. Behind him came several more men, similarly attired.

They proceeded to set out their wares on one of the tables, and when they were done, they had set out the finest jewels that Europe had to offer.

"I don't understand what's happening," Nina muttered, but she was looking around with a sort of hunted look on her face.

"I suspect you do." Zeus went to take a seat next to her on the sofa she had chosen. He only smiled when she shot a fairly outraged look his way as his weight tipped her closer to him. He waved his hand at all the open briefcases, sparkling with rows upon rows of priceless, impossibly stunning rings. "Choose one."

Beside him, Nina simply…shut down.

"I wouldn't know where to begin," she said, and she sounded…different, somehow.

As if, unbowed by the entire house of Haught Montagne, and not too impressed with Zeus while she was at it, what had finally brought her to her knees was a private shopping expedition.

The woman was a revelation.

"If I may," said one of the men, looking closely at Nina. "I think I have just the thing."

He turned all the briefcases around and then did the choosing, presenting Nina with a selection of five rings instead of ten times the number. And every time she reacted, he switched the presentation until, at the end, only one remained.

And it was clear that no other ring could possibly have done.

It was lovely. Delicate, though it boasted a large, marquise-cut diamond set horizontally. It looked as if it had been designed for Nina's hand, so it nearly sang. Zeus watched as she looked down at it, an expression he couldn't read on her face.

Yet when the men had left, Nina pulled that beautiful ring off her finger and set it on the table before her with a decisive click.

"I can't wear that," she announced.

"Of course not," Zeus agreed, lazily. "I have yet to present it to you. On bended knee, very likely. It's a classic romantic gesture for a reason."

"No."

It registered on him that she actually seemed distressed, but before he could reach for her, she pushed herself off the couch and onto her feet.

"I can't wear that, Zeus. Look at my hands." And then, disconcertingly, she lifted her hands toward him, as if warding him off. "I spent ten years of my life scrubbing floors."

"No one will ask you to scrub floors while wearing a ten-carat ring, Nina."

"This whole thing is ridiculous," she threw at him. "No one will believe for one second that you're marrying a *servant*. A scandalous former servant. Because why would you?"

"I told you. This is a love story."

Because he needed it to be to really pour salt in his father's wounds.

That was what he kept telling himself.

She looked down at her bump. Then she lifted that same grave gaze to him. "No one will believe that, either," she said quietly. Yet with conviction—and he found he disliked it. Intensely. "I'm sure no one will have any trouble believing that I somehow fell in love with you, in my mercenary way, as gold diggers are wont to do. But anyone who has ever met you knows how impossible it is that you would ever fall in love with anyone."

Everything she said was true. And yet he wanted to argue—against the premise, against the names she called herself, against her description of him. Even though all of that was precisely why she was so perfect.

He opted to shrug instead. "And yet, why else would I marry if not for love?"

Nina only fixed him with that same look, much too grave for his liking. She stroked her belly. "I can't think of a single reason. Can you?"

She looked as if she was about to say something else, but then she squeaked a little. Her hands moved on her belly to press down, and because she was no longer wearing a tent, he could see the way her belly rippled.

When Nina looked at him again, her whole face was changed. Light. Shining.

And it hit him, suddenly, that when she wasn't wearing masks and pretending the way she'd had to do for so many years, this was what she looked like. Those brown eyes so bright they seemed shot through with sunshine. Her lovely face, open and happy. And that smile of hers, so charming that it lit up the whole of their hotel suite and likely outside as well, rendering Paris something other than gloomy this February day.

Rendering him...undone.

"Ouch," she said, but she was laughing. "Apparently our child would like to weigh in on this discussion. I'm almost certain it voted for no ring, no marriage, and no more of this silly game."

Zeus moved without thinking. He rose, moved to her, and then slid his own hands onto her warm belly. And he didn't so much hear the way she caught her breath. He felt it, as if she was inside him.

And he felt his child again.

He *felt*, and instead of shoving the feelings away, he stood in them a moment. He kept his palms against her belly and felt her breath come faster. He let all of that wash around in him until he hardly knew who he was, and then he kept on.

"I don't think you're translating correctly," he said as he felt the little drumbeat kick beneath his hands. "The child clearly wishes his parents to marry. He's adamant."

"*She* thinks that she would be just fine as an independent entity," Nina replied.

She pushed his hands away, but then their hands were tangled up together. That wasn't any better.

Zeus wanted to laugh at himself, because if anyone had ever dared try to tell him that there would come a day that simply *touching hands* with a woman would so nearly destroy him, he would have laughed.

But everything with Nina seemed charged like this. One slip away from total detonation.

Little as he liked to recall it, it had always been like this. From that night in Haught Montagne when he'd pressed into a moment that had bloomed between them, thinking she would frown and dismiss him, but she'd laughed. It had seemed preordained.

This had always been impossible to resist.

If she hadn't disappeared so completely after that night, walking away from a castle with little more than a backpack, by all accounts, Zeus would have found her. He had tried.

He didn't like to admit how hard he'd tried. He didn't like to think of that strange autumn at all, when he'd been…not himself.

But he needed to remember his endgame. That was what he'd told himself then. That was what had to matter now.

He needed to keep his promise. He would.

For a moment he could see his mother's face, tipped back in that marvelous laughter of hers that had become so rare near the end. He had been so small, and she had danced with him, around and around to the music of the sun and the sea. He remembered how she'd swung him up into her arms and kept going, twirling until they were both dizzy.

Then they'd done it again.

And by the time Zeus had grown to a tall eleven, she didn't laugh any longer, and she certainly didn't dance, so it had taken coaxing for her to let him pick her up and spin her around in his arms, trying not to notice how frail she was. How tiny.

How destroyed.

Zeus let go of Nina's hands and stepped back. For a beat, he didn't know what he would do. Maybe run? Shout? He did neither. Though it hurt.

He smiled at the woman he would marry, and soon. To fulfill the destiny he'd made for himself not long after that day in his mother's chamber. Then he went and assumed his typical position on the couch, as if it had taxed him sorely to stand.

And he opted not to notice that Nina looked at him for much too long, her expression gone grave again, as if she could see straight through him.

When he knew no one could.

He'd made certain of that.

"Now," he said, with his usual dark humor, though it stung more today than it should have. It made his ribs feel dented. "Let me tell you how this will go."

CHAPTER SEVEN

Nina learned a lot about Zeus over the following weeks.

When he mounted a campaign, he did not play around. He had made their hotel in Paris their home base, and she quickly realized why. Its little-used front entrance was on a busy street, but its back entrance was gated and equipped with a security officer. That meant that Zeus could decide when and if to play paparazzi games.

First he started telling his stories.

He did not get down on one knee. Instead, he slid the ring on her hand over breakfast their first morning there and told her to get used to wearing it. Then he called in what appeared to be the entire Parisian fashion world, paying Nina absolutely no mind when she protested, and insisted they use the front entrance.

"You must mean the back," she said when he ended the call. The ring was heavy on her hand. It dazzled her, catching her eye with its sparkle every time she breathed. The more she gazed at it, the more impossibly magical it seemed.

Even on a hand like hers.

"The more of a commotion out in front, the better," Zeus said. He offered her that wicked curve of his mouth. "Trust me, little hen."

"Well," Nina said, blinking at the blinding jewel on her finger. "That's very unlikely."

Zeus only laughed, low and hot, so that it rolled around inside her and made her feel shivery. Everywhere.

By the time they came, in a horde, Nina certainly wasn't *ready*. But at least she'd eaten and tried her best to get used to the idea.

Ten slender and severe-looking men and women, almost all in black, took over the suite's small ballroom. They wheeled in racks stuffed with fabrics and garments. They conferred with Zeus, pursing their lips and frowning at her, but then murmured appreciatively when they draped certain fabrics over her.

They did not appear to need *her* input at all.

"I don't need all of this," she complained, in the middle of the melee.

But Zeus only eyed her as if she was something adorable. Yet edible.

"I do," he said.

It wasn't as if Nina hadn't witnessed a fitting like this before. She'd sat through far too many of them, in fact. What she hadn't experienced, however, was a fitting like this in which she was the center of attention.

Gown after gown, fabric after fabric. Her measurements were taken, then retaken, while theatrical arguments in French swirled on all around her.

At one point, standing on a raised platform while

a crowd of fashionistas revolved around her, she thought, *This is how a queen must feel.*

The ring on her hand seemed to buzz a little, as if it knew she'd actually dared to imagine herself in the role.

She sneaked a look at Zeus and found him watching her. He was leaning back against the far wall, another one of his dark suits looking as rumpled on him as ever. His ankles and arms were crossed, giving him the look of a sort of fallen angel.

But his green gaze was as hot as it was dark. And it was focused on her.

Nina flushed. And burned.

And yet she couldn't look away.

Almost as if she wanted him to see what he did to her.

When the fitting was finished, they left her with what seemed like an entire wardrobe that very same day. Yet promised to come back with what one stylish gentleman told her were *the important pieces.*

Nina both wanted and didn't want to know what those might be. Because she still couldn't quite accept that this was happening, maybe. Or because she and Zeus were left alone in a ballroom filled with racks of clothes. With no one else in this suite apart from his unobtrusive security detail.

He was still leaning against that wall. Like a taunt.

And all the things she felt, all the ways she burned, bubbled up inside her like a sob. She wanted to explode. She wanted to launch herself at him. She wanted—

"You must change into one of these new options,"

Zeus told her idly, though his gaze was still hot. Too hot. "You like art, do you not?"

She couldn't tell if she welcomed the shift in conversation or did not. And her cheeks were too pink either way.

"I question anyone who does not like art," she managed to reply.

"Then your task is to change into something appropriate for looking at art in Paris."

Nina lifted her chin. "Define *appropriate*."

He didn't smile, but his green eyes grew warm. He waved his usual languid hand, but this time at the racks of clothing.

But when she took too long, only staring at him like she couldn't quite comprehend anything that was happening—because she couldn't—he went and chose a few pieces himself.

Nina went up to the room he'd given her the night before, but she hardly saw it. She put on the simple dress he'd chosen, then sighed. Because it looked like nothing on the rack, but it fit her like a dream. The fabric was soft yet held enough of a shape that, once again, she could see the difference between her belly and her body.

And she blamed her hormonal state when she got a little teary at that.

She wrapped a bright scarf around her neck, knotting it carelessly, then pulled on the trench that slid over her shoulders like a hug. She looked in the mirror and thought it was all so beautiful that maybe, if she squinted, she was beautiful, too.

Just in case, she went and fixed her hair, too. And swept some mascara over her lashes.

When she came down the suite's winding stair, Zeus was waiting at the bottom. He took her hand and kissed the ring she wore, and she thought she wasn't the only one who felt shivery inside.

Then he led her to the nearest chair and helped her sit.

And she felt her mouth go dry when he knelt before her.

"I'm already wearing the ring," Nina managed to say. And she waved it at him, in case he'd forgotten in the twelve seconds since he'd kissed it.

"And it suits you," Zeus rumbled in reply. "But you will need shoes, I think, to brave the city."

Nina watched, then, as Prince Zeus of Theosia slid a delicate shoe, itself a near-operatic work of art, onto one of her feet. Then did the same with the other.

Like another prince she used to dream about. When she'd still believed in fairy tales.

She cleared her throat and reminded herself that these shoes, however stunning, were not made of glass. "I don't know if I can walk in these."

He pulled her up to stand in them, and she swayed, gripping him tighter.

"See?" she demanded. "It's a tragedy waiting to happen."

"Then lean on me, little hen," Zeus murmured, as she clung to him. "I promise, I will not let you or my child fall."

My child, she marveled. He'd actually said *my child*.

And the moment between them seemed dipped in

gold. He stared at her for what felt like a millennium or two, then lifted her hand and the ring to his lips once more.

"You do understand that no one will believe this is real," Nina whispered, though she felt…fragile and beautiful, both not herself and more fully herself than before. "Since when have you wanted to do anything in private? Yet you supposedly proposed to the servant you knocked up where no one can see?"

"But of course." He lowered her hand and guided it to his arm. "This will only add to your mystery."

And that night, he took her on a private tour of several of Paris's most famous museums. She found that once she decided she could walk in her shoes, she did. And they were more comfortable than the heels she'd had to trot in while chasing Isabeau around. So comfortable she kept forgetting where she was, or who she was with, the better to tumble heedlessly into one masterpiece after another.

"What made you think to do this?" she asked at one point, her eyes almost overflowing with the marvels she'd seen tonight.

"The time you don't spend in the library you spend walking the halls, looking at the art on the walls and in the gallery," Zeus replied. Then smiled when her mouth dropped open. "I know. It is so difficult to imagine I could pay attention to such things, but I assure you, I do."

"Thank you," she managed to say. Awkwardly. But heartfelt all the same.

And he didn't look like himself then. No lazy smile, no laughing gaze. He only looked down at her as if they could have been anyone. Just a man and a woman in front of a painting so famous it had its own merchandise.

Just a man and a woman, a pretty ring, and the baby they'd made.

Deep inside Nina, a voice whispered...*what if?*

But his security detail entered the room, and the breathless moment was gone. And afterward, Zeus took her to a restaurant so exquisite that there was no name on its door, and when he ushered her inside, the maître d' nodded as if they were regulars, then greeted them both by name.

And it was later, much later, when Nina felt drunk on good food and great art. And, if she was being honest, the man beside her.

"I'd like to walk back," she said when the car pulled up before them on the narrow side street. "Either my feet don't hurt or they've gone completely numb."

"Very well," Zeus said and then looked behind her, doing something with his chin to alert his team.

Her hand still felt strange with the ring on it, so she kept curling it into a fist and holding it up. As if, were she not careful, the ring would tip her sideways and take her tumbling down to the ground.

But then he solved the problem by taking that hand in his, and that was...

Nina told herself that she was drunk, even though she hadn't touched a sip of alcohol. She felt that giddy. As if she was graceful enough to turn cartwheels, walking down the street in the dark with a man so beautiful that every passerby who saw him stopped and looked twice.

And there were so many things she wanted to say to him, out here in these old streets. Points she needed to make, and then, while they were out here in the dark and the cold, perhaps a confession or two.

She was saved from all that, in the end.

Because by the time they arrived back at their hotel, a crowd had formed. Almost before she registered that all the people were waiting—and for them—the flashbulbs began popping.

It was as violent as it always was, and that was before they started shouting.

Her heart slammed against her ribs. She almost tripped over her own feet and was grateful she was holding on to Zeus for dear life as he pushed on through the wall of noise and disorienting bright lights.

It was a fight to make it into the hotel lobby, where it was mercifully hushed—but Nina could still hear all the shouting from outside. Zeus's security detail led them across the lobby until they reached the private elevator that brought them directly up to their rooms at last.

Nina was shaking. She didn't realize until they were inside their rooms with all the doors locked that Zeus was laughing.

Honest to God *laughing*.

"Why do you think it was funny?" she asked him, letting go of him to hold on tight to the nearest wall. She tried to reach down to take off her shoes, but she'd forgotten that her belly was in the way.

And she had to hold herself back from kicking him when he came over and knelt down to remove them.

Just as she had to *not* punch him, hard, on his shoulder when she had the opportunity.

"You are shaking," Zeus said as he rose, his gaze narrow as it scanned her face.

"That was..." She shook her head. "I've been near scrums like that before, obviously. The last time they were shouting my name, I was half-asleep. This time I actually heard all the vile things they were saying about me. Or to me. I don't know how you can find it the least bit entertaining."

And somehow it felt right when he moved his hands to grip her shoulders. Gently enough, but they were still his hands. Holding her.

"Because that was all it took," he said, gazing down at her. "One evening out and here they are."

She could still hear the shouting in her ears. Her eyes were still dazzled by all the cameras. "Why do you want that?"

He looked confused—or whatever *confused* was on a man so convinced that if there was an answer worth giving, he already knew it. "We discussed this."

"We did not discuss it. You ranted on about telling stories and twisting narratives, but I didn't think..." But her voice trailed off.

"What, then, did you think it would entail?" he asked, his voice a gruff thread of sound. She didn't know why it sounded so loud when she'd heard real volume outside. And when she knew he wasn't shouting himself.

But all Nina could do was shake her head. "I don't know."

"Trust me." His hands gripped her a little tighter,

then he let her go. And she remembered, suddenly, that bronze mask in the halls of his palace. He had never resembled it so much as he did now—and there was no trace of laughter on his face. "This is exactly what I wanted."

But that was the thing, she thought later, shut away in her room with the lights of Paris pouring in through the raindrops that coated her window, like the tears she refused to let herself cry. She did trust that all of this was what Zeus wanted. But how was she meant to trust that what he wanted was any good for her or the baby?

I don't believe he asked you to trust that, came a voice from inside her. *He only asked you to trust* him.

Nina curled herself up in a ball and tried to sleep, but when she did, her head was filled with images of Zeus on his knees, playing Cinderella games.

The headlines started pouring in the next morning.

And Nina quickly realized that Zeus did not intend to give any supposedly soul-baring interviews to carefully vetted, sympathetic journalists. That was one way of rehabilitating a reputation, though one rarely used to good effect by royalty. Instead, he made certain that he and Nina were seen out every night, taking in Paris like lovers.

To drive the point home, he doted on her. He held her hand as they walked. He was always leaning close when she spoke. He helped her into cars. He gazed into her eyes over dinner tables, smiled fondly when she spoke, and looked—in every photograph Nina saw of them—like a man besotted.

This strategy, he informed her with glee, allowed

the tabloids and their readership to compare and contrast for themselves the difference between the arranged engagement to his Princess that he had clearly never wanted anything to do with, and the pregnant woman everyone now suggested he'd left Isabeau for. And would convince anyone who looked that the two of them were mad for each other.

He didn't need to announce any engagement, because the papers took care of that with their zoom lenses. The speculation about the ring she wore went on and on, and the more people carried on about it, the more Nina was described as not only the mercenary gold digger of yore, but something of a femme fatale besides. She was called a dangerous beauty, having hidden in plain sight for years before she'd taken her shot. Most agreed this was evidence that she was nothing but an evil whore. Still, others countered, her mix of innocence and beauty and a handy sob story made her the only one in all the world who could turn Prince Zeus's head.

Nina found it was less upsetting to read these stories about herself than she'd anticipated. Because it was still nothing more than a character she was playing to match the character Zeus was playing, wasn't it? It was no different than wearing her odd clothes and haphazard hair in a royal court.

Though every night she went to her bed alone and wondered just how much each one of them was playing.

By the middle of the second week, the stories were already changing. Who was this woman who had claimed the unclaimable Prince? Was she truly the disgrace of Haught Montagne, as advertised, or had the wicked Prince simply fallen in love with the lonely orphan girl? For how else was she able to succeed with Zeus?

She had to admit that the paparazzi were thorough in their research. There was a round of pictures she hadn't known anyone had taken, from a hostel she'd stayed at in Spain. But rather than creating a scandal out of the photographs of her at a party, the pictures made her into a different kind of heroine on the ravenous internet.

"Apparently I'm the introvert's mascot," Nina said from her favorite sofa, where she was enjoying another phenomenal tea. "It makes a change, as mascoting goes."

Zeus came over from whatever he was doing on his tablet and plucked the paper from her grasp, peering at the grainy pictures. "You look like a librarian shushing the obstreperous children."

"That's more or less what I was doing, if memory serves." Nina shrugged. "Apparently I'm relatable."

"So my team tells me daily." He handed back the paper, his gaze as warm on hers as if they were out in public where photographers were always lurking. But they were in private. "You're making quite a splash. And not a hen in sight."

But the real test, Nina knew, was the upcoming ball.

At the end of their third week in Paris, they left France and headed to the tiny kingdom of Graciela, tucked away between France and Spain, where the country's newly crowned Queen was having a birthday ball. The expectation was that the guest list would be a who's who of European royalty.

"You look nervous," Zeus said with that lazy drawl that made it clear he was not.

Outside, Graciela was shrouded in clouds as Zeus's pilot circled the small airport, waiting for their turn to land.

"Not at all." Nina tried out a laugh that came out tinny. "Who doesn't love a bit of a swim, surrounded by so many sharks?"

"The trick is to pretend the sharks are minnows," Zeus told her, that green gaze of his a simmering fire even as he gave her that half smile. "And treat them like minnows. Most find it so confusing they spend the rest of the evening trailing about after you, begging for more."

"Sometimes," she said softly, "your cynicism about the human race is heartbreaking."

It was Zeus, so all he did was shrug. No matter how many times she thought she saw something else in those green eyes of his. She told herself it was the hormones They were making her see things that weren't there. And would never be there.

She had to stop looking at pictures of them in the tabloids and imagining what she saw was real, because she knew better.

Nina had to keep reminding herself that she knew better.

There was no what-if here.

"Whatever you do," Zeus told her, something darker in his gaze, "never show the sharks your heart, Nina."

She hoped she wasn't that hormonal.

Nina braced herself once they'd landed and were whisked to the royal castle, but she was surprised to find that the stuffy manners that she'd always found so tedious—mostly because it had been her job to use them in the wake of Isabeau, who did as she liked—were an excellent stand-in for the sorts of masks she used to wear. At first she wondered why it was that royal personages she'd met many times before were suddenly capable of being kind to her as they all lined up to be introduced into the ball.

"What a pleasure to meet you," said a queen here, a sheikh there, and excellencies everywhere. "Many congratulations on your most happy news."

Then she realized, it had nothing to do with her. It was all about Zeus.

Because he might be one of the biggest walking scandals in Europe, but he was still the Crown Prince of Theosia. And everybody knew that King Cronos was not doing well.

"They're already lining up to kiss your ring," Nina murmured as she and Zeus waited for their turn to be announced. Graciela's castle was, like all castles, all about its ramparts and keeps. The ball, thankfully, was being held in the new annex—which meant a grand covered gallery festooned with heat lamps and circulating attendants.

She wanted to laugh, maybe a little hysterically, at the fact that even the rulers and figureheads of Europe had to line up like so many partygoers outside a club.

"A kingdom is a kingdom, after all," Zeus told her, leaning down the way he did now. His mouth so close to her ear that goose bumps prickled down her neck. Or maybe that was because he had curled his hand over her nape. "Theosia might be small and unthreatening, and unlikely to wage war in the traditional sense, but there are always economic pressures that can be brought to bear."

"It's like you're a king already," Nina said with a sigh. She lifted a hand to rub at her neck, as if that could make the shivery sensation dissipate. It didn't. "Already plotting out your wars."

"You have not been paying attention." Zeus gazed down at her, unusually grave. "I've been at war my whole life."

She caught her breath, and her heart pounded—

But then they were being announced.

And she understood why he'd waited for this moment as they stood there at the top of a long stair. Because he had to do nothing but stand there, looking resplendent as ever in his formal attire. He looked even more impossibly beautiful than usual. And he had Nina on his arm, dressed in a gown so outrageous it had taken staff to help her into it.

This was the point all along, she understood as their names were called out and they started down toward the waiting crowd.

This was Zeus's engagement announcement. He'd planned it this way.

But when they reached the floor of the ballroom, he looked down at her and smiled as he took her by the hand.

And Nina…forgot. That all of this was planned. Plotted out ruthlessly by Zeus and his public relations people to create a story. This story. Just as he'd said.

She knew better than to believe any of it.

She knew better, but he tugged her straight out onto the dance floor, then pulled her into his arms. She knew better, but he gazed down at her…and suddenly it didn't matter what kingdom they were in, what ballroom. Who might be watching, or what the papers might say tomorrow.

There was only the way he held her, smiling down at her as he made the belly between them part of the dance instead of an impediment to it.

And Nina wanted fairy tales, the kind she'd dreamed of when she was a little girl.

She wanted all of them, she realized then, as she danced with her very own prince. She *wanted*, when she thought she'd gotten rid of that sort of thing long ago.

Because a girl who wanted in an orphanage was only destined for despair. And a girl who wanted anything at all in service to Isabeau would find nothing but pettiness and backstabbing.

Just like the girl who was foolish enough to have feelings for Prince Zeus was proving herself no kind of shark at all, but a minnow, through and through.

Nina knew all of that, and oh, did she know better. And still, as the music swelled and they danced around and around, she let herself pretend that this was real. That none of this was for show. That the way he looked at her meant what it should.

Tomorrow could do its worst. She had no doubt it would.

What if? she asked herself.

And tonight, she let herself believe.

CHAPTER EIGHT

Nina was sitting at one of the tables set up in semiprivate alcoves dotted around the main ballroom. This part of Graciela Castle was clearly a more recent addition—meaning the last century or two—because each alcove was carefully situated with views out over the tiny kingdom's sweeping valley, covered in snow and dotted with light.

And to make the fairy-tale evening even better, she was waiting for Zeus to return with food. Because, apparently, in the role of Prince Charming that he was playing tonight, he not only danced with her... he fetched things for her.

It was all part of the fantasy she was letting herself believe tonight.

Nina took a deep, steadying breath and wondered if this was what it felt like to truly be happy. No expectations, no regrets. Just that look on Zeus's face and the fire that seemed to burn brighter between them by the hour.

She had no experience with happiness. The closest she'd come was out there on her brief travels—

though even then, she'd still been so aware of what she'd run from.

Tonight she was only aware of Zeus.

And the way she felt when she was with him, the focus of all that bright green intensity.

Nina shivered a little, then laughed at herself. She patted her belly. *I think your father might be a good man*, she confided silently to her child. *When pressed. You'll see.*

The music was glorious, a full orchestra playing music to beat back the winter dark. And Nina almost felt as if she was a queen already, sitting here in sweet solitude as she waited for Zeus's return.

When she looked up and saw Isabeau descending upon her, her usual entourage fanned out behind her, her first thought was that she'd fallen asleep at her table and this was a dream. A dream she'd had more times than she could count. All of those haughty and imperious faces, some already alight with malice. If Nina had been with them, she would have been shuffling along at the rear of the pack, far enough back that she could avoid the poisonous looks they liked to throw her way.

Because they had gained their position with Isabeau through the usual channels—that being by the lucky accident of having noble blood that stretched back through the ages in Haught Montagne, as was proper. Nina had wondered many times if her presence was an insult to these other ladies-in-waiting even more than to the Princess.

The way they were all glaring daggers at her now, she had to assume the insult was universal.

Princess Isabeau came to a stop before Nina in a dramatic manner that she knew very well made her skirt swirl about her while showing her legs to best advantage. She practiced it. And it occurred to Nina that it felt a lot like power to know the things she knew about this woman and no longer have to hold her tongue.

Not that she had to descend to Isabeau's level. But she *could*.

"I can't believe you dare to show your face," the Princess said in her usual cutting tone. "Especially in your revolting state."

Nina understood that she was to take from that the clear message that her face was unpleasant, shown or unshown. Because Isabeau was a classically beautiful, tiny little brunette with a heart-shaped face and perfect bone structure, and she loved to make sure others knew how ugly they were in comparison. She particularly liked to let Nina know this.

It only occurred to her now that Isabeau would not have spent so much effort slapping Nina down about her looks—or her offensive lack thereof—if she hadn't felt threatened in some way. And why would she feel threatened? Only if Nina actually looked the way Zeus made her feel.

The revelation made her smile, far too brightly.

But "Pregnancy is quite natural" was all she said in return. "Some find it very beautiful."

And what a joy it was to say whatever she liked without having to second-guess her words or her tone or the expression on her face. She was no longer Isabeau's little pet. Her pocket orphan that she could pull out whenever someone accused her of being exactly who she was as evidence that once upon a time, she'd had a benevolent impulse.

Nina couldn't seem to tamp down her smile, and Isabeau...actually looked uncertain for once. She brushed back a tendril of her lovely hair, her blue eyes narrowing.

Always a warning sign.

"Who do you think is buying this act? If Prince Zeus was capable of impregnating anyone, he would have had a parade of bastards by now." Isabeau sniffed, then looked crafty. Another red flag. But tonight Nina couldn't seem to work up the necessary concern. "The people of Theosia will rise up in revolt against a grubby commoner trying to pass off her baby as heir to their kingdom."

Nina had not seen that one coming. Maybe she should have. She laughed and took her time standing up from the table, propping one hand on the belly before her, big enough that Isabeau looked askance at it. "I assure you, Isabeau. There is absolutely no doubt about the paternity of this child."

And she wasn't sure she meant to, but she said that in such a steady, distinct way that there could be no doubt that she was announcing—in no uncertain terms—not only her relationship with Zeus but exactly how their baby had been made.

All right. Maybe she did mean to.

It felt...liberating.

Isabeau looked as shocked as if Nina had hauled off and slapped her. "You're nothing," she hissed. "You'll never be anything but a charity case. Don't you know that by now, Dumpy?"

Nina sighed. Not because the nickname hurt. It didn't. It never had. But it was only now that she'd stopped hiding herself that she realized how silly it was that she ever had. And how pathetic Isabeau was to issue taunts like they were on a playground.

That wasn't entirely true. She'd known it all along.

"We could have been friends," she said quietly. "Companionable, at the very least. Instead, you took every opportunity to prove how petty you are. I feel sorry for you."

Isabeau reared back. "*You* feel sorry for *me*? I am a *princess*. My father is a *king*."

"And so will my husband be," Nina replied coolly. "Making me a queen, yes? You will have to forgive me. I don't eat and sleep your hierarchies, but I believe I'll shortly outrank you."

Amazingly, the little coterie behind Isabeau actually...tittered.

Nina could feel everything change in that moment. Not because the courtiers had turned, the way courtiers always did. But because, at last, she truly felt free.

All this time, all the effort she'd spent, whether hiding from Isabeau or, periodically, attempting to placate her—all that was over now. And whatever happened next, she finally understood something she should have realized all along.

Her child would never find itself the plaything of a creature like this. Her child would never be lost. Her child would always know who and what it was.

A prince or princess of Theosia. One day its King or Queen.

Nina had gotten lost after her parents died. But that would never happen again. Not to her and certainly not to her baby.

And once she understood that, how could anything else matter?

"I'm done with you," she said to Isabeau, then swept past her, thinking that she would head across the ballroom to search for food herself.

But she was brought up short to find Zeus standing there just outside the alcove with an expression she couldn't read on his face. Clearly having witnessed the entire interaction.

"Look at you," he said admiringly. He didn't say *little hen*, but it felt as if he had. "It appears you've found your claws."

Then he was looking past her and shifting where he stood, obliquely blocking her from Isabeau. Making his sentiments known.

Again.

"You're supposed to be with me!" Isabeau hissed at him. She stamped her foot. "Our fathers decided it. You can't possibly think you belong with that— that—"

"Princess," Zeus said, in the kind of quiet voice that made a wise person's hair stand on end, "I would advise you not to finish that sentence." He drew Nina closer, and if possible, looked even more like a bronze statue than ever before. When he spoke, his voice carried. "Nina is to be my wife. And, in due course, the Queen of Theosia. She belongs with me. Always."

And as declarations went, it was something. It was even more than *something* coming from him. Nina knew full well that some part of that statement would be on every tabloid around come morning. Maybe that was part of his plan. But she didn't care.

She belongs with me. Always.

Her whole life, Nina had wanted to *belong*. Of all the precious gifts this man had given her, this was the one that made her heart ache.

She didn't care if it was true. She cared that he'd said it.

Nina forgot all about Isabeau. She had the vague impression that her entourage herded her away, but she didn't bother to confirm it. She looked up at Zeus, and suddenly it was as if her belief in fairy tales had spilled over into…everything.

As if maybe it was all real. Complete with a vanquished villainess.

Because she felt powerful and beautiful. Their baby was safe and protected and always would be. And she had Zeus, looking at her as if she was magic.

She belongs with me.

"Remember when I told you not to kiss me?" she asked.

He looked devilish and amused at once. "I remember you spouting such nonsense, yes. I did us both a favor and ignored it."

"You haven't kissed me since."

"But if I'd wanted to, I would have," he said, all lazy drawl and a simmering heat in his beautiful eyes. "That's the key point."

"Zeus," she said. He looked down at her, lifting one marvelous brow. "Stop talking."

And then Cinderella lifted herself up on her tiptoes, leaned forward, and kissed Prince Charming herself.

Because it was *her* fairy tale.

He kissed her back with all the same heat. And then he pulled her with him, laughing, back to the dance floor.

"We cannot leave yet, my wild little hen," he told her. Sternly. "So we must dance."

But the moment they could leave without offending their hosts, he hurried her out of the ballroom and followed his waiting aide to the rooms set aside for them in Graciela's ancient castle.

"What is it?" he asked as they walked in, when Nina laughed. He shut the heavy door behind them and leaned against it.

Nina looked around. Stone walls, tapestries, and an old standing suit of armor in one corner. A fire crackling in an old fireplace. A weathered yet polished wardrobe. And thick, soft carpets thrown all over to mask the chill of all the stone.

"It's just…castles," she said, because it was somehow perfect that they were here, tonight. Making fairy tales real. "They are always the same."

She walked farther into the room, making her way over to the canopied bed that stood against one stout stone wall and running her fingers over the embroidered coverlet.

"Second thoughts?" Zeus asked, his voice a dark temptation, and she remembered that. He had asked that same question on their first night together, but then he had been poised above her.

The hardest part of him notched between her legs, the pleasure already unbearable—she remembered every moment.

She looked over her shoulder at him and smiled. "Not a one," she whispered.

And then she watched him come toward her, dark blond like one of the gods his people sometimes claimed his family had descended from. Green eyes that were darkly intent now and laced with that fire that was only and ever theirs.

He came toward her, then turned her in his arms, and Nina thought that surely now she would feel unwieldy again. Swollen and awkward.

But Zeus held her in his arms, he bent her back, and he kissed her.

Ravenously.

And Nina felt as light as air, as graceful as a dancer.

She met his kiss, all the fire within her bursting into spirals of flame that licked through her body, making her fight to get closer. To feel *more*. To glut herself on this man all over again.

He kissed her, and she kissed him, and it was different now. Better.

Laced through with a kind of reverence, as if neither one of them could believe that they were here again. In a castle, near a bed, just like last time. Nearly seven months gone by now, and it felt like yesterday.

"I looked for you," Zeus said against her lips. "You hid well, little hen."

"I wasn't hiding."

But then she was laughing as he lifted her up as if she weighed no more than a feather and sat her down on the edge of the high bed. His hands were busy beneath her long skirts, and she sighed as he ran his palms up her legs, over her thighs. And sighed again when he only brushed, gently, the place where she needed him most. Then moved on.

She remembered this, too. That Zeus liked to tease.

"Were you not?" he murmured, trailing his fingers up the sides of her dress. "You were hard to find, then, for a person who was not hiding."

But he seemed distracted. He spent extra time on her belly, then found her breasts. Once again, only a glancing caress before he eased her back so he could attend to the complicated fastening of her gown down one side.

"I suppose I was running," she said, because this room felt like a confessional. This night felt like a brand-new start. "But I didn't know where I was going."

His hands stilled. "You only knew you wished to get away."

Nina smiled again. She couldn't stop smiling, really. She lifted a hand and slid it over his hard jaw, strong and solid. And, tonight, with that faint rasp against her palm that made all the fires he set within her kick a little higher. Burn a little hotter.

"Not from you," she said softly. "It never occurred to me that you would come looking. It was my one night with the wickedest, most notorious prince alive." She felt his lips curve as he turned his head so his mouth was against her palm. "That is the Prince Zeus promise, as far as I'm aware. One night. Never more."

"That is a very strict rule indeed." He pulled her dress away from her body and then left it open on either side of her, so she felt as if she was being presented to him on a platter of fine Parisian fabric. He moved so he was standing, positioned between her outspread legs. His gaze was a dark blaze as he looked at her, lying before him so wantonly with little more than a scrap of silk between her legs. "But it is for dastardly courtiers. Horrid princesses. Vapid celebrities of all stripes. Little hens are exempt."

Nina didn't feel like a hen, she felt like his, and perhaps that was the same thing.

She pushed herself up on her elbows, watching him greedily as he slowly, deliberately, set about ridding himself of his own clothes. Slowly, with that half smile on his face, he stripped himself down and tossed his discarded garments toward the cases his servants had set up. Then he was standing before her, naked.

Far more beautiful out of his clothes than in them.

Zeus came down beside her on the bed. She could feel his sculpted chest against her as she turned toward him, and once again, his mouth found hers.

And for a while there was only that slick heat, that mad spin. As potent as the first kiss. As irresistible as the last.

But he pulled away and directed his attention lower. He concentrated on her breasts first, gazing at them in wonder.

"You astound me," he whispered in a rough voice, his green eyes nearly black with desire.

Then he used his mouth and his tongue, even the scrape of his teeth. His big, hard hands. Every trick at his disposal to coax her into wave after wave of impossible sensation. It raced from his mouth straight down between her legs and had her moaning.

Nina hadn't known how much more sensitive she was now.

But Zeus did.

And he took his time, showing her all the ways her body had changed.

She began to move her hips, pressing herself against his hard thigh, there between her legs.

And he laughed, the way she remembered him laughing before. That sound of dark, endless delight.

It made her burn all the more.

Outside, the snow came down, but in this room the fire that crackled in the grate was no match for the heat between them. Nina couldn't think what could be.

Zeus worked his way down her body, so slowly she wanted to cry. Maybe she did. And finally he found her belly and laid kisses behind him, everywhere he touched.

Something in her seemed to glow almost bright enough to hurt. That there could be all this heat, all this mad, greedy desire, and yet in the middle of it, a tenderness. Affection. She was making love to a father, not just a man.

This was no fairy tale she'd ever heard of. This was hers, and it was theirs.

And it was real.

But then he wiped all those thoughts away when

he moved even lower, crawling off the side of the bed so he could pull her hips to his face.

His mouth closed over the mound of her softness, and she jolted, even though he had yet to remove her panties.

This was only a test. A temptation. And it still punched through her, a lightning bolt of pure sensation.

Nina made a sound that was neither a sob nor a scream, but somehow both. She lifted up her hips, begging him mutely.

Zeus laughed again.

Then he tugged her panties from her hips, peeling them off her with exquisite slowness. Down one leg, then the next, taking his time.

Only then did he move back into position. He gripped her hips with his strong hands, tilting her toward him. And then licked his way into the very center of her heat.

And this was not the waves of sensation from before. This was a thunderstorm. A whole hard crash.

Nina shattered at the first lick and then never quite came down again.

Zeus, naturally, settled in. He took his time.

And wanting him was nothing new, but Nina knew she had not been this sensitive before. That every time he breathed, her body reacted like this. With a greedy, encompassing joy that she couldn't have contained if she'd tried.

It felt like a gift.

She was limp and sobbing when he finally rose up. He looked down at her like that bronze mask, passion making his features almost stern. If it weren't for that glittering heat in his green eyes, she might have found him frightening.

But she could see how much he wanted her. Looking at the hard jut of his sex made her flush hot all over again.

Zeus pulled her legs around his waist, then angled himself down onto the bed. He propped himself up on one arm and gazed down at her. His chest was moving like hers, like breathing was hard. His gaze was possessive. Commanding.

And all she wanted to do was melt against him, then ask for more.

He gripped his sex with his free hand and guided himself to her entrance. Then he stroked her there, with that hardest part of him that felt to her like bronze.

For a moment their eyes met, and the blaze of intensity there almost sent her over the edge again.

Almost—but then he thrust inside, filling her completely at last.

At last.

Nina could no longer tell if she was at the edge or over it, so intense were the sensations, so wild was this fire.

She gripped his arms as he moved over her, setting a slow, deliriously intense pace.

A rhythm she could feel everywhere, inside and out.

And the dance had been a fairy tale, but this was something better. She didn't think it was hormones any longer, not when her chest ached the way it did and every stroke seemed to open her up more inside. Her heart. Her poor heart.

But it was worth breaking if she could have this.

He dropped his head to pull one nipple into his mouth, hard enough that the electric jolt of it seemed to travel straight down her body into the place where they were joined. And once again, she was sent hurtling.

Hurtling and hurtling, and she heard him shout out her name as he followed.

He flooded her, and she cried out as she shook and shook.

It wasn't until she'd recovered herself some little bit that she realized what she'd said. The secret she'd been carrying all along.

"I love you," she had told him, again and again. "I love you, Zeus."

And she was terribly afraid she'd ruined everything.

CHAPTER NINE

Her words echoed inside of him like doom.

Or grace, whispered a voice within.

Zeus had almost forgotten himself, and that never happened. But the taste of her had exploded through him. She had rocked him. He had found no defenses when usually he was the king of them.

The kiss in the ballroom had nearly undone him. He, who had spent his life chasing every sensation available, had nearly been brought to his knees by this woman. In the middle of a ballroom, with the eyes of the world upon them.

And he wasn't sure he would have cared.

Zeus had never cared about making a scene. On the contrary, he went out of his way to cause as many as possible. But he could not bear the idea of further exposing Nina to the same censure.

He'd already done that.

And he, who regretted nothing, had regretted the scene he'd set up in Haught Montagne ever since.

But he shoved those things aside. The rest of the evening had passed in a blur, of faces and names he knew he ought to know, because she'd kissed him.

Nina had dismissed the Princess who had caused her so much trouble with a wave of her hand. Then she'd looked around, every inch the perfect queen, and smiled when she'd seen him.

Then Nina had kissed him.

Entirely of her own volition.

With all that melting, glorious heat.

There could be no concerns that he had seduced her this time. There were no worries that he was exerting pressure on her in any way. Zeus would have sworn to anyone who asked that such things did not concern him—so confident was he of his appeal—but Nina was different.

She had been different that night, and he hadn't been prepared for it.

And now she was the mother of his unborn child. She wore his ring. And she had kissed him like she was the one who'd chosen him from the first.

It was as if that kiss had woken up a part of him he had come to believe no longer existed. Or had never existed. She had chosen him, and she made him believe that he might have a soul after all.

And, more unimaginable still, a heart.

He had felt it pound in him, like it was pounding out her name.

Then they had come to this room of stone and fire, high up in yet another castle filled with so many of the same people doing the same tedious things, and once again, she had humbled him.

She had done it that first night. She did it with ease. She made him new, scrubbed him raw, and he didn't like it. He told himself he *couldn't* like it.

He didn't know what to do with it.

So Zeus had done the only thing he could. He had closed the distance between them, the hunger in him a wild and uncontrollable roar, and he had taken her in his arms at last.

Here, where there were no witnesses. No paparazzi and none on call. There was no press release, no story. No narrative to tinker with.

There was just this beautiful woman who was only his, who had danced with him tonight as if he was a dream come true.

He wanted to be that for her in every possible way.

And then, finally, he'd placed her on the bed and taken her the way he'd begun to imagine he never would again.

It had felt sacred.

Like a vow.

Like a simple, honest truth, stark and irrevocable.

And when she cried out those words she should have known were forbidden, Zeus couldn't bring himself to react the way he knew he should. Instead, he moved them both up in the bed, then pulled the coverlet over them so they could lie there, together.

Because he needed to gaze at her as if he expected, at any moment, that she would be taken from him again. And that, once again, it would be his fault.

"We never talk about that night," he managed to say. His eyes were so greedy on hers, he felt so torn, that he was surprised she could stand to hold his gaze at all. But she did.

"What is there to talk about?" He thought that was a slap, a dismissal. Instead, Nina rolled closer to him and piled her hands beneath her face so she could smile at him. It felt like a miracle. *Maybe she is the miracle*, something in him whispered. "We both know what it was between us. How intense it was. What it meant. Yet it was always going to end the way it did. Because you'd already called them."

The last time she'd mentioned this, he'd deflected. *Were you truly under the impression that I was or am a good man?* And maybe he would never be a good man. Not by any reasonable measure.

But for Nina, he would try.

"I did," he said. Simply enough.

And of all the things he'd done in his life. All the sins, all the scandals. They seemed like nothing to him. It was this admission that cost him the most.

But her smile didn't waver. *I love you*, she'd said. And unlike the many who had mouthed those words before, she knew him. She'd seen him do more than flatter and cajole a night away.

She'd chosen him, not his reputation.

"Zeus," Nina said quietly, her brown eyes soft. "I understand."

Then she leaned toward him, kissing him again. And it was as if she'd flung open the windows and let the noonday sun inside. He felt that light all over him. He felt bathed in sunshine.

He knew that if he bothered to look, it would still be dark outside. A cold winter's night, with snow coming down as if it might never stop, up here in the mountains.

And Zeus had spent his entire life, it seemed, finding new ways to be worse. To be even more terrible than reported. To live down to every low expectation his father had ever set him.

He'd come to think that the reason it came so easily to him was because that was who he was. That all along, he hadn't been acting at all.

But the way Nina looked at him, as if he was the miracle here, made him feel something he had long been certain he would never feel again.

Hope.

"You shouldn't understand," he told her fiercely, his hand going to her so he could grip her, to make sure she was real. "You should hate me. Why don't you hate me?"

"I've tried," she admitted, with that smile of hers. "Believe me, I did try. But it turns out, I don't know how."

What could Zeus do but kiss her again then, with all those things he thought he'd lost. His soul. His heart. Himself.

And he knew that morning would come. As morning always did. He knew that his endgame marched closer every day, regardless of what work he put into selling the world love stories. It would all come full circle soon. He was ready.

But here, now, far away in this castle room where no one could see who they truly were with each other, he let himself be the one thing he'd never been. In all his years of pretending to be this or that. Or everything.

Here with Nina, his Nina, he let himself be nothing more or less than a man.

Not just any man, but the one she loved.

Again and again.

There was a faint hint of light in the sky outside when Zeus woke again to find Nina curled up next to him. The sight caught at him, hard enough to leave marks. This woman who gave all of herself to him, when she, more than any other, should never have let him near her again. That big, round belly where his child grew, safe and warm. He kissed them both. Nina on her cheek, so she smiled a little while she slept. And his baby, too.

His baby. Zeus hadn't let himself truly take in what that meant. That in only a couple of months, he would be able to hold a child of his own in his arms.

He would be able to do it differently. To do it better.

Take what had been done to him, but turn it inside out.

The heart he'd just rediscovered seemed to crack open inside of his chest. He tried to imagine Nina in the role of his mother. Or himself a king like Cronos. He tried to imagine letting all of that weight land on the tiny life inside Nina's belly, and he couldn't. It was too much. He wanted to rage. He wanted to punch the stone walls surrounding him.

He wanted to go back and change everything. Save his mother. Save himself.

And somehow find a way to keep his father from walking the path that had led them here.

Maybe what he couldn't accept—what he'd never been able to accept—was that, given the chance, he'd save his father, too.

He didn't want to feel these things. He didn't want to *feel*. He had always chosen to see himself as a finely honed weapon of a particular vengeance. Nothing less, nothing more. As he had vowed over his mother's grave he would become, so he had done.

Yes, yes, such a weapon, his friend Vin, more commonly known these days as His Royal Majesty, the King of Arista, had said with an eye roll when they'd all gotten together for a drink in Paris.

Perhaps the weapon has grown a bit blunt now that you're impregnating women and parading them about Paris with statement jewelry, Prince Jahangir Hassan Umar Al Hayat had murmured, lounging in the chair opposite in the private club. Jag had grinned. *I recall a time when all you could do was extol the virtues of prophylactics.*

Rafael Navarro, bastard child of the former King of Santa Castelia and long its regent, had laughed. Vin had joined him. Zeus, who knew exactly why they were laughing, forced himself to smile when he would really rather…not.

There are a great many virtues in impregnating the wrong woman and making her a wife, Rafael had said. As he would, having recently scandalized the whole world by kidnapping his own woman from her wedding to another man. Another man who had happened to be Rafael's half brother. *I recommend it.*

I second this recommendation, Vin had said, sounding revoltingly happy.

I have no intention of settling like the two of you, Jag had said, shaking his head at them. *I prefer the time-honored practice of not making my lovers accidentally pregnant.*

His friends and he often cleared their schedules and

made drinks happen in various cities, all these years after Oxford. Zeus had been surprised at how little he had wished to leave Nina in their hotel for even so short a time. He, who had never turned down the opportunity for a social event in all his days. Particularly not when it was with these men. His closest friends.

His only friends.

But he had only shrugged languidly, as if he was still the same *him* he had ever been. *I believe you are all mistaking the matter. I salute your fecundity, truly. Yet I assure you—my situation is not emotional, however accidental. It fits in nicely with my plan or I would not have moved forward with a wedding. Have you met me? Do I seem the marrying kind?*

And he had pretended not to notice how Vin and Rafael had looked at each other then.

He couldn't seem to get that look out of his head now.

Because the way his friends had gazed at each other had seemed ripe with a kind of emotion Zeus would have sworn neither of them could feel.

Yet maybe what he'd been worried about after all was what *he* felt.

What he had always felt.

Zeus kept circling back to the fact that whatever the shape of the weapon he'd made himself into, that hadn't been what he'd wanted. It had never been what he'd wanted.

He'd gone to great lengths to deny it, but at heart, he'd wanted what any child did. His mother. His father. His family.

And it only occurred to him now—here in this

room with a woman who had knocked him off balance from the start—that maybe it wasn't the vow that he'd made at his mother's grave that had motivated him all this time. Not entirely.

Maybe it was the longing of a child, after all.

Zeus told himself he was horrified at his own mawkish sentimentality.

He made sure Nina was covered as he left the bed. He moved over to the fire, pulling the quilt that they'd long since kicked off around his waist. And then he sat, stared into the flames as they danced before him, and, for the life of him, could not understand how things had come to this point without him realizing what he was doing.

Not his own feelings, which he assured himself he could dismiss as he should have long ago. But to *her*. To his Nina. For a man was no man at all who hurt the woman he should protect. Hadn't he learned that when he was young? In the worst possible way? He knew he had. It had changed the course of his life. It had made him who he was.

How could he possibly justify using the woman who loved him, despite what he'd done to her, as a pawn in this bitter game?

The fire gave no answers.

Zeus kept imagining holding his baby for the first time. Staring down into the eyes of his own child. And it was so powerful that it threatened the favorite image he'd been carrying around for more than half his life now. Of staring down at his father on his deathbed, diminished and humbled, and making sure the old man knew that despite everything, Zeus had won.

It was like the two things were at war, ceding no territory.

Tearing him apart.

"You look cold," came her voice, so soft it cut right through him. "Are you all right?"

And Zeus had no idea how to answer that.

Nina was beside him in the next moment, kneeling down with him on the thick, priceless rug before the fire. She drew the coverlet with her, wrapping it around the both of them while she slid her legs beneath the quilt.

He thought she would ask questions, but she didn't. She only sat with him, her thigh against his, until he shifted her so he could hold her before him. She sat between his legs and leaned back, resting her head against his shoulder.

Even then, she only gazed into the fire. As if she knew that simply sitting with him soothed him, somehow. It was as if the heat of her body was hope itself, curling its way into him whether he wanted it there or not.

Whether he wanted to believe in it or not.

He rested his chin on the top of her head. He wrapped his arms around her.

It was only then, in a room dark save for the fire, that he found himself able to talk.

"They say my mother died of heart failure," he told her, amazed at how easily the words came after so long spent holding them in. And letting them poison him. "And in the end, she did. But it was more complicated than that."

"I'm so sorry," Nina murmured.

Somehow that made him want to go on rather than stop, when he would have said he was allergic to pity.

"I told you what a joy she was, but there were many others who did not think so. My father chief among them." He heard Nina murmur something and held her tighter. "I cannot say when I began to understand that the way my father spoke to her made something in her die a little. He was so much older, you see. She had been given to him after his first Queen died, taking his hopes of extending his bloodline with her. That was what he cared about. Bloodlines. The throne. The kingdom. What he did not care about was his young, silly second wife, who he took on purely to breed an heir."

"Maybe he didn't know how to care about anything but those things," Nina said softly. "Do you know what his relationship was like with his first wife?"

That walloped Zeus. Hard. Because in all this time, across all these years and all the bitter hours he had spent cataloging his father's many sins, it had never occurred to him to think of such a thing. He knew about the Queen who had come before his mother. He knew her name and some part of her story. But he'd been so focused on the wrong that had been done to his mother that he had never asked too many questions about the woman who had preceded her.

"I always assumed she suffered the same fate," he said.

"But you don't know?" Nina sighed a little. "Maybe he loved her. And hated that he couldn't have her but felt he needed to have a child."

"Nina." Oddly enough, he wanted to laugh. "Do not defend him."

"I'm not defending him," she replied. "It's not his heart I'm worried about."

His own heart kicked at him unpleasantly. But he kept going. "My mother was soft. It was part of what made her sweet, but she was no match for life at court. The courtiers and sycophants took their cues from my father, and she wasn't like you. She didn't know how to hide herself away. She didn't know how to protect who she was inside. And each harsh word, each bit of malice, each laugh at her expense took more and more from her."

Zeus couldn't remember now why he'd started to tell her this story. But as she nestled in closer against him, something in him eased. Or made room, maybe, so that he could keep going.

"First she would harm herself," he said. "Bruises. Cuts. Not where anyone could see when she was in public. But I saw." He shook his head. "Over time, it became clear that she wasn't eating. That every time someone criticized her, she punished herself for her flaws by taking away food. And then, I suppose, it was not so much a punishment any longer, but how she made her point. How she got the last word."

"Zeus…" Nina whispered.

"They tried to intervene. But in the end, I suppose it was the one place she could assert her will, so she did. And eventually, her heart gave out."

He heard her whisper his name again. He felt the touch of her lips at the side of his neck.

And he had never told anyone this story before.

It was the only story that mattered, and he peddled his stories to anyone who would run with them, but he never gave them this one. Maybe it was that Nina knew tragedy, too. Or maybe it was that she was Nina. And the simple fact of her, sitting here and bearing witness to this tale, made it better.

Not what had happened. But how it sat in him, even now.

"I was eleven years old." Zeus pulled in a breath. "And I was the one who sat with her at the last. And in my rage and grief, that day and into her funeral, I made a vow. I promised her as she was laid to rest that I would keep it."

Nina slid her hand over his chest. It took him a moment to realize she'd put her hand over his heart. He covered it with his.

"It was my father who could have helped her. Who, if not the King? Her husband? He could have stopped what was happening. He could have thrown out anyone who dared speak ill of her. He could have stopped criticizing her himself. There were any number of things he could have done, but he didn't." Zeus heard that roughness in his voice. He knew it told too many truths about him—more than he liked to share. Perhaps even with himself. "I vowed that I would ruin the one thing that mattered to him."

He heard her quick, indrawn breath, though Nina said nothing. But she didn't have to.

"Yes," he said. "I made it my mission in life to tarnish the throne. So that the Throne of Ages would find itself polluted by the most disreputable, irresponsible, unworthy occupant of all time."

That wasn't all of it. But it was enough. Zeus's heart was still jarring against his ribs. He felt outside himself, and that was before Nina turned to kneel before him so she could meet his gaze.

"I know that's the role you play," she said quietly. "But is that really you?"

Something swelled at him, so sharp he assumed it must have been bitterness—though he worried it was something much worse. *Hope*, something whispered in him. "Do you not know? And this the man you claim to love?"

But if he imagined she might look away, or be shamed in some fashion, he was disappointed. She only gazed at him as steadily as before.

"I know what I believe," Nina said with that quiet conviction that made him ache. "The question is, what do you believe?"

There was a roaring in him then. On and on it went. And her gaze was on him, in him.

And he *felt*. He felt...everything.

This woman had haunted him for seven months now, and she haunted him still. And Zeus understood then that it was entirely likely she always would.

Still, that storm raged on inside him. Still, the roar of it was loud enough to blow this stone castle to ash.

Zeus did the only thing he could think of to do.

He bent his head to hers, taking her mouth in a kiss that said all the things he could not. All the things he would not.

Everything he wished he could say to her. Only and ever to her.

Over and over again, he kissed her.

And he moved within her there, before the fire, until the shuddering took them both. Sweet this time, and more dangerous for it. Then he lifted her up, carried her to the bed, and took her once again.

Hot and hard.

As if in the taking, the sweet glory of this maddening fire, he would find the answer. What he believed. What he wanted. Who he was.

And in the meantime, he would hold her like sunshine between his hands and warm himself until hope felt as real as she did.

They had fallen asleep again when a great pounding came at the door.

Zeus rose, pulling on his discarded trousers as he stalked to the door. He flung it open to find the better part of his guard standing outside.

"Your Royal Highness," said the head of his security detail, bowing his head. "I'm afraid there is news of the King. His condition is grave."

For a split second, Zeus thought he had missed it— but no. There were rituals for that. His guard would have knelt. They would have called him *sire*.

He could see from their expressions that they would do these things. Soon.

"How long?" he asked curtly.

"A matter of hours," the man replied.

Zeus nodded, then closed the door. He turned to find Nina watching him, and he braced himself for her reaction. She would fly to him. Offer condolences that he would reject. Try to comfort him, and it might send him into a rage.

But she only gazed at him with what he was terribly afraid was compassion.

"I will find my things and dress," she said.

All Zeus could do was nod. All he wanted to do was reach for her. Turn back time, live in this night forever.

But his father was dying. It was time to go home.

And, whether he liked it or not, honor the vow he'd made so long ago.

CHAPTER TEN

THE FLIGHT BACK to the island was terrifying at first, as the pilot fought the winter weather to get them aloft. But once out of the mountains, everything was smooth. And, to Nina's mind, almost frighteningly quiet the rest of the way until they landed in the bright sun and soft breezes of Theosia.

The moment they returned to the palace, Zeus stalked away, surrounded by his aides. And looking more alone than she had ever seen him.

Nina found herself left to her own devices. Standing in the middle of a palace that was now hushed in dreadful anticipation.

And she'd spent her life mourning her parents' deaths. She had no idea how a person *prepared* for such a thing.

She walked, not sure where she was headed, in and out of the glossy, exquisite rooms that seemed to glisten with their own history. And it was perhaps unsurprising that she eventually found her way into the gallery of family portraits. The Kings and Queens of Theosia, stretching back into antiquity.

Nina looked at all of them, starting as far back in

time as the pictures reached. Slowly, slowly she advanced through the ages until she found her way to the small collection of portraits on the farthest, emptiest wall.

She recognized Zeus immediately. Only a small child in the painting, but undeniably him. The same green eyes. A smile made more of mischief than of studied wickedness, but his all the same. His hair more blond than dark, and the hint of all that austere bronze yet to come.

Then she studied the painting of King Cronos, who she had never met. He had been too ill the whole time she was here. Yet she could see Zeus in the face of the proud man she gazed at now, dressed in all his finery. The same forbidding features. The same hard, sensual mouth.

Beside them hung two very different portraits. One was of a dark-haired woman with eyes of violet and a reserved curve to her lips. Next to her hung a young blonde with emerald eyes and the biggest smile yet in this room full of portraits.

And Nina's heart hurt.

For all of them. But mostly for Zeus. For the little boy with such a big name in the portrait in front of her and the man she'd sat with so early this morning, feeling the clatter of his heart against her back. Hearing each and every betraying scratch in his voice.

She didn't know how long she stood there before she gradually became aware that she wasn't alone. When she turned to look, she saw Thaddeus, Zeus's sniffy butler who had so disdained her on sight.

"Madam," he intoned by way of greeting.

Nina sighed. Maybe it was time for more sad antechambers. "Have you come to encourage me to leave the portrait gallery to my betters?"

But even as she asked the question, she saw that his gaze was on the portrait of Cronos's first Queen, not on her.

"Did you know her?" she asked.

Thaddeus looked surprised for a moment, then something like resigned. He put his hands behind his back and stood taller. "Which 'her' do you mean?"

Nina looked back at the portraits. The reserve in one, the irrepressible life in the other. And the portrait of the King, looking young and mighty. "Either one of them."

"It was my very great honor to have served them both in some small capacity," Thaddeus replied in reliably frosty tones.

Nina smiled at him. Winningly, she hoped. "What were they like?"

"Madam. Of all days, this day cannot be the appropriate—" He stopped himself, but not until Nina had seen what looked like genuine emotion in his gaze. He looked down at once. "I beg your pardon."

"One day my portrait will hang on this wall," Nina said quietly, looking at all the space on this white wall. And trying to imagine her contribution to this long line of people who didn't seem like people any longer, not once they were captured in oil and framed. "And I would hope that if anyone asked, you or someone like you would tell them who I was."

Thaddeus drew himself up. "I would never dream of attempting such an impertinence."

"I'm sure I'll look suitably grand, like everyone else," Nina said, looking over at the rest of the gallery. "But a portrait can't show the truth of things. That I showed up at the palace gates six months pregnant with snacks in my purse. My hair in a mess, and no apparent decency at all. Wouldn't it be a shame if there was no one here to tell *that* story, Thaddeus?"

If she wasn't mistaken, she saw the faintest hint of a thaw in the old man's bearing. Only a hint.

But eventually, the butler cleared his throat and indicated the first Queen.

"Queen Zaria was a childhood friend of His Royal Majesty," Thaddeus said. "They grew up together here on the island and were promised to each other when they were very young. No more than five, as I understand it, and from that time they were always together. By the time they married, it was very clear that they were not only great friends, but very much in love."

Love stories, Nina thought, her heart clutching in her chest. They always ended badly. It was only fairy tales that ended well. *How do people survive these love stories?*

How was she planning to survive the one she was currently living, for that matter? She looked down at her ring, adjusting the way it sat on her finger, and admitted to herself that she just didn't know. Maybe she wouldn't. Not in one piece.

Last night had made it clear that she was all in here, in the very last place she should ever have risked herself. But there was no taking it back.

Nina acknowledged that she wouldn't take it back if she could.

Thaddeus was still speaking, his gaze on Queen Zaria. "They tried for many years to have an heir, with no success. It is my understanding that they were finally successful, but something went wrong. Both the Queen and the unborn heir were lost."

Nina found she had her hands on her own unborn child. "That's a terrible story."

"Look around," Thaddeus invited her. "Look at all the people who hang here. More often than not, they are all terrible stories. Crowns and palaces do not protect anyone. Not from life."

And she couldn't tell if that was pointed or simply true.

"What of the second Queen?" Nina asked.

Beside her, Thaddeus seemed to grow more grave. "The King mourned for some time. Years passed, but he felt he had a duty to his people. Queen Stevi was from a noble, aristocratic family. She had been raised to marry a man of stature. She was innocent but not unprepared." He blew out a breath. "The papers love to pretend otherwise."

"The papers love to pretend," Nina agreed.

The butler bowed his head slightly. Then continued. "The palace had become…dark. It was a place of grieving, with no place for the brightness of youth. The Queen produced an heir quickly and was soundly praised. But it is my understanding that once the task was accomplished, it was felt that she had very little to offer."

And Nina could hear all the court gossip behind those words. All the pain and misery. It was not hard to imagine a bright, happy girl gradually reduced to one more tragedy in a place like this. All the white walls and sunlight in the world couldn't make a toxic environment better. It only made it shine.

Is this really what you want? she asked herself. *For you or your baby?*

But there was a different king then, she reminded herself. A different king than the one who would ascend soon. A different king. Not hers.

"And the King?" she said now, her voice small. She almost didn't dare ask. "Does he yet live?"

"His Royal Majesty clings to life, madam," Thaddeus said. "But barely."

"And Prince Zeus?"

"Has only now left his side."

They both stood there a while longer, staring at the same four portraits, until something dawned on Nina. She turned to look at the crusty old man, standing beside her looking deeply aggrieved he was here.

"Did you come to find me?" she asked. "On the Prince's behalf?"

"Not on his behalf, madam. No."

But Nina understood. She smiled, so wide she made herself laugh. "That does make a change, doesn't it? You tracking me down and then wanting to take me to the Prince. Who could have guessed, all those weeks ago in that musty little antechamber?"

Thaddeus only inclined his head. He looked as if he smelled something rotten.

But Nina felt warm inside. Because she knew, somehow, that this was the beginning of a beautiful friendship. She almost said so, just to see him sneer again without actually sneering.

He didn't lead her to Zeus so much as he walked out of the palace, headed into the extensive grounds, and wound his way down to a secluded cove. Where he left her at the top of a set of stairs with a significant look.

Nina padded down the stone steps cut into the hillside and found Zeus at the bottom.

He was still dressed in the clothes he'd thrown on back in Graciela. He stood and stared out at the sea. Perhaps wishing it would turn stormy and turbulent instead of its offensive deep blue and calm turquoise.

She walked across the sand, then stood by his side, and waited.

"He sleeps," Zeus gritted out.

"Did you speak to him at all?"

Zeus did not move, and yet Nina felt as if he was turning deeper into stone as he stood there. "It is not certain he will wake again."

She remembered asking him about loneliness that night so many months ago. Because she knew her way around it, having had little company but her own her whole life, no matter how many people were around. Much like him, she supposed, if for very different reasons.

But she had never seen anyone more lonely than Prince Zeus now.

It was not lost on her that her declaration of love had not exactly gone down well. Nina had been surprised by it herself. She'd never said those words to another person, not as long as she could remember. She already whispered them to her baby. But they had simply poured out of her mouth last night.

Because somewhere between the ballroom and the bedroom, she had come to understand that it wasn't make-believe with Zeus. It wasn't stories told, or publicity stunts. Not for her. Once they looked at each other, really looked at each other, in Haught Montagne that night, everything that came after had been inevitable.

It felt good to finally admit it.

She had loved him then. She loved him still. And the baby growing ever larger within her was simply one more manifestation of that love. Nina couldn't wait to see who their child would become.

And these seven months of pregnancy had taught her something else, too. It wasn't necessary to know every last detail about a person to love them. It was not even required that love make rational sense. Sometimes it was a look. A quickening. An instant understanding of life forever altered.

Her life was altered. There was no denying it.

She wouldn't take that back, either.

Nina moved closer and took his hand, there before the water that the Theosians beckoned daily, even in these less godlike times. And when he looked down at her, somewhere between shock and astonishment, she squeezed his fingers harder in hers.

"I love you," she said.

And Zeus seemed to shatter, even as she watched. He gritted his teeth so hard she saw the hard cords of his neck stand out. She felt his hands clench, though he did not grip her hard enough to hurt.

"Do you know what I plan to say to my father

should he regain consciousness again?" he growled, his voice gone raw.

But Nina did not let go of his hand.

"I've been planning it since you came here. It is the crowning achievement of my lifetime of disappointing the man." His hand flexed in hers. "And it is all because of you."

He turned to face her, so Nina took his other hand. He stared down at where they were linked and made a low noise, like an animal in a trap.

But he didn't pull away.

"I have all the pictures to show him," Zeus gritted out. "Every scandalous paparazzi shot from the summer, to refresh his recollection. He was apoplectic when it happened. And I've been biding my time, waiting for his final moments to tell him that it is all much worse than he could imagine. Much worse than some pictures in the papers."

She could see that he wanted her to say something, but she couldn't find the words.

"I have been looking forward to this," Zeus continued. "To telling him I'm marrying a commoner, a nobody. An orphan girl who was cast aside by her own country but bears the heir to the throne he loves so much. It will be a masterstroke."

Nina wasn't sure, then, if she felt relief or a hollow sort of despair. Relief, because she'd known that all of this had to be a game. She'd known all along. And little as she minded Isabeau's taunts and gibes, name-calling and spitefulness, she found she minded much more that this was how Zeus truly saw her.

Even if he looked like it tormented him.

But beneath that, that sense of despair. Because she believed he was a better man. The man she'd seen in snippets, here and there. The glimpses she'd seen of him in what looked like the sort of meetings no one would believe the notorious Prince Zeus could sit through, much less command. The man who had slid shoes on her feet so gently and had stood just outside that alcove so that she might handle her former life on her own. The man who could have found her a few gowns for his pictures but had ordered her a queen's wardrobe instead, and who took an obvious delight in dressing her. The man who not only told her she was beautiful but made her feel it.

The man who made love to her like it was a sacred ritual, burning them both clean and new.

She believed all of these things fully. And it felt like a kind of agony that he did not.

"If you wish to say all these things to your father, why are you here?" she asked quietly. "Down on the beach, where if he stirs, it might very well take you too long to race to his side so you can hurt him one more time."

Nina could see the storms in his eyes. The glaze of grief. "You don't understand."

"I do," she replied calmly, though she felt anything but inside. "You saw me choose not to take my revenge on Isabeau. It would have been easy enough to do. It doesn't occur to her yet that I know all her secrets, but it will. I get to take pleasure in not sinking to her level."

He pulled his hands from hers, but he didn't stalk away as she half thought he might. He only stood there, letting the wind move over him while his green eyes were like thunder.

"It is hardly the same thing."

"It doesn't have to be the same thing. I still understand. That's called empathy—but I know they don't teach much of it in prince school."

"Nina."

The broken way he said her name pulled at her, but she pushed on anyway. "I learned some things about your father today. That he loved his first wife. Probably all of his life. And that she died, taking his unborn heir with him."

"Everybody knows this story," Zeus gritted out. "I learned it as a child."

"But you are only paying attention to the *story*, Zeus. I want to talk to you about a man." Nina shook her head when he began to speak again. "To you, he's larger than life. Your father. Your King. The man you blame—and possibly rightly—for making your mother's life so very difficult. All I am asking you to remember is that at the end of the day, he's just a person. And people are complicated. Good and bad. Kind and vicious. They can be all things. And your mother died so young herself, when you were just a child. It's only natural that you hated the person you felt was responsible."

"Because he is responsible. He could have stopped it." He looked ravaged then, but he sounded worse. "He could have *helped* her."

Nina went and took his hand again. She held it between hers, close to her heart.

"Do you have any idea what I would give for a single hour with my father?" she asked, holding his gaze no matter that the look in his eyes was painful. "With either one of my parents? I spent a lifetime wishing I could have another moment. Just one more moment, just enough, so I could tell them the only thing that really matters."

He said something, and she thought it was her name, but the wind stole it away.

"That I love them," Nina whispered. "That I will always love them. That no matter what happened to me, no matter what the years without them were like, I could never let that be what little I have of them. I would regret it forever."

He shook his head, as if warding her off.

"Zeus," she said, low and urgent. "Don't do something you'll regret forever."

"And what if I'm not the man you think I am at all?" he demanded, bringing his face in close, torn apart with emotion. No bronze mask. Just…him. All of him. "What if I am, instead, the creature I have always played? No regrets. No compassion. No love. What then, Nina?"

She reached up so she could hold his beloved face between her hands. And she gazed up at him, only dimly aware of the tears that wet her cheeks.

"Then I will regret it all for you," she promised him. "Your commoner queen, who will love you anyway, no matter how little you love yourself."

And for a moment, he only stood there, as if caught in his own storm. Nina thought she heard the ominous roll of thunder.

Then, as if it caused him physical pain, he pulled

away from her. He staggered back, his green gaze locked on hers.

It felt like a lifetime.

But then Zeus turned away and left her behind on that beach.

Nina wrapped her arms around their baby, promised it all the love neither she nor Zeus had known, and stayed there.

Until her tears were gone.

CHAPTER ELEVEN

KING CRONOS WOKE in the evening, and Zeus was there. The nurses made him comfortable, fluffing his pillows until he frowned and waved them away. Then they left father and son alone in the King's traditional bedchamber.

Zeus had always hated this room. Everything was too martial, too imposing. All about history and tradition. He preferred sunlight and space to all this heaviness.

But he had never thought to ask *which* history his father was mired in. He had always assumed it was all Theosian history and had never cared for the yoke of it himself. But now he wondered if these stout furnishings reminded the old man of something else. Something personal.

Someone.

He didn't ask now. He stood against the nearest wall and gazed down at what age had done to the man he recalled as far mightier than the sun. The true god in this palace dedicated to them.

Back when he had been so small and useless.

Nina's voice sounded in his head. *He's just a person.*

Zeus could admit that he had never thought so.

"I did not think I would see you again," Cronos rasped. And did not look as if he was best pleased to see Zeus now.

Because even at a moment like this, he knew how to provoke his son. Zeus reminded himself that he had not become who he was out of nothing.

"I've been waiting for this moment," he drawled, lounging against the wall in the indolent way that he knew had enraged his father since he was little more than a sulky youth. "Surely you know that. A most indecorous deathwatch, I think all your acolytes would agree."

Cronos only laughed, though it sent him into that rattling cough that had slowly taken him over this last year. "Such is the weight of the crown, my boy. You must wait for the moment of my death to rise. And you cannot mourn for even a moment. You must rule."

Zeus wanted to launch into one of his diatribes. He'd been practicing them for years. He had looked forward to this moment with all that he was. Before Nina, he had planned to vow, here on the old man's deathbed, that he would never have a child. That he would make sure the throne passed out of this family forever, so that all the old man's machinations had been for nothing.

With Nina, he'd thought he'd have an even better knife to stick in, deep.

Because he could still remember sitting with his mother as she slowly faded away, that little smile on her face. So pleased that she had, in her death, done

one thing to please herself completely. He could remember every moment of her last days.

He had been holding them close ever since. Hoarding them so he could build his fury about what had happened, year by year.

But now he was in another room in this palace, at another bedside, and yet his head was still back on that beach. *I will love you anyway, no matter how little you love yourself*, she had said.

And Zeus found he could not bring himself to say the things he should.

"Do you believe I will mourn you, old man?" he asked, almost idly.

And for a moment, he saw again the canny, shrewd King who had ruled his country long and well, through wars and plagues and famines alike.

"It is all mourning, in the end." That gaze of his still packed the same punch. "Remember that, Zeus. If you have any stake in this life at all, sooner or later, you mourn."

And maybe that was the word for what tore Zeus apart. Maybe it was all mourning, after all. For what he'd lost. For what he'd found but had intended to betray in this way. Maybe that made sense of the heaviness in him and the heart he'd only just discovered, broken into pieces.

And all of that wrapped up in an eleven-year-old's rage and grief for the mother who might not have left him if anyone beside him had loved her.

He cleared his throat. "I planned to send you off into the afterlife with the knowledge that I have not only impregnated Princess Isabeau's scandalous orphan, but I will also be marrying her in short order. Forever tarnishing your throne, your reputation, and therefore all you hold dear."

Cronos stared for a moment, and Zeus expected him to start in with the usual outrage. But he didn't feel even remotely as entertained as he'd always thought he would. He felt no rush of glee. No cleansing rush of spiteful triumph.

And it had never crossed his mind that he might find his revenge…underwhelming.

His father began to laugh again, though it made him hack and sputter. It took him a long time to catch his breath again. For a moment, he looked as if he might slip back into sleep. Instead, he roused himself, and when he looked at Zeus again, it was with an expression Zeus had never seen before.

As if his father was almost…bittersweet.

It had his throat tightening up.

"There is no throne in this world that is not tarnished," Cronos said. "It is only that, once the tarnishing has occurred, we all rally about and claim it as gold."

Zeus's pulse picked up then, though he was still. Very still. "And here I thought the only thing that mattered to you in this world was that throne."

"Because it was all I had," Cronos blurted out, as if the words had been tamped down inside him a long while. And the saying of them seemed to exhaust him. He collapsed against his bed, his breath coming harder. But he kept on, looking determined. "I lost everything. The throne was all that remained. And it took me too long to understand that a throne is nothing but a bloody chair. What matters is who sits upon it—and what he does when he is there."

They held each other's gaze for what seemed like forever. Zeus knew that these were words his father never would have said if these were not, perhaps, his final moments. But then, he knew that he would not have listened otherwise. And as they gazed at each other without rancor for the first time in more years than he cared to count, Zeus felt as if a thousand more unsaid things passed between them.

"Father," Zeus began.

The old man lifted a trembling hand. "You have nothing to apologize for, my son," he said, still holding Zeus's gaze. "It is the regret of my life that I did not see what I was doing to your mother, so lost in my own misery was I. And that I remained lost for far too long. I want you to know that if I could, I would go back and change what happened. I would change…" He broke off and smiled, faintly, though his eyes were sad. And his voice was fading. "I would change everything."

And then Zeus found himself doing something he would have sworn he would never, ever do.

He went and sat by his father's bedside. He took the old man's hands and looked deep into his eyes. Because he had stood on a beach and told Nina what kind of man he was, and she had loved him anyway. He knew the power of it.

And how could he deny it to his father now? When he knew how it had felt to hear Nina say those words to him?

I am sorry, Mother, he said inside. *I have been choosing you for a lifetime. But this is the end of his.*

A moment he had been waiting for, thinking he would taint it with revenge. But now he was here, and it was happening, and he couldn't find the will to do it.

He had chosen bitterness his whole life. What would happen if he chose peace?

If he let himself love his father a little, too?

"Father," he managed to say, though his voice was raw. "Rest now. I love you."

And when Cronos's eyes closed again, there were tears on his creased face.

Zeus did not know how long he sat there, but he thought it no more than a handful of minutes. And then his father breathed his last.

And Zeus did not move.

His heart was racing, his ribs too tight. And he knew that he only had a moment left. He only had a single, solitary moment left. One final moment when he was a son sitting beside his father. One last moment when he was who he had always been. Prince Zeus of Theosia.

Not a good man, perhaps. But he had great plans for his future.

First, however, he would step out of these doors and everything would change.

But then, everything had already changed. He was to be a father. There was a woman who looked at him as if he was worthy of her. She did not need him to save her. She wanted only for him to love her.

"I wish we had done it better," he said to his father,

in this last moment that was only theirs. "I wish we'd changed everything together."

He set the old man's hand down. And then he sat back and thought of his mother. His laughing, lovely mother. He was older now than she'd been then. And he had his own child on the way.

So he whispered the words he'd never thought he'd ever utter, not to her. "I forgive you, Mama."

For leaving him. For, in her way, taking him on as harrowing a journey as his father had.

Because in the end, both of them had been too locked in their own misery to care for their child as they should have. He understood that now.

But he did not intend that history should repeat itself. His child would know exactly how much it was loved. Always.

Zeus gave himself one last moment in his chair. Then he rose and blew out a breath. He looked at his father one last time as a son. Then he turned and opened the door.

He had stepped through it a prince. He would exit a king.

And he swore he would do a better job with the new title than he had with the old.

But as his father's attendants rushed inside, he didn't stand there and wait for them all to drop to their knees and "Long live the King" him the way tradition dictated they should. He was moving, rushing through the palace, because he was already King. It didn't matter who acknowledged it.

What mattered was her. Nina.

She was not in her rooms.

She wasn't in the library or any of the galleries.

Zeus was heading back to the beach when he finally found her standing in one of the palace's main halls, contemplating a large bronze mask.

And a thousand things he needed to say stormed within him. He wanted to tell her everything that had happened. Everything he'd understood, almost too late. Everything said and unsaid.

She turned as she sensed him coming, or perhaps he made some noise, and he knew she could see what had happened. Right there on his face. He expected her to call him *Your Majesty*. He expected her to curtsy. He expected that, like every other person in this palace, she would look to his rank first.

He should have known better.

"Oh, no," said his Nina. His perfect little hen. "*Zeus.* Your father. I'm so sorry."

She opened her arms wide, and he moved into them. And then, somewhere in that mess of grief old and new, there was still Nina, and he was kissing her—the heat undeniable.

But all of these other things as well.

And so it was that the brand-new King of Theosia knelt before his scandalous orphan in a hallway where anyone could see them. He wrapped his arms around her.

"Nina," he said, very solemnly. "I love you."

She was crying, and he would have to do something about that, but she was smiling, too.

"I suspect I am very bad at it," he continued. "But I think, if I try, I will figure out how to love you as well as I pretended to disdain everything else."

"Just love me," Nina whispered. "Love us. Everything else is negotiable."

He stayed where he was, his face against her belly, hugging his child and his woman at once.

And when he rose, he wiped away her tears. Then he reached down and retrieved the ring he'd put on her finger. This time, he held her hand while he held the ring up between them.

She was still smiling, though her eyes were still wet. "You already did this, Zeus."

"I did not. Not properly."

"But—"

He lifted her hand to his lips, and she subsided.

"Nina, I love you," he said again, because it could never be said enough. "As I have told you before, I could command you to marry me. But I would rather you do it because you wish to."

And this was harder. So much harder than he'd imagined. Nina was gazing at him, her eyes damp and filled with all the things she'd taught him. Love. Hope.

Forgiveness not because it was deserved or earned, but because it was necessary.

"The King of Theosia will need a queen," he managed to get out past that tightness in his throat, "but I need you. My people will expect me to fail, for that is what I've taught them I do. But you expect me to fly, Nina. And I think that the better I love you, the easier it will be to spread our wings. And I already know that a man is only as good as a woman who imagines him better."

"It has always been yes, Zeus," she whispered. "It will always be yes."

"And in return for these services to man and crown," he continued, though there was light in him now, beating back the shadows. Sunlight, at last. "I will take all the time and energy that I have dedicated to my foolish plans and leverage them on you instead. We will raise our child together, and we will be happy, Nina. If I have anything to say about it, and I do. *We will be happy.*"

"We will be us," Nina said, moving closer so she could reach up to pull his face to hers. She kissed him then. His forehead. His jaw. "Not our histories. Not what happened to us. Not the things we did before we found each other. We will be you and me and the family we make together. We will be *us*, Zeus."

"Forever," he vowed.

And the hall was getting crowded. There were matters of state to attend to—and there could be no more putting off this moment.

Zeus slid that ring back onto Nina's finger, where it belonged. And when she took his hand and held it tightly, all he saw was sunlight. He felt it, deep inside.

I will do it right this time, he told his parents. *I promise.*

"We'll do it together," Nina whispered, as if she'd heard.

And then, hand in hand, they turned to face the future.

The way they always would.

CHAPTER TWELVE

THE FUNERAL PROCESSION took over most of the island. The citizens of Theosia came out in force to mark the passing of their King, whose reign had been long and stable.

They were less sure about their new King.

But a week after his father was laid to rest, Zeus married Nina at last. They stood together in the island's cathedral and spoke all the old words to each other. And new ones that were only theirs. That was the day he made her his Queen, though the coronation would come later.

Not without telling a few stories along the way. The papers were filled with all kinds of theories about the fall of wicked Prince Zeus—and how, perhaps, the most unlikely bride was the only one who could civilize the savage beast.

"This is utter nonsense," Nina complained, sitting with him at the table in his morning room, the light he loved so much making her blond hair gleam like gold. Her brown eyes danced. "You were never a *savage* beast."

Zeus took that as a challenge. And by the time he

was done, she was limp and smiling in the vast bed in the rooms they now shared—his rooms. Neither one of them wanted to move into the King's traditional chambers.

They both wanted that light.

As much of it as possible.

"Your friends have all made a point of telling me that they're disappointed you didn't officiate your own wedding," Nina said at the grand reception after their wedding.

Zeus looked over the press of well-wishers who'd crowded into the palace and saw Jag, Rafael, and Vincenzo standing together. They all lifted their glasses in a mocking toast. He inclined his head in return and reminded himself that he was a king now. He could summon his best friends and call it a treaty summit. He made a mental note to do just that.

"Pay them no mind," he told his wife. "They are shocking reprobates, every one of them."

She made a face at him. "No wonder you all get along."

He and Nina danced and danced. And every day, she was lovelier to him. But perhaps never lovelier than she was then, wearing her stunning white dress, round with his child, and beaming with happiness.

Later that night, they stood on their balcony, looking out over the island that had always been his and was now hers, too. There were fireworks going off in all the villages, celebrating the kingdom's new start.

And what it represented.

Hope.

"You're mine first," he told her, standing behind her

as he had so many times—so he could put his arms around her and hold both her and their future close. "But from this day, you're also Theosia's. You belong to us all now, Nina."

He wasn't surprised to find tears on her cheeks again, even as she smiled with all her might.

"I will do you all proud," she promised.

But Zeus was already proud.

Their son was born late, prompting idle speculation in all the usual places that the new Prince intended to take after his father. And maybe he would one day. But first, there in the palace with the medical staff standing by, he was a miracle.

Maybe an everyday miracle, but a miracle all the same.

Zeus held the tiny bundle with wonder and awe and looked down at the perfect little boy who he knew would take after his mother. If he had anything to say about it.

And they loved each other as best they could, year after year. Wholly. Fiercely. They didn't always see eye to eye, but they fought hard to get back there. Every time.

The commoner Queen of Theosia gave the kingdom not only an heir but three spares. And they loved her for it. She made her royal children work with their hands as much as possible and treated any hint of laziness as a violent illness that required immediate attention. She insisted on kindness. She applauded thoughtfulness. She also loved them all to distraction, made them all feel adored, and was, without contest, the heart and soul of the family. And so, too, in time, the kingdom. Her passion was orphanages and lost children of any kind, and she became a patron of too many struggling organizations to count—at home and abroad.

Princess Isabeau of Haught Montagne, when reached for comment about her once-fiancé and the orphan girl she'd taken into her court so benevolently, never had a thing to say except that she wished them every happiness.

Not in public, anyway.

For his part, Zeus tried to learn from the first part of his life. He tried to love more. He worked hard at being good at all three of his important roles. Husband. Father. King. He hid himself less and less and found it more amusing than anything else how surprised people were to discover that in private, he'd been an excellent prince all along.

He took his stewardship of Theosia seriously but ruled with compassion.

He loved his children. He delighted in them.

But most of all, he loved his wife.

"Are you lonely?" she asked on their wedding anniversary, some twenty years into their beautiful future.

"Never," he replied at once, holding her in his arms in that very same Parisian hideaway where he'd first put his ring on her finger.

"That's a good thing," she replied, turning in his arms and wrapping herself around him with the same bright, hot passion that only grew between them. "But even if you were, I know the cure."

Because she healed him, the way she always did. And over time, he found ways to return the favor.

Mostly by loving her so much and so hard that she never again doubted he always would.

"This is our fairy tale," he told her. "We make the rules, little hen."

"Fairy tales end happily," she liked to tell him as he swept her into his arms. "That's the most important part."

Zeus had to say he agreed.

And that was how a common, possibly scandalous orphan—from nowhere with nothing—married the wickedest, most notorious prince in all the land.

Then tamed him. Just like that.

* * * * *

COMING SOON!

We really hope you enjoyed reading this book. If you're looking for more romance be sure to head to the shops when new books are available on

Thursday 23rd October

To see which titles are coming soon, please visit
millsandboon.co.uk/nextmonth

MILLS & BOON

FOUR BRAND NEW BOOKS FROM MILLS & BOON MODERN

Indulge in desire, drama, and breathtaking romance – where passion knows no bounds!

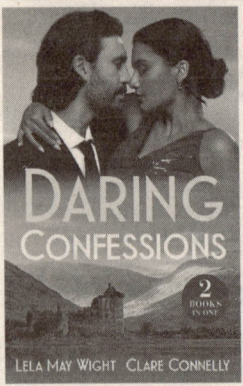

Demand from a Greek — Lynne Graham & Jackie Ashenden

Crave Me — Michelle Smart & Lorraine Hall

Daring Confessions — Lela May Wight & Clare Connelly

With his Ring... — Lucy King & Millie Adams

OUT NOW

Eight Modern stories published every month, find them all at:

millsandboon.co.uk

MILLS & BOON TRUE LOVE IS HAVING A MAKEOVER!

Introducing

Love Always

Swoon-worthy romances, where love takes centre stage. Same heartwarming stories, stylish new look!

Look out for our brand new look

OUT NOW

MILLS & BOON

OUT NOW!

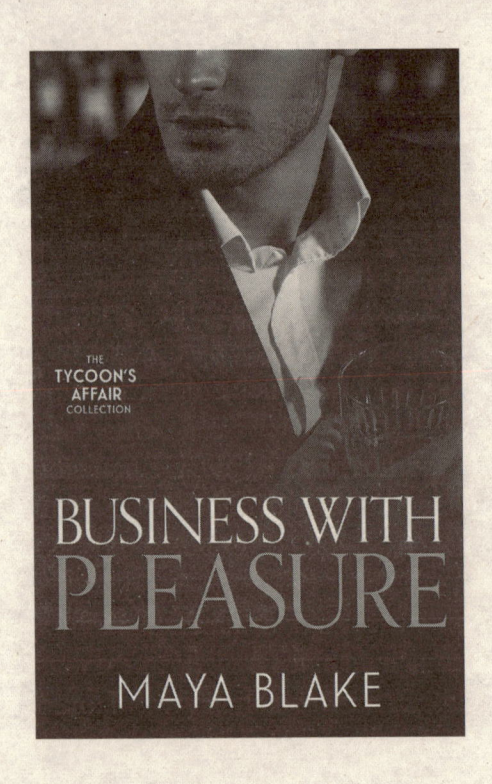

THE **TYCOON'S AFFAIR** COLLECTION

BUSINESS WITH PLEASURE

MAYA BLAKE

Available at
millsandboon.co.uk

MILLS & BOON

OUT NOW!

3 BOOKS IN ONE

In the Spotlight
★★★ FAME'S TEMPTATION ★★★

RACHAEL STEWART SOPHIE PEMBROKE ABBY GREEN

Available at
millsandboon.co.uk

MILLS & BOON

OUT NOW!

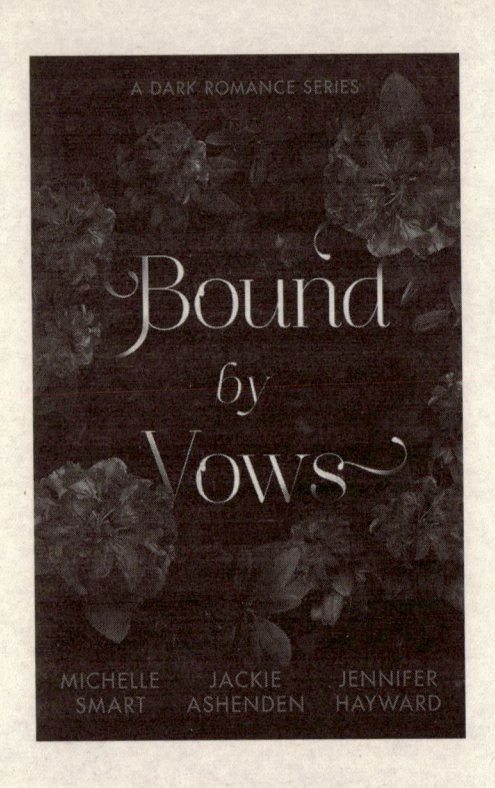

A DARK ROMANCE SERIES

Bound by Vows

MICHELLE SMART JACKIE ASHENDEN JENNIFER HAYWARD

Available at
millsandboon.co.uk

MILLS & BOON

MILLS & BOON

THE HEART OF ROMANCE

A ROMANCE FOR EVERY READER

MODERN — Prepare to be swept off your feet by sophisticated, sexy and seductive heroes, in some of the world's most glamourous and romantic locations, where power and passion collide.

HISTORICAL — Escape with historical heroes from time gone by. Whether your passion is for wicked Regency Rakes, muscled Vikings or rugged Highlanders, awaken the romance of the past.

MEDICAL — Set your pulse racing with dedicated, delectable doctors in the high-pressure world of medicine, where emotions run high and passion, comfort and love are the best medicine.

Love Always — Celebrate true love with tender stories of heartfelt romance, from the rush of falling in love to the joy a new baby can bring, and a focus on the emotional heart of a relationship.

HEROES — The excitement of a gripping thriller, with intense romance at its heart. Resourceful, true-to-life women and strong, fearless men face danger and desire - a killer combination!

afterglow BOOKS — From showing up to glowing up, these characters are on the path to leading their best lives and finding romance along the way – with plenty of sizzling spice!

To see which titles are coming soon, please visit

millsandboon.co.uk/nextmonth

afterglow BOOKS

Afterglow Books is a trend-led, trope-filled list of books with diverse, authentic and relatable characters, a wide array of voices and representations, plus real world trials and tribulations. Featuring all the tropes you could possibly want (think small-town settings, fake relationships, grumpy vs sunshine, enemies to lovers) and all with a generous dose of spice in every story.

♪ @millsandboonuk
◉ @millsandboonuk
afterglowbooks.co.uk
#AfterglowBooks

For all the latest book news, exclusive content and giveaways scan the QR code below to sign up to the Afterglow newsletter:

SCAN ME

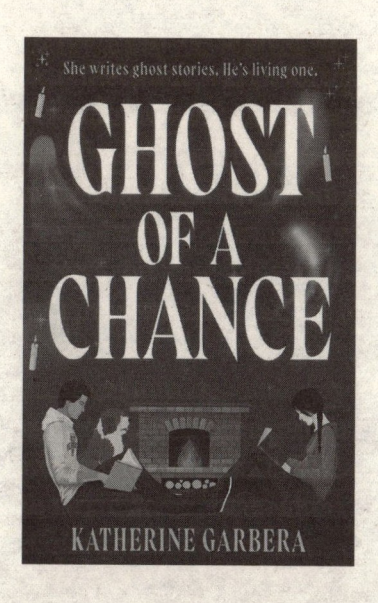

afterglow BOOKS

GHOST OF A CHANCE

She writes ghost stories. He's living one.

KATHERINE GARBERA

- 🛏 One night
- 💕 Second chance
- 🎭 Secret identity

OUT NOW

To discover more visit:
Afterglowbooks.co.uk

GET YOUR ROMANCE FIX!

Get the latest romance news, exclusive author interviews, story extracts and much more!

blog.millsandboon.co.uk

MILLS & BOON
A ROMANCE FOR EVERY READER

- **FREE** delivery direct to your door
- **EXCLUSIVE** offers every month
- **SAVE** up to 30% on pre-paid subscriptions

SUBSCRIBE AND SAVE

millsandboon.co.uk/Subscribe

LET'S TALK
Romance

For exclusive extracts, competitions and special offers, find us online:

- **f** MillsandBoon
- **X** @MillsandBoon
- **◉** @MillsandBoonUK
- **♪** @MillsandBoonUK

Get in touch on 01413 063 232

> For all the latest titles coming soon, visit
> millsandboon.co.uk/nextmonth